A SEASON FOR MURDER

Also by Ann Granger

Say It With Poison

A SEASON
FOR MURDER

Ann Granger

St. Martin's Press
New York

Library of Congress Cataloging-in-Publication Data

Granger, Ann.
    A season for murder : a Mitchell and Markby village mystery / Ann Granger.
        p.   cm.
    ISBN 0-312-07079-9
    I. Title.
PR6057.R259S4   1992
823'.914—dc20   91-41548
                                                                            CIP

First published in Great Britain by Headline Book Publishing PLC

First U.S. Edition: April 1992
10 9 8 7 6 5 4 3 2 1

To John, always my first reader

A SEASON
FOR MURDER

One

The tall young woman jumped back and put her thumb to her
mouth to stanch the bright spurt of scarlet blood. When she took
her thumb away the puncture mark was clearly visible in the
reddened flesh and had begun to throb. She glared resentfully at
the cause of the damage. Affixed with sticky tape to the front
door of the cottage was a large, garish plastic holly wreath. The
leaves were lime green and daubed with white paint and silver
glitter. The wreath had luminous puce plastic berries protruding
on bits of wire, one of which had been driven into her thumb,
and it was topped with a bird of unrecorded species inadequately
disguised as a robin, with all the charm of a carrion crow. A
banner across the centre of the wreath read: 'Merrie Xmas'.

She made a second and more cautious attempt to remove the
seasonal decoration. She was not against Christmas goodwill
but this thing went beyond the bounds of acceptability by any
yardstick. She could not imagine who had put it there. The
cottage had been empty for some weeks, awaiting her arrival.
She leaned the wreath against her suitcase on the path beside
her and felt in her pocket for the key and turned it in the lock,
pushing against the door as she did so. It swung inwards and
there was a soft shuffling sound as it caught against papers lying
on the hall floor. She squeezed through, carrying suitcase and
holly wreath, and found herself in someone else's home which
would be, for the next year at least, hers.

The unretrieved morning mail littered the carpet. She picked
it up and riffled through it. Three circulars, a free newspaper, a
letter for the Russells, owners of Rose Cottage, which she would
have to send on and one large white envelope addressed to
'Miss Meredith Mitchell, Rose Cottage, Pook's Common near
Bamford' and postmarked 'Oxford'.

'That's me!' she said aloud, her voice echoing in the empty
hall and turned the envelope this way and that, wondering who
knew she was expected here. She had just finished a stint as

1

British consul in Yugoslavia and had received what all Foreign Service personnel know must come eventually: a home posting. It was not surprising. She had been abroad for a number of years. But it meant a new kind of life altogether. Now it would be her turn to struggle into London with other commuters every morning and spend a desk-bound day there before fighting her way home again at night. Her turn also to find suitable accommodation which she could afford.

But here she had been lucky. The Russells, to the female half of which pairing she was related, were currently in Dubai where Peter had taken up a medical post. They were happy to let her have their home at a peppercorn rent and, although it would mean getting up at six sharp every morning to get into Bamford where there was a mainline station, she could – just about – commute from here. If she lived modestly, she had calculated grimly, she would be able to afford the price of a British Rail season ticket.

If the availability, comfort and cheapness of Rose Cottage had been the chief reasons for her decision to take up the Russells' offer, she had to admit that secretly the name 'Pook's Common' had exerted its own lure. 'Pook' appeared in other place names up and down the country and was, she assumed, the same as 'Puck' as in 'puckish' and of course, as the character in Shakespeare. She had looked it up in a dictionary and found that the word existed also as 'pooka' and that it meant a hobgoblin which generally appeared or was depicted as a horse. The chance to live for a while in a spot haunted by the spirit of a magical horse wasn't to be turned down lightly.

Certainly Pook's Common, even today, had a slightly wayward and unreal air to it. It was one of those strange places with no obvious *raison d'être*, hardly worthy of bearing individual names since they contained so few buildings. Obviously of ancient origin, it had somehow survived into the twentieth century without either being abandoned and going under the plough or being absorbed by larger communities nearby. It lay on the B road between the village of Westerfield and the market town of Bamford. She had even driven through it several times on her previous visit to the area when she had stayed at Westerfield, and scarcely realised it was there. On the B road itself, Pook's Common consisted of a signpost, a row of six pre-war council houses and a garage. The garage buildings were surprisingly smart and declared themselves on a brightly painted hoarding as

'J. Fenniwick. Repairs. Estimates. Exhausts. Tyres. Taxis.' The last presumably came into use when all attempts at repairs failed or the estimates priced them too high.

But this was a false Pook's Common, an offshoot. 'Real' Pook's Common lurked down a side turning, a narrow single-track lane, ill-maintained (probably with the connivance of the inhabitants to discourage casual visitors), and lined on either side by hedgerows. When you reached it, it consisted of a smattering of cottages built of solid stone. They were all well kept up and had neat, tidy gardens. Little to see in these at this time of year but in spring purple and mauve aubretia would cascade down over the drystone walls which bordered the road, orange marigolds would sprout, self-set, all over the place, delphiniums would raise royal blue spikes of blossom, wisteria and clematis would burst into flower and the rose bushes come into bud.

Significantly, unlike true cottagers' gardens, none of these showed any sign of vegetable beds. No last abandoned cabbage stalks rotted on the ground. In spring no upturned, holed bucket would force a crown of rhubarb and in summer no runner bean frames would stand like Indian tepees in an alien land. In addition, one or two of the cottages and gardens were more than a little 'twee'. One had a palpably false wishing well in its front lawn, another an old hand-turned mangle, painted bright blue and standing sadly out-of-place by the front porch. Pook's Common had survived at a price. The price was to have become in part a resort of 'second homes' belonging to people lawfully engaged all week in town who came out here at weekends or during holiday breaks. To be fair, the Russells had lived here all year round before departing for Dubai. But that was because Peter Russell, a doctor, had worked out of the medical centre in Bamford and commuted there from Rose Cottage every day. Meredith would strike out even further and go up to London. It would be, she realised ruefully, a tiring business. Most people's work meant they had to live somewhere a good deal handier and less isolated.

The result of this was that for much of the time Pook's Common must be pretty well abandoned, a ghost hamlet. Perhaps the pookas returned, when the humans departed in their Volvos and BMWs, and pranced round the false wishing well on their tiny hooves and tried in vain to curdle the UHT milk in sealed waxed packets.

Meredith made her way down the narrow hall and opened a

door at the far end. It led into the kitchen, immaculately tidy and basking in pale winter sunshine. It still had its original stone-flagged floor which struck cold through the soles of her shoes. On the scrubbed pine table, propped against a potted plant, was a note. It said, 'I have put some food in the fridge to tide you over. M. Brissett.' The plant was a kalanchoe and probing it with a finger Meredith found the compost to be bone dry and the fleshy leaves rubbery. She carried it to the sink, turned on the tap with an effort, filled the dish in which the pot sat and put it on the windowsill in the light. The action gave her a glow of virtue as if she had done someone a good turn.

She next turned her attention to the fridge. It contained a vacuum pack of streaky bacon rashers, half a dozen eggs, butter and a jar of home-made marmalade. She opened the freezer compartment and discovered a sliced loaf which she took out and put to thaw on the table. Further investigation turned up a motley collection of tins and bottles in the larder probably left behind by the Russells and including, she was thankful to see, a jar of instant coffee and a tin of evaporated milk. Meredith filled the kettle at a recalcitrant tap and while it heated went in search of the gas-fired boiler which controlled the central heating. It was in a cubbyhole under the spiral staircase together with hand-written instructions for its use. An air vent had been punched in the outside wall beside it and a cold draught streamed through. No wonder the cottage was like an icebox. After bumping her head painfully on the stairtreads above and barking her shins on the newel post against which the boiler was wedged on the other side, she managed to light it. By now the kettle summoned her with a shrill shriek and she scuttled back, unhooked a mug from a wooden rack and made her coffee. Now at long last she was able to sit down, still well muffled in her anorak, and open the letter addressed to her.

It turned out to be a rather pretty card with a picture of fuchsias on the front. Inside was written 'Welcome back! Alan'. She should have deduced what it would be. Sherlock Holmes would have worked out the likely contents in five seconds flat from a mere glance at the envelope, plus a complete description of Alan Markby himself. All post in the area went through the sorting office at Oxford and the Russells must have told him they had let the cottage to her. An image of Alan formed itself in Meredith's head. She pictured him buying the card, his tall thin figure stooped suspiciously over a rack in some shop, picking through for one which appealed to him. That would be one with flowers or plants on it but not one of those fanciful concoctions with a vague impression of a floral group in unlikely pastel shades. No, this card reflected the man who had bought it. It was specific, a highly professional photograph, and on the inner side of the cover in tiny print was the name of the particular strain of fuchsia depicted. It was called Dollar Princess. Meredith allowed herself a moment's wild speculation as to whether some kind of compliment was intended, then smiled wryly at her foolishness. Dollar Princess! She couldn't think of a more unlikely description of herself. She realised belatedly she had been smiling fondly at the card so frowned severely and dropped it back on the table.

Warming her chilled fingers on the hot coffee mug, she told herself that it was to be expected, now she'd returned to this part of the world, that she and Alan would run into one another again. The prospect filled her with mixed feelings. Their previous connection had been semi-official. He was a chief inspector, CID, at Bamford station and they had met through a murder case. A violent death in which one had been closely involved wasn't something easily forgotten and even just thinking about it, Meredith felt a sharpening of her senses and a slight prickling of the hair on the nape of her neck. She also felt the dull ache in her heart of recalled personal loss. Yet all this had formed the cement in her previous relationship with Alan, the reason for meeting, the reason for a certain kind of closeness, for asking any number of personal questions, for frank exchange of views. For, in fact, becoming pretty well acquainted. But without the underlying excuse of a murder enquiry, any relationship this time would be based on a blunt acceptance of mutual attraction. That was not something she was prepared to think about. If she must meet Alan, it would be nice if there were some excuse for it. She realised, to her dismay, she was therefore implicitly hoping for another crime. She shuddered – she'd had her fair share of trouble. And one murder in a lifetime was enough. That was not an experience to be repeated.

She dismissed her thoughts of murder but allowed her mind to continue to run on Alan as she sipped her coffee. It was still too hot and burned the end of her tongue. She blamed the undeniable slight hopping of her heart on this. It couldn't, she told herself sternly, be the idea of Alan that did it! But she had liked him, liked him a great deal more than she had let him see. He'd been showing signs of being far too keen and, in the circumstances, following on the horrifying sequence of events surrounding the deaths at Westerfield, it really hadn't been the moment to contemplate romance. She had let him down tactfully, or so she hoped. She had told herself at the time that this was because she didn't wish to hurt his feelings. If she were to be honest, it was also because she hadn't really wanted to drive him away for ever.

All these inconsistencies in her own reactions annoyed her. She was supposed to be good at handling problems; though other people's problems always seemed easier to settle than her own. She'd left her last post as consul with the congratulations of all ringing pleasantly in her ears after several years hard and efficient work. Even the Foreign Office had been very nice about her achievements. But they hadn't, for all that, given her the kind of posting she'd wanted! They'd assigned her a desk in London, a fate worse than death in her book. What a stupid expression, she immediately thought. She'd just been reflecting on an episode of violent, ugly death and it wasn't easy to suppose something worse.

But the FO might have shown its gratitude by offering her some task other than a dreary trek up to London and back every weekday. It wasn't because she hadn't done well, they'd assured her. They had even heard about her last emergency, a case involving a visiting British tourist, a local girl and a jealous boyfriend.

It had all taken place a couple of weeks before the end of her tour and led to her going out in a blaze of glory. Normally she was happy to let yobbos fend for themselves. Unfortunately this one had been aged barely seventeen, technically under-age, and she'd felt obliged to help him out. She'd first persuaded the Croatian police to waive their resolve to lock him in the cells. She'd promised he would pay compensation to the girl's battered boyfriend and to the bar where the fracas had taken place for broken furniture. That had meant organising the arrival of the said money from England from her protégé's long-suffering mother. Toby Smythe, the vice consul, had been all for letting him be locked up, pointing out gloomily that she was making herself responsible for someone totally unreliable. Meredith stuck to her guns. She collected her boy from the hospital which had taped up his broken nose, and even persuaded the grumbling Toby to give him a bed overnight on the floor of his flat. The next morning she had personally escorted the errant youth to the airport. He had not shown himself particularly grateful for any of her efforts on his behalf as he'd shambled along beside her. His natural intelligibility worsened by his broken nose, he had indistinctly articulated a desire for the revenge of which he felt he was being robbed while shouting abuse at other travellers.

Meredith, clinging to the consul's dictum of 'my countryman right or wrong' steered him firmly into the café area with a view to buying him some breakfast which might at least stop the flow of profanities. But there they had been cornered by relatives of the aggrieved boyfriend who, it afterwards turned out, had tracked them from the hospital. Her initial reaction had been dismay especially when lagerman beside her, overjoyed at finding himself back in a familiar situation, had immediately seized an abandoned beerglass. It had been a very hairy moment. Meredith found herself standing between two brawny six foot bauxite miners from the Banat and her gleeful British subject, brandishing his glass cheerfully.

It certainly was the moment for some nimble footwork and wits. Meredith dived into the middle of the group, thanking her lucky stars she spoke a basic Serbo-Croat and was five foot ten herself. She pressed English cigarettes she kept handy for emergencies into the massive paws of the miners, detached her boy from his beerglass, delivered herself of a pithy speech and manoeuvred him, as he protested at being rescued, through the gates of the departure lounge. There, safe, he had gestured graphically at the two miners beyond the glass partition. He hugged Meredith and informed her she was 'all right' and clumped his way off, a noticeable cordon sanitaire of clear space creating itself between him and fellow-passengers. She had taken comfort in the thought that he wouldn't be allowed back in, especially as the two miners were still in the main hall watching suspiciously and had been joined by a pair of hefty airport policemen summoned by the woman in the cafeteria. Meredith took refuge in a time-honoured process for mending fences. She bought them all a drink. They bought her a drink. They bought one another drinks. By the time she left, slightly unsteadily, they had all been on the best of terms.

Bolstered by the memory of this success, Meredith turned her attention back to Alan's card which now appeared merely a gesture of friendship, like lagerman's hug. Yes, kind of Alan and thoughtful but really nothing more. For a brief moment Meredith toyed with the possibility that he might also have fixed the abominable plastic holly wreath on the door. But she knew he would never be guilty of such a crass lapse of taste. She took another look at her martyred thumb. It had stopped throbbing but it was sore and still red and angry. She wouldn't be surprised if she developed verdigris poisoning from that wire. An inauspicious beginning to Christmas. Perhaps the creature on the holly wreath was a bird of ill omen.

As if prompted by the idea, Meredith was suddenly transfixed by a new sound. It was so quiet here that any noise struck the ear like a thunderclap. But this was a distinct, sinister crunch of slow heavy footsteps purposefully approaching the back door. She tensed, and a trickle of nerves ran down her spine. She had been so certain Pook's Common was deserted. And if it was – apart from whoever was approaching her door – she was in all the more vulnerable a position. She jumped to her feet and, taking a leaf from lagerman's book, grabbed a meat mallet from a row of kitchen utensils hanging on the wall.

A chesty wheeze was audible, followed by a scrabbling. Then a key was inserted noisily in the lock. Meredith felt a small wave of relief wash over her and put down the meat hammer. She still didn't know who the visitor was, but the caller had a key and presumably therefore some bona fide reason for entry.

The door opened with a rattle and revealed a stocky female form. Meredith forced back an impulse to giggle, largely at her own foolishness, and at the contrast between the figure standing before her, and the one she had constructed in her panicked imagination. The visitor advanced, ample contours encased in a beige quilted raincoat. A knitted green bobble cap perched atop her tight grey curls and a pair of suede winter boots with zips protected her feet.

''Ullo,' she said agreeably. 'I thought you'd turned up. Mrs. Russell, she wrote me you was coming this week. Get here before Christmas, she said, and that you'd want me coming in to clean for you like I done for her.' She was nodding emphatically as she spoke, in constant agreement with herself, and the bobble pom-pom rolled back and forth, loose on its wool moorings. 'I seen the car when I come out of Miss Needham's, the lady what's opposite,' she added in final explanation.

'Mrs Brissett?' asked Meredith.

'That's right, dear. And you're Miss Mitchell. I put some things in the fridge. Did you find 'em? Oh yes, so you did, there's the

8

bread. You'll have to go into Bamford if you want to stock up with a bit more because we haven't got no shop round here. Tomorrow being Friday Bamford will be fair crowded, what with Christmas almost on us an all. The money people spend on Christmas! Mind you, it's nice to see all the pretty things, that's what I think.'

A small puzzle solved itself. 'Was it you who, who so kindly put a Christmas decoration on the front door?'

'Oh, you seen it then?' said Mrs Brissett, relieved. 'I thought someone had pinched it. As I say, I like to see things Christmassy and, knowing you was coming from abroad, I thought it would be nice. I don't know if they does things like that abroad. I don't like to think of Dr and Mrs Russell out there in the desert and not a Christmas tree for miles, just camels and such. Where's it gorn?'

'It fell down,' lied Meredith. 'I don't think the sticky tape was strong enough. I'll put it back when I find a tack, or perhaps I ought not to knock nails in Dr Russell's door. I am only renting, after all.'

'Pity it fell down,' said Mrs Brissett regretfully. 'I got it off a stall in the market last week, ever so cheap. Better fix it up indoors somewhere. I'll bring some more things. I got loads at home, paper chains and a nice big Chinese lantern and up in my loft there's a big plastic Father Christmas stands oh, two feet high, sort of holding his tummy and laughing. I could bring it over and put it in your front window.'

'I really shouldn't like to deprive you, Mrs Brissett!' said Meredith hastily.

'It's no trouble. Make this place look cheery, especially you being on your own. Spending Christmas alone, are you?'

'Probably. I don't mind, really.'

'I shouldn't like it. Got my grandchildren coming over.'

'I must settle with you for the food in the fridge,' said Meredith, putting a stop to a conversation which threatened to end with an open invitation to drop in at the Brissetts over the Christmas period. She reached out her hand to her shoulderbag lying on the table.

'No need now, dear. I'll be in tomorrow. I clean here on Tuesday and Friday and I clean at Miss Needham's on Monday and Thursday. I just thought I'd pop in and see if you'd got the heating going.'

'Yes, thanks.' It seemed she had at least one neighbour, then:

9

the Miss Needham who shared Mrs Brissett's services.

'It don't take long to warm through,' pursued Mrs Brissett. 'These old walls is near on two foot thick and keep in the heat wonderful. And there's a gas fire in the living room besides. Put that on, I should. Oh, and I made up a bed but I should stick a hot water bottle in that, if I was you.'

'Thank you,' said Meredith again, breaking firmly into the stream of instructions.

'All right then,' Mrs Brissett prepared to leave at last. 'I'll see you tomorrow. Half past eight I come along and generally go at twelvish. Got me own key, as you see.'

'Fine, thanks. I'm on leave – holiday – until after Christmas so I shall be here, although tomorrow I'll probably go into Bamford and stock up with provisions.'

'Go early,' advised Mrs Brissett. 'If you wants to park your car. Market day, remember!' She departed, closing the door noisily behind her. A regular, slowly fading squeak, indicated she had cycled here, it would seem likely from Westerfield.

Meredith signed deeply in relief. But Mrs Brissett was right in one thing and the cottage was already noticeably warmer. Meredith unzipped her anorak and set out to inspect the rest of it. Downstairs there was only the living room, besides the kitchen, and a tiny cloakroom. She climbed the spiral stair and found herself on a minute landing. Bathroom, very cramped, to her right and two bedrooms corresponding to the two rooms below. Mrs Brissett had kindly made up the bed in the larger room above the living room. It contained a double bed, obviously the Russells' own. Meredith wrinkled her nose in doubt at the thought of sleeping in someone's marital couch. She walked across to it and sat down on the edge. It was a pretty room with roof beams and a funny little dormer window. A late Victorian wash basin and ewer, just for show, stood on a stand in one corner. A clothes closet had been built in under the eaves. Meredith spread her hand over the flower-sprigged duvet.

She was glad that Peter had been able to build a new life for himself. But she understood the still newlywed Russells quitting Pook's Common for Dubai as they had. Sometimes, to start anew, you have to go away and begin among strangers.

Meredith was pleased for the Russells. They needed one another, lent one another support. But what suited them wouldn't necessarily suit her. She was used to being alone, fending for herself. She didn't need a permanent relationship.

But, she thought ruefully, there were undeniable attractions in a temporary one. The bed looked extremely comfortable and she found herself thinking about Alan Markby again and wondering whether to phone to let him know she had arrived and thank him for the card. Christmas was a time for being with friends, not alone. After all, she reasoned obstinately, temporary didn't have to become permanent and Alan was not the sort of thick-skulled egotist who imagined the slightest sign of friendship on the part of a woman signalled a burning passion. If she was going to be some time in Pook's Common, she needed to set about creating a social life for herself. To do that she'd have to build on the slender foundations laid down in her previous visit, and she'd have to look towards Bamford. In Pook's Common itself there didn't appear to be much going on.

'This place,' she observed aloud, 'is dead.'

Her return had been the subject of some conversation elsewhere, that previous Sunday afternoon.

'You can't spend Christmas on your own, Alan!' said his sister reproachfully. 'Christmas is a family time.'

'You don't say,' Alan Markby said bleakly. His gaze moved towards a newspaper-covered heap on the sofa which represented his brother-in-law. The newspaper rose and fell gently and regularly. Markby returned his gaze to his sister, curled up in her armchair with feet tucked beneath her, and smiled. Laura wore a bright scarlet sweater and black cord pants and her long blonde hair hung curling on her shoulders. She was short-sighted and large spectacles perched on her nose but only made her look endearing.

'You look less like a legal-eagle,' he said, 'than an owl.'

'I am more family-minded than business-minded just at the moment, I have to confess. There's always so much to do at Christmas.' There was a snort from beneath the newspapers. Laura contemplated her sleeping spouse. 'You are coming to us for Christmas Day at least, aren't you Alan? You cannot, really cannot, spend it all on your own talking to plants. Paul's cooking the meal so it will be good. He's got a recipe for some sort of chestnut stuffing for the turkey and he's spent ages decorating the cake.'

Markby looked doubtful. 'Well, you know, Laura, some of my colleagues are married men with families so it seems only fair to let them have Christmas Day and work myself. Morton and his wife have got a new baby. As I understand it, the baby has something called "six months' colic" and his wife is suffering post-natal depression but I dare say he'd like Christmas at home even so – '

'You don't have to go in – so long as they have your telephone number and can reach you. You're a senior CID man, not Mr Plod. You don't propose to sit on the desk and take details of lost kittens? Of course you don't. Unless someone robs a bank or murders their lover, you're superfluous.'

'What makes you think violent crime doesn't take place at Christmas, Laura? It's one of the busiest times of the year as regards violence in the family circle. How many clients come to you wanting a divorce in the New Year saying that Christmas was the last straw?'

She was not to be put off. 'I expect you here mid-morning on Christmas Day. A place will be set for you. The children are counting on your being here.'

Markby shuffled about in his chair. 'To tell you the truth, Laura – now don't go making more of this than it means – but I've a friend who will be staying near Bamford and I rather thought – '

Behind her outsize glasses, his sister's eyes gleamed as if she had just spotted a loophole in a contract. 'Meredith Mitchell! You kept saying you didn't know whether she was coming or not, you lying dog. You've fixed up to spend Christmas with her!'

'No I haven't. I think she'll be here. I was going to ring – no! She's not due until the end of the week!' This last came out as a shout because Laura's eyes had turned to the telephone and her mouth opened. From beneath the newspaper came a gurgle and the top sheet twitched. 'I feel,' Markby went on quickly, 'I ought to see what Meredith is doing over Christmas. She doesn't have any family here and she might be alone and so I thought I ought – '

'Absolutely no problem, Alan. You can bring her here.'

'Here . . . ?' His heart sank and he stared at his sister dolefully.

'For goodness sake! It can't be that bad! Paul is a professional cookery writer and his food is guaranteed to be edible which is more than can be said of mine. A family Christmas, she'll love it.'

'It's just that I – she might have other plans.'

'How? No, bring her here. I insist.'

He stared at her miserably. 'I hardly know how to ask her, Laura. She's really only a – a slight acquaintance. I ought not to have called her a friend, to be honest. It's a long time since we saw one another last and a lot of water's flowed under the bridge in between. She might think it a bit pushy of me. She might not want to come and not know how to refuse.' He paused. 'It would put her and me, frankly, on the spot a bit. Perhaps she doesn't want to see too much of me. Why on earth should she? Actually asking a person to join a family party . . . it might look as if I were trying to stake a claim of some sort. Which I'm not!' he concluded hastily.

His sister's reply was crisp. 'Honestly, Alan, I never knew anyone make so much fuss over nothing! You're being inconsistent. It's a simple invitation. You said yourself you think you ought to see if she's fixed up for Christmas. If she isn't and she'd like to be, she'll be delighted at being asked. If she really doesn't want to see you, she'll refuse. I'm sure,' said Laura tartly, 'she's perfectly capable of speaking her mind!'

'Yes,' he said in a depressed voice.

The newspaper heaved and rustled again, this time more vigorously. Paul's head appeared, bleary-eyed. 'Wassatime? Football . . . telly . . . cuppa tea . . .'

'You'll enjoy a family Christmas,' said Laura in final judgement. She pressed the remote control and the television screen flickered. 'We'll all watch *The Wizard of Oz* together and play games. We'll have charades, Matthew and Emma are big enough to join in this year. We'll light a real fire and bake chestnuts on the fender, provided you and Paul go out in the yard and saw up plenty of logs. It will be such fun.'

The telephone rang for Meredith the evening of her arrival as she was washing up after her bacon and egg supper. The sound of his voice at the other end was not unexpected but she took time to compose her voice before replying.

'Yes, yes, I did have a good trip, thanks . . . well, I am a bit tired. It was a long drive.'

His voice at the other end was cautious. He was asking if she would like to come out for a meal the following evening. He was asking in that careless way which was meant to indicate that it wouldn't matter if she couldn't make it, but couldn't disguise that he hoped she would.

His evident nervousness increased her own self-possession. She was back in charge of the situation, where she was used to being. 'A pub?' she said cheerfully. 'No, I don't mind eating in a pub. You'll pick me up at seven? Yes, I'm looking forward to seeing you, too. Oh, and Alan!' She pulled back the receiver she was about to put down. 'Thanks for the card.'

The receiver clicked softly back into its cradle. Meredith beamed into middle distance and congratulated herself. That hadn't been difficult, had it? She'd been friendly, casual, hadn't gushed, twittered or giggled. He was a mature man and wanted a correspondingly mature relationship. Ditto herself. Her brow crinkled. She sounded like an ad in the personal columns of a magazine. Who really wanted mature relationships anyway? She did, she told herself again firmly.

She pushed herself resolutely away from the telephone console and went back into the living room. Dimly lit by the gas fire and one lamp, its chintz cheerfulness in the mellow glow from the fire looked warm and comfortable like a nest. Whatever went on outside, one could feel safe in here.

The noise of a car engine leaping into life fell on her ear. With idle curiosity Meredith went to the window and tweaked the curtain aside to peer out. Across the road stood a cottage very like this one. Its front door stood open letting out a stream of yellow light which outlined the dark silhouette of a woman standing in the porch. She was waving goodbye to a visitor about to drive away in a large car. It looked like a Granada. The car roared off into the night, headlights sweeping the lane ahead. The woman turned back into the cottage and closed the door. Darkness fell over the road outside, almost total darkness which made Meredith realise for the first time how little in the way of street lighting existed in Pook's Common. In this stretch of lane there was just one faint glimmer from a lamp-post at the corner. As for the woman's appearance, of that she had made out little, just a tall, athletic figure. She thought, 'Miss Needham' and was a little surprised. For some reason – quite illogical – she had imagined Miss Needham to be an elderly spinster of genteel appearance and retiring habit, not someone much younger and in the receipt of visits by drivers of large cars. But perhaps Miss Needham was thinking the same about her, she thought wryly.

Meredith turned from the window, switched out the fire, checked the front and back doors and went up to bed, falling effortlessly asleep in the wide double bed.

Across the road, the light went out in Miss Needham's dormer windows, too.

In the Brissetts' council house Mrs Brissett awoke and dug her spouse in the ribs. 'Don't you forget to go up in the loft and bring them decorations down for Miss Mitchell, Fred.'

Laura Danby lay awake and wondered whether, if there would be an extra guest at Christmas, she ought to order a larger turkey.

Alan Markby, several miles away in Bamford, rolled over in his own over-large double bed. He wondered whether, when he went to collect Meredith tomorrow and take her out as arranged, he would find she had changed, or she would think he had, and what on earth they would find to talk about. And how he would broach the invitation issued to her by Laura. And what she would say. He fell asleep, torn between all these worries and the simple glow of pleasure which arose from the thought that he was going to see her at all.

Two

Bamford on a Friday morning before Christmas was everything Mrs Brissett had warned it would be. Meredith counted herself lucky to catch a space in the car park behind the supermarket as some other shopper pulled out. A glance through the plate glass doors of the supermarket itself sent her heart plummeting to her boots. A solid struggling mass of shoppers pushing unwieldy trolleys stacked high with goods, dragging along wailing children, bad-tempered, hot and tired, milled about in a frenzy.

Meredith turned her back on it. She'd go there last, when she had done all her other errands. With luck, the press might have thinned out. She walked down to the open market itself. But here the crowd was almost as bad. Stalls brandished stacks of holly and decorations of the kind beloved of Mrs Brissett. Unwholesome pink and yellow candies were sold from trays. Cut-price toys in boxes and cellophane wrapping spilled out of cardboard boxes. Vegetables seemed to have reached a record price. Meredith bought two pounds of satsumas and retired defeated. But she couldn't live on satsumas and the last of the bacon rashers until after Christmas. She pushed her way down the High Street, swinging her shopping bag against the legs of others and being clobbered in return. A young woman ran a pushchair into the back of her legs painfully and, when Meredith turned round, treated her to a furious glare which clearly said she had no business to be in the way. The High Street was bedecked with strings of coloured light bulbs and skeletal Christmas trees which would spring to life at dusk. Christmas carols blared tinnily from a loudspeaker system overhead and from every shop window, or so it seemed, the public was reminded that only four more shopping days remained until Christmas.

Meredith came to a halt by the florists and stared mistrustfully into the window. It was likely, more than likely, that Alan Markby might buy her some kind of Christmas present. He might even hand it over tonight when he called to take her out for a

17

meal. It would be embarrassing to be given a gift if one hadn't bought one in return. Buying aftershave or deodorant seemed much too intimate. A plant, however? He was a very keen gardener. Meredith pushed open the door and went in.

Inside resembled an untidy greenhouse. In anticipation of bumper Christmas sales, new stock had been crowded on to every available surface and spilled across the floor. The atmosphere was damp and suggested decay. There was a smell of wet peat compost and commercial plantfoods. A young woman in a pink overall emerged from the back, looking harassed.

'I want a potted plant,' Meredith explained. 'Something which blooms at Christmas. Perhaps something a bit unusual?' Her eye fell on a group of poinsettias. They seemed a bit obvious with their red leaves.

'How much do you want to pay?' asked the girl in practical tones.

'I don't know. How much are they?'

Some of them, it turned out, were very expensive. In fact, most of them were. She came out with a Christmas cactus.

As she forced her way back along the pavement, laden with shopping bag and plant wrapped in paper, Meredith sudden realised she was being hailed.

'Excuse me!' called a voice determinedly. 'Have you got a minute?' A tall spindly youth in a grubby ex-army greatcoat, blue jeans and a woolly hat, pushed his way in front of her. He was unshaven, not particularly well washed and appeared severely undernourished, but the voice was educated. 'Would you like to sign our petition?' he demanded aggressively.

She saw now that he held a clipboard. 'What's it about?' she asked with suspicion.

'To ban hunting on council-owned land.' He held out the clipboard impatiently as if she quibbled over a minor detail.

The crowd swirled round them and she found herself struggling to make sense of what he said. 'Hunting what?'

'Foxes. Or anything else. But foxes mostly. Because of the local hunt.'

'I didn't know they had one.' Someone cannoned into her shoulder and she nearly dropped the cactus. 'Look,' she said. 'I haven't got a hand free and I don't know what it's about . . .'

'The Bamford Hunt,' he said truculently. 'All you've got to do is sign here!' He pushed the clipboard at her. It had a stub of pencil attached to it by a string and the paper list was grubby, most signatures illegible. 'If we can keep them off council land it will make it nearly impossible for them. They're wrong, blood-sports are wrong. It's immoral. Everyone ought to be up in arms about it.' He thrust his whiskery countenance impatiently at her. Clearly he felt time wasted explaining his cause was time lost gathering signatures.

'I don't know anything about the Bamford Hunt,' Meredith said, suddenly finding him unattractive and pushy, his manner hectoring, and disliking both the way he assumed she would agree with him and the arrogance he displayed in failing to give any reason why she should do as he asked.

'Here, take a pamphlet!' He shoved one at her, ill-printed. 'Sign the petition, every signature helps. It's wrong. Fox-hunting is wrong.'

'You may be right or not,' she said crossly. 'I've never thought about it. And I certainly don't mean to sign anything before I have. So I won't if you don't mind. I'll read your pamphlet,' she added in a spirit of Christmas goodwill.

'Don't you care about wildlife?' he demanded furiously. 'Don't you care how barbaric it is? Don't you think animals matter? You ought to. You should. Everyone ought to sign!' He fixed her with a glittering eye. In it judgement was writ large. Nothing now would have induced Meredith to sign his petition, whatever it had been for. She didn't like him. It was as simple as that.

'Yes, I like animals but I don't like being told what to think before I've had a chance to make up my own mind!' Meredith thrust her way unceremoniously past him.

He scowled at her and then lurched away to trap some other person with his clipboard and pamphlets. As luck would have it, a strapping young woman was coming towards them. She had a head of flowing auburn hair and carried herself in a self-possessed manner touching on the arrogant. She wore no make-up but had classic features, a straight nose, full lips and fine eyes. She wore a well-used wax jacket over tight breeches and riding top boots. In jargon she would have understood, she was a thoroughbred. Bloodstock with sire and dam in the Form Book.

'He wouldn't . . .' thought Meredith dismayed at his temerity. 'He couldn't . . .'

But he did. The anti-bloodsports campaigner threw himself in the Amazon's path, brandishing his clipboard. Meredith could not hear what was being said but she could more or less guess at it. The stable yard fraternity is seldom short of the picturesque word. The auburn-haired equestrienne delivered herself of a pithy speech, gave the young man, now scarlet beneath his whiskers, no chance to reply, put out a hand and thrust him physically aside with such force that he staggered back and bounced off the door of Woolworth's behind him, and strode on.

'I could have told you that would happen,' said Meredith unsympathetically to him.

He gave her a dirty look and then threw an even dirtier one after the young woman. 'Toffy-nosed bitch!' he said. Then added in a mumble as if to himself, 'Just wait . . . just wait till you try it on Boxing Day. . . .' He shambled off.

As for Meredith, she forgot about him once she had ventured at last into the supermarket. From now on, it was every man for himself. She began by saying 'excuse me' politely and trying to manoeuvre her trolley round people. But it quickly became apparent she was wasting her time. The trolley also had a mind of its own and a tendency to advance crablike, sideways. The sheer volume of goods offered for sale added to her sense of disorientation and frustration. She had, after all, just spent some years in a country where shortages were common and varieties of goods few. Diplomatic staff such as herself depended heavily on goods brought in specially by their embassies for their use or on block orders from firms which existed to supply the needs of expatriates. Now to see three or four brands of tinned meat and half a dozen of coffee, all stacked up in profusion, was bewildering. She found it vaguely shocking to hear mothers ask small children what they wanted and casually add the often quite arbitrary choice of the child to the pile of goods already in the trolley. Within five minutes, Meredith was not only as hot, bothered and bad-tempered as the rest, she was angry too at people who did not seem to appreciate what they had. She stood fuming in the check-out queue in a cloud of righteous indignation, fuelled by the discovery that she had forgotten the washing-up liquid.

'Drat it!' she said aloud.

'Forgotten something?' asked a male voice behind her.

She glanced round guiltily. The voice was that of a bespectacled man of indeterminate age and appearance wearing a parka coat and standing behind her in the queue. He held a wire basket with a modest stack of provisions. He smiled pleasantly at her. 'I'll hold your spot in the queue if you want to go back and get it.'

Meredith looked back at the heaving throng on the shop floor.

'No, thanks. I don't think I could face it. Thank you all the same.' On impulse she added, 'There's so much to buy – they don't realise how lucky they are!'

He smiled. 'Some are. Some can't afford it. To see a shop window full of goods when you haven't the money to buy isn't much fun.'

Meredith frowned, considering this. For some reason she felt she owed him a serious answer. He was only a man in a queue but something in his voice suggested that what she had said struck a chord in him. He cared about this.

'People aren't as poor now as they were years ago,' she said. 'I know some aren't well off, but a hundred years ago they starved on the streets.'

'Some still live on the streets. Not here in Bamford admittedly. But in big cities. . . . Been up to London recently?'

'No, not yet,' said Meredith gloomily, thinking of the FO desk which awaited her. 'After Christmas I shall be travelling up every day.'

'Take a look in shop doorways early in the mornings. Count the sleeping bags.' The queue shuffled forward a little. 'Perhaps they aren't starving,' the man went on, 'but they feel failures.' He pushed his spectacles up the bridge of his nose. They seemed to have a tendency to slide down it. 'There's so much, as you say, and everyone else seems to them to be doing well enough to enjoy it all. Fifty years ago it wasn't a disgrace to be poor – it was a shared misfortune with thousands of others. Now the poor are made to feel ashamed, that it's their own fault, some shortcoming which they have. Many of the youngsters feel resentful, that society is kicking them out. You can't blame them.'

'No, I suppose not,' Meredith said slowly.

He gave an embarrassed smile. 'I didn't mean to lecture you. The subject is by way of a special interest of mine.'

'That's all right.' She was moved to offer, 'You've only a basket of a few items, you might as well go in front of me. I've got a trolley-full.'

'Oh, that's all right. I'm not in a hurry. You carry on.'

'Next person please!' requested the check-out girl snappily and Meredith was forced to move up and hastily unload her goods on to the conveyor belt.

Her shopping paid for, Meredith pushed the grumbling trolley out to her car. There were ominous dark clouds gathering overhead now and a chill wind. She packed everything away and returned her wire chariot to the 'trolley park' shivering in the air which struck so cold after the oppressive warmth of the supermarket. Meredith backed out slowly to avoid other shoppers making for their cars with their overladen squeaky trolleys and set off out of town.

She was surprised at how relieved she felt when she reached Pook's Common. It felt like quite a haven of peace in comparison to Bamford. Rose Cottage did not have a garage, but it had a parking space formed by sacrificing most of the front garden. She got out and shivered in an icy blast which struck right through her anorak. The dark clouds had become more compact and although it was still only late morning, it was as dark as a gathering twilight. Meredith rubbed reddened fingers together and went round to the boot to unload her wares. As she did there was a screech of brakes and another car drew up outside the cottage opposite, causing her to glance up. The driver's door slammed and to her surprise a figure she recognised got out.

It was the red-head she'd seen in town. She looked across the road, saw Meredith, smiled and came striding athletically towards her.

'Hullo,' she said. 'I'm Harriet Needham. I live over there in Ivy Cottage.'

'Meredith Mitchell,' Meredith said, disentangling herself from a welter of plastic carrier bags.

'Been into Bamford, have you?' asked Miss Needham sympathetically. 'Bloody awful, isn't it?'

'Pretty dreadful. I had to stock up for the holiday break.'

'You've taken the cottage on from the Russells, haven't you?' Harriet tossed back her mane of red hair. 'Come over and have a drink sometime.'

'Thanks, that's kind of you. I will.'

'Why don't you come over now and have coffee? It's going to bucket down with rain later.' Harriet squinted up at the dark sky with businesslike appraisal. 'Mud!' she muttered, Meredith realised not to her but in response to a thought triggered by the weather and important to the speaker.

'Thanks, I will. I've to unload all this first of all.'

'Sure, fine. I've got my lot to unpack as well. I'll leave the front door open. Just come in when you're ready and yell.' Harriet strode back to her own side of the road.

Meredith went into the cottage, arms full of bags. A faint clatter from the kitchen indicated Mrs Brissett was just finishing up. There was a smell of wax polish in the air mixed with lavender from the downstairs cloakroom. The living room door stood ajar and Meredith, staggering past on her way to the kitchen, stopped abruptly, transfixed. 'Oh, dear . . .' she said faintly, unable for the moment to come up with any stronger remark although Miss Needham could probably have obliged. 'Oh my goodness, whatever am I going to do about this?'

Mrs Brissett popped out of the kitchen door. 'You leave them groceries, Miss Mitchell. I'll put them all away.'

'Thank you . . . and thank you for . . . for. . . .' Meredith faltered.

'Knew you'd like it!' said Mrs Brissett.

Harriet's door stood open as she had promised. An inviting smell of coffee wafted into Meredith's nostrils. She called, 'I'm here!'

'In the kitchen!'

She followed Harriet's voice. Ivy Cottage had originally had much the same ground plan as Rose Cottage. But someone had built on a large extension to the rear and this housed the kitchen, which as Meredith was to discover, was large, modern and furbished it seemed with every kind of modern gadget. The former kitchen had been made into a small dining room almost entirely filled with an early Victorian table and set of six chairs which were undeniably the real thing. There was a buffet across the top of which was ranged a set of blue and white plates of equally antique origin and in the middle of the table stood a Georgian silver chafing dish. It looked as though Harriet liked to entertain.

This thought was reinforced by the sight of Harriet's groceries, strewn across a worktop in the kitchen extension – French bread and a large packet of chicken breasts, two bottles of good wine and several unusual cheeses, plenty of fresh, out-of-season and expensive salads and all the trimmings of a dinner party. But for how many? wondered Meredith, remembering the departing car of the previous evening.

Harriet noticed her looking at the groceries and said cheerfully, 'I took one of those cordon bleu cookery courses. Useful. I couldn't boil an egg before.'

A little embarrassed because it looked as though she had been prying, Meredith murmured, 'I'm not much of a cook.'

'It's fun, I like doing it. And there's time enough here at Pook's Common for things like cooking. You need time and not to be rushed.'

'Yes, it's certainly quiet enough here,' Meredith observed a little ruefully. 'Away from it all.'

'That's what I thought when I first came.' Harriet set the cups and cream jug on a tray with brisk efficiency. 'But funnily enough, it's not. It's surprising what's around in Pook's Common!' She did not elaborate on this tantalising hint but picked up the tray. 'We'll go in the drawing room. More comfortable.'

Harriet's drawing room, the equivalent of Rose Cottage's humbler living room situated in the front of the building, was furnished with a mixture of modern comfortable easy chairs and several nice old pieces, a Victorian roll-top desk and a little Regency card table among them. Had they come together with the antiques in the dining room from a larger house, a family home? Meredith wondered. On a purely practical note, all this added up to quite a bit in value and Ivy Cottage did not appear to have any extra locks or catches at the windows.

Yet the thing which struck her most of all here in the drawing room was that Harriet seemed to have a passion for photographs. In every kind of frame and occasionally jammed, a smaller snapshot in front of a larger, in the same frame, they spilled across the mantelshelf and over tabletops, shelves and cupboards. Several of them pictured Harriet or others with horses.

'Do you keep a horse yourself?' Meredith asked.

'Old Blazer.' Harriet picked up a newish picture. 'This one. Tom Fearon keeps him for me at the livery stables. He's a nice old chap.'

Meredith wasn't sure whether Harriet meant the horse or Mr Fearon so she murmured politely.

Harriet poured out the coffee. 'You certainly need something to buck you up after dealing with that scrum in Bamford. I loathe shopping. But none of the shops delivers and there's no village store around here.'

'Do you live in Pook's Common all the time?' Meredith asked as she took the cup. It was pretty bone china sprigged with rosebuds. 'Some of the cottages look like weekend homes.'

Harriet had returned to the kitchen. Her voice came muffled. 'Some are. There are only eight of them all told, four on each side, as you've probably observed.' She came back, this time carrying a plate with home-made biscuits on it which she held out to Meredith. 'Help yourself, "Viennese whirls" they're called. My problem is that I like to make the things but can't

24

possibly eat them all myself. Well, if I did, I'd need to sell old Blazer and buy a shire horse to carry me! Hang on, I'll get you a napkin.'

The napkin was damask and perfectly laundered. Harriet did everything right. Efficiency about the house on the part of others always inspired wistful envy in Meredith who was efficient about the office and rather at sea about the home. I, she thought disconsolately, offer people packet biscuits if I've remembered to buy any and generally only have paper napkins. But Harriet had returned to Meredith's query about the cottages.

'The semi-detached pair on the right of yours, looking at them from the road, belong to one of the Oxford colleges. One of those gets used by various people, no idea who any of 'em are. But the other is used by Dr Krasny. He comes down when he has a lot of writing to do because it's quiet. One doesn't see much of him even when he's here. He's a pleasant enough chap, though, and generally looks in to say hullo and have a glass of sherry on his way out to tramp over the common looking for flowers. I believe his subject is rare wild orchids.'

'There is an actual common, then?'

'Oh yes. Although it's not strictly grazing land any more. More like open moorland. The cottagers of Pook's Common used to have grazing rights but I'm the only one to keep an animal now and I keep mine in a paddock belonging to Tom. Turning out a valuable beast on the common today would be asking for trouble. We had rustlers round a year or two back. Sounds like the Wild West, doesn't it? It still goes on, quite a bit. The poor brutes go for slaughter, horsemeat steaks for the continent.'

Harriet sipped at her coffee. 'The one on the left of yours is Mrs Sowerby's. She's elderly and hardly ever puts her nose out of the front door. Her daughter drives out from Bamford once a week but around this time of year she goes to stay with some other relative, I'm not sure where, so I dare say she isn't there at the moment and you haven't got any immediate neighbours resident. This is a pretty lonely spot, As regards this side of the road, looking towards mine. The cottage next door to this on the right, it's got a ghastly fake wishing well in the front garden, belongs to the chap who runs the garage up on the main road, Joe Fenniwick and his wife. They're permanent residents, like me. Joe's a good mechanic incidentally and you can take your car to him with confidence. The cottage on the left here was bought by some business type who was going to weekend here with his girlfriend. He spent a fortune doing it up and then his girlfriend bolted and now he wants to sell. Bottom's fallen out of the market, though, just now. That only leaves the one at the far end, which belongs to a couple who plan to retire here in the spring. Hope they like things quiet. In the meantime it's empty, although they generally turn up at weekends and mess around the place, painting bits and pieces and knocking in nails. So it is rather deserted. I like it that way myself.'

'I'm going to have to travel up to London every day of the week,' Meredith said with some regret. 'I don't start until after New Year. I'm beginning to wonder if I've bitten off more than I can chew.'

'Rather you than me,' Harriet said frankly. She paused. 'What do you do?'

Meredith explained. Harriet gazed at her thoughtfully. 'I admire anyone who can hold down a job,' she said suddenly. 'I worked for a bit when I was about eighteen. It was in Liverpool, because I lived in the Wirral then and I used to travel over there every day to put in my hours. I say I worked, but I mean it was for a charity which ran one of these centres where they try and help the socially deprived. They had an old people's day room and a young mothers' club and a crèche and all kinds of projects for youngsters. I'll be honest, I couldn't stick it out. I only did mornings but even the mornings were too much for me.' She pulled a slight grimace. 'I have independent means. You haven't to say that these days. People look at you as if you'd said you had plague. I have turned my hand to trying a bit of writing and I keep meaning to take it up again. I prefer being out of doors, though, that's my trouble, and writing takes up so much time. Wish I could say I did do something organised and worthwhile on a regular basis.'

'You could!' Meredith said promptly. 'You just haven't found the right job for you.'

Harriet looked thoughtful again. 'Perhaps I will one day. And perhaps I've found the thing for me already. I don't mean a job, but something which needs doing, all the same.'

Her gaze had drifted as she spoke and seemed to rest on one of the photographs displayed nearby. Meredith followed her line of sight and saw that it rested on an oldish-looking photo. It showed three little girls in sandals and sundresses grouped together with a spaniel dog. One little girl had familiar red curls.

Harriet glanced at Meredith and saw that she was looking at the picture. 'That's me,' she said pointing at it. 'You can always tell by the carrotty hair.' She got up and picked up the frame and brought it over to Meredith. 'That's my cousin Fran next to me. We were much the same age and more like sisters than cousins, really.'

'And who is that?' Meredith pointed at the third child, a pretty little girl with dark hair and an engaging, impish grin. 'She looks a happy child.'

'Oh, that's Caro, Caroline Henderson, a friend of ours.' Harriet's voice was still casual but it struck Meredith its carelessness was now a little forced. 'She was a happy child. We all were. It was a good childhood. I'm glad Caro was happy then because she sure as hell wasn't later on!' She withdrew the photo abruptly and returned it to its place on a table.

'I'm sorry,' Meredith said awkwardly.

Harriet looked slightly abashed. 'I didn't mean to snap. Sorry. It was just that we were all so fond of her. Caro was a diabetic.' She seemed to be making an effort to speak in a dispassionate practical tone. 'And just to make things more difficult, an heiress. Her father died when she was a kid, as did her uncle, which meant that her grandfather who was as rich as Croesus had no one else to leave his ill-gotten gains to. It wasn't a blessing!' Harriet's voice had grown bleaker as she spoke and finally broke off on a clipped note of finality.

'I can imagine that. Diabetes is quite a burden to carry through life.'

'The money was a worse one. But she didn't carry it for long,' Harriet drained her cup and set it down noisily on the tray. 'She was only twenty-three when she died from an overdose.'

'I'm sorry,' Meredith said awkwardly. 'Was it to do with the diabetes?'

'Not really. They said it was depression. She had been treated for depression. The doctors prescribed all kinds of pills. I told her to throw the lot away. I wish she had done. You know, once a woman's got a name as a neurotic no one takes her seriously any more. No matter what's wrong, they prescribe more pills and tell her to take it easy. Nobody listens to her. No one believes her any more but they're ready to believe anything anyone else says about her!'

'It's a tricky problem,' Meredith said cautiously. 'Dealing with a neurotic person is well-nigh impossible. They do go off the deep-end and tell you extraordinary tales. I've had to deal with a few.'

'Oh, I know it's like crying wolf,' Harriet nodded. 'But if you know that person, you can generally disentangle what's really happening from the rest. I'm not a fanciful person. I suppose I'm quite hard-headed in a way. But I don't lack sympathy. The reason I packed in the charity job wasn't because I didn't sympathise. It was because I got so frustrated. I'd slave my guts out on a case and think I'd got it settled and a week later the woman would turn up in my office with the same dreary tale. Working for an outfit like that helps you tell the real from the fraud.' She paused. 'But you still get it wrong, sometimes. I don't like being made a fool of!'

Outside in the little hallway, the telephone rang. Harriet said 'Excuse me!', got to her feet and went out to answer it. She closed the door behind her and the conversation came to Meredith as the muffled indistinguishable sound of Harriet's voice. Meredith was relieved to be spared the embarrassment of unavoidable eavesdropping. Harriet's voice rose aggressively and then the receiver was slammed down. She returned, flushed, and walked to the drinks cabinet. 'Would you like a glass of sherry? Or something stronger? Wish each other Merry Christmas and all that!' She was reaching for the glasses already. Clearly, she meant to have a drink.

'All right, a sherry would be fine,' said Meredith who really didn't like drinking in the middle of the day.

Harriet pushed back the whisky bottle and poured out two sherries. They toasted one another in Croft Original.

'Absent friends,' Harriet added before drinking hers. 'May they never be forgotten.'

As foreseen by the dark clouds, it began to rain during the afternoon and by the time the headlights of Markby's car illuminated the front windows of Rose Cottage, it was fairly tipping down. He dashed up the short front path at a run and shot through the door Meredith held open for him.

Squashed against her in the tiny hall, he dripped water and spluttered apologies. She thought that he hadn't changed a bit. It was the same thin, intelligent slightly wary face and as far as she could tell the same old Barbour jacket. He was the sort of man who loathed new clothes. His hair fell over his forehead in a damp straight lock and his blue eyes were screwed up as if in concern or alarm.

'Have you got a mac?' he asked anxiously. 'We have to get from the pub car park into the pub. It's bucketing down.'

'I've got my anorak and it has a hood. I was afraid it might rain for Christmas.' Why was it when English people met again after an absence, they talked so determinedly about the weather? But he had spotted the wreath, hung up in the hall.

'That's a bit – bright.' He stooped over it, peering down. It hung at the level of his chest.

'It's Mrs Brissett's. She threatened to bring a plastic Father Christmas too. As it is, look in here.' Meredith threw open the door to the living room.

'Good grief,' he said faintly.

Paper chains, turquoise, acid yellow and flaming scarlet, were draped about the room from corner to corner and back and forth. A large puce Chinese lantern dangled from the ceiling and a silver tinsel Christmas tree stood on the coffee table.

'She did it all while I was in Bamford shopping this morning. It's so kind of her and she must have worked so hard . . . I can't possibly take any of it down. She said she was sure I must have missed an English Christmas abroad all these years. I don't know how she got up to fix the ceiling chains.'

'It's, ah, cheerful . . . and talking of Christmas – ' He broke off and looked embarrassed, then said, 'I'll explain later. Shall we go and get that steak?'

He took them by a tortuous route to a pub called The Black Dog, which made a change from horses and pookas, until she recollected uneasily that a black dog was one of the devil's traditional earthly disguises. Meredith, trying to use her bump of direction thought they had gone in a circle and as far as she could tell through teeming rain and darkness, were in the middle of the open moor or common. For all its slightly sinister name and the murk and the remoteness of its location, The Black Dog presented a brightly lit oasis suggesting welcome and hospitality. A string of multi-coloured lights gleamed beneath the overhanging thatch and bright yellow light was streaming from its tiny windows. Several cars were already parked in the yard at its side.

'Christmas,' said Markby gloomily. 'Mind you, I think we're getting the "don't drink and drive" message across. Not so much by getting them to understand as frightening them with a

Breathalyser test and losing their licence. Everyone needs to drive these days.'

A blast of warm smoky air struck Meredith's face as she preceded him into the one large room inside. The Black Dog had abandoned the old distinction between saloon and public bars. The 'public' which frequented it had become an amorphous mass. Very few true locals could be distinguished here: a car-borne young-ish, free-spending town-based clientèle supplied the bulk of the trade. They were sharp-faced and casually clad. The older people there looked well-dressed and prosperous. All mingled together and jostled for their drinks or huddled round tables over plates of food. Food was obviously as important a commodity as drink in The Black Dog. It would be interesting, thought Meredith, to know at what point exactly a 'pub' became a 'restaurant'. But in the latter establishment customers would have demanded more space and comfort. Here they accepted others cannoning into their backs as they ate and occasionally dripping overflowing beer glasses on to their tables or even down their necks.

The bar was against the far wall, plentifully stocked and presided over by a bleached blonde in a white beaded sweater. A slim youth with curly hair pushed his way round, collecting used glasses, and a young girl with a notebook was taking orders for food at the bar. The place was fairly crowded and noisy with chatter. There was the inevitable piped Muzak but it was mercifully unobtrusive.

The building itself was obviously very old. Its walls were of thick stone blocks and bulged and its low ceiling criss-crossed with smoke-blackened oak beams. A fire blazed in a huge hearth beneath an oak lintel which, to judge by its thickness, must have come from a tree already at least a hundred years old when it was felled to help build this ancient building. Horse brasses had been tacked along the length of the oaken lintel and gleamed in the firelight. There was a framed poster above it, advertising a livestock sale of the 1860s. Meredith craned her neck and saw behind her an even older notice announcing a trio of public hangings, two of them for offences which in some circumstances would not even have warranted a custodial sentence today. She wondered if it was an original or a reproduction. It was brownish-yellow and very tattered and looked as if it might be the real thing. An unpleasant thing, too.

Meredith wrenched her gaze from the sad little scrap of paper and looked about her. Despite the noise and the modern dress of the customers, it was not difficult to imagine men with clay pipes sitting around the hearth of The Black Dog on windy, wet nights. But modern marketing had laid its hand on the old tap-room. The chairs were upholstered in crimson dralon 'velvet' and a newer, brighter, and considerably less literate notice on the wall advertised the coming attractions of regular Saturday 'gigs'. The menu, judging from plates already on tables, was surprisingly sophisticated for such an out-of-the-way establishment.

'It's getting popular,' said Markby as they squeezed into a corner settle near the fire. 'You all right there? Not going to be too hot? Give me your coat, there's a place to hang them over there. What would you like to drink?'

'I'm sorry, I was gaping at all the knick-knacks!' she smiled up at him. 'I'll have a glass of white wine if I may.'

'I was hoping you'd like this place.' He gave a rueful grimace. 'Just sorry it's so crowded. Hang on, I'll be back in a jiff.'

She watched him fight his way across the room to hang up the coats and then to the bar. He did it without pushing and shoving but with competent authority. People moved out of his way and didn't seem to mind doing so. He always thanked anyone who did, she noticed, and felt a return of the respect he had inspired in her at their first meeting. Not, she recalled, that he couldn't be awkward. But then, she admitted honestly, so could she!

Meredith sat back, feeling the heat of the flames play on her face and relaxing. It was noisy and crowded but it was nice to have it so and Alan needn't have worried that she'd dislike that. A large black cat with tattered ears appeared and strolled unconcernedly through the maze of feet to rub itself against her legs. Not a dog, devilish or otherwise, she thought with some amusement but then remembered tales of witches and their black feline familiars. All this superstitious nonsense was getting to her.

'Hullo,' said Meredith, stooping to scratch one battle-torn ear. The cat mewed up at her, displaying a fearsome and off-putting set of teeth. A voice from a nearby table floated towards her.

'Keep them out of the hands of the police, that's the thing. What we need are proper assessment centres. They need help, not locking up. Once they've served any kind of custodial sentence so much damage is done . . .'

A fresh burst of noise cut off the end of the sentence. Meredith lifted her head from her feline acquaintance, pushed back the curtain of dark brown hair which obscured her vision and looked curiously in the general direction of the voice. But it was impossible to tell now who had been speaking or even to be sure at which of the small crowded tables the speaker sat. Of the two tables nearby, one was occupied by a mixed group of men and women, all young and casually clad, the other by two men, one with a beard and guernsey sweater in which, in this warm room, he must be sweltering and the other with thinning hair, bespectacled and somehow familiar.

I know him! she thought. He was the chap behind me in the supermarket.

'Sorry to take so long!' Markby was back, holding a pint in one hand and her glass of wine in the other. He also had a plastic-covered book under his arm. 'Menu,' he said. 'Take it, can you?'

Meredith pulled it free and opened it up. Goodness, this wasn't a menu, it was a volume. She supposed that she wrongly still thought of pub meals in terms of bread and cheese or pasties. As in so many other things, she decided with a sigh, being out of one's own country for such long stretches of time, left one behind the times. She remembered her experience in the supermarket. It made one critical, too.

Markby said helpfully, 'The steaks here are generally all right, which is one reason I come here. Or the salad and cold meat is okay.'

'I'll settle for the rump steak, then.'

Markby battled his way back to the bar to place their order and when he came back they sat and looked shiftily at one another. Food ordered, the obvious subject of conversation gone, neither was quite sure what to say now.

'How was your drive back across Europe?' he asked.

'Pretty uneventful. I'd rather drive at this time of the year than in summer when there's so much tourist traffic.'

'Settled in all right at Rose Cottage, Christmas decorations apart?'

'Oh yes. Mrs Brissett's a treasure, as they say. I'm very lucky.'

Two avenues of conversation neatly blocked off, silence fell. My fault, thought Meredith despondently. She ought to expand but how?

'Dirty night,' said Markby determinedly, falling back on the British standby, the weather.

'Yes. Nice and warm in here and I like to see so many people.

They're busier than usual, I suppose.'

'Oh yes, Christmas . . .' He fiddled with a beermat. 'I was going to ask you about that. Are you staying around here? I mean for the actual Christmas period, Christmas Day, Boxing Day and so on.'

'I imagine so. I haven't anywhere else to go.' That sounded wistful so she added robustly, 'I know I said I liked seeing the crowd in here but that doesn't mean I can't manage on my own. I don't mind it being quiet!' The last words came out defiantly. She hoped he didn't interpret them as telling him to mind his own business. She didn't mean to sound brusque. Perhaps he just made her nervous.

She saw with some dismay that his expression had grown sombre. 'Oh,' he said, 'Quiet.' Whatever else Christmas Day at Laura's might be, it couldn't be guaranteed to be quiet, he thought.

'Pook's Common is virtually a ghost settlement, did you know?' Meredith burst into a relentless rattle of meaningless information, determined to keep the conversation going. 'Hardly anyone lives there full time. It's a bit like coming back to Britain and finding you've committed yourself to living in Brigadoon.'

'A bit creepy?' he asked sympathetically.

'Not so far.' She didn't want to give the impression she was in need of company at the cottage. Then, thinking she sounded brusque again, added, 'But I imagine it could be, in the right circumstances.'

Markby nodded sagely, raised his beer glass and then, in a surprised voice, said, 'Hullo!'

She glanced up. He was staring at the two men at the nearby table.

'Who are they?' Meredith asked curiously in a low voice. 'I met one of them earlier today.'

'Did you?' he sounded startled. 'Which one? Where?'

'Only casually in a supermarket. He was behind me in the queue. The one with the spectacles.'

'That's Colin Deanes. I don't know the other chap, the bearded one. But I'd happily put a quid on his being a social worker. Deanes writes and lectures about teenage delinquents.' Markby was beginning to sound animated. 'He's got a bee in his bonnet about keeping them out of remand homes and prison. I'm not against that, but you can't leave young thugs loose to go round terrorising honest folk. As far as I can make out, Deanes doesn't believe that young people should be expected to know the difference between right and wrong. Expecting people to know it's wrong to mug old ladies doesn't seem unreasonable to me, but I'm just a copper. Deanes says it's a cry for help.'

Chief Inspector was slightly more than just a copper, Meredith thought wryly, amused at his apparent self-abasement. From her experience of him he certainly wasn't unaware of his own competence!

'Such modesty!' she teased him gently.

'A public servant, that's me. So are you. You should know as well as I do the public can be a very difficult master!' He took a purposeful swig of his beer and set it down.

'Hum, yes. I take it you've had dealings with Mr Deanes?'

'He's rented an old farmhouse right out in the middle of nowhere on the common, beyond your place and even more isolated, believe it or not. He's been writing his latest book there. He shows up in Bamford from time to time at the station. He likes to take up my time, looking for copy. He'd call it doing research. It's impossible to discuss anything with him. His view is entirely blinkered. I'd say his heart was in the right place if I didn't doubt that, since he has so little sympathy for the victims of his young tearaways. I'm not against anyone trying to help put youngsters straight, but people like Deanes never want to hear any point of view but their own. He seems to assume I'm about as liberal-minded as Genghis Khan and the annoying thing is, when he talks to me, I start sounding like the worst sort of reactionary. He provokes it. I take up points of view I don't actually support strongly and start defending them to the hilt. Even when I do agree with him, he makes it extraordinarily difficult for me to say so.'

Meredith smiled to herself at his mounting vehemence. This was the Alan Markby she remembered! She almost commented on the irony of the last charge he laid against Deanes. It was a bit like the pot calling the kettle black. At the time of the Westerfield poisonings he had sometimes been a difficult man to agree with, and he'd more than once annoyed her by his attitude. Perhaps, she reflected ruefully, she was just easily irritated. She recalled the young man she had met campaigning in the street that morning. He hadn't meant any harm but his few words had set her against him. On reflection, she had been too quick to judge him and she regretted it now.

'I met someone today,' she said, 'who affected me a little as you describe Deanes affecting you.' She told him about the anti-blood-sports campaigner. 'He was a harmless sort of youth really, just trying to do what he thought was right. But he was so ham-fisted about it. He annoyed me and I'm afraid I didn't sign his petition.'

'Oh yes,' Markby said. 'The Boxing Day Meet.' He sounded glad to get on to another subject. 'The Bamford Hunt always gathers in the Market Square on Boxing Day and after downing a glass or two of something sustaining, moves off for a day's sport, watched by the local populace. It is possible that this year we'll have hunt saboteurs to contend with. They try and throw the hounds off the scent and generally disrupt things. They may turn up in a show of force in the Market Square.'

The return to a seasonal topic seemed to have prompted him to tackle something obviously on his mind. 'About Christmas. The reason I asked you just now what you planned to do was that Laura, my sister – you remember her, don't you? She's a partner in a firm of solicitors in the High Street – well, she thought you might like to join us for a family Christmas dinner. The food will be all right,' he added hastily, 'because Paul, my brother-in-law, always cooks it. That's his line, cooking. He writes about it.'

'It's very kind of Laura,' Meredith said doubtfully.

He seized on the doubt. 'You don't have to. I mean, it's up to you. Of course, she'd be delighted and so would I, since I've got to be there. She's got youngsters . . .'

'Yes, I seem to recall you told me about your sister and her kids, three of them, right?'

'Four – there's been an increase. The littlest one leaks at both ends incessantly. Matthew, the eldest, is quite a bright chap and Emma, the next one age-wise, is all right but learning the recorder. She's practising "Jingle Bells" for a Christmas solo. Vicky doesn't do much except break things. A sort of potential lady-wrestler. They're all right, really, but if you'd prefer peace and quiet, you might find them a bit exhausting.'

He looked so comically apologetic that she had to burst out laughing. 'I should love to come. Tell Laura, and I'll give her a call myself.'

'Fine, that's okay, then.' He looked relieved. 'I'm glad you're coming.' Hastily he added, 'Because it means Laura keeps the kids in better order if there's a visitor. I don't count.'

'Oh, I see.'

35

The girl arrived then with their steaks and there was a welcome break in conversation, during which they observed Deanes and his companion departing from their nearby table. They began to squeeze their way towards the door and in doing so, passed by Markby.

'Ah – hullo, Chief Inspector!' Deanes said. He stopped and pushed his spectacles further up his nose with a forefinger in the gesture Meredith recalled. Now that she took another look at it, it was a rather insignificant sort of nose on which any pair of spectacles might be expected to slip. He had pulled on his fur-lined parka ready to brave the elements. 'Policeman's night out?' he asked humorously.

'We do get some time off!' Markby said brusquely.

'Hope you enjoy your meal.' Deanes looked towards Meredith and a surprised expression crossed his face. 'Small world! We met briefly in the supermarket in Bamford. Perhaps you don't recall me?'

'Yes, I do.' Meredith smiled.

'Glad to see you got out of there in one piece, Mrs Markby.'

'Oh, but I'm not!' began Meredith and Markby at the same time exclaimed, 'She isn't!' so that their denials chimed in unison.

Deanes chuckled. 'Oh, I see. Well, enjoy yourselves. Happy Christmas.'

He followed his guernsey-sweatered companion out, leaving the two diners in unhappy silence, avoiding one another's eye.

'We didn't handle that very well,' Meredith said at last.

'He is a silly blighter,' Markby said irritably, taking a gulp from his pint.

Meredith, recalling her brief conversation with Deanes in the queue, felt compelled to defend him. He had shown, or so it had seemed to her at the time, genuine concern for others. Such a man earned a good word on his behalf. 'Are you sure you're fair to him?' she ventured disastrously. 'Or are you predisposed by your calling to see him as interfering – trespassing on your patch?'

A warlike gleam entered Markby's blue eyes. He jabbed a forefinger at her. 'Listen here, Miss Smart-Alec, you haven't seen him in full flight! Put him on the telly, give him a bit of limelight and away goes our Colin! No one else can get a word in edgeways. And he's not always entirely fair to the poor foot-slogging copper, either.'

Meredith drew herself up. 'People are entitled to their opinions, I suppose. And anyway –' Meredith was aware of her own tone growing argumentative. 'Take a look at that!' She pointed at the poster announcing the public hangings. 'Penal reform has certainly been needed in the past and probably still is. Ideas of how society should treat its criminals change just as ideas of justice change. Once upon a time a man could hang for setting fire to a hayrick! Thank goodness for people prepared to stand up to authority and tackle the system they believe is wrong.'

'Even if they stop you on a busy shopping morning and ask you to sign petitions?' Markby countered craftily.

'That's unfair!' Meredith said indignantly. 'All right, yes! Even if it means you've got to inconvenience the uncommitted. Although fox-hunting on council land isn't quite what Deanes campaigns about, is it?'

'Deanes campaigns for causes which have a high profile,' said Markby drily. 'That may be pure coincidence, of course, and I may be a sceptic.' He glared at her over his beer, daring her to agree with his last assertion.

Meredith was not to be led away from the point at issue. 'The causes may have a high profile because Deanes campaigns for them! Good for him, he's doing his job.'

He was gazing at her with an infuriating world-weariness suggesting he'd heard her argument a hundred times before. 'This is turning into one of those mediaeval disputes which split hairs endlessly,' he said. 'Are you playing devil's advocate, by any chance?'

'No, I'm not!' exclaimed a heated Meredith, bouncing about in her chair. Her hair fell over her face and she glowered at him. 'I'm not saying the man should be considered as a candidate for sainthood. Just that perhaps he ought to be respected!'

Her companion gave a muffled grunt and attacked his steak vigorously. After a mouthful he seemed to relent. 'All right, then, I'll admit to a degree of prejudice against people who seem to make a living out of being agin the establishment. But I'm certainly not against anyone taking up arms against an injustice. It's when people are opinionated, as opposed to having a properly argued opinion that I lose patience with them. Or when they refuse to face unpleasant truths, like good and evil. They try to blend them together when they're really opposites!' Danger of choking stopped him at that point. After a moment or two when he had swallowed his steak and could speak safely, he went on, 'Modern theology doesn't help, I dare say. To say nothing of modern educational notions. But sometimes a chap is a wrong'un, pure and simple.' He gave a decided nod as if to approve his own argument.

'You believe in evil, then?' Meredith asked curiously. She had often wondered whether policemen did believe in something it was now so fashionable to doubt.

'Oh, yes.' Markby put down his knife and fork and regarded her seriously. 'Oh, yes, indeed. Very much so. Hoofs, horns, forked tail and all,' he added with a grin. Meredith didn't respond to his attempt to lighten the conversation but merely sat staring at him thoughtfully. Serious again, he went on, 'A real presence sometimes, at any rate, even if not quite like the folk image. I've had occasion to talk to men who have committed appalling crimes and sometimes I swear I've felt it there in the room with us, wickedness.'

'And good? Does that exist as a real force?'

'Oh, certainly. Good too. There are more good people about than the world gives credit for.'

'So where does that place Deanes? On the side of the angels or the other lot?'

Markby chuckled, his customary air of self-deprecation returning. 'I can't say, "somewhere in the middle", can I? Not after the other things, I've said. I didn't mean to divide the world into black and white, you know. Of course there's a grey area. I was talking of extremes. As for Deanes, there's an old and venerable tradition of the holy fool. But Christmas is upon us and I shall be charitable. The fellow means well. Just keep him out of my hair. Would you like another drink?'

'Only if you're having one.'

'Can't. Driving. Have to set a good example. Never do if I was ordered to pull over and blow into a bag.'

'We can go back to Rose Cottage, always supposing Pook's Common is still where we left it, and I'll make coffee,' she offered, aware that she should contribute to the peace that had broken out between them.

He smiled at her. 'That sounds nice.'

They sat over the coffee, talking more easily in the cosy intimacy of the cottage than in the crowded bar of The Black Dog. Meredith told him what she had been doing since they last met and Markby gave a summary of his own activities. 'Sadly routine, I'm afraid,' was his verdict. 'Not as interesting as yours.'

Meredith demurred.

'Mine aren't always all that interesting. People think my job's full of excitement. But mostly I'm pushing bits of paper around. Some of the exciting things I could do without. And then there's the gruesome. They turn up from time to time.'

'Yes, they do, don't they?' Markby smiled. 'Or at least they do in my job.'

Their eyes met and they looked away from one another. Both knew the other was thinking of their first meeting and the case of murder in which Meredith had found herself so painfully entangled. Absence from the scene, thought Meredith, and being involved in other countries in other people's affairs had made it all seem rather long ago. But it wasn't: only eighteen months.

The relaxed air which had reigned in the warm little living room of Rose Cottage seemed suddenly to have evaporated. Markby stirred and made signs of being about to take farewell. 'I really must go. It's been . . . it's been very pleasant. Nice to see you again.'

Suddenly they were formal.

'Yes, likewise. Thanks for the meal.'

It had stopped raining but the night was dark and damp.

'Don't stand about on the doorstep,' he said. 'You'll catch cold.'

Nodding obediently – slightly idiotically – she thought, Meredith went back indoors and watched through the window as he drove away. Across the lane, the windows of Ivy Cottage were dark. Not tonight, Harriet's dinner party, Meredith thought. She remembered the muffled telephone conversation in Ivy Cottage that morning. Or did he ring to cancel? she asked herself and for some reason, felt uneasy.

Three

The following morning the overnight rain had cleared away. Meredith peeped out of the dormer window at the sun sparkling on the wet slates and road. As she watched, a small car drove slowly past and made for a cottage at the far end and on the other side of the narrow track. A middle-aged couple got out and began to unload a motley collection of boxes and bags. They must be the pair who proposed to retire here one day, Meredith deduced, come to check on the property or possibly even to spend Christmas here. They obviously didn't mind the isolation. She also noticed Harriet's upstairs windows were all open. A curtain flapped wildly out of one of them.

Meredith showered, dressed and breakfasted and turned her attention to the washing machine in the corner of the kitchen. She had a pile of laundry but was unused to having a machine at her disposal. She peered at its various buttons and dials and wondered if it were possible to wreck it by unintentional mis-setting. A hunt in a drawer produced a handbook. She sat and sipped her tea and read it. It all seemed fairly simple. She loaded it up. First attempt to get it to go failed because she hadn't plugged it in to the electricity supply. A second attempt did better. It began to chug away, her underwear rotating past the little window in the door. Meredith, feeling quite pleased with herself, put on her anorak and set out to explore a little more of Pook's Common. The road continued past the cottages so there must be something down there and it ought to be the common itself.

She walked past Ivy Cottage and down the narrow roadway. Before the last cottage she paused as a woman appeared in the doorway.

'Good morning,' she called. The woman peered at her short-sightedly and looked bewildered. 'I'm living at Rose Cottage!' Meredith shouted.

'Oh, the Russells' cottage!' The other scurried down the garden path towards Meredith. 'Have they sold? I didn't know.'

'No, just gone away temporarily.' Meredith explained.

'Oh, I see.' The woman looked relieved. 'I'm so pleased they haven't put the cottage on the market because that would leave it empty. Yet another empty cottage here would be just dreadful! How nice that you're going to be here. Pook's Common could do with a few more people, don't you think? Such a lonely spot.'

'Have you come to spend Christmas?' Meredith asked, puzzled.

'Oh, no!' The woman looked horrified. 'We're going to my daughter's for Christmas! We've only come today to make sure everything is all right. We're going to retire here as soon as we've sold our house.' She sighed. 'My husband likes the . . . the quiet of Pook's Common. Forgive me, I ought to have introduced myself. I'm Lucy Haynes. Geoffrey!' she called out suddenly.

'What do you want?' came an irascible voice from inside the cottage in return.

'I want you to meet someone, Geoffrey!'

There was a further irascible grunt and a short, stocky red-faced man appeared.

'My husband,' said Lucy Haynes with a touch of resignation in her voice. 'This lady, Geoffrey, is renting Rose Cottage.'

Mr Haynes approached mistrustfully. 'I thought the Russells had taken off. Where have they gone?'

'Dubai,' Meredith informed him.

Mr Haynes gave another snort of disgust. 'I've no desire to go running round the world. I can't wait to settle down here permanently. Peace and quiet, that's the thing! We're just down for the weekend to air the place out and run the heating. Got to watch out for damp in these old places.' He stamped his feet like a restless pony, obviously anxious to get back to whatever he had been doing.

'Nice to have met you,' said Meredith tactfully and moved off.

'I hope we'll see a bit more of you, Miss Mitchell,' said Lucy Haynes, it seemed to Meredith a trifle wistfully.

She walked on, wondering whose decision it had been to buy a retirement home in such an isolated spot. Geoffrey's, she suspected. Lucy Haynes was going to find it lonely. Geoffrey was probably a ranting misanthrope so it didn't matter. Not a good idea to shut yourself away like this once you got a bit older, thought Meredith. You depended on your car unless you fancied walking two miles to Westerfield to catch the bus. No shops. No doctor's surgery. Lots of fresh air and not much else.

After a few minutes' walk it seemed she had truly left the hamlet of Pook's Common behind. Hedgerows grew straggling on either side, bare now in mid-winter, black, grey and brown instead of green. But here was something. An acrid odour mingled with the unmistakable smell of farmyard manure struck Meredith's nose. She had reached a five-barred gate and a notice board nailed on a tree trunk proclaimed 'Pook's Stables'. That seemed fitting. Meredith leaned curiously on the gate and looked over.

It was a stable yard all right. The loose-boxes were set around three sides of a square and away to the right, half-hidden, was a neglected-looking dwelling. There was a small horse-box parked in one corner of the yard and just on the other side of the gate a large Mercedes. Its wheels and the lower half of the bodywork were splattered with mud. It looked pretty impressive, even so, in these rural surroundings.

'Hi!' said a voice behind her.

Meredith turned. Harriet stood there in breeches and waxed jacket, holding a rope halter and a plastic bucket. She smiled at Meredith's surprised expression.

'I followed you down. I would have caught up with you earlier but I saw you talking to that poor downtrodden mouse of a Haynes woman and waited till she'd gone. I can't stick Geoffrey.'

'He seems a bit brusque.'

'He's a real old misery. She really ought to stand up to him. I'd give him the order of the boot. But she hasn't got the gumption. And I know what's going to happen as soon as they really move in. He'll want to change everything. He'll want the road made up and start pestering the council. He'll want proper street lighting instead of our present hit or miss lamps. He'll complain that the horses deposit muck outside his gate. He'll want a bus service and a pavement.' Harriet glanced past Meredith and raised the hand holding the rope halter in salute to someone unseen behind her.

Turning, Meredith was just in time to glimpse a man standing by one of the loose-boxes. She had a brief impression of a swarthy, handsome face and strong build, a quilted body-warmer and well-worn sweater, the inevitable riding breeches and boots. Then he ducked into the loose-box out of sight.

'Tom's in one of his funny moods,' said Harriet with a shrug. 'Come and meet Blazer.'

They walked on past Pook's stables and reached open fields. From behind a hedge a sudden whinny made Meredith jump.

'He's heard us,' said Harriet. 'He knows I'm on my way for him.' She opened a gate and held it for Meredith. Fastening it behind her she started out across wet turf. Meredith whose walking shoes, though practical enough for most surfaces, were not really adequate for squelching through boggy terrain, made her way along behind her as best she could, seeking out the firmer spots. Rushes grew here and there in clumps across the pasture. It must be very low-lying. She asked if there were a river nearby.

'Just down the road a little way. There's a bridge.' Harriet stopped and whistled. Two horses came plodding into view, one a handsome chestnut with a startling blaze down its face and the other a grey, following behind. As they came up, Meredith was surprised at the amount of body-heat coming from them in the low outside temperature. They seemed to steam slightly.

'Here he is!' Harriet stretched up to pat the chestnut neck. Blazer put down his head and nuzzled at her coat pocket. 'All right, you greedy brute. Hang on.' She delved in her pocket and produced a wrapped boiled sweet. She managed to unwrap it with difficulty, Blazer trying to scoop it neatly out of her hand with his flexible upper lip. The grey stood back a little, watching. 'I've got one for you, too.' Harriet said. She pushed Blazer away from her. 'Get out of the way! It's not your turn!'

The grey was more cautious. It approached sideways on and flung up its head, eye rolling. 'He can,' warned Harriet, 'whirl round and give you a kick, this fellow. Here, come on . . .' She clicked her tongue.

The grey sidled up and took the proffered titbit and then suddenly bucked and danced away. 'Tom's horse,' Harriet said. 'He's a bit like old Tom in character. You can get round him if you go the right way about it. But he can cut up rough and turn a bit nasty if he's got a mind to. I'm fond of him, though.'

This time Meredith asked, 'Tom or the horse?'

Harriet glanced at her and laughed. 'I'm fond of Tom and the horse. But you haven't to let either of them get the better of you! They'll play on it.' Blazer had come ambling up again. Harriet threw the rope halter over his head. 'You and I, old chap,' she said softly. 'We get along just fine, don't we?'

They returned to the gate, Harriet leading the horse. 'I keep my tack up at Tom's place. I'll see you later, perhaps?'

Meredith waved goodbye and watched her set off back the

way they had come in the direction of Pook's stables. She continued her own walk down the lane. She came to the river after about five minutes and stood on the bridge, leaning over the parapet to watch the water race by. The level looked quite high. Further down the lane the fields came to an abrupt end and an expanse of open ground stretched in front of her. The grass was coarse and tufted, crossed here and there by narrow, half-obliterated footpaths. Isolated trees struggled, windswept, for survival. A large bird, a crow as far as she could tell, flapped up from picking at something on the ground and wheeled away high above her. The prospect did not encourage one to wander further. The common seemed somehow unfriendly. If the pookas were out there, they were welcome to it. Meredith was not sorry to turn back.

As she re-passed the stable yard, she heard the sound of voices, a man's and a woman's, raised in some altercation from inside the buildings. Suddenly Harriet's clear tones rang out. 'I'll do as I damn well please!'

'You owe me at least – ' the man's voice began angrily.

'I don't owe you a thing! And I'm not going to discuss it with you while you're in this foul mood. You can call by later if you've got over it – and not if you haven't!'

'Attagirl!' thought Meredith with a grin. Mr Fearon wasn't getting the better of Harriet, certainly.

As she passed the Haynes' cottage, it seemed something was amiss there, too. But this time it was Geoffrey's voice which rumbled on aggressively, with occasional mild squeaks of protest from his wife. They had probably been married for some thirty-odd years, perhaps longer. Difficult now, Meredith thought, to change habits established over the best part of a lifetime. Perhaps after all there was much to be said for remaining independent, carving out your own orbit. Lucy Haynes was as tied to her bad-tempered spouse as a satellite moon to its planet. Geoffrey led and Lucy followed. Harriet, by way of contrast, wasn't a follower but a leader. How did one stop a person like Harriet, headstrong, independent, beholden to no one? Short of tripping her up and hitting her over the head, goodness only knew.

Independence. It was easy to surrender your independence in ways which you hardly realised until too late. Even by accepting Laura Danby's kind invitation, Meredith's own fiercely maintained independence could be said to have been undermined. It was different for Alan, the Danbys were his family. Although

45

once he'd had a wife of his own. Meredith allowed herself a moment's speculation about this never-discussed time in Markby's life. Or at least never discussed with her. Did he ever speak of it with anyone? His wife's name had been Rachel, that much Meredith knew, and it was all. He'd tell her about it one day, she thought. But he clearly wasn't ready to yet.

She returned her thoughts to the Danbys. What would they make of her? How did they view her? As Alan's girlfriend? God forbid. That wouldn't suit either Alan or herself! Perhaps she had already compromised herself beyond recall by accepting the invitation. The thought sent an uneasy shiver down her spine. Back at Rose Cottage, Meredith consulted the calendar, frowning.

It was Saturday, half over already, and that meant only three more entire days remained before Christmas Day, the coming Wednesday, when she had committed herself, she now feared rashly, to festivities with the Danbys. It was generous of them to ask her along, she didn't deny. Or perhaps it was kind of Alan. He may well have asked his sister to invite Meredith. That thought made Meredith even more uneasy. She hoped that she did not appear to others like a worthy cause. Poor old Meredith, all on her own. Can't leave her to spend a solitary Christmas . . . It was possible they thought nothing of the sort, but she still felt she had to do something to show she was not entirely alone and friendless. Going away for just a day before Christmas to visit a friend or relative, just to let Alan Markby and Laura Danby know that she did have someone else, would bolster her morale. The trouble was that now, after so many years abroad, most of her friends were Foreign Service personnel like herself and nearly all abroad on postings at the moment. As for family, she had few of them. No one close unless, of course, one counted Aunt Lou.

Dear old Aunt Lou! Meredith's finger, running down the calendar, retraced its path and lingered over Sunday. She must be, what, over eighty? She wasn't a real aunt but a courtesy one, the widow of a former colonial service administrator and a friend of Meredith's late parents. But it would be nice to go and see the old lady. She lived an easy drive away, near Newbury. Meredith had brought her back some embroidered handkerchiefs, as it happened. She could take them along. Indomitable Aunt Lou, whom nothing could shake.

Meredith hunted down Aunt Lou's telephone number and

dialled it. The old lady had been deaf for years and had what she called a 'thing-gummy-jig' on her telephone receiver which was intended to help her hear her callers more clearly. Aunt Lou was inclined to mistrust the device and confuse it with what she had read of 'bugged' telephones in the newspapers. It certainly didn't appear to be much help to her. If people visited the house and the old lady answered the telephone while they were there, the visitors in their armchairs five yards away could hear the caller distantly but clearly, but Aunt Lou on the phone still yelled, 'Speak up!'

'Who?' screeched Aunt Lou down the telephone now.

'Meredith, Aunt Lou! Meredith Mitchell!'

'Oh, Merry! How are you, my dear? And why are you calling from so far away? Think of the expense!'

'I'm not far away, Aunt Lou. I've just got back to England. I thought I'd come and see you tomorrow, if that suits you.'

'Right you are, dear. If you come about twelve, I shall be back from church.' With that she abruptly rang off before the thing-gummy-jig wrought any mischief.

Aunt Lou's house looked exactly as it had always done. Meredith, looking up at it in the sunshine, felt five years old again. It was a large, rambling, gracious Edwardian building. It had been a wonderful place for exploring. It had had its own peculiar smell, compounded of wax polish and the pot-pourri Aunt Lou made and put out in little dishes in every room. There had been a brass dinner gong in the hall and oh, the delight when allowed to strike it, just once, with its little hammer.

Necessity had led to changes since those days. The house had become far too large and expensive to maintain for Aunt Lou and so it had been altered, the top half being made into a separate flat on the first floor and a studio apartment created in the former attics. Both had been sold off and Aunt Lou remained in residence on the ground floor which she'd had converted into a suitable flat for herself. The arrangement had not proved perfect. Aunt Lou seldom approved of the people who lived above her, but it worked after a fashion.

The house next door, similar in style, did not seem to have suffered the same mutilation. It had the quiet secluded air of a gentleman's private residence about it. In its drive stood a Japanese four-wheel-drive vehicle and as Meredith looked across the laburnum hedge at it, a woman of about her own age came out of the house, slamming the door crossly, got into the vehicle and reversed out into the road, driving off at speed. Meredith had only time to see that she was expensively dressed, sharp-featured and bad-tempered in looks. She dismissed her from her mind and rang Aunt Lou's bell.

'Come in, my dear,' said Aunt Lou, dragging open the door.

Aunt Lou had never looked young, at least not to the child Meredith. She had always had grey hair, scraped back into a no-nonsense knot and wore baggy knitted suits. The hair now was white, but the baggy suits hadn't altered in style a jot and she had changed remarkably little except that, as Meredith was distressed to see, the old lady now had a walking stick which accompanied her everywhere. With her stick Aunt Lou moved quite briskly, however.

'I have,' said Aunt Lou fortissimo as she led the way into her ground floor flat, 'made us bean casserole.'

'Oh, still vegetarian, Aunt Lou?'

'Naturally!' snapped Aunt Lou testily. 'What else should I be? Do you think I should have lived as long as I have on meat?'

The living room hadn't changed much. The same antique plates gleamed behind the glass doors of a walnut cabinet. The muffled tick of the grandfather clock echoed in one corner. Crocheted antimacassars graced the backs of all the chairs although it was many years since a gentleman with pomade on his hair had sat in one of them.

'Those,' said Aunt Lou, lowering herself stiffly into a chair and pointing with her stick at the walnut cabinet, 'are yours.'

'Oh, the plates?'

'Yes, they're in my will. I was intending to give them to you when you married. But you haven't married and I dare say you won't do so now.' Aunt Lou scrutinised her visitor. 'You're not a bad-looking girl. Aren't there any young single fellows about where you are? When I was young and Roger was in the colonial service, young single European women were much in demand. Girls who couldn't get themselves a husband in this country were sent out to find one in the colonies and it seldom failed.'

'Yes, Aunt Lou. But I'm not thinking of marriage.'

'Aren't you?' said Aunt Lou unkindly. 'Chance would be a fine thing, I dare say. It's not what you think, my girl, it's what the man thinks. Or don't girls wait to be asked these days?'

'Not always, I believe, Aunt Lou. I think it's quite common now for them to do the asking.'

Aunt Lou looked mildly taken aback but not for long. 'Yes, well, common is probably the word to describe that sort of behaviour. Your trouble, my girl, is that you're too independent by half. It don't do. Of course a woman should know her own mind and few men really relish a life with a clinging vine, but it can be taken too far.'

'Good job I'm able to earn my living, wouldn't you say?' Meredith pointed out.

Aunt Lou looked glum. 'It was different in my day. Mind you, I'm not saying everything's for the worse. Lots of girls married in haste and repented at leisure then because they were afraid of being left on the shelf. But now it's all divorce and even the married ones carry on in a very odd way. I read about it in my newspaper. That woman upstairs,' Aunt Lou's walking stick made an aggressive stab at the ceiling. 'Men coming and going. Lost count of 'em. And take Mr Ballantyne next door – he's a very nice, well-mannered old gentleman, must be oh, seventy something.'

'He's got women coming and going?' Meredith asked innocently.

'Behave yourself!' ordered Aunt Lou. 'Of course he doesn't.'

'I saw a young woman leaving as I arrived, rather narrow face, nice clothes, looking cross.'

'That will be his daughter, Felicity, I was about to tell you about her, don't keep interrupting,' said Aunt Lou sternly. 'Mr Ballantyne comes in here sometimes for a glass of wine.' Meredith knew Aunt Lou meant by this thick sweet sherry. 'He's a widower. Quite a wealthy man, I believe. He lives in that big house all on his own with a woman coming daily to clean and cook his lunch. He hasn't done as I did and chopped his house in half. I wish I hadn't. Such odd people upstairs and one has no control over who lives there. I was ill-advised.'

'You couldn't manage the whole house, Aunt Lou.'

'Well, I could have made some other arrangement. However, I was telling you of Mr Ballantyne. He has just the one daughter and that girl has given him great cause for concern. He tells me about it. He likes someone to confide in. She married a very unsuitable fellow. I've seen him a few times and he's never made a favourable impression on me! But he doesn't come often, only when he wants Mr Ballantyne to put up the money for one of his schemes or projects, which Mr Ballantyne usually does for the sake of his daughter. It's all wrong. Generally Felicity visits her father alone. No children. Poor Mr Ballantyne can't make it out. He says that they more or less go their separate ways, Felicity and this green fellow she's married to. He says it's entirely the fault of the green man and he doesn't approve of his ideas at all really and only backs them because of a natural wish to support his daughter. I've told him, he shouldn't do it.'

'I would have thought,' Meredith murmured, 'that as a life-long vegetarian, you'd approve of green ideas.'

'What's that?' Aunt Lou hadn't caught the words. 'Mr Ballantyne is most unhappy. He's thought of changing his will and his investments – but she is his only daughter. One understands that. The wine is in that sideboard, Meredith. Pour it out.'

They sipped at the sherry and Meredith presented the hand-embroidered handkerchiefs which were well-received. Wine disposed of, they proceeded to the kitchen where the bean casserole was making its presence known by a savoury odour.

'I'll take it out of the oven!' Meredith said hastily, seeing Aunt Lou wrestling with walking stick, oven gloves and oven door. Privately she wondered how much longer the old lady could continue to live alone, even in this flat. But to wrench Aunt Lou from the home which had been hers for such a long time would be to kill her.

They ate in the kitchen. The bean casserole really wasn't bad and was followed by a savoury because Aunt Lou did not believe in sweet puddings.

They sat gossiping in the afternoon. Meredith described Rose Cottage. Aunt Lou said it sounded very nice but to make sure the bed was aired because old places were often damp. She hoped Meredith would look after herself. She supposed Meredith still ate meat, which couldn't be helped, 'but according to the newspapers so many cows are going mad. Roger, I remember, had to deal with the tsetse fly and I suppose it's something similar. It caused endless trouble because of all the bride-prices being paid in cattle. Meat-eating causes so many problems.'

They parted with expressions of mutual affection.

'So nice of you to come and see me, dear. Do drive carefully,' were Aunt Lou's parting words.

Meredith stooped and kissed a faded cheek and smelled the sweet perfume of rose pot-pourri. Sadness swept over her. This might be her last visit. Even if she saw Aunt Lou again, the circumstances were likely to be much altered. Behind the old lady in the hall stood the little brass dinner gong, but even that looked much smaller than in memory. It was still brightly polished.

Meredith drove home to Pook's Common. The visit intended to boost her morale had had a very different effect. It had reinforced her awareness of time racing by, running like grains of sand through your fingers.

Monday before Christmas and the sense of urgency had even reached Pook's Common. Meredith supposed Harriet would be fully committed socially over the Christmas period but she wanted to offer some token of hospitality, so she went across the road after breakfast and asked if Harriet would like to come over to lunch.

'Not that I'm a great cook, I'm not like you. It will be make-shift.'

'That's fine.' Harriet smiled. 'I'd like to.'

From the kitchen behind them came the sound of Mrs Brissett cleaning up vigorously and singing 'The Holly and the Ivy'.

'Mrs B. has got the Christmas spirit,' said Harriet.

Meredith knew herself no cook but, inspired by the thought that even Aunt Lou at eighty-three could produce a bean casserole, she managed to produce leeks rolled in thin slices of ham, topped with a slightly lumpy cheese sauce. It was a dish which was one of her standbys if faced with a guest.

Harriet arrived with a bottle of wine. Away from her home ground she seemed surprisingly ill at ease at first, almost shy. She was polite about the leeks and lumpy cheese and said a similar thing could be done with endives and it looked at first as if the lunch was going to prove a slightly awkward affair. But then Meredith discovered that the way to get Harriet relaxed and talking was to introduce the topic of animals. Harriet tossed back her luxuriant mane of auburn hair, drank deeply of her wine and launched into tales of the ponies she had learned to ride on and grown up with, and of Blazer, her current horse. She did not talk much about people, once mentioning her cousin Fran in connection with a horsy narrative, but otherwise saying nothing about family or friends.

Beneath that assured exterior, thought Meredith, she's vulnerable. Perhaps that was why she acted so aggressively sometimes. What had gone wrong? she wondered. A love affair which didn't work out? A personal loss? A family quarrel? It would be interesting to know, but Harriet would never tell, that was clear.

They turned to the subject of Christmas and the festivities nearly upon them.

'I'm not religious,' Harriet said. 'And I don't go for the fancy decorations and general hoo-hah. I'm a sad disappointment to Mrs Brissett in that respect. She insists on tacking up a bit of tinsel and so on and I see she's done the same for you. I just like the food and the booze and turning out on Boxing Day for the hunt. You must come along and see us move out.'

'I might,' Meredith said.

Harriet glanced at her watch. 'Hell's teeth . . . I promised Tom I'd be at the stables at two. I must dash. He'll dive into a prolonged fit of the sulks again. Thanks for the lunch.'

As in the ballad, Tuesday was the night before Christmas. Christmas Eve, when the Victorians sat round and told ghost stories. When Meredith had been a child, her father always read *A Christmas Carol* aloud to his family on Christmas Eve. As a youngster she had always been truly terrified at the point in the narrative when Marley's ghost clanked in.

She supposed she was feeling a bit down in the dumps, apprehensive too about celebrating Christmas Day at the Danbys. She peered at the Christmas cactus she had bought for Alan and decided it looked distinctly sorry for itself. It had looked all right in the shop. But it hadn't flowered and as far as she could tell, had no intention of doing so. She also felt the tiniest bit muzzy and hoped that she hadn't a cold coming on. In the end, she made herself a drink of hot milk with a dash of brandy and took it up to bed, taking along the hot water bottle for good measure.

Either it was the brandy or it was the heat, but she went out like a light. As sometimes happened she awoke equally suddenly. It was dark, chilly, her hot water bottle was now a clammy unwelcome intruder in her bed, and it was quiet. Meredith pushed out the cold bottle and lay listening. Slowly she became aware that it wasn't quiet at all. There were a dozen different kinds of squeaks, creaks, groans, clunks and rattlings. Mice? She hoped not. Old wood settling in changing temperature? Much more likely. Or the pookas, emerged on this Christmas Eve to make mischief?

Horse-like pookas, thought Meredith. Their symbolism must be ancient. Horses were a sacred beast once. All those carved white horses on chalk hillsides. Fertility symbols, also. Did the pooka bring good or bad luck? It was while she was trying to decide this one that she heard, or thought she heard, a faint clop of a hoof.

Meredith sat up in bed and listened. She had just decided it was imagination when there it went again. Clip-clop. Outside. In the night, in the darkness. She rolled over to see what time it was by the luminous numbers on the clock-radio. Just a little before two in the morning. Clip-clop. And now, faintly, a whinny.

A sudden chill rippled the length of her body from head to toes. She slid out of bed, reluctant but inexorably drawn to the window.

Outside the moon shone down brightly, casting a weird pale light over the cottages and the trees and fields beyond. The fields shimmered, unearthly silvered, the trees raised bare tormented arms to the sky. No lights showed at any windows. But half these cottages were empty anyway. So few people. Herself, Harriet, Joe Fenniwick and his wife and possibly the Haynes also, staying over. Six souls. All alone. The total population of Pook's Common. Human population, anyway. Meredith's breath had fogged the window and she rubbed a clear circle. That wasn't good enough. She opened the window altogether and leaned out, shivering as the night air struck icy through her thin nightgown. She looked to the right, towards the junction with the B road. Nothing. She looked left, down towards Pook's stables. Nothing. Right again . . . my God, there it was!

Scudding clouds had temporarily obscured the moon, but now they flitted aside and revealed against the horizon the black outline of a horse. It stood, head high, tail flowing, ears pricked, silhouetted against the silvery grey backdrop at the junction with the B road. As she watched, holding her breath, it reared up, threshed at the air with its forelegs, and then leapt away and was lost to her sight beyond a rise.

Meredith closed the window and sat down on the edge of the bed. Her knees felt weak and she was shaking. It was all very well to laugh at ancient superstitions by light of day and in company. All alone at dead of night was another matter. Pook's Common. The place wasn't called that for nothing.

Meredith went downstairs and made a cup of tea. She felt better afterwards. But she wouldn't tell anyone what she thought she'd seen, least of all Alan. He'd think she was crazy. Or dreaming. But it hadn't been a dream.

*

Christmas Day fell on the Wednesday. Meredith had told Markby she would rather like to attend Westerfield church on Christmas Day morning before going to Laura's if he didn't mind, so Markby drove out from Bamford after breakfast to accompany her. They walked there from Pook's Common across frost-crisped fields.

It was too late to be worrying over any implications inherent in spending Christmas with the Danbys and now the day had dawned Meredith was rather pleased she was going to be with company, especially after her sighting of the whatever-it-was during the night. But the lingering memory of the ghostly horse and a nervousness which couldn't be denied at the thought of meeting the Danbys made her feel more than a little awkward. Markby asked twice if she were cold and she knew he'd noticed and was politely trying to find out what was wrong. She assured him she was quite warm and felt fine, and silently hoped he didn't think she was regretting her promise to spend Christmas with him and the Danbys. He probably did, but it couldn't be helped. She was glad when Westerfield church hove into view and sensed that he was just as relieved.

The church was not in permanent use and had no resident vicar but it held occasional services and now at Christmas an elderly cleric in retirement had volunteered to conduct a sung Eucharist at nine-thirty with the help of a volunteer choir assembled from the Women's Institute. A large number of people had turned out for it. Cars were parked all along the grass verge outside the church. People's voices, exchanging Christmas greetings echoed on the clear air.

Markby nodded towards the line of people ahead of them on the flagged pathway to the church door. 'Good turn-out.'

'Glad it's not raining.'

'Should hold off.'

The weather to the rescue again.

The elderly cleric was standing in the doorway in his surplice to welcome them. He was indeed very old, white-haired, pink-cheeked and frail in appearance.

'He ought not to be standing about in that cold church porch!' muttered Meredith as they strode towards him.

They had reached him and he grasped their hands in turn and beaming, chirped, 'Welcome, welcome!'

'I think he's enjoying himself,' whispered Markby.

He sat back in his pew and looked around the church which

the indefatigable ladies of the WI had transformed with flowers and holly sprays. There was even a Christmas tree set up by the altar.

'Nice mixture of the Christian and the pagan,' he observed casually. 'I haven't been in this church for years.'

Meredith was suddenly struck by the thought that a local man by origin, he might have married Rachel here in this very church. The possibility filled her with horror. Supposing in innocently requesting him to escort her today, she'd unwittingly committed a crass blunder? She peered cautiously at him.

He was now studying the crayoned pictures of the nativity by local children which were taped up on the pillars. From the nearest one Mary and Joseph stared out with large round eyes. The ox was very small in proportion to the adult figures, rather like a large dog with stubby horns. It was smiling. The donkey was as big as the ox and its ears were short like a pony's. Its hooves were crayoned jet black and it looked oddly mischievous, slightly malicious. Pooka-like. Of the baby all that could be seen were two stiff arms poking up out of a manger well supplied with bright yellow straw.

'What,' asked Meredith hoarsely, 'are you thinking about?'

'To tell you the truth, I'm uttering a private prayer that Laura's children will be on their best behaviour for you. Let's hope Matthew hasn't been given any of those battery-operated toys which make irritating noises and Vicky doesn't mangle everything.'

'Oh, is that all?' exclaimed Meredith in relief.

'Why, what did you think I might be thinking about?'

'Nothing. Well, I thought you might, you might know this church well and have personal, um, memories of it.'

'Yes, I've got some of those. But all childhood ones. I haven't been to a service here for years.'

Meredith experienced an absurd sense of relief. Not married here then. She was glad when someone, after a false start, struck up the organ. The WI choir plunged shrilly into voice. Markby hurriedly opened his hymnbook and burst into a stentorian 'Hark the Herald Angels Sing', considerably disconcerting the old lady in front of him.

Next to him, Meredith made a feeble stab at joining in. She had warned him beforehand that she couldn't sing, he recalled. She was right, he thought, as she got underway. She wandered all over the stave and produced a curious counterpoint to the tune. It wasn't a question of singing flat, he decided, but of simply singing the wrong notes. He felt a new bond between them. He liked some music but generally wasn't musical and was always slightly put off to find himself in the company of those who were. As the sopranos of the WI soared off into the upper atmosphere he began to feel for the first time that this Christmas had meaning. And it was nice to be here with her, of course.

Festivities at Laura's house were already well underway by the time they arrived there. The lounge floor was a sea of discarded, brightly coloured wrapping paper. Matthew had acquired a tank which trundled over the carpet emitting small but sharp percussive explosions accompanied by a shower of sparks. Emma was experimenting with atonal motifs on a xylophone and Vicky had been given a doll but had pulled the arm off. She presented it trustfully to her Uncle Alan as he came in, to be mended. He tried to introduce Meredith, holding the broken doll and shouting above xylophone clamour and a relentless pop-pop from the toy tank.

'Happy Christmas!' yelled Laura happily. 'Like a glass of sherry?' She was wearing a jade green velour 'leisure suit' and her blonde hair was twisted up in a knot on top of her head. Long strands escaped and hung fetchingly round her flushed face. 'Paul's in the kitchen. He was up at the crack of dawn doing something unspeakable to the turkey, but the kids were up anyway. I made the brandy sauce for the pud but I think I've put too much brandy in it and now Paul won't let me back in the kitchen. I'll go and get the sherry. Make yourselves at home!'

She disappeared towards the dining room. Markby hastily jammed dolly's arm back into its socket. 'There you go, Vicky, don't bust it up again, there's a good girl. Give me your coat, Meredith. And, um, do you want to put down your bag?'

They had both of them brought mysterious plastic carrier bags about which they ostentatiously avoided asking one another.

'It's my presents,' said Meredith. 'Not much of interest, I'm afraid.' She stared at him with defiant hazel eyes.

'Oh, yes, well I . . .'

'Sherry!' announced Laura reappearing with a tray. 'Paul will join us in a minute.'

Meredith delved in her plastic bag and produced a bottle of wine and – because she had not been sure whether her hostess drank – a box of chocolates.

'Oh, lovely!' said her hostess who showed every indication of drinking like a fish, grabbing the wine. 'And chocolates, super.'

'And I brought a tin of biscuits for the children, I didn't know what else . . . Alan told me how old they were but I'm a bit vague about kids, I'm afraid.'

'Absolutely marvellous. They'll love them. I've got you a present but I have to find it – and yours, Alan. Just a sec.'

She vanished again. There was still a bulge in the bottom of Meredith's plastic bag. She gave him a hunted look and began to burrow in its depths to extract what was obviously going to be his present. Markby summoned courage and delved in his own sack. They came up together, clasping their offerings.

'It's a Christmas cactus,' he said, getting in first.

'So's this one, mine – I mean – my present for you.'

'I see. Well, um . . .'

Solemnly they exchanged cactus plants.

'I've always wanted one of these,' said Meredith.

'So have I.'

They smiled uncertainly at one another and he wondered whether he could kiss her, just on the cheek in a Christmas sort of way. In front of all the kids no one would be misled into thinking it romantic. He drew breath and leaned forward and he thought she actually knew what he meant to do and wasn't going to object.

Then Vicky tugged at his pullover. 'Dolly's head come off.'

After that, things looked up a bit. Paul's dinner was excellent. Matthew ran out of percussion caps for the tank. Emma played 'Jingle Bells' on the recorder quite nicely, or perhaps a mixture of wine and the brandy sauce mellowed the ear. They all sat down in front of the television to listen to the Queen's Speech, feeling at peace with one another and the world. Dolly's limbs lay strewn about the carpet but Dolly's assailant had gone to take a nap and slept. Baby Emily had arrived but sat peaceably chewing the head of a blue rubber rabbit. The two older children were playing some board game and arguing in a fairly friendly manner.

That was when the telephone rang. Laura hauled herself up from the sofa and went to answer it.

'It will be for me . . .' said Markby resignedly. 'I'm on call.'

Laura appeared in the doorway. 'It's Tom Fearon at the livery stables for you, Alan. He sounds pretty cross.'

'So am I, pretty cross. He'd better have a good reason for ringing me up on Christmas Day! Excuse me, everyone . . .'

'Bad luck,' said Meredith with sincerity, having suffered similar inconveniences in the course of consular duty.

Markby snatched up the telephone receiver lying on the table in the hall. 'Tom? Happy Christmas!' he growled down it.

'Not so bloody happy here!' retorted Tom's furious voice at the other end. 'Some joker got in here last night. Let all the damn horses out – I've spent all morning going round the lanes rounding the brutes up again!'

'Bad luck. Sure someone didn't forget to close a gate?'

'Come off it. This time of year they're all stabled at night and with a good lock on the door. Especially after that rash of rustling last year – you remember? I tell all the owners who keep animals here to get them freeze-branded. The slaughter houses are chary of taking freeze-branded animals. They check them out first and the thieves know it and generally leave branded animals alone. So it wasn't rustlers. It was downright malicious! Someone smashed the lock with a tool of some kind and let the horses out deliberately. They must have chased them out of the yard and made sure they took off in all directions. I found two of them in some old dear's garden at Cherton! And I know who did it! Those blasted hunt saboteurs!'

'Tom,' Markby said, carefully controlling his voice. 'Whilst I appreciate the trouble it's caused you, you could have reported it to Bamford station and not rung me up, you know. As for whether it was hunt saboteurs or home-going Christmas drunks, the station will make all possible enquiries. But it's hardly CID . . .'

'There's a letter, too, shoved through my door. Threatening God knows what. If I could get my hand on the dirty little tyke who wrote it – '

'It was signed?' Markby interrupted sharply.

'Like hell it was! Of course it wasn't. The writer didn't have the guts to put a name to it! Look here Alan, I'm ringing you because I want your personal assurance that the local nick will have people on hand tomorrow in the Market Square when the meet assembles.'

'You've kept the letter, I hope?'

'Yes. Listen! I know disturbing you on Christmas Day is a bind but's it's more than that for me! And I've got to go now. I promised to spend Christmas Day with – with someone. I had to ring up and explain about chasing horses and that I'd be late. It didn't go down well. Christmas dinner ruined and so on – she's hopping mad. So I must get over there now. I want someone in the square tomorrow, Alan!'

'I'll see what can be done,' he promised. 'Though it's not my department. I'm fairly sure that there will be someone on duty there as a matter of course but I'll check.' He hung up. Blast Tom and blast all his nags. To perdition with the Bamford Hunt and every one of its hounds. Good job Tom had got all the horses in, though. There could have been a serious road accident with a dozen or so frightened animals careering about country lanes. The irresponsibility of the people in question! Then he gave a little smile. Tom Fearon, an odd moody person at times, nevertheless had a considerable reputation as a lady's man. The morning's adventure had apparently left him in hot water with the lady of the moment. Tom would have to turn on all the charm to talk her round but if rumour were true, his success rate was high.

Markby went back to the living room where the Queen's Speech was finished, Matthew and Emma were watching a film and Emily had been sick. She was cleaned up and the four adults sat round the table and played Scrabble. Then Paul produced mince pies and in due course there was ham salad and Christmas cake. But the earlier glow Markby had gained in the church had been dispersed by Tom's call. Something had gone wrong with this Christmas and whatever it was, it affected him. But he didn't know what it was, that was the trouble. Just a feeling. A feeling of something unpleasant, waiting. And real, very real.

'You're a bit quiet,' said Meredith as he drove her back to Rose Cottage that evening. He'd been quiet since the phone call. She hoped it hadn't been anything serious but if it wasn't then he ought not to have brooded over it for the rest of the day. She was annoyed, slightly, and she knew her remark sounded a little resentful.

'Sorry!' he apologised. 'It was just something on my mind.'

'Indigestion?' she enquired crisply.

'Don't let Paul hear you suggest such a thing! No, not indigestion.'

'Didn't think so. He is a good cook, isn't he? Wish I was as good. Was it the phone call?' she added after a moment, more sympathetically.

'In a way.' He drove on for a few minutes, the headlights cleaving a way through the darkness. 'Drat it,' he said after a bit.

'Why?'

'Because I looked forward to this Christmas, knowing you'd be here. Did you enjoy today?' Hope entered his voice.

Meredith's resentment was replaced by a warming sense of friendliness. It was nice to think he had looked forward to her company. Also that he thought highly enough of her to want to present her to his family. Her earlier haverings now struck her as selfish. She'd been so obsessed with viewing today's arrangements from her own position. He'd taken her to church, he'd taken her to lunch and she hadn't been particularly gracious about any of it. She hoped she hadn't let him down in any way. 'Yes, I did enjoy it!' she said enthusiastically. 'Thanks. Laura gave me a box of some very nice soap. That was kind of her.'

'She's a good sort. I'm glad you enjoyed it.' He cheered up visibly.

They turned off the B road at the junction and drove down the narrow track to the cottages. Outside Harriet's the big car was parked again. Meredith couldn't see it properly in the absence of proper streetlights and wondered if it was Tom Fearon's Mercedes. The other night she had fancied the car which drew away was a Granada. Beside her, however, Alan seemed suddenly to have sunk back into grim-faced absorption.

'Is it still the phone call?' she asked gently.

'Yes, in a way,' he confessed. 'Tom's a good fellow, if unpredictable and inclined not to give a damn for anyone else. Ringing me up on Christmas Day, I ask you! But that's Tom for you. I've known him most of my life, since we were boys. His family was by way of being a bit notorious locally. I don't mean in a bad way, just different. Other kids called Tom a gipsy, but only when they were out of his reach! There's certainly gipsy blood there but it's way back. Sometimes though it has a way of surfacing.' Markby smiled. 'Tom always had a couple of lurcher dogs tagging along at his heels when he was a kid. He was always one for the girls and as soon as he was a bit older, instead of the dogs he always seemed to have besotted females hanging round him. I think he treated the dogs better than he treated the women, actually – ' Markby broke off embarrassed. 'I shouldn't have said that. But I do think Tom's animals have always meant more to him than people. Last night someone let all the horses

out of his livery stable so you can imagine the state he was in
when he rang.'

'What?' she shouted, jumping in her seat.

He stared at her in astonishment. 'Yes, stupid trick.'

'You've no idea!' Meredith caught her breath. 'I haven't gone
bananas. It's just that last night . . .' She explained about the
moonlit vision of the rearing horse. 'And it was a real one, after
all! I knew it was in my heart. Well, seventy-five per cent of me
knew it was real and the rest of me, well, silly though it sounds,
I almost believed in the horsy hobgoblins.'

'I don't blame you for getting jittery. Christmas Eve and so
on. Spooky. Tom had to go racing round all morning rounding
them up again. Luckily none of them was hurt and none caused
any accidents.'

'Accidents . . .' Meredith said ruefully. 'I should have rung
the police and reported a horse on the loose on a public highway
in the middle of the night.'

'Doubt anyone would have found it – them – before daylight.
We don't know about damage. I understand a couple got into a
garden. Tom's a chap with a temper on a short fuse anyway. Bet
the air was blue. It led to an upset with a girlfriend, too, I gather.
It all made him late for her Christmas lunch. He was just going
off to make amends. Hope that didn't end with Tom slinging the
turkey out of the window!'

He didn't mention it to Meredith but he was more worried
about the anonymous letter in fact. Preventing a repeat of the
episode letting the horses loose meant tighter security at the
stables and Tom could, if necessary, hire himself a private security guard. The letter though . . . anonymous letters had a habit
of turning very nasty. Only one so far – or this was the first he
had heard of, but the affair could snowball and sometimes this
kind of thing took an unforeseen twist.

He realised he was in danger of appearing rude and dragged
his attention back to present matters. 'You wouldn't, I suppose,
like to go and see the Bamford Hunt meet in the Market Square
tomorrow morning, would you?' he asked. 'The Boxing Day
Meet is a tradition, and worth seeing. I won't pretend there isn't
an element of duty in it. Tom wants someone on hand but I
don't want to ask for extra men on Boxing Day in case of trouble
which might well not happen. There will already be a couple of
chaps in a patrol car down a side street as a matter of course.
And if I'm there myself . . . just as an observer, you understand.

But you might like to see it. Provided it doesn't rain, of course.'

'Yes, I'd like to see it. Harriet suggested I go along.'

'I'll pick you up then.'

'Can't I drive myself in and meet you somewhere – in the square?'

'Fair enough. They foregather about eleven.' He smiled awkwardly. 'Well, I look forward to it. Goodnight, then.

'Goodnight and thanks. It was a nice day. See you in the morning.'

'Yes.'

He was going to kiss me at his sister's, Meredith thought. When he handed over his present. He would have done if that kid hadn't interfered. She wondered if he would now? It didn't look like it. She was relieved but paradoxically slightly annoyed, too. She opened the car door determinedly and got out. 'See you tomorrow!'

'I'll wait here and see you safely inside. In case of any more mischievous pookas around!' He grinned at her.

'Don't make me feel sillier than I already do.' She walked quickly up to the front door, opened it, turned and waved. He couldn't turn in the narrow road here because of the car parked opposite. He drove a little way further on and turned using the grass verge after the last cottage. She waved again as he drove past towards the junction, and went indoors.

She was restless, still feeling she had made a bit of a fool of herself. She boiled some milk for a cup of cocoa, resolving to steer clear of the brandy and hot milk: all that talk of pookas in the car had made her sound neurotic! Meredith took the cocoa upstairs by the hall light and into the bedroom without putting on the lightswitch there. In the half-light shining in from the hallway, she went to the dormer window to pull the curtains and found herself looking out directly at Harriet's cottage opposite. Someone was in Harriet's bedroom. Two people. They were outlined clearly against the blinds, locked in an embrace so abandoned that it was obvious neither suffered from the hang-ups she and Alan did.

Meredith, with a surge of embarrassment, jerked her curtains across cutting off the sight. She undressed and got into bed and sat up with her cocoa mug, sipping at it. She supposed most normal people in a situation like the one she and Alan had been in all day, would have ended up in bed together, here in this comfortable bed at Rose Cottage. Perhaps he'd even hoped so, poor chap. And had he been almost anyone else, that's how the day might have ended because anyone else wouldn't have mattered. It would just have been having a good time. But with Alan there was the dreadful yawning pit of caring in the way. It was the sort of pit once set for tigers, with stakes on the floor on which you got impaled if ever you fell in. And she was never going to get impaled on those stakes again.

'I'm never going to let him matter!' she muttered. 'I'm better off on my own and that's how I'm going to stay! He's better off on his own, too, and he knows it. Nature's singletons, that's us.'

Outside a car engine revved up and purred away into the night. Harriet Needham wasn't one of Nature's singletons. 'Wonder who the bloke is?' thought Meredith sleepily, pulling the duvet up round her ears. 'Wonder if it was the same one as the other day? Looked like the same car . . . Tom's Mercedes? Not sure. Couldn't really make it out. None of my business . . . Wish I hadn't messed up every relationship I ever had.' And then, quite suddenly and unwished, the thought: 'Wish I hadn't come back.'

Four

Boxing Day morning was grey and overcast but the rain promised to hold off at least until the evening. Good news for the Bamford Meet, thought Meredith, scooping her boiled egg out of the pan. It might be chilly, though, standing about in the Market Square and she had put on a thick pullover. She had overslept which was not surprising given the amount of rich food and drink consumed the previous day at the Danbys so it was as well the meet did not assemble until eleven-ish. She glanced at her wristwatch. Twenty past ten. Time enough, just.

She arrived in Bamford a little after eleven and parked in the almost empty car park to the rear of the supermarket. It seemed desolate now. Inside appeared a dark labyrinth of ravaged shelves behind plate glass still festooned with the posters advertising special Christmas bargains.

She put her hands in her pockets and briskly walked the short distance to the square. It was already full. The riders, about a dozen so far, had gathered together in the middle. The horses all looked spruced up for the occasion with plaited manes, even the two disgruntled piebald ponies on which perched two identical solemn-faced small girls. The crowd was about fifty in number and stood about chatting and watching the riders. In and out of their feet and the horses' hooves scurried the hounds in cheerful disorder. Occasionally one would disappear in the direction of the High Street, casting about for an interesting sniff, hoping perhaps to discover a fox in the vicinity of the cut-price chemist. The kennelman, a small dour wiry figure, would bawl orders after it and when it came loping back within reach, seize it and drag it, claws scraping on the flagstones, back to rejoin the main pack. It would then escape again, almost at once. One such came lolloping up to Meredith, a silly grin on its face. It was distinctly smelly, kennel-kept as opposed to a household pet dog.

She heard her name called and saw Alan Markby in his green

weatherproof on the far side of the square beckoning to her. He was standing beside a burly man in a duffel coat whom he introduced to her as 'Jack Pringle, a local doctor.'

'Hullo, Miss Mitchell,' Pringle said. 'You've taken Peter Russell's cottage out at Pook's Common, I understand. We used to be in the same practice, Peter and I. Now he's doing his stuff under the desert sun. Nice little cottage that, but Pook's Common is really the back of beyond. Far too cut-off to suit me. You don't mind the isolation?'

'Not really,' Meredith said, shaking a hand like a shovel which was extended towards her. 'I think I'm going to like it there. And of course, after New Year I shall be commuting up to London every day.'

Pringle grimaced sympathetically and nodding towards the riders, asked, 'What do you think of our local hunt?'

'Not quite as I imagined. More relaxed and informal.'

'We ain't the Quorn, you know. Bamford Hunt just about keeps going, nearly broke. Costs a fortune to feed all those hounds and keeping a horse isn't cheap these days. I used to follow a bit but I had to give it up. Mind you, I think they've had a bit of luck lately with a couple of wealthy chaps coming to live in the area and showing signs of interest.'

'Rupert Green, you mean?' Markby said non-committedly.

Pringle chuckled. 'Oh, yes him, the playboy. Bright chap, mind you. And he's got guts, I'll say that for him. He's far from the best rider around but he sticks to it, or to the horse which is more important I suppose! I suspect he's happier in sports cars, but he's determined to be a country gent!'

'Which is he?' asked Meredith, looking around.

'Over there.' Markby touched her elbow and pointed.

Beyond the crowd, almost out of the Market Square altogether, two male riders waited as if they mistrusted the milling crowd. They were both immaculately turned out, top-hatted, gleaming-booted.

'Green is the chap on the left,' Markby said. 'He's a big financial fish in the city. He bought the old Cherton Manor about a year ago and has set about turning himself into the local squire.'

Meredith turned her attention from Green and his companion to the rest of the assembly. Goodness, that was a familiar face! Geoffrey Haynes, his red features as furious as ever, stood on the opposite side of the square with his hands in his raincoat pockets and glowering at anyone who had the temerity to walk in front of him. Christmas with their daughter had lasted just the one day, it seemed. Was that because Geoffrey wanted to return to the hermit-like seclusion of Pook's Common, or because the daughter and her family couldn't stand more than one day of Geoffrey? There was no sign of poor Lucy. Perhaps she'd stayed behind to enjoy her grandchildren. But Geoffrey wasn't the sort to tolerate independent action on the part of his wife. He would have dragged the unfortunate woman back here with him. Meredith was beginning to share Harriet's feelings towards Geoffrey Haynes.

Her attention was distracted by a clatter of hoofs as a rider on a grey came up to them. The rider bent down and reached out a hand to shake that of Markby and of Pringle.

'Morning, Tom,' Markby called up to him. 'No more alarms?'

'All quiet, but we kept a round-the-clock watch on the stables last night, just in case. Took shifts. If I'd caught the buggers I tell you, there would have been murder done.'

'Tom Fearon,' Markby said to Meredith, introducing her. 'Who keeps Pook's stables.'

She had already recognised him and the grey. The horse was immaculate, mane braided, tack buffed to perfection. He complemented his rider who, viewed nearer to hand, was indeed a strikingly handsome man in a slightly foreign, gipsy fashion, black curls bunching round the rim of his hard hat, his skin tanned walnut by an outdoor life. Meredith felt, rather than saw, his dark eyes run appraisingly over her. Instinct would have told her even if Markby hadn't that this was one who liked the girls. She felt defensive hackles rise on the back of her neck.

Fearon leaned smiling from the saddle and reached out his hand. 'Nice to see you here. You're Meredith Mitchell, aren't you? Harriet was telling me you'd taken the cottage opposite hers. Settled in all right?'

'Yes, thanks.'

'Come down to the stables some time. I'll show you round. And if you're interested in riding, we can certainly find you a suitable mount.'

'That's very kind.' She knew she sounded rather sniffy but she couldn't help it. If Fearon fancied she could be lured into a loose-box for a quick romp in the hay, he was wrong. Beside her, Alan Markby was grinning to himself as if he knew what she was thinking.

Pringle interrupted the conversation, perhaps fortunately,

exclaiming, 'There's Harriet!'

Fearon twisted abruptly in the saddle and the grey stamped a nervous hoof. Meredith, bearing in mind Harriet's warning that this horse might kick, prudently moved away a little.

The crowd had parted to let Harriet through to the centre of the square. She looked magnificent, her athletic figure showing to its best in the tightly fitting black jacket and her red hair confined in a velvet snood beneath her hard hat. But she also looked, Meredith noticed, very pale and rather subdued. Fearon turned his horse's head and rode towards her. He leaned across and spoke to her, his face and gestures urgent, but she shook her head.

'Harriet looks a bit ropey,' said Pringle thoughtfully. 'Must have sunk a bit of booze yesterday.' He sounded deeply concerned and Meredith glanced curiously at him. Pringle raised his arm and beckoned, calling, 'Harriet! Over here!'

Harriet rode slowly towards them. When she saw Meredith she said, 'Oh, hi!' slurring the two syllables together and smiling uncertainly.

'Good morning,' Meredith returned. Harriet really did look far from well.

'Take it from me as a medico,' called Pringle up to her, 'no stirrup-cups today! Sure you will be able to keep up?'

'I'm all right, Jack. Don't make a fuss!' said Harriet brusquely, making an obvious effort to pull herself together.

'You look distinctly hung-over, my lovely.'

'Then fresh air and exercise is the best thing for it. I'll know when I can't sit in the blasted saddle.'

'I'll follow behind with the stretcher!' said Pringle drily.

'Happy New Year!' said Miss Needham tartly by way of response and rode away.

It was at that moment Meredith caught a glimpse of another familiar figure. From somewhere the anti-bloodsports protesters had arrived. They must have assembled in a side street and now they were here, mostly young and apparently in fairly good mood. Two of them carried a banner proclaiming their cause and on the outer ring of the group stood Meredith's whiskery acquaintance, minus his clipboard today, but defiantly carrying a placard of his own, declaring the hunt to be a bastion of class privilege. His grubby ex-army greatcoat flapped around his spindly legs in the shabby jeans, underlining the contrast between him and his fellow-protesters, most of whom were clean and reasonably dressed in country wear. It was as if he had mounted the wrong protest in the wrong place, or was simply the wrong person to do it. It struck her that he seemed to have tacked himself on to the others. None of them talked to him though they chatted otherwise amongst themselves. Occasionally one of them would glance the youth's way as if expressing some general unease about him.

Meredith caught hold of Markby's sleeve. 'That's him! The one I told you about. He stopped me last Friday in the High Street and wanted me to sign his protest. He looks just as unhinged today as he did then, poor lad.'

'He looks as though he could do with a decent meal,' Markby observed. The police had arrived now in the shape of a wpc who was talking amiably to the protesters who moved back a little apparently in response to her request. 'Wpc Jones, that one,' murmured Markby as if to himself, 'and doing her job very well.' But Meredith noticed that the movement of the group backwards had served further to isolate her adversary with the placard and the beard. He now stood alone, grim-faced.

'You know,' Pringle said in worried tones. 'Harriet must have had a real skinful yesterday. She does look less than secure aboard.'

Both Meredith and Markby looked towards Harriet. Whilst they had been watching the protesters, a waitress had come out of The Crossed Keys hotel on the corner of the square carrying a tray of interesting-looking glasses. She took it from rider to rider. Harriet had picked up one and tilting back her head, drained it at a single gulp.

'Told her not to have any of that, didn't I?' growled Pringle. 'She's the most difficult, awkward, obstinate woman I ever came across, even if she is one of the best-looking.'

Fearon was watching her too and looking concerned. As if aware of his scrutiny and annoyed by it, she jerked Blazer's head round and turned the horse's tail towards Tom. This led her to stare straight towards Rupert Green and his companion who still waited on the outskirts of the throng. Then she turned her head deliberately aside from them, touched her heels against the chestnut's gleaming flanks and moved away.

'I just hope,' Meredith said, 'that she doesn't see the chap with the placard. He asked her to sign his wretched petition on Friday after he asked me, and got sent away with a flea in his ear. If she sees him today she might go over there and tell him his name for nothing again.'

'Had a bit of a set-to, did they?' Markby sounded interested.

'Oh, I don't know about that. But she did give him a hefty shove and he nearly fell. The silly chap ought to have expected it. I mean, she was all kitted out in breeches and boots and he surely didn't think he had a likely candidate for a signature?'

She fixed a doubtful gaze on the whiskery young protester, willing him by some telepathy to keep back out of the way. That he had quite the opposite intention was obvious. The placard was swaying in the air, his lean face was twisted in excitement. Thrill of the chase, she thought. What motivates him is the same thing as motivates the riders. He's got a quarry and he means to run it down.

Out of the corner of her eye she was aware of the group of horses and riders. One horse had detached itself and ambled towards the line of protesters but it was not for a moment that Meredith realised, with a pang of dismay, that it was Blazer carrying Harriet. Miss Needham was now slumped slightly in the saddle. At first, just for a second, Meredith thought she had seen the placard and was going over to argue the point. But one look at the lacklustre picture presented by the normally spirited Harriet convinced Meredith that she was not even aware the protesters were there, let alone that she had approached so close. Meredith found herself involuntarily raising an arm to attract attention. She wanted to shout out, 'No, Harriet – not over there!' But even if she had, it was unlikely Harriet would have heard her.

The protesters themselves seemed surprised and, as a group, moved back out of her way by some joint instinct. Blazer was a large animal. The one person amongst them who didn't move back was the young man with the whiskers and the private placard of his own. He was already standing apart and when he saw Harriet coming, he alone moved forward as if to challenge her.

It all seemed to happen at once. Meredith thought, he's recognised her! The silly idiot is going to shout some sort of stupid abuse at her and she'll bite his head off!

Pringle exclaimed, 'Who's the silly sod with the placard! Harriet!' he yelled.

At the same time, Markby muttered, 'She's going too close! Where's Wpc Jones and her partner?'

Wpc Jones was in fact several yards away and for the moment unaware of any change in the situation. But her partner, a young constable with a fresh complexion, spotted a potential flashpoint and began to walk briskly towards the group.

They were all too slow. The whiskery young man gave a sudden outlandish yell, causing everyone to look that way, several horses to dance skittishly and their riders to curse. Perhaps Harriet had been roused by Pringle's stentorian cry. Whatever the case, it seemed she only then became aware of the protester as he flourished the placard. She hauled on the reins and tried to back Blazer, his eyes rolling white, out of trouble. But the protester hurled himself forward, brandishing his placard under the startled chestnut's nose. Blazer snorted wildly and reared.

As Harriet fought for control, the Master rode forward shouting, 'Stand clear! Get back there!' and from the constable came a shout of, 'Oy, you, stop that!'

But the youth seemed possessed by his own particular demon. He darted forward, heedless of the flailing hooves and cursing rider and struck out towards her with his placard.

Time froze and events unrolled before Meredith's horror-struck gaze as if in a slow-motion and silent film. All noise was muffled and cut out. Blazer's forelegs cut through the air almost with grace as if he were swimming. Vaguely Meredith was aware that the protesters and the other surrounding crowd members had parted like the waves of the Red Sea, falling back on either side leaving Harriet, Blazer and the protester isolated.

Then Harriet fell . . . toppling slowly sideways, losing reins and stirrup, flinging out her hands, her hat falling off, the snood loosening so that a lock of flaming auburn hair fluttered like an oriflamme above her collapsing body.

Then she landed on the Market Square flagstones with a sickening crash to lie motionless.

Noise, after a moment's horror-filled hush, returned. Now everything seemed to happen at top speed. Faces frozen in the crowd became animated. Limbs caught and held stiffly in awkward attitudes jerked into life as if an electric current had been applied to them. They surged forward around the prostrate figure on the ground and then shrank back.

Pringle bellowed the classic formula, 'Let me through, I'm a doctor!' and hurtled across the square, scattering dogs and horses, his duffel coat flapping to either side like great brown wings.

Blazer had bucked away riderless, empty stirrups flailing, reins trailing loose. Someone, Meredith saw it was Fearon, grabbed at the bridle. It must have been an automatic reaction because he was looking down at the motionless figure and shouting, 'Harriet!'

The protesters looked appalled, suddenly all very young and frightened, huddling together pathetically beneath their joint banner. The bearded youth stood alone over his victim, seeming swept up in a euphoria of victory. He turned, like a winning boxer, and raised up both arms, still brandishing the placard. The constable grabbed it from him and grabbed his arm at the same time. Wpc Jones ran up, the Master dismounted and hurried towards the huddled figure on the ground. Markby started forward and the rest of the crowd fell back, silent. Even the hounds sensed something was amiss and became still, tails pressed between hind legs, watching.

Pringle had reached her first and dropped on to his knees beside her. Markby had come up behind him. Wpc Jones was keeping back the crowd and he called to her, 'Send for the ambulance!'

'Get up, Harriet,' Meredith whispered uselessly. 'Move . . . please move . . . just move a hand . . .'

But it was obvious Harriet was not going to get up and remount. 'Has she broken something?' asked an anxious voice in the crowd.

Pringle looked up at Alan Markby stooping down beside him. He spoke quietly but in the silence which had fallen his words were all too clearly heard.

'She's dead!' he said. As he spoke a dark pool of blood began to gather under the luxuriant mane of Harriet's auburn hair which had escaped from the loosened snood and spread slowly over the ground.

The clip-clop of a hoof came almost like a gunshot in the quiet which followed. Rupert Green had ridden forward from his position to the rear of the crowd. He looked down at Harriet's motionless body and took off his top hat. The traditional, yet so unexpected, sign of respect in the presence of death shocked Meredith almost more than anything else that had happened. The other male riders, all of whom looked stunned, seemed jolted by Green's gesture and there was a scramble to imitate it. Fearon, his swarthy face as white as a ghost beneath the tan, removed his hard hat slowly, the last to do so, and with an angry look at Green as if he felt the financier had somehow insulted rather than honoured the lifeless form sprawled on the flagstones.

Holding his top hat to his chest, Green leaned from the saddle towards the bearded young man, securely grasped between the two constables.

'You killed her!' he said in cold accusing tones. 'You killed her and you meant to!'

Markby began, 'Just a moment – '

But before he could finish a clang of metal and a shattering crash of glass caused them all to spin round. The waitress from The Crossed Keys, unsuspecting, had come out with a fresh supply of punch. Harriet's body lay directly in her line of sight. She had promptly dropped her tin tray and her shrill shrieks began to split the crisp winter air.

Geoffrey Haynes, forgotten by Meredith and unseen by her for some time, strode out of the crowd, up to the waitress and slapped her face. 'Stop that, you stupid woman!' he ordered.

'All right, sir, all right, I'll take care of her!' Wpc Jones shouldered him brusquely aside.

Faintly, in the distance and coming nearer, growing louder, the two-tone cry of a siren announced the imminent arrival of the ambulance. It really need not have hurried.

'I tell you, I didn't know she was going to fall off, did I?' Simon Pardy mumbled for the third or fourth time in the aggressive undertone which seemed to be his preferred manner of replying to any remark. He accompanied his words with a defiant glare from beneath his brows and chewed at the corner of his lip.

'What did you think might happen?' Markby returned, increasingly irritated.

Everything about this sullen youth annoyed him and it was hard not to show it. But a rational discussion with the young Pardy was not something easily achieved. He understood now what Meredith had meant. Simon naturally put people's backs up. He had entered the police station in a storm of self-righteous protest and had been by turn hectoring, belligerent and spiteful. As the reality of his situation dawned on him, he turned whinge-ingly self-defensive. Underneath it all, Markby suspected, Simon was badly frightened at the result of his action – but that did not mean he had not intended to do it. A deed planned in cold blood may appear very different to the perpetrator if he ever gets round to carrying it out. Young Pardy could be terrified at his own success. Markby had seen such things before.

Simon, for all his shambling manner and muttered speech was

a highly articulate young man and Markby had learned upon enquiry that he was the product of a minor public school – although it was doubtful whether the school would have cared to broadcast his presence amongst its alumni. In appearance he was singularly unprepossessing. His age, Markby now knew, was twenty. His clothing was grimy. His nails were bitten to the quicks. His face was gaunt and unshaven. He had a nervous twitch which jerked at a muscle at the corner of his thin-lipped mouth and a malevolent stare. The nervous twitch might well be newly acquired and the result of present circumstances.

'I didn't know she'd fall off like that!' Simon repeated again. 'Those people are supposed to be good riders, aren't they? Anyway, they're always falling off riding across country and they know how to fall. You know, like acrobats do, head tucked in and roll over. But she went down like a sack of spuds and cracked her head open. I didn't expect that, did I?'

Markby hissed and frowned. The annoying thing was that the revolting youth had put his finger on a significant point. Harriet had indeed gone down 'like a sack of spuds'. He had seen her fall with his own eyes but he doubted any other witness would have disagreed with the description. Even Tom Fearon, who ought to know how good a rider Harriet had been if anyone did, had said wonderingly and without the slightest intention of *double-entendre*, 'Harriet had a first-class seat. I didn't expect to see her coming out the side door like that.'

So why had she? Just bad luck? Or was it in some way connected with her pallor and unsteadiness remarked upon by Dr Pringle?

'Did you,' Markby asked patiently for about the third or fourth time, 'intend to make her fall?'

'No, of course not!'

'Was your action pure stupidity – ' He saw Simon's eyes gleam with hatred at him. ' – stupidity, as I say, or did you act hoping to make her fall off?'

'Oh great,' said Simon sarcastically. 'Either I agree with you that I'm thick – which I'm not, incidentally. Or I say, yes, Chief Inspector – ' His voice took on a mincing mimicking tone. Markby hoped it wasn't intended to imitate him. 'I intended her to fall, and if I said that, where would it leave me? Facing a murder charge, I suppose.'

Markby tapped his fingers on the table top and hissed with exasperation. It was impossible to tell whether this youth was very shrewd or rather simple.

The law recognises degrees of homicide other than murder and is observed with some nicety on the matter of recklessness or assault with intent to cause bodily harm. The element of 'mens rea' – that is to say, what was actually in the accused's mind at the time of the assault – is of utmost importance. Pardy had certainly behaved recklessly as the law understood that term. If Pardy had stood in the middle of an empty field shouting and waving his placard, he would have committed no offence. If he had done so because he genuinely believed himself to be alone and was unaware that a mounted rider was behind a clump of trees nearby, though the horse as a result took fright, he might still plead that his action was not reckless.

But Pardy had known he was in a crowded place and that animals were involved which might very well react with panic at his action. Yet he had gone ahead. Reckless, certainly. But had he intended to make Harriet fall? Had he been bearing a grudge against her since the previous Friday when she had pushed him against the door of Woolworth's? Had he singled her out or had she simply been the unfortunate rider nearest to him? Had Pardy, in a nutshell, just been carried away and thoughtless – which might result in a lesser charge – or had he set out to harm Harriet with such deadly results that this might even finish up as a trial for manslaughter?

I'm not a barrister, Markby thought, nor judge nor jury. But he was the first step on the path to those persons and he had to get this right! If he didn't, some clever lawyer would get the boy off on a technicality. On the other hand, perhaps the youth was just plain stupid and hadn't realised what would happen when he started waving that placard about. People could be amazingly stupid. Further enquiry into Pardy's activities might well hold the clue to the truth. Markby set out on a different line of approach.

'Ever send any letters to members of the hunting fraternity?'

'Send them letters? Valentines, I suppose?' Simon jibed in his sarcastic way. But he looked startled for the moment. He had not been expecting the change in subject. He had his answer to questions about the events of that morning but he had not prepared an answer to any others. He gave Markby a look of pure dislike, rooted, the chief inspector suspected, in anger at having been out-manoeuvred.

'Don't try and be clever,' Markby told him, hanging determinedly on to his patience. 'It's not a laughing matter and no time to make jokes. Nor are you in any position to make them. Have you, at any time, sent threatening letters to members of the Bamford Hunt or people connected with it? To Mr Fearon who runs the livery stables at Pook's Common, for example?'

'No, I didn't!' said Simon defiantly. 'And you can't say I did or prove anything.'

Out of the corner of his eye, Markby saw Pearce, taking notes in the background, shift in his chair. 'Fearon kept his letter and we have it here,' Markby said.

'So? Going to compare handwriting, are you?' Pardy sneered insolently.

'Supposing I said, yes? What would you say?'

'I'd say you couldn't do it!' Pardy returned triumphantly.

'Oh?' Markby's voice was deceptively pleasant. 'Why?'

But Simon had belatedly realised the trap into which he had already put a toe – and drew back. 'I dunno. What I meant was, you couldn't prove it was my writing because I didn't write it.'

'Indeed?' Pardy was right and he couldn't prove handwriting, because the letter had been formed of scraps of newsprint in the classic way. A tabloid paper. Pardy had almost admitted that he knew that – but had stopped just short and wouldn't be fooled into such a damning admission now.

'Where did you spend Christmas Eve?' Markby asked.

'At home mostly. Went down the pub first for a drink.'

'Anyone see you there? Which pub?'

'Bunch of Grapes. Several people saw me there. My mates – Micky was there and Trace and Cheryl – I share the house with them. And the landlord will remember me. Miserable old bastard that he is.'

'What time did you leave?'

'Dunno, half ten-ish.'

'And went – ?'

'Home!'

'Alone?'

'Yes!'

'Any one at home to witness your return?'

'No! I told you, Trace and Cheryl and Micky were all down the pub. I left them there. Cheryl was pissed.'

'Were you – drunk?'

'No, I was not drunk!'

Markby abandoned this tack. It would lead nowhere. If Simon

had gone to the stables and let out the horses, it would be difficult to prove it. Christmas Eve is a time of flux, like New Year's Eve. The youthful population ebbed and surged like a floodtide in and out of public houses and discos. Invariably some of them were drunk, others high on some weed, some too randy to notice anything but the opposite sex, and the remainder were too self-absorbed to notice anything.

'All right, let's go back to the events in the Market Square, Or rather, let's go back to the Friday before that. Last Friday. You were in Bamford, collecting signatures for a petition.'

'Yes, I was!' Simon looked surprised, displeased and wary by turn. 'Who told you?'

'Police foot patrol saw you and half of Bamford. You approached Miss Harriet Needham, the deceased lady.'

'Did I? I don't remember. I asked a lot of people. Is that her name?'

'You approached Miss Needham,' repeated Markby evenly, 'whether or not you knew at the time that was her name, and you asked her to sign. She spoke brusquely to you and pushed you back against the door of Woolworth's.'

'Oy!' burst out Simon, aggrieved. 'Who says that? Load of cobblers!'

Markby kept his gaze steady.

'A very reliable witness.'

'Yeah? Well your reliable witness can – '

'Did you speak to Miss Needham?' Markby almost shouted before Simon could finish. 'And as she walked away from you, did you utter the words, "Wait until Boxing Day" or any words similar to that?'

'I don't remember.'

'Yes, you do. You were angry. You had some cause to be. She pushed you. She made you look a bit of a fool in front of anyone else who was watching. Didn't it make you angry? Wouldn't you have liked to get your own back?'

Simon ran a tongue across his dry lips. 'I want a solicitor.'

'Oh, why?'

'Because it's my right, that's why. I want my solicitor. I'm not saying another word until he gets here and you lot can certainly forget any idea that I'll sign anything.'

'So, what's his name?' Markby asked, nodding at Pearce.

A gleam of malice shone in the detainee's eye. 'Colin Deanes,' said Simon and had the satisfaction of seeing the chief inspector momentarily struck dumb.

It was later that evening that Simon Pardy, released from custody for the time being with a stern warning not to leave the town, went home. This was a terraced house in Jubilee Road, a street of run-down Edwardian villas. Number forty-three where he lived with three other youngsters was more dilapidated than most. It had no inside lavatory. No matter the weather, one had to go out to a privy next to a coalshed in the backyard. The stonework around the bay windows was crumbling and the upper front bay had developed a distinct list. All the brickwork needed repointing and the paintwork was faded and peeled. In the state it was, the landlord would have had difficulty in finding respectable tenants and was happy to let it out – at a fairly stiff rent – to youngsters.

Simon lived here as a result of a chance meeting with Mick Leary in a pub. He had been looking for a place to live. Micky and the two girls were looking for a fourth person – someone having just moved out and on. They needed four to make the rent affordable. Simon had moved in at once.

Micky worked locally as a storeman; the two girls, Tracy and Cheryl, as supermarket assistants. When not working the girls dressed alike in black tight pants, black leather jackets and black suede boots. They had spiky black-dyed hair and ears drilled full of holes to take a forest of earrings. Both were short, dumpy and energetic and, seeing them scurry together down the street in their black garb, they looked like a pair of hunting spiders. Simon was not interested in them or in girls generally. Nor was he interested in young men. He was not, basically, interested in people at all. He had always been a loner, even at school. He had early become addicted to radical causes but latterly had settled on those related to animals. Yet curiously enough, he was not particularly interested in animals for their own sake, either. A couple of cats hung around number forty-three, but they avoided Simon – who in any case never fed them. Mick made a fuss of them and the girls brought home tins of catfood from the supermarket for them. On the whole, the cats did quite well out of number forty-three. But they did so without Simon, the animal champion.

One cat, a sinewy black and white, crouched on the crumbling brick wall in the lee of next door's straggly privet hedge as Simon strode, greatcoat flapping, through the gap where a gate should have been. The other, a tabby of more enterprising character, lurked in the porch hopefully. Simon let himself in and shut the door before the cat by his feet could squeeze in after him.

Voices could be heard from the kitchen – the only room in the house which had any heating and so the one where they all assembled. Simon made his way over the cracked linoleum on the hall floor and pushed the door open.

The other three were seated round the rickety kitchen table, its surface covered with empty coffee mugs, lager and Coca-Cola cans and an overflowing ashtray. Their heads were close together and as he appeared they all looked up in unison with startled faces and fell silent. It was obvious they had been talking about him.

Simon didn't care whether they had or not. Recently he had begun to suspect they would like him to leave and, if they could have been sure of finding a substitute fourth, would have asked him to do so. But he was used to people not liking him or his company and so took their attitude as expected. He had not the slightest intention of going. He went over to the kettle and filled it.

'How did you get on with the filth?' Micky asked. 'We heard all about it down the pub.'

'All right.'

'She's dead, that's right?' Cheryl asked, her mouth remaining half-open when she finished speaking. 'Everyone was saying she was dead.'

'Yes.'

'What, an' they let you go?' demanded Tracy, the more aggressive of the two. She shook her crest of rusty-black spikes and blinked eyes rimmed with thick black circles like a nautch dancer's.

'You bet they did,' snarled Simon. 'I got Colin on to them.'

'What, Deanes?' Tracy sounded sceptical.

'Yes, Deanes!' Simon turned to glower at her. 'He sorted them out quick enough!'

'Him?' Her scepticism increased. 'He couldn't sort himself out of a paper bag!'

They were all startled by his reaction. Simon launched himself towards the table and crashed both clenched fists down on its surface, making it rock dangerously and all the mugs and cans rattle.

'Don't you say anything against Colin! He knows what he's doing! He tells the sodding establishment where to get off! He's the best bloke I know and if there were a few more like him, we'd have a decent society in this country – instead of the crap we've got!'

There was a silence, then Micky said peaceably, 'All right, keep your hair on. Good job you could call him up.'

Simon looked from one to the other of them. Cheryl ran the tip of her tongue round her parted lips. Tracy blinked her kohl-rimmed eyes rapidly.

'All right?' he demanded truculently.

'All right!' they chorused obediently in reply.

Simon pushed himself away from the table and went back to the hissing kettle to make his coffee. They could not see the glow of triumph in his eyes. His heart danced with pleasure in his chest and all the fear he had experienced at the station turned to joy. They were afraid of him. They were afraid he'd turn violent and do one of them some actual physical harm. They had never feared him before. They had despised him, tolerating him for his share of the rent. But now the Needham woman had died and they were afraid of him. There would be no more hinting now that they would like him to leave. They'd like him to go, all right, but were too scared now to ask it of him. From now on he could do and say what he liked – they wouldn't raise a squeak.

Simon poured hot water into his mug, his lean face creasing into an unattractive, self-congratulating smile as he began to consider the perks of power.

Five

Markby drew up before Rose Cottage and switched off his engine. He got out but before going to knock at the door, crossed the road and stood for a moment contemplating Ivy Cottage. It was Friday morning, following the accident. They had traced a relative of Miss Needham's already, a Miss Frances Needham-Burrell. Bit of a mouthful, that, thought Markby. She was also, it appeared, Harriet's executor in the matter of her will and was making arrangements to come to Bamford immediately. He had not spoken to Miss Needham-Burrell himself and had no idea how old she was. Probably a stringy old battleaxe in tweeds.

Harriet's solicitors were Duckett & Simpson, one of Bamford's three legal firms. Mr Theo Simpson, the senior partner, personally handled Miss Needham's affairs. Mr Simpson it was who, hearing of the accident in the Market Square, had telephoned Markby to confirm what had happened and to inform him that he, Mr Simpson, would be getting in touch with Miss Needham-Burrell. Markby thanked him for his prompt intervention and help. He had dealt with Mr Simpson on several occasions. The solicitor was a scrupulously correct elderly man with no sense of humour and a dislike of being hurried, although he'd moved quickly enough this time. His devotion to his clients' interests was outstanding. So much so that on several occasions when obliged to contact him on police matters, Markby had found him positively obstructive. This time poor old Simpson had been caught off-balance by events and had sounded distinctly agitated on the telephone.

'Old Theo?' Laura had said once, when he grumbled to her about Mr Simpson. 'He's a bit stuffy, I suppose, but he's very sound on his law. Wish I knew a tenth as much.'

Markby found himself wondering now of what, apart from Ivy Cottage, Miss Needham's estate consisted. As for Ivy Cottage, it was attractive, old-world, in a good state of repair and with a nice little garden behind it. It was guaranteed to make any estate

81

agent's eye light up, even with the current slump in the property market. He realised that asking Mr Simpson about the will without a court order would be a waste of time. He'd tried, in a roundabout fashion, on the telephone to get some information as to Harriet's means of support, pointing out that there might be others who should be informed of the tragic event. The most Mr Simpson would concede – with the greatest reluctance and sounding scandalised at the impropriety of the question – was that his late client had been in receipt of a private income from a family trust. What level of income this had been, he did not feel he could reveal. It was, he said testily, sufficient. Which same meant, thought Markby, that he was saying Harriet wasn't a kept woman.

So Harriet hadn't worked at a regular job. She had done a little freelance journalism for such magazines as *Horse and Hound, The Field* and *Country Life*. For this information he was indebted to Jack Pringle. Harriet was also, he had been surprised to learn this time from Laura, the author of a saga entitled *Briony Rides at the Horse of the Year Show*. It was aimed at a readership of little girls at Pony Club age but also attracted those who didn't own a pony but just felt passionately about horses – a stage little English girls are prone to go through and some never grow out of. His niece, Emma, was apparently entering such a stage and owned a signed copy of *Briony Rides at the Horse of the Year Show*.

'It was jolly nice of Harriet,' Laura said. 'Emma saw her in Bamford and asked her if she could send her the book to sign and Harriet said yes, of course. So Emma sent it over to Pook's Common and Harriet sent it back with a very nice inscription and a signed photo of herself on her horse. Emma's got it framed in her bedroom. This accident is a rotten business.'

However, this remarkable literary work – even given an army of fans as keen as his niece – would not have brought in very much income, nor would the journalism, and it was to be assumed the trust provided the rest.

What he was also wondering was whether Harriet had received any letters of the kind received by Tom Fearon and if so, whether she had kept them? But he had little reason yet to ask for a search warrant and Mr Simpson would go purple in the face and throw every legal book in his considerable library at him if he so much as tried. But it would be worth making contact with Miss Frances Needham-Burrell when she arrived and asking her –

when sorting out her cousin's effects – to keep an eye open for letters with a threatening or abusive content.

Markby retraced his steps to Rose Cottage and Meredith opened the door as he came up. She seemed pleased to see him.

'I was watching you through the net curtains – how's that for snooping? Would you like a cup of tea or coffee?'

'Tea would be fine.' He sat down in the living room into which she ushered him and observed, 'You've taken down the decorations.'

'Yes, it hardly seemed right to leave them there in the circumstances. Mrs Brissett's very upset about Harriet's death. She's been crying and I sent her home. She was very fond of Harriet. It seems that a few years ago Mrs Brissett's daughter's husband left her and she had trouble finding a job and had no money . . . and Harriet helped her find a job somewhere. The Brissetts are eternally grateful. It sounds kind of Harriet.'

'I think she was kind . . .' Markby said, remembering the signed copy of *Briony Rides at the Horse of the Year Show*. Meredith went out to fetch the tea and when she returned he went on, 'This is an official visit, actually.'

Meredith smiled quickly. 'I guessed as much. What's happening about that boy?'

'You mean the wretched Pardy – that's his name, Simon Pardy. I've let him go pending further enquiries – he set his solicitor on me. Your friend, Colin Deanes, no less. He arrived in record time and accused me of bullying tactics. I wasn't going to get anything else out of Pardy anyway so I had a statement typed up and after Deanes had put a magnifying glass over it, the lad signed and was ushered out by Deanes doing a mother-hen act over him.'

'Is Deanes a solicitor? I thought he was a writer and a sociologist?' Meredith asked, surprised.

'Also, it seems, a qualified solicitor who used to be in partnership up North somewhere, but quit to make a fulltime career of saving wayward youngsters. I didn't know, either.'

'Is Pardy wayward? I mean, has he been in trouble before?

Markby grunted. 'Not around here. Minor things elsewhere.'

Pardy's previous convictions were of a relatively trivial nature, being ordered out of several county towns by magistrates for persistently collecting without a licence in the street – rattling his tin in support of a variety of causes but only very recently turning his attention to those connected with animals. That Markby found curious. One might claim Simon's heart was in the right place, but his head – so it appeared to Markby – was all over the place. An irrational young man. The causes he pursued so vigorously no doubt satisfied some deep, emotional void. Estranged from family, probably, and with few real friends. Even the local hunt saboteurs were vague about him.

'He just turned up one day,' said their leader. 'None of us knows anything about him.'

On the other hand, warned a little voice at the back of Markby's brain, the lad's manner and appearance could be a sham. He may be just naive and well meaning. Or he may know exactly what he's doing – and be doing it for reasons his companions know nothing of, his meaning anything but benevolent. It might be worth enquiring of other departments whether Simon had ever been known to associate with anarchist groups. Just a thought.

'Listen, Meredith,' Markby leaned forward now. 'You were a witness of the incident in which Harriet died and the previous one when she and Pardy met. Tell me how you remember the incident in the Market Square first.'

Meredith poured out the tea carefully, gathering her thoughts. She pursed her lips and rubbed a hand over her thick brown hair. She was wearing a knitted pullover in some kind of fluffy yarn and jeans. 'Well,' she pushed the sleeves of the pullover up to her elbows. 'It's a funny thing. Although I can see the whole thing unrolling in my mind's eye like a silent film, I can't really be precise about where everyone was and that sort of thing.'

'I don't expect you to be. People never can be. At least you admit it. The worst kind of witness is the one who swears to a fact about which he is quite wrong though quite sincere, and absolutely refuses to be shaken. It's extremely difficult to remember something which takes place suddenly, unexpectedly and in distracting circumstances. Try your best.'

'Let's see. Harriet rode close by the demonstrators, which surprised me. It was as if she didn't see them. They went back – except for Pardy who came forward – or was it that the others went back and he was left alone in a forward position? I couldn't swear quite to which. He waved the placard in a wild and thoroughly stupid manner. The horse reared up. Harriet came off . . . Pardy just stood there, looking pleased with himself – he waved his arms in a kind of salute. Fearon caught Harriet's horse, didn't he? He was holding it by the bridle a minute or two later. Then Green rode up. He must have ridden through the crowd but I didn't see him do it. Suddenly he was there, taking off his top hat and looking down at her.'

'What did you think of Green's gesture?' Markby asked her.

'To tell you the truth, it gave me the creeps. It made me think of that voodoo thing which hangs round graveyards and wears a top hat.' An image of Green's bared head as he looked down at Harriet's body came into her mind and of his face and expression. Shocked? No, she thought, he looked relieved, that's it! But now she was imagining things, she decided immediately and kept this impression to herself. 'What did you think?' she temporised.

'Me? Strictly between us I thought his action grotesque. Although it was correct, I dare say, and he no doubt intended it as a mark of respect. I don't think Tom Fearon liked it much.'

'No, I noticed he looked angry. Perhaps it's Green himself he doesn't much like.'

'What makes you say that?' Markby looked at her curiously.

She flushed. 'Just a thought. It's very warm in here. Do you mind if I turn down the gas fire?' She got up and stooped to reach the tap. 'That's how I recall it. Sorry I can't do any better.'

'Did it strike you just before the accident that Harriet looked woozy or unsteady in the saddle?'

'Yes, it did, very much so, and quite unlike her normal self I would have thought. Although of course I didn't know her very well or for very long. I'm no judge.'

'Just using your powers of observation, how would you have described her? Hung-over? Still tiddly?'

'I don't know, Alan!' Meredith burst out crossly. 'I'm not qualified to make a guess. And you shouldn't ask me – it's a leading question and if you asked me that in court the judge would intervene and tell the recorder to strike it out! Why don't you ask Dr Pringle – he knew her better than I did and he can give a medical opinion!'

'Oh, Jack . . .' said Markby vaguely. 'He's gone a bit quiet. I don't know what he's thinking. All right, I won't ask leading questions. But you said you saw her in Bamford the previous Friday. How did she look then?'

'In fine fettle. And she was all right because when I got back here, she drove up and asked me over for coffee. She had bought all kinds of food for a dinner party. She'd taken a cordon bleu cookery course, she told me. Perhaps I should take one of those . . .' added Meredith, going momentarily off at a tangent. 'I'm not much of a cook at all. Pretty rotten, really.' She pulled

herself together and back to the subject. 'She probably enter-
tained a lot. She had a visitor on Christmas Day evening,
anyway.' She fell into a sudden awkward silence.

'How do you know?'

'I – saw them. On the blind, their silhouettes.' Meredith's face
flushed and her jaw set aggressively. 'It sounds dreadful, real
voyeurism. I wasn't snooping from behind the curtains though,
I assure you. I was going to draw the curtains, upstairs in the
bedroom about ten minutes after you dropped me off here. He
– it was a man – could tell you what sort of a state she was in –
oh lord, that sounds like something I don't mean. I meant, if she
felt ill. She wasn't acting as if she felt ill.'

'As if she were drunk?'

'I really couldn't say!' The words came out sharply. More
mildly, she added. 'But I would have guessed she had a good
head for holding her drink. I saw her twice between that Friday
in Bamford and seeing her silhouetted on the blind on Christmas
Day.'

'Oh?' he raised his eyebrows.

'On the Saturday morning I saw her outside Pook's stables.
I'd gone for a walk. She caught up with me and took me along
to a paddock to see her horse. Then we parted, I went on and
she went back with Blazer to the stable yard. And on Monday
she came over here and had a quick lunch with me because Mrs
Brissett was cleaning over at Ivy Cottage. We just sat and natt-
ered, about various Christmas holidays we recalled from our
individual childhoods. Actually, I talked mostly about that.
Harriet didn't say much about family. She had the measles one
Christmas and put the entire household in quarantine – that was
about the only purely family story she told. She asked what I did
abroad. Then I got her talking about horses. She'd always owned
a horse or pony since a kid. She'd saved Blazer from slaughter.
Saw him at a sale being knocked down to a known horsemeat
dealer and stepped in and outbid him at the last moment. She
felt very strongly about animals being exported live to the continent for slaughter, horses or cattle. She explained Common
Market regulations to me. It seems they aren't as strict as British
ones and people here are worried the rules governing transport
of livestock may be relaxed to put us in line with Europe. Harriet
was concerned it would mean suffering for the wretched animals
and it does seem wrong that, for example, under EEC rules the
poor beasts don't even have to be fed and watered so frequently

during transport as under our rules. The really stupid thing is that Pardy got everything so wrong. I mean, she did care about animals. She cared a lot and she did things to help, practical things like buying Blazer and writing to MPs and others about this animal transport business.'

Markby sat glowering at the gas fire which had dulled its bright flames and hissed in a soft insistent way. 'I suppose,' he asked without any real hope, 'she didn't mention to you anything about anonymous letters?'

'No, nothing.' Meredith looked and sounded surprised. 'Did she receive any? What about?'

'I don't know. Tom did and other subscribers to the hunt may have. I'll have to wait for Miss Needham-Burrell.'

'Who?'

'The deceased's cousin and her executor. Probably an old biddy with a moustache and a shooting-stick.'

'Oh no,' said Meredith, remembering the photograph of the three little girls, 'She's – ' She broke off and finished meekly, 'She's probably very nice.'

'Nice and, I hope, cooperative.' Markby got up. 'Thanks for the tea. I hope this isn't going to cast too much of a blight over seasonal festivities. Will you be able to come out for a drink on New Year's Eve, next Tuesday evening?'

He wanted to see her again. She ought to be wary but despite this she felt pleased. 'Yes, thanks, if you're not still busy with this.'

'Oh, we'll have it cleared up by then.' said Markby, cheerfully.

Meredith waved him goodbye from the gate, watching as he turned outside the Haynes' cottage and until he had driven off out of sight towards Fenniwick's garage and the B road turn. As the sound of his car died away she found herself staring at the blank windows of Ivy Cottage across the lane. Yesterday morning Harriet had got out of bed and made herself ready to go hunting behind those upstairs windows. Today Harriet lay dead. And on Christmas day night Harriet and a man had been locked in passionate embrace behind those windows and she, Meredith, had glimpsed them. Where was he now, Harriet's lover? What was he thinking? And did he know the reason or could he offer any explanation for her unusual demeanour at the meet? If there's an inquest, Meredith thought, he ought to come forward and give evidence. There would be an inquest, wouldn't there?

A sharp breeze blew around her and brought on it a faint but unmistakable odour of horses. Meredith looked thoughtfully down the lane. Pook's stables were invisible from here but were making their presence known by other means. She reprimanded herself sharply. She shouldn't interfere. But why not? She'd liked Harriet. She wanted to know the truth. Tom was Harriet's friend. So he should want to know the truth too. Or did he know it already?

She returned indoors to fetch stout shoes and anorak, tied a headscarf over her bobbed brown hair to stop it flying about in the wind, and set off down the lane.

At Pook's stables the yard was empty although she could hear the horses in their stalls. Meredith pushed open the five-barred gate and refastened it carefully behind her. Fearon's Mercedes was parked under the roof of a hay-barn to her left. He was around somewhere unless he had ridden out on the common. That was more than possible. Meredith peered into a couple of loose-boxes and called 'Mr Fearon?' but only found herself staring into surprised equine faces. She hesitated, thought 'In for a penny, In for a pound!' and began to walk towards the ramshackle bungalow behind the stables.

There was a field just behind it containing red and white poles and some painted oil drums. They lay about higgledy-piggledy but were obviously intended to be set up as practice jumps. The whole place seemed to be organised chaos. Horses mattered here, horses first and foremost. The humans and their needs had to be squeezed in when time and space permitted. The front door of the bungalow was ajar. Meredith hesitated again in the porch and then rapped loudly on it.

'Mr Fearon!'

There was no reply. She could imagine that Tom would go out and leave his door open if he was working about the place but not if he had quitted it, and in winter it seemed foolhardy to say the least to leave it and let the cold air invade the house. She stepped into the narrow hall and called again, 'Mr Fearon, are you here?'

A faint moan from the door to her immediate right answered her. Alarm seized her. Was he hurt or ill or even, given recent events, overcome by grief and distress? He had been closely involved with Harriet over the horses. Poor man! thought Meredith in a sudden burst of commiseration. She tapped on the door and receiving no further reply, pushed it open.

She found herself on the threshold of Fearon's bedroom: that was a bit tricky and she knew she ought to retreat there and then. The curtains were drawn still and on this winter day it was almost as dark as night in here. But then she heard another faint groan and saw that a figure was sprawled immobile across the double bed in the centre of the room. Meredith edged cautiously towards it.

'Mr Fearon?' She came to an abrupt halt, stooped and sniffed, wrinkling her nose at the odour of whisky. Hurt or ill? Distressed? Nothing of the sort. He was drunk!

Meredith uttered an exclamation of disgust. She turned on her heel and strode to the windows, jerked back the curtains to allow the grey daylight to flood the room and surveyed her surroundings. What a mess. Tom's riding hat hung on the brass bedknob at the foot of his bed. One pair of riding boots, presumably his best ones, lay propped against one another by the dressing table looking as inebriated as their owner. His white shirt from the previous day had been discarded on the floor. Tom Fearon, fully dressed, lay across the unmade bed, his feet in muddy boots on the coverlet, unshaven, eyes closed.

Meredith marched across, grasped his pullover in both hands and dragged him off the pillows to shake him violently. 'Wake up!' she ordered sharply.

Tom's eyes opened blearily. She released him and he fell back on the crumpled bedclothes to stare up at her at first blankly. Then after a moment his gaze cleared and a puzzled look entered his eyes. 'Who the hell are you?' he muttered hoarsely from the pillow.

'Meredith Mitchell from Rose Cottage!'

'Oh, sure, yes,' Fearon blinked. 'Remember you. In the square, yesterday . . .'

'Get up, Mr Fearon! This is disgusting! You have livestock to care for!' Meredith said furiously.

That struck home. Fearon's eyes opened fully and he sat up with a jerk, swore, rubbed his hand over his black curls and squinted at her. 'I was out there at six this morning seeing to the horses. Don't bloody lecture me!'

'There's no need to swear!' Meredith said crisply.

Fearon swung his legs to the floor, put his hands on the edge of the bed and grimaced up at her. 'What are you doing in here, anyway?'

'I came to see you but you weren't in the yard. The front door is open. This place is icy cold. Haven't you any heating?'

'Don't need any, I'm outdoors all day!' Fearon lurched to his feet. She was tall but Tom was an awful lot taller, he must be six-two in his socks, Meredith calculated. She tried to visualise the silhouetted figures on Harriet's blind. The man had been tall, but as tall as this? Difficult to say.

Her gaze fell on the mud-stained coverlet. 'Tchah!' she said crossly.

Fearon glanced in that direction to see what had upset her, looked vaguely surprised, slapped half-heartedly at the mud with his hand and mumbled, 'It'll brush off . . .'

He walked past her, scratching his ribs absently, and disappeared into another room. Tap water splashed into a basin. Meredith walked out into the hall and waited. Fearon reappeared holding a towel, his black hair glistening wet and rivulets running down his swarthy skin. He rubbed at his jaw and the back of his neck with the towel and said, 'I'm not drunk, I was dog-tired, not that I owe you any explanation. I only had a couple of hours sleep last night.'

'I smelled the whisky.'

'One drink, I had one drink! And it's no damn business of yours! Who the hell gave you the right to breeze in here and order me about?' He suddenly exploded into anger, jaw thrust out pugnaciously, dark eyes gleaming.

'You invited me yesterday. You said I should come down and see the stables.'

Fearon looked temporarily nonplussed, then shrugged, tossed the towel back into the bathroom behind him where it presumably landed on the floor and growled, 'All right, I'll show you around. Let me get my jacket!'

The jacket was a well-worn Harris tweed with leather patches on the elbows. Fearon dragged it on over his sweater, tugged a disreputable flat cap over his wet hair and set off briskly towards the yard. Meredith found herself scurrying along to keep up with him.

'Tack room!' said Fearon laconically, throwing open the door as they reached it.

Meredith looked in. Saddles, gleaming immaculately and stirrups irons polished, hung neatly on pegs. Bridles hung above. Compared to the bungalow the tack room was a miracle of neatness.

'I've only five horses here at the moment,' Tom said moving

on to the first loose-box. 'The old mare here should do you all right.'

He said this suspiciously blandly and Meredith glowered at him. He had opened the loose-box door and disappeared inside, returning leading a bay horse of about fifteen hands by the halter.

'She's twelve years old, nice old girl, good mouth and nice manners which puts her ahead of some women – and she won't set you down in the dirt. Let me known if you're interested and I'll throw a saddle over her for you.'

'Thank you,' said Meredith, patting the mare's nose.

'Got a side-saddle back there in the tack room if you prefer,' said Tom in that bland way.

'All right!' said Meredith crossly. 'I'm not simple! You can pack in the jibes.'

Fearon's tanned cheeks stretched into a grin. He returned the mare to her loose-box and, coming out again, leaned against the closed door with his arm folded and regarded her steadily from beneath the dragged-down brim of his flat cap. 'All right, Miss Mitchell, what do you want to know?'

To her annoyance, Meredith felt the blood surge into her face. She drew a deep breath and said quickly, 'I came to talk about Harriet.'

'I rather thought that was it.' Fearon pushed himself away from the door. 'It's warmer in the tack room. There's an oil stove in there.'

She followed him back into the little harness store and sat down on a bench while he lit the paraffin stove which soon filled the room with its smell and heat.

'Isn't that thing dangerous? I mean, I would have thought you'd worry about fire.'

'I'm careful.' Fearon gave her a dry glance. 'And you try cleaning tack with frozen fingers.' He sat down on a bench against the opposite wall and rested his arms on his knees, hands loosely clasped. He had surprisingly fine hands, long, slender and strong, but there were tell-tale scars across the knuckles, pale against the tanned skin. He'd been in his share of fistfights had Mr Fearon. But how long ago? Were the scars just mementos of boyhood?

'I'm sorry about Harriet,' said Meredith slowly. 'I was looking forward to knowing her better.'

'Were you now?' His tone was almost insulting, not quite.

Meredith kept her temper. 'Yes, I liked her very much.'

Fearon grunted. 'Shook me up a bit, that yesterday,' he said unexpectedly.

'Yes, I'm sure it did. It was horrifying to see her fall.' Meredith paused and added, 'I'm not surprised you had a drink and I'm sorry if I was critical just now.'

'Keeps the cold out.'

'It doesn't, actually. It's a misconception. You just get an illusion of warmth and afterwards you're colder. The veins expand or something and you lose body-heat.'

'What are you, for chrissake?' he asked. 'A ruddy Mother Superior?'

'No, I was just wondering about Harriet. She seemed ill at the meet just before the accident. Didn't you think so?'

He grew cautious. 'I never knew her ill. She was pretty fit.'

'But she wasn't fit at the meet, was she?' Meredith persisted. 'She was slumped in the saddle and slurring her words. Would she have been drinking before she arrived there, do you think?'

'Now you listen to me, Meredith, or whatever your name is!' Fearon said fiercely. 'Harriet might have had a glass or two that morning but she wasn't drunk! In five years I never saw Harriet the worse for drink. I saw her knock back a few glasses but never saw her tight! Have you got that through your head? I don't know why she was the way she was just before that young blighter with the placard made Blazer rear up, but she wasn't ill and she wasn't drunk, got that?'

He was really angry now and in the close proximity of the tiny over-filled tack room he loomed distinctly dangerous.

'All right,' said Meredith meekly.

Fearon relaxed marginally but was terminating the interview. 'I've got work to do. Phone if you want me to saddle up the mare and I'll have her ready for you by the time you get down here.'

'Thanks.' They had both risen to their feet.

'See you around, I dare say,' said Fearon with heavy politeness.

'Yes, good bye!' Meredith escaped through the door he held open and walked quickly home feeling both discomfited and dissatisfied. Silly idiot! she chided herself. Barging in there! She sighed. And I still don't know if he was the man I saw outlined on Harriet's blind. She frowned. If Harriet wasn't ill and she wasn't drunk, then what was wrong with her?

*

At that moment, back in Bamford, Chief Inspector Markby was about to be given the answer to that question.

'The post-mortem report is in on the Needham business!' Pearce greeted him.

Markby, taking off his overcoat and sticking it haphazardly over a peg, grunted. He paused by the windowsill on the way to his desk to peer at an African violet in a pot. A row of smaller pots alongside it contained leaves from this parent plant from which he was hoping to strike new plants, so far without result.

He sat down and picked up the sheaf of papers neatly set out on the top of his desk. After a moment he whistled softly under his breath, then called sharply, 'Pearce!'

'Yes, sir?'

'The deceased lady was brim full of tranquillisers.'

'They wouldn't have mixed well with booze,' said Pearce. 'They were all drinking some stirrup cup or other, you said.'

'Yes, they were. Tranquillisers . . .' Markby leaned back. 'No wonder she fell off. She certainly looked and acted odd beforehand. It lets young Pardy off the hook, I suppose. We can still charge him with reckless behaviour. But the reason she fell so easily and so heavily would seem to be that she was light-headed from a mixture of drink and pills. Funny . . .' He screwed up his eyes and stared unseeingly at the calendar on the further wall. 'I wouldn't have thought she was the type to take tranquillisers. Very self-possessed, confident – not nervy or depressed.'

'Never can tell,' said Pearce wisely.

'True. If it results in young Pardy being charged with a lesser offence, Deanes will be highly satisfied. Or disappointed, perhaps. That book of his has been finished some time, by the way, and is about to appear in the bookshops. It's called *Revolutionary Youth*.'

'I'll look out for it,' said Pearce expressionlessly.

'It deals with kids who take up causes and get drawn into violent activities as a result. They raid research labs and let out the animals, that sort of thing. Or demonstrate . . . like Pardy. I'm being uncharitable possibly, but I wonder if Deanes wasn't looking forward to a little publicity over Pardy's case to promote his book? He may well be disappointed that the whole thing seems likely to fizzle out as death by misadventure.'

Markby turned his eyes back to the report. 'She'd had a dickens of a lot to drink. Not just the one stirrup cup I saw her take.

She must have had several tots before she started out. If she'd been stopped in a car with this level of alcohol in her, she would have lost her licence for a year at least and got a hefty fine. In view of this, I can't see the coroner bringing in any verdict of unlawful killing. Pardy was stupid and the results were tragic. But she would have fallen off anyway once the hunt started out in earnest. At the first hedge she tried to clear.'

'What about the letter Mr Fearon got, sir?'

'Ah, that's another matter and I want to follow it up. I'm pretty sure Pardy sent it but so far can't prove it. I'll put my last dollar on it there were others. I've arranged to drive out and have a word with the Master tomorrow morning. So much for my Saturday. He might have received some – or know who has. You'd better go round and ask some of the other hunt sub-scribers. The letter Fearon got was a very nasty piece of threatening mail. Pardy, if it was Pardy, may have slipped up and written one by hand. Although if they use newspapers to do it, they generally stick to the one method. We'll see.'

'Come in, my dear chap, come in,' invited Colonel Stanley. 'Excuse me if I don't get up. Ruddy sciatica has got me today. Can't move off this confounded sofa. I feel like a damn old woman. Have a drink?'

'Normally, I'd say, not on duty,' Markby said with a smile, shaking the Master of the Hunt's hand.

'Of course you would. But this isn't normal. I was at school with your father, you know. Of course, he was senior to me. I was just a squib and he was a six-former, very fine chap and took no notice of grubby little oicks. Quite right too. So you'll have a whisky? You'll have to do the honours. Pour me one too, dash of soda, don't drown it.'

Markby 'did the honours' and settled down in a vast, chintz-covered, feather-cushioned armchair. The walls of the room were hung with sporting prints and photographs of men and women in riding garb. A dull grey winter Saturday morning was kept out by tall windows hung with faded velvet drapes. There was a distinct lingering odour of tobacco and dogs. A log fire roared in the open hearth, spitting out sparks. It was untidy, comfortable and very English.

'Don't need to ask what's brought you!' said Stanley abruptly.

'Yes, I'm sorry about it.' Markby cupped his hands round the tumbler of tawny liquid.

'No need to tell you how I feel. Or other folk. She was a fine girl, fine girl!'

'She'll be much missed.'

'My dear chap – ' the Master paused. 'Indeed, yes, indeed. What are you going to do about it?'

'Well, you've heard about the traces of tranquillisers found in the deceased's blood?'

'I have. I don't mind telling you, I find that a bit rum. Harriet wasn't the nervy type. I've seen that girl ride straight at an obstacle would make many a man blanch.'

'It does confuse the issue. Would she have fallen, off, but for the mixture of drink and pills?'

'I would have said,' the Master observed grimly, 'that with a bloody great placard waving under the horse's nose, there was every likelihood she'd fall off!'

'Good horsewomen, though, would you say? You spoke of her riding straight at difficult obstacles.'

'Excellent. I take the point you're trying to make. But I certainly hope that odious little twerp with the placard isn't going to get away with it!'

'Oh, he'll be charged with something, but quite with what, we're not yet sure.'

'Personally, I'd call it murder!'

'Yes, sir.' Markby paused tactfully. 'In a court of law, however . . .'

'Yes, yes,' Colonel Stanley interrupted testily. 'I understand. The law's an ass. Dickens wrote that. He was right.' He shifted awkwardly on his sofa and his face contorted in pain. 'Her cousin Frances telephoned me last night. She's abroad but is getting the first available flight back. Naturally the news came as a terrible shock to her. She heard it from that dry old stick, Simpson. She's shocked and she's unhappy, Alan, about the post-mortem report. She swears Harriet never took those fool pills and she wants to know if anyone has found any in the cottage. No chance of a mistake, I suppose?'

'By the pathologist? No, none. It's not that uncommon. People get careless about mixing drink and pills. Especially at Christmas.'

'We were discussing it, my wife and I. She must have taken the things that morning before she set out. Seems very odd. What for?'

'I am looking into that, sir.'

The Master glanced at him. 'I've every confidence in you, dear chap. I'm not criticising. I know you won't let it go until you're satisfied.'

Markby put down his tumbler on a small table, laden with copies of *The Field*. 'There's another matter I'd like to discuss, if I may?'

'Go ahead.'

'You heard that someone let the horses out of Tom Fearon's stables on Christmas Eve?'

'Yes, I did! Damn fool thing to do!'

'A letter of sorts was also pushed through Tom's letterbox. Very abusive. I was wondering, would you know if any other subscriber to the hunt had received similar hate mail? It's an offence to send such stuff and we'd certainly try and put a stop to it.'

It seemed to him that his host looked even more uncomfortable and it wasn't, thought Markby to himself, because of the sciatica. He knew something about other letters.

'I did receive one myself,' he said at last. 'About a month ago. Threw it into the fire. Lot of half-baked nonsense. I didn't want my wife to come across it, though – you understand. That's why I destroyed it straight off.'

'If you should receive another, could I ask you to pass it to us?' Markby asked.

'Well, I suppose I could. But one gets those things from time to time. One doesn't have to worry about them.'

'Would you know if anyone else got any?'

'Can't say I do.'

'I see. Yours, was it written or typed or what?'

'Neither. Lots of newsprint cut out and stuck on. Rather messily, incidentally.'

'That sounds similar to Tom's. Well, we'll see if any more turn up.'

Stanley sighed. 'I'll be frank with you. I'd rather it were kept quiet if any more do. The hunt can do without a report like that in the local press. It would inspire the cranks and a shoal of other letters.'

'I promise you we'll be discreet.'

'Discretion,' said the Master slowly. 'Not much of that about these days. Things one reads in the press! People seem to have some urge to tell everyone else all the things which in my day we kept quiet about! Dirty linen washing in public isn't in it!

Things change and not for the better, to my mind. But I'm getting on and who cares what I think? Different sort of people turn out on the hunting field these days, too. Some of them hardly seem to know one end of a horse from another. No hunt manners. Not their fault, they just don't know the drill. They barge around upsetting other, nervous horses and young riders. The language too, in front of ladies and children, I mean . . . and some of the behaviour at hunt balls. Not that in my young days there were never some wild moments. But it was a different sort of wildness, if you take my meaning.'

'I think I do. Still, it's a good thing from the hunt's point of view that new blood is coming along, surely? The sheer expense of keeping hounds and so on. The more people contributing, the merrier, I'd have thought.'

'Oh, I don't deny it. And some of the newcomers have money to throw around, so I'm not going to prevent them throwing some of it towards the hunt. That fellow Green's been very generous. Know him?'

'I've met him, only once.'

'Big financial wizard in the City, I understand.'

'So I've heard.' Markby drained his tumbler and stood up. 'I'm obliged to you for giving me your time, especially in the circumstances. Hope the sciatica improves.'

'I'm happy to help if it means the right thing is done by poor Harriet. My wife is very upset about it. Ah, well . . .' The Master turned a shrewd pale blue eye on Markby. 'How's that pretty sister of yours? Family well?'

'All very well, thanks.'

'That husband of hers, still doing the cooking? Saw him on telly the other day, local station, after the news. He had an apron on. Seems a rum sort of go. In my day we left cooking to the women unless, of course, it was a fancy French chef. Can't he do any other job?'

'He likes doing the one he's got. He writes about it, too.'

'I know. My wife's got one of his books. Takes all sorts, I suppose. Give little Laura my love.'

'Tomorrow, Sunday,' Markby said to Pearce on his return, 'I am going to have free. Let no one mention horses to me or they will get very short shrift.'

By Sunday morning the grey skies had cleared away. The wind had dropped and air was fresh and crisp. Markby telephoned

Meredith and asked her if she was interested in a country walk that morning.

'Yes,' she said, adding rashly, 'you can come back here to lunch afterward.'

That was a pretty daft offer, she thought as soon as she had put down the phone. She was a rotten cook. There were pubs all over the place which served perfectly acceptable Sunday lunches. Why couldn't she have let him take her to one of those? She resisted the thought that she liked the idea of him sitting at her kitchen table. Instead she told herself that it was only fair to offer hospitality. He'd taken her to dinner at The Black Dog and through him she'd spent Christmas at Laura's. Besides, she ought to be able to manage a lunch. Hadn't she cooked for herself and Harriet last Monday?

That was only a few short days ago but now seemed light years away. To produce the same lumpy cheese sauce dish would be morbid, to say the least and not exactly a Sunday-lunch menu. Meredith was suddenly swept up in an insane desire to impress, well, produce something decent. A hunt through larder and freezer turned up frozen chicken Kiev. No one could go wrong with frozen ready-prepared Kievs. Just stick them in a hot oven. A packet of savoury rice. Meredith read the instructions. That didn't seem to present any problems. You just put it in the pan with water and let it boil itself dry. 'Until all liquid is absorbed' the packet said. She had tomatoes and half a head of expensive out-of-season lettuce. She could make a side salad. Pudding? Meredith dived back into the freezer and rooted about. A cheesecake lurked at the bottom. It looked good in the picture. That would do.

He turned up shortly after ten in gumboots, corduroys, pullover and the trusty green weatherproof. They climbed the stile into fields beyond the Haynes' cottage and set off.

'Do you know where we're going?'

'More or less. Mind the barbed wire!' Markby warned, pointing at the fencing to either side of the stile.

Meredith, stranded inelegantly with a foot on the wooden step and the other leg half over the topmost bar, said crossly, 'I can see it.'

'Not unless you've got eyes in your – in the back of your head.'

She negotiated the rest of her descent with dignity and without the unpleasant sensation of wire tearing a hole in the seat of her pants.

'You don't mind cattle, do you?'

'I don't like 'em very much.'

'I mean, you're not scared of them? There are some cows in this field.'

Meredith peered into the distance. 'That's all right, they're far enough away. It seems strange to me to see cattle out in a field in mid-winter. In central or Eastern Europe they're all under cover.'

'Winter's been mild.'

They trudged over long, wet grass, Meredith glad she was wearing wellington boots. The hedgerows were dank and dark, here and there still white-rimed with the morning frost. Her breath and his rose into the air in clouds and there was that peaty smell which she had last smelt at the florist's. She wished that it didn't now make her think of graveyards.

'The post-mortem report is in on Harriet,' Markby said without warning and without looking at her. 'I'm not meaning to talk shop but I thought you might be interested.'

'I am!' He didn't answer at once so she prompted impatiently, 'Well?'

'Her manner was due to a mixture of drink and tranquilliser pills. She'd had a cocktail of them at some point that morning.'

'What!' Meredith stopped short and stared at him in disbelief. 'I don't believe it!'

'Why not? Think we haven't got competent doctors at police disposal?'

'Yes, I know – I mean, I'm shocked. It's not what I would have expected.'

'One would have thought she'd have more sense certainly. The Master and next of kin have expressed similar surprise so you're not alone.'

'I'm surprised she took such pills at all. Harriet? She seemed so – cheerful and positive, although I suppose . . .' Meredith cast her mind back over her last conversation with Harriet, 'One can't know what's in a person's mind.' Another thought occurred to her. 'I wonder how Tom Fearon will take this?'

'Tom?' Markby glanced at her.

'I – had a word with him the other day. He was adamant she wasn't ill or drunk and keen to defend her reputation as having a cast-iron head where whisky was concerned.'

'Tom knew her as well as most, I dare say,' he returned ambiguously.

'Do you know if a date is set for Harriet's funeral? Will it be local?'

'I don't know.' Markby swished at a trailing bramble with a piece of stick. 'I would like to know more about those tranquillisers. What if she had had a threatening letter which worried her enough to make her turn to pills?'

'She didn't strike me as worried.' Meredith paused. 'If you could find out who the man was, the one who was there on Christmas Day evening . . . he might have a few answers.'

'Not that easy, unless he comes forward. And why should he? You will keep an eye out, won't you, Meredith? I mean on the cottage. I want to know when Miss Needham-Burrell arrives.'

'Oh yes, cousin Fran. I want to see her too. She can tell me if the funeral is local or private. I would like to attend.'

'Why do you call her "cousin Fran"?' he asked curiously.

'What?' Meredith gave a guilty start. 'Oh, Harriet mentioned her. She called her Fran.' She felt impelled to add, 'I don't think she's that old.'

'Oh well, hope for the best. I mean – some of these old ladies can be sticky about protocol. I'd like to snoop in Harriet's personal papers – to see if she received any hate mail, like Tom.' He turned a speculative gaze on Meredith. 'If you should see Miss Needham-Burrell . . .'

'Yes?'

'You could nip across and introduce yourself – chat her up a bit and try and mention the possibility of anonymous letters. It might come better from you – not official. And of course, if you could actually get into that cottage – '

She looked at him coolly, unsure if she wanted to be used in this way. 'Isn't this all very irregular?'

'I've got so little to go on.' He struck out again with the stick, knocking back a bunch of frost-blackened nettles. 'It's just that I have a particular dislike of anonymous letters. They really are nasty things. They upset people terribly. A lot of victims who've received them have told me what an eerie feeling it is. As though someone out there is watching and waiting. They really felt threatened. The one Tom received was a pretty foul-worded composition. I shouldn't like to think many of them were floating around. And it's surprising how reluctant people are to go to the police. They feel guilty – quite wrongly. As if the police, or anyone else, will think there must be something wrong with them for them to have got such letters in the first place.'

'No smoke without fire,' she said thoughtfully.

'That's it. We don't think any such thing, of course. Such letters are the product of twisted minds. The most innocent people can receive them.'

'All right then, I'll watch out for Frances Needham-Burrell. I'll drop hints if I can. It's a bit tricky, though, Alan. I can't go clod-hopping through a bereavement.'

'You'll do it tactfully. You're a consul, aren't you? You've had delicate situations to deal with.'

'Such confidence. I'll do my best. Those beasts are coming this way!'

Markby stopped and stared across the field. The cows were approaching in a long, strung-out line, plodding purposefully along beneath clouds of steam rising from their muddy flanks. 'They probably think we've come to call them in for milking.'

'I don't fancy them up close, if you don't mind. Can we walk a bit faster. The gate is over there.'

They quickened their pace. The following cows obligingly quickened theirs. 'You know what,' Markby said mildly. 'They think we want them to hurry so they're pacing themselves to keep up with us. Slow down and they will.'

'Nice theory.'

'I've got an even better one – told me by a cowman years ago – when charged by a bull, stand your ground and when it gets close enough, grab it by the nose. Cattle have very sensitive muzzles. Grab it by its nostrils and you can lead even the most awkward blighter around, meek as anything.'

'If you think I'm standing waiting for a charging animal the size of a tank to reach me . . . how on earth do you grab its nose before it tramples you into the turf? That cowman was having you on. The brute has got to be right up to you before you can reach its nose.'

They had reached the further side of the field during this animated discussion and Meredith hopped nimbly over the gate with twice the speed and dexterity with which she had negotiated the stile. Markby joined her on the further side and they both stopped to watch as their bovine companions lumbered up and stood in a row staring at them expectantly, tossing muddy heads.

'You see? They're waiting for us to open the gate.'

'Let 'em wait.'

'Marning!' piped a voice.

They both jumped round. A small grubby child in a woolly

pullover dotted with holes, faded jeans and gumboots had emerged from nowhere.

'Good morning to you,' said Markby. 'What are you out looking for?'

'I come to let them cows out – take 'em back fer milking.' The infant threw back the rope securing the gate and wrenched it open competently. 'Come on, you daft buggers!' he encouraged the cows which had begun to plod forward.

Meredith and Markby stood by the hedge as the parade ambled past, the child at the rear, a minute figure compared to his charges, whistling, shouting insults and slapping the laggards on their muddy behinds.

'I feel embarrassed,' said Meredith as the group disappeared down the lane. 'If it gives you any satisfaction to know that.'

'You see? You should have believed me. I'm delighted you're embarrassed. You deserve to be.'

'Do you or do you not, want my help in dealing with Miss Needham-Burrell?'

'Point taken. Pub's open – a quarter of a mile down this lane. I'll buy you a pint.'

Meredith followed him down the lane. Whatever happened to champagne in your slipper or even cocktails for two? Gumboots, muck, I'll buy you a pint . . . that was clearly her level. She squelched along in the muddy ruts left by the cattle, avoiding other more unpleasant tokens of their passage. He had it right, anyway. It was about her mark. She was no Harriet – Meredith wouldn't have minded betting a few men bought her champagne. Poor Harriet, laid out in a drawer in the morgue or being worked on even now by the undertaker to repair the more obvious signs of post-mortem investigation before friends and relatives viewed the body. Meredith speculated whether or not her dinner guest would go to her funeral. What was he thinking now, she wondered?

It was half past one before they got back to Rose Cottage and there was no denying a brisk long country walk built up the appetite. The pub at which they had finally arrived and had their pints had been serving up bar meals. The smell of the plates of food as they were borne past had been tantalising and caused pangs of hunger to strike Meredith's stomach as though she hadn't eaten anything for a week.

'Sure you wouldn't rather we ate here?' Alan Markby asked her. 'Or have you left something cooking?'

'No – but it won't take long to prepare. If you don't mind waiting till we get back.'

'No, fine by me.'

So, thought Meredith grimly when she had arrived back in the kitchen of Rose Cottage, do we rush on madly to our doom.

The first discovery she had made on return was that she had forgotten to take the cheesecake out of the freezer. She put it on the kitchen table now but suspected it would still be lumps of ice when they came to eat it. According to the packet, the chicken Kievs only took about twenty minutes in a hot oven. She turned it up as hot as it would go and put them in on a tray.

They looked rather nice. She tipped the rice into a pan and put it on the top on a low number and retreated to the living room where Alan was sprawled on the sofa reading the copy of a Sunday newspaper they had collected from a garage shop next to the pub.

'Won't be long!' she said brightly. 'Would you like to open the wine?'

'Sure, where is it?' The paper rustled.

'Don't move.' Fat chance. 'I'll bring it in here.'

She gave him the wine and corkscrew and returned to the kitchen to make the salad. A pungent smell of garlic filled the air. Kievs were doing all right. She went back to the living room to share a pre-prandial glass of wine with her guest.

'Cheers,' he said. 'This is a nice little cottage. I really hadn't taken much notice of it before, in detail, I mean.'

'It's a super cottage. I can understand why the Russells didn't want to sell when they went to Dubai.'

'They were lucky to have you to let it to. I've heard some pretty grim tales from people who've let property complete with furnishings to strangers. Holes knocked in the walls, furniture ruined. Place has been a wreck when they've got it back.'

'Mrs Brissett will make sure I don't do anything like that. I'm very fortunate. I have all mod cons and Mrs B. All I have to do is relax. Well, till Monday after New Year and then I start my daily London trek.'

'Bamford railway station at seven in the morning is no place for weaklings, let me warn you.'

'Thanks for the encouragement.'

'I don't,' Markby said tentatively, 'like to interfere with the chef's methods, but ought there to be that burning smell?'

Meredith raced out into the kitchen. It was filled with smoke.

She flung open the window, grabbed a tea-towel and hooked the red-hot rice pan off the burner. The Kievs were shrivelled up like lumps of coke, burst open, and all the garlic, herby butter filling had run out on the tray and burned. The savoury rice was bone dry, half cooked and stuck to the pan. The only thing all right was the salad.

Meredith howled in despair and rage. 'Oh no!' she moaned, staring at the burnt offerings before her. 'Oh, what the hell am I going to do?'

Hands gripped her shoulders and moved her gently to one side. 'Hullo?' said Alan's amused voice in her ear. 'Or as policemen are supposed to say, Hullo, hullo, hullo . . .'

'Shut up!' she said fiercely. 'I can't cook. I cannot cook. Other people can, most people can, I can't. Harriet was a cordon bleu cook.'

'No reason why you should be because she was.'

Her shoulders sagged and her voice deflated. She supposed he was right. It didn't make her feel any better. 'Sorry, that was your lunch. We should have eaten at the pub. My fault. I can make you a sandwich.'

'Come on,' he turned her neatly and propelled her back into the living room. 'I suggest you have another glass of wine and sit there and I'll sort it out. Not for nothing have I a brother-in-law who cooks professionally. The main thing I've learned from him was how to deal with disaster. Professionals have disasters, too. Just wait. No! No arguments.'

Meredith closed her mouth and accepted the new glass of wine. She watched him go back to the kitchen and when he had shut the living room door firmly, she sank down on the rug in front of the gas fire with her back propped against the armchair and sipped gloomily at the wine.

He came back after a while with a tray bearing two plates. 'That's yours, that's mine.' He handed her a plate, a napkin, a knife and a fork. Then he settled down on the rug opposite her with his.

Meredith poked mistrustfully at the colourful heap on her plate with the fork. 'What did you do?'

'I stripped off the breadcrumb coats from the chicken things and threw that away. I chopped up the chicken itself and I put it and what I could rescue of the rice and a bit more rice which was in the cupboard into a frying pan with a stock cube and some water and I sort of poached it all together.'

He paused as she tasted it gingerly.

'And I took your tomatoes out of the salad and put them in as well.'

She swallowed appreciatively. 'It's not bad. Different.'

'You see?' He waved a fork at her. 'All was not lost.'

'It was for me. I'm hopeless in the kitchen. Never was any good.'

He studied her thoughtfully. 'Look here, you hold down a difficult and sensitive job. You deal with difficult foreign authorities, desperate stranded tourists, all manner of accident and disaster, reams of paper work, issue passports, invade foreign gaols with help and succour for Brits behind bars, all in a day's work. Why on earth should you be able to cook as well?'

'Most women can. Harriet could.'

'She didn't do a great deal else, did she? Except ride round on a horse and pen a few articles when the mood took her. I think,' he went on quietly, 'you are upset about her. You liked her, didn't you? Got along well with her? Seeing her die like that, it's hit you badly. Delayed shock.'

'I did like her. We didn't have time to get to know one another well. But we did get along all right. I think we would have been friends. Funny – ' Meredith paused. 'She knew a lot of people, probably had quite a few lovers, but I think she was short on real friends. People you can relax with, talk to about anything or nothing, even argue with and it doesn't matter. Friends, you know.' She paused. 'Like you and me.'

'Oh, yes . . .' he said in a flat voice, turning his attention to his plate, 'like you and me. As you say, friends.'

Six

Meredith awoke to the sounds of a Golden Oldie from the clock-radio assuring her with tuneful if gloomy repetition that it was Monday. She sat up. A few minutes before seven-thirty. Nearly time for the news bulletin. Then she would get up, not because she had to but because lying in bed once she had awoken in the morning always seemed wrong, making her feel uneasy. Surely she had some reason to leap out of bed and dash around getting ready? And if she hadn't, why not? What had she forgotten?

She could never get used to not having to go into the office, that was the trouble. A glance at the clock on a weekday morning, if it discovered the hour to be past seven, always inspired panic, believing she was late. In a way, she would not be sorry for New Year to be over and for a return to some regular routine, even the extra-early rising necessary to get herself up to London. Everyone likes a holiday but she missed her work, her pattern. That's what comes, she thought, of living on your own. Alan would be getting up – had probably got up by now. He might be having his breakfast, or shaving, or showering, or checking the house plants before leaving . . . He was another who lived on his own and made out pretty well doing so. As she did.

But she wasn't alone. From below came a rattle of crockery, then a creak on the stair and a knock at the bedroom door. But before she had time to get alarmed, a familiar voice sounded muffled through the door panels.

'Miss Mitchell? You awake? I brought you a cup of tea.'

'Come in, Mrs Brissett!' Meredith called out startled. She pushed herself upright on the pillows and when the cleaner, her solid form wrapped in a flowered overall, pushed open the door bearing a tray, added, 'This is a surprise! It's not your day – '

And then she remembered that Monday was – or had been – Harriet's day – and silently cursed her clumsiness.

'I hope you don't mind me coming in, Miss Mitchell,' said Mrs Brissett, setting down the tray. 'The fact of the matter is, I went

107

to Miss Needham's on a Monday for years. And it got to be a habit. Only I can't go there any more – well not until Miss Needham's cousin comes and tells me what she wants doing. Mr Simpson he rung me – that's Miss Needham's solicitor, in Bamford. Very nice old gentleman he is, the old school, you know? He handled our Dawn's divorce for her – Miss Needham saw to all that. She was very good to our family, Miss Needham.'

Mrs Brissett rubbed a reddened work-worn hand over her face. 'Mr Simpson said Miss Needham's cousin would be in touch with me. What would you like for your breakfast?'

'Oh, but I can get – ' Meredith broke off. The poor woman obviously wanted something to do. Her distress at Harriet's sudden death had in no way diminished and as for Meredith herself, the regular pattern of her life was important to Mrs Brissett. 'Why, how kind – just a boiled egg. I like them boiled hard, really hard. Like golfballs.'

'Right-o, Miss, I'll see to it. Don't you let that tea get cold now.'

Mrs Brisset plodded out and down the stairs. Oh dear, thought Meredith. Poor Mrs Brissett. What a rotten business it all was. She sipped at the tea thoughtfully.

Downstairs in the kitchen, Mrs Brissett had laid out a breakfast place at the kitchen table and the kettle was hissing cheerfully. Toast, neatly cut into triangles, was already wedged in the toast rack, butter had appeared in a glass dish and the egg was knocking noisily against the side of its pan.

'You did say hard,' said Mrs Brissett, removing it carefully, spooning it into the eggcup and finally crowning it with a knitted hat very like the ones she wore but in miniature. 'Like concrete, this one.'

'I really do like them like that. Thank you.'

'I did just go across,' said Mrs Brissett, running water into the egg pan. 'To Miss Needham's – and call in to tidy round, before her cousin come.'

Meredith looked up quickly, eggspoon in hand. 'Tidy up?' Her heart sank. 'You, um, didn't throw anything away – wastepaper, that sort of thing?'

'No, Mr Simpson said to leave everything. But I just put a duster round to make it decent. Mind you, I was there on Thursday, the day that poor Miss Needham – I tidied then. It was all just as she'd left it to go hunting that very day. I washed up, cleaned the kitchen, made the bed, that sort of thing.'

'Was there a lot of washing-up?' Meredith asked, she hoped artlessly.

'Usual!' said Mrs Brissett abruptly.

Meredith took the rebuke meekly and ate her egg. Mrs Brissett clattered about the kitchen with a determined energy. It was obvious there was something more on her mind. Eventually Meredith ventured to ask, 'Is there something worrying you, Mrs Brissett?'

Mrs Brissett swung round. 'Yes, there is! And it's no good, I've got to talk to someone about it. I talked to Fred, my 'usband, of course, but he just says, fuss about nothing. But it's not, I know it. And I knew Miss Needham!'

'Why don't you sit down?' Meredith invited. 'And have a cup of tea. There's plenty in the pot.'

The cleaner collected a cup and joined her at the table. Leaning her brawny elbows on the cloth, she leaned forward and said confidingly, 'It's on account of what Mr Simpson asked me.'

'The solicitor? Was it – would he mind your telling me?'

'Shouldn't think so. It will be public knowledge anyroad, as soon as the inquest is held. Wicked!' snorted Mrs Brissett suddenly.

'The inquest?'

'No – what's being said. Mr Simpson, he asked me – did Miss Needham take them tranquillisers often? Of course, I said, no – never! She never took no medicines. She had a friend once as died, something to do with the wrong medicine or too much – I don't rightly recall. Anyroad, she never had so much as an aspirin in the house and I told Mr Simpson so. So he says the post mortem – nasty thing, cutting up poor Miss Needham – he says, the doctor what done it, he found she had tranquillisers in her blood and there was drink, too. Now, Miss Needham, she did like a drink. It's no secret so I'm not telling tales. But take them pills, never! I said, that's wrong – he's got it wrong that doctor. And Mr Simpson said, "I assure you, Mrs Brissett, the doctor is quite firm on that point". But I say, doctors can be wrong, can't they?' Mrs Brissett stared defiantly at Meredith across the toast rack.

'Well, it's possible – but I shouldn't think that the doctor who conducted the post mortem is wrong on that point. You are quite sure, Mrs Brissett?'

'Course I am!' insisted the cleaner. 'I cleaned for Miss Needham for three years and she never took no pills of any kind in all that time. What she used to do, was have a glass of brandy. Cure anything, she reckoned. Mind you, she was a lady! She held her drink like a lady and all – you'd never know she'd had a few.'

'I see . . .' Meredith said slowly. 'I didn't know Miss Needham well, but what you say certainly seems to make sense to me. Do you mind if I mention this to Chief Inspector Markby? He's by way of a friend of mine – and I think he knew Harriet, too.'

'Oh, Mr Markby,' said Mrs Brissett. 'He's a gentleman. They used to live round these parts, Markbys, years ago. Landowners they was. But it's all gone now. Down where them old folks' bungalows are – that used to be land belonged to Markbys and a big house. It got knocked down after the war an' the bungalows built there. 'Course the time I'm talking about, when the Markby family lived there, was well before the last war. Sixty year ago or so, when my mother was a girl. Yes, you can tell Mr Markby, o' course.'

'Were you born in Westerfield, Mrs Brissett?'

'Oh, yes, dear. And Fred.'

'And Miss Needham – when did she come here?'

'Let's see, she come about four, maybe five, year ago,' said Mrs Brissett. 'First of all she had Cissie Lumsden clean for her until the arthritis stopped her working and then I took the job on. Miss Needham, she come from the North somewhere. She was ever such a nice lady.' Mrs Brissett sniffed noisily. 'To think of her being done to death like that.'

'I don't know that "done to death" is quite the expression to use – ' began Meredith, but was summarily interrupted.

'Well, I do! He killed her, that wicked young man! Waving them posters in front of her horse! Anyone knows you don't do that in front of horses! Bound to make them jump about.'

'Miss Needham was a very good rider, though. In normal circumstances – '

'I know when dirty work's been done,' said Mrs Brissett crushingly. 'And dirty work's what's did for Miss Needham. Truth will out.'

Meredith rang Markby when Mrs Brissett had left and relayed the gist of the cleaner's conversation. 'I thought you'd like to know.'

'Yes, thank you.' He paused. 'I don't quite know where it

110

leaves us, but I'd better have a word with Mrs Brissett. She may have to give evidence at the inquest. What I'd like to do is get hold of the bottle or packet which had the tranquillisers in it. Any sign of Miss Needham-Burrell yet?'

'Not yet. I keep peering out of the window. I must look a regular nosy-parker.'

'Keep peering. Ring me when you've contacted her. I want a word with her myself. Tell her not to throw anything away!'

Meredith put down the telephone and rubbed a hand over her hair. As she did, the sound of a vehicle drawing up opposite fell on her ear. She dashed towards the window and stared out eagerly. Across the road, outside the gate of Ivy Cottage, a Range Rover was now parked. She was just in time to see a young woman jump down into the road, a young woman so uncannily like Harriet in build and manner that it gave Meredith quite an unpleasant shock. She watched the newcomer walk up the path to the front door of Ivy Cottage, pause, fiddle and then open the door. She had the keys. Fran Needham-Burrell without a doubt.

Meredith sat down and wondered how long she should decently wait before going across the road and making herself known. Too long and Miss Needham-Burrell might have started throwing away what might prove vital evidence. Evidence of what? Meredith stirred uneasily. Truth will out, said Mrs Brissett. Truth about what? Suppose all their poking and prying merely finished with an embarrassing and sleazy revelation of who Harriet's man friend had been, and Harriet's personal and very private life in particular? He could be married. Coming and going so furtively it seemed very likely that he was. Meredith pulled on her anorak and walked diffidently across the road to knock at Ivy Cottage's door.

'Yes?' She was like and yet unlike Harriet, viewed close to hand. She was about the same height and build and had the same assured, free and easy manner and there was a certain facial similarity too. But her long curling hair was corn-blonde and she had startlingly beautiful eyes, sea-green and fringed with dark blonde lashes. Meredith managed not to gawp, but only just.

'I'm sorry if I'm disturbing you.' She found herself stammering. 'I live across the road. I thought you must be Harriet's cousin – I came over to say how sorry I am and to offer any help, if I can help.'

'Thanks,' Fran stood back, holding the door open. 'Come on

in. I'm Harry's executor – you may know that. I've got the unenviable task of clearing out her stuff.'

Meredith followed her into Harriet's drawing room, trying not to recall her last visit and to imagine Harriet standing by the drinks cabinet pouring out the sherry. 'I ought to tell you that Chief Inspector Markby of the Bamford station – he's a sort of friend of mine and he knew Harriet and he and I were both there when – when it happened – he asked me to pass the message to you that he'd like to have a word sometime.'

'Oh? What does he want?' The sea-green eyes were momentarily cool and eyed Meredith appraisingly.

'Well, amongst other things I think he'd like to have the packet or bottle which held the tranquillisers . . .' Meredith broke off in embarrassment and hoped her obvious familiarity with the result of the post mortem, ahead of the inquest, would not strike Fran as impertinent. 'He asked, requested, that you don't throw anything away. He meant papers and so on.'

Fran was frowning. She put up a hand and pushed back a heavy switch of blonde hair. 'You know, it's really odd. I would have sworn Harry would never have taken that kind of pill – any kind of pill, for that matter. It's just not in character for her.'

'That's what Mrs Brissett – the cleaner – says. She cleaned for Harriet and she cleans for me.'

Fran eyed Meredith again and seemed to make up her mind. 'Come into the kitchen. I'm going to make a cup of tea. And then I'm going to collect all Harriet's clothes and take them to Oxfam. You can give me a hand with that, if you like. He won't object to that, will he, your police pal?'

'No, I don't think he meant keep all her clothes. Certainly I'll help.'

Meredith followed Fran into the kitchen and once again had to make a determined effort to blot out the image of Harriet making coffee here as she watched Fran make the tea. Harriet's living presence in Ivy Cottage was so recent and still so real that the tragic event of Boxing Day seemed impossible.

'It seems all wrong, doesn't it?' Fran remarked in echo of Meredith's thoughts. 'As if we were poking and prying in Harry's things and making free with her kitchen.'

'Yes, it does.'

'I don't think I'd turn a hair if she walked in the door there.' A nod of the blonde head. 'It seems all wrong for Harry to be dead at all. I still can't accept she's really and truly gone for good. I keep feeling that there must have been a mistake. I couldn't believe it when Theo Simpson rang through. I was at Klosters. I came back to the hotel and they said there was a call from England for me. I made poor Theo repeat everything. He was distraught. But it was the last bit of news I'd have expected. Harry was – was aggressively healthy, if you know what I mean. That's why I can't accept that she took those pills. She led an outdoor life. Always down at the stables – although there might have been an added attraction down there, I suppose,' Fran added drily.

'Oh, yes . . .' Meredith murmured uneasily.

'Don't look so shocked. I'm not spilling any secrets. Harry was always quite open about him – you have met Lover-Boy down at the stables, haven't you?'

'I've met him – but only very briefly.'

'Keep it that way, if I were you. I used to warn Harry to watch herself with that one. Not that I blame her. Very sexy, our Thomas. But he's the sort who believes in his women walking ten paces behind and carrying all the baggage, if you know what I mean. That type can cut up very rough if he doesn't get his own way. Wonder how he's taking this.'

'I think Harriet realised that. I got the impression she knew how to keep him in his place,' Meredith said frankly.

'Probably.' Fran fell silent and stood for a moment with two mugs, one in either hand, lost in her own thoughts. Then she gave her hair a shake, put the mugs on the table and said, 'Well, it hardly matters now, does it? Water under the bridge. Take milk?'

'Yes, thanks.' Meredith accepted her mug of tea.

'You say you saw it happen?' Fran settled down at the breakfast bar. 'Tell me. I'd like to have a first-hand account. Perhaps I'll start believing it then.'

Meredith took a deep breath. 'The horse reared up when the placard was brandished under its nose and she came off. It was a terrific shock to see her fall. Everyone was stunned. I must say, she did seem unsteady beforehand, slouching in the saddle and not looking herself at all. But the young man's action was inexcusable.'

'She liked a drink, we all know that,' said Fran bluntly. 'That's what really knocks me out. I mean, if someone said she fell out of the saddle blind drunk, I would have said poor old Harry had lost her control over the hard stuff but I would have accepted it.

But drink and pills? Not in a hundred years!'

'There's something else, too,' Meredith said hesitantly. 'I think Alan – Chief Inspector Markby – wondered if Harriet had received any anonymous hate mail. Some other hunt subscribers have. That's why he hopes you won't throw anything away.'

'Hate mail?' Fran stared at her across the steaming mug of tea. 'If she did, she would have chucked it out straight away. I doubt it would have worried her unless it was from an outraged wife accusing Harry of dire adultery with an erring hubbie. Anything to do with the hunt she could have coped with all right.'

'Well, it's for the police – I mean, I'm just passing on the message.'

'Sure.' Fran put down her mug. 'Let's go and take a look in the bathroom. As I told you, I'm curious about it, too.'

They went upstairs. In the tiny bathroom Fran pulled open the door of the medicine cabinet to reveal a predictable range of shampoo, skin cleansers, eye-brow tweezers, mixed make-up items and toothpaste. Also a packet of disposable plastic razors for men. Thoughtful of Harriet, that, opined Meredith silently. The only medical items, however, were a pack of sticky plasters and a bottle of TCP.

'In the bedroom?' suggested Meredith.

They hunted through bedside cabinet and drawers which revealed, embarrassingly to Meredith though not apparently to Fran, several packets of condoms together with a couple of paperback novels, handcream and a tube of ointment intended to relieve soreness and sprains.

'She was a great rider to hounds,' said Fran, waving the ointment tube. 'Got plenty of bruises. That's about it for medicine, though. We won't find any tranquillisers, you know. Nor will your copper friend. Harry didn't take them. Don't care what the sawbones says.'

'So how – ?' Meredith frowned.

'Don't know. Shall we ever find out, that's the thing? Do you want to help me with Harry's clothes? Say if you don't. It's a bit grim. She left me this cottage, by the way, and all the contents. I don't know what I'll do with it. I don't see myself weekending in Pook's Common. There's what you might call a shortage of entertainment on hand. Unless you fancy a roll in the hay down the road.' Fran was opening the nearer of two wardrobes as she spoke.

'I had to do all this when my parents had both died,' Meredith said to her, remembering. 'I know how it feels. It seems such an impertinence. I felt so guilty about throwing anything out, even rubbish. I felt if they had kept it they wanted it – I had no right . . . Then someone said to me, "a life isn't about things". After that, I saw it in perspective more. It didn't seem to be such a betrayal of trust.'

'Harry wasn't bothered about things, either!' came in a muffled voice from inside the wardrobe door. 'She cared about all animals and some people. I admit she made this cottage decent and she was a jolly good cook and marvellous hostess. But she wasn't one for shopping. Although,' Fran backed out of the wardrobe, hair mussed and breathless. 'For someone who didn't give a toss about material possessions, she had enough dresses! Someone must have been taking her out on decent dates. I mean, she wouldn't have needed to dress up like this – ' Fran pulled out a flamboyant brocade evening skirt – 'just to go and shovel manure with Tom Fearon!'

And Harriet was open about her relationship with Tom, too, thought Meredith. Tom didn't come and go surreptitiously, parking his car in dark stretches of lane and never appearing in daylight. So who did?

They spent the next hour taking Harriet's clothes from the wardrobes and downstairs cupboards and sorting them out. As Fran had remarked, there were some beautiful evening gowns amongst them and expensive casual wear which suggested week-ending in more luxurious surrounds than Pook's Common.

'Lucky old Oxfam,' said Meredith, reverently hanging up on a hook behind the door an emerald green shot-taffeta on a hooped skirt and having a very famous label in it. She adjusted the plastic tent in which the gown was shrouded.

'Take it, if you like it,' said Fran carelessly. 'It would fit you.'

'I don't like to.' Meredith hesitated, tempted.

'Go on. Harry wouldn't have minded. She was always giving frocks away. She and I used to swap them regularly. Well, you can't wear the things more than once or twice, can you? Everyone remembers them. So we wore each other's for years. I think I borrowed that one once. It would suit you. It's one less to jam into the back of the Range Rover.'

The thought of this beautiful dress crammed into the back of the Range Rover clinched it. 'Thank you,' said Meredith. After a few moments she said awkwardly, 'I wanted to ask about the funeral. Will it be family only?'

'I've run into a bit of a problem with that.' Fran bundled up expensive silk and lace lingerie and stuffed it all efficiently into a Harrods plastic bag. 'I thought I'd like to have Harry buried in the churchyard at Westerfield. She enjoyed living in the area and that's the nearest I can get. But it seems it was decided ages ago to discontinue burials there and it's been grassed flat. They've advised me to bury her at Oxford. I don't see why I can't bury her where she would have wanted, least I can do! I was fond of Harry, we were very close as kids.'

'What about her original home – before she moved here?'

'No point, no family left up there.' Fran paused. 'Harry would have liked to be buried here and I'm going to raise a ruckus until I get permission. What's the use of a churchyard you can't bury anyone in? I'll get on to the Diocesan office, county council, Lambeth Palace if I have to. You watch me!' She gave a determined nod and Meredith fully believed that the assembled synod of the Church of England would quail before Miss Needham-Burrell in full cry.

Together they lugged plastic sacks of Harriet's clothes down the narrow stair and out into the lane to pack them in the Range Rover. As they returned indoors, Fran said, 'I'll let you know about the funeral – write your phone number down for me.'

'Right – oh, I haven't got a bit of paper.'

'Try the desk.'

Fran ran back upstairs and Meredith, stifling her excitement at the unexpectedly helpful turn of events, opened up Harriet's Victorian roll-top desk.

Harriet had been untidy in paperwork matters but that too might prove to be a blessing. The desk's capacious pigeon-holes were stuffed with all kinds of correspondence. Meredith pulled out a writing pad and opened it. A loose sheet fell out, partly scrawled across. Curiously she spread it out.

'. . . plaster-saint you've got another think coming. You're a dirty two-faced liar and – '

There was no more. Evidently the passage was part of a draft. Harriet had reworded it – either to make it milder or stronger – at least, Meredith supposed this to be Harriet's handwriting. A quick hunt amongst other papers confirmed that it was. But it did not reveal any similar scraps. Meredith sat with it in her hand, thoughtful. This was, by any standard, a turn up for the books. When talking of abusive mail, Alan had meant letters to Harriet – not from Harriet. Meredith glanced guiltily over her shoulder. Handing this over to Fran might not be a good idea. Alan would certainly like to see it, even if he later excluded it from any investigation. But Fran might not like her cousin's private letters of this nature to be bandied about. Fran's footsteps sounded on the wooden stairs. A decision had to be made quickly.

Meredith folded the scrap of paper and pushed it into her anorak pocket. Hastily she scrawled the phone number of Rose Cottage on the next blank sheet and handed it to Fran as she came in.

'Enough for one day, I think,' Fran said with a sigh. 'I've got to go into Bamford and call on old Simpson, anyway.'

'Where are you staying?'

'Not here – I've taken a room in Bamford at The Crossed Keys.' Fran put Meredith's phone number away in her shoulder-bag. 'I'll call you when I'm coming out here again.'

'So what do you think?' asked Meredith impatiently.

'I think if Theo Simpson finds out we – you – abstracted this piece of paper from Harriet's desk, we're in trouble. But we'll cross that bridge when we get to it. Whom was this intended for, do you think? You're a woman. Whom would you write to like this?'

'I don't know! I don't think I'd've ever written to anyone like that. I can't imagine – unless, someone who had let me down?'

'A man? Cheating on her? Promised her something – marriage? Chickened out?'

'Do men promise girls marriage nowadays? I mean, like they did once.'

'Well, since breach of promise ceased to be an offence in law, sobbing young things reckoning they've been let down and their prospects are ruined are not a category we get to deal with nearly so much. Where's Miss Needham-Burrell staying?'

'At The Crossed Keys in Bamford.'

'I'll call in on her when I get back.'

'You mean, sir,' said Pearce, 'that Miss Needham didn't receive abusive letters, she wrote 'em?'

'She wrote at least one and take another look at this letter Fearon got. It's pretty strong. But it's also pretty vague about what he's actually supposed to have done. He's a swine, he's a decadent parasite, he'll get his come-uppance one of these days . . . four-letter words galore . . . but what's he done? It doesn't actually say anything about the hunt by name. Fearon assumed it was about the hunt. We took his word for it.' Markby picked up Fearon's letter. 'Of course, I realise it's composed of stuck-on clippings of newsprint and this piece Miss Mitchell found is handwritten – but one reason Harriet rejected this hand-written piece might have been a sudden decision to do it anonymously and use chopped-up newspapers. Fearon has a reputation as a lady's man. We know Harriet had a passionate male visitor on Christmas Day evening. Fearon told me he was late meeting with a lady friend because of chasing horses round all Christmas Day morning. Perhaps Tom was two-timing her and she found out?'

'I would have thought,' Pearce said slowly, 'that if she'd found out he was deceiving her she would have gone down to his stable yard and pushed him in the horse trough. More her style from all I've heard. She wasn't one to write anonymously, I'd have said.'

'Actually, so would I. But you never can tell. But we're forgetting the letter the Master got. I wish he'd kept it. Harriet wouldn't have written to him like that. Scrub the theory about her writing the letters. It wasn't her. Tom's was probably from a hunt crank and this letter is a one-off and about something else.' Markby scowled at the scrap of paper Meredith had given him. 'Incidentally, did you have any joy with other hunt subscribers? Anyone get any letters?'

'Not to admit it, sir. One or two acted a bit furtive. But all swore blind they hadn't received any.'

'Damn. Well, one thing at a time. I'd very much like to know who Harriet's dinner guest was – and whether he was there the next morning. He might hold the clue about the tranquillisers which are so much disputed by everyone who knew the deceased well. Miss Mitchell heard a car leave. But what if he came back later or turned up for breakfast?'

Markby put both letters into the folder on his desk. 'In the meantime, I'm popping over to The Crossed Keys to see if Miss Needham's cousin is there.'

It took only five minutes to walk from the station to The Crossed Keys. He asked for Miss Needham-Burrell at the desk.

'Room twenty,' said a receptionist with heavily mascara-ed eyes. 'Would you like me to ring up?' She laid scarlet-tipped talons on the phone by her and cast him a speculative look.

'If you would. Say, Chief Inspector Markby – she'll know who I am.'

The girl spoke into the internal phone. Putting it down, she said, 'She says, go up. We haven't got a lift but you can go up those stairs there – they'll bring you out at the right end of the corridor. Second floor.' A flash of scarlet nails to indicate direction.

Markby made his way up two flights of what had once been service stairs. The Crossed Keys was an old building. Its floors sloped disconcertingly and it was a rabbit warren of little rooms with low door lintels. It catered mainly for travelling businessmen of one kind and another and people who broke journeys here on impulse. As a result it had that uncared-for look, although it was clean enough. But with its guests, one- or two-nighters, there was no call for luxury or anything but the basic necessity of a bed and a bath.

Number twenty had a pot of African violets outside it on a rickety wooden table. Markby paused to gaze covetously at the violets, a colour he didn't have, and to wonder if anyone would mind if he abstracted a leaf to try and strike some cuttings. Oh well, Miss Needham-Burrell first. He had to do this strictly by the book. Lots of polite enquiry and expressions of sympathy and coax out the permission to go through Harriet's papers. Perhaps he should offer her tea downstairs in the lounge?

He lifted his hand and knocked. A quick, light footstep and the door opened to reveal to his startled eye a stunning blonde in a towelling wrap and mule slippers.

'Hullo,' she said, sea-green eyes widening. 'Don't tell me you're Mr Plod?'

'I'm – Chief Inspector Markby . . .' he heard his voice say, curiously strangled.

'Policemen are getting handsomer! You're Meredith's friend, right? And your name is Alan.'

'Yes, it is,' he confirmed sheepishly and made an effort to cast off his confusion and stop looking at this luscious beauty like a mesmerised rabbit at a stoat.

'Great. I'm Fran, to you. Why don't you come in, Alan? And we can – talk. I've got a bottle of whisky.'

He followed her into the room and took the armchair offered. She was pouring out drinks efficiently from a collection of bottles and glasses on a tray. 'Water in mine, if you don't mind!' he said hastily.

'Say when . . . okay?' She handed him a tumbler. 'What do you want to ask me?' She sat down and crossed her legs. The towelling robe slipped a little, not much but enough. 'I was just going to run a bath,' she explained, the corners of her full lips turning up slightly.

Markby's mind briefly cast up a forbidden image and then went totally blank. He rummaged in its depths for the reason which had brought him. Letters, pills, he wanted to ask about both. Wonderful slim tanned leg. Keep your mind on your work. What did he want to ask her? To tell the truth, just at this minute, nothing to do with police work.

'You know the results of the post mortem, of course,' he said doggedly, staring straight into her slightly amused sea-green eyes.

He saw the amusement fade. Her expression stiffened and she sipped at her whisky. 'Yes. Meredith said you were asking about tranquillisers. We – Meredith and I – searched the cottage but we didn't find any or any empty packets and, frankly, I'm not surprised. Harriet didn't take that kind of drug, any kind of drug. She didn't believe in them. She believed in this – ' Fran raised her glass. 'I'm not doubting the results of the post mortem. But like you, I'm very curious to know how and why.'

'I wonder if the dustbin's been emptied?' he murmured, more to himself than her.

She answered anyway. 'No – it's the holiday period. Everything is tied up in a plastic bag. You can rummage through that if you like.'

'I'll get my sergeant on to it. There is also the question of some letters.'

'Oh, yes, hate mail. I haven't had time to go through her papers. I'll keep an eye open.'

He swilled the remains of his whisky and water round his glass and said carefully, 'I know this appears to be a straightforward unfortunate accident following a piece of very foolish behaviour by a young demonstrator. I'm not suggesting it's anything else. I have no reason to do so. But there are a couple of loose ends and if I seem to be asking impertinent questions about your cousin, it's because I don't like untidiness – not because I'm prying.'

'Ask away.' She shifted slightly in the chair and retrieved the fold of towelling robe which had earlier slipped, drawing it back over a shapely knee. The result was twice as erotic than if she had left it as it was. 'I don't, incidentally, promise to answer. But I'll listen.'

He gave her a wry grin. 'That's fair.'

She met his eye. 'Oh, I'm always fair.'

'Yes – well, we have reason to believe – ' he saw a slight smile touch her full mouth. 'What's wrong?'

'Sorry – it's the police jargon. Do go on. What have you reason to believe, Alan?'

'That Harriet had a male visitor on Christmas Day in the evening. He would seem to have left that night. I'm wondering if you would know who he was. He might be able to shed some light on the mystery of the tranquillisers.'

She rotated her topmost foot, flexing the bare toes which protruded through the mule slipper. 'No, I don't know. I'm not being obstructive. I don't, really. She had a lot of friends.'

'I see. Well, if you should find out – I'd be grateful . . . and I'll send my sergeant over to check out the waste and Miss Needham's desk, if that's all right with you.'

'Certainly.'

'I hope you're managing to arrange everything,' he said, remembering the sad duty which was hers. 'Mr Simpson being helpful?'

'Dear old Theo?' She gave a throaty chuckle. Then she pulled a face. 'Actually I'm having trouble about the funeral. I want to bury Harriet at Westerfield in the little churchyard but that's not allowed, I'm told. It all seems damn stupid and petty to me. It's been secularised or whatever. Flattened out and turfed over like a park. No more burials.'

'Oh? Oh, yes, so it has.' He reflected. 'The Markby tombs haven't been flattened. That's my family's private corner of the churchyard. It's railed off. I mean, no one has been buried there for years but the graves are still there, headstones, monuments, all the usual . . . There might be a space there and I don't see why anyone should object, especially if the family – i.e. myself – agrees. Try that tack.'

'Thanks!' The sea-green eyes glowed with genuine warmth. She followed him to the door and stood in the open frame, one hand on the doorjamb. 'I'll try it, as you say, how can they object? And as I told you, I'm fair. If someone does me a good turn, I like to return it.' The smile touched her mouth again. 'I owe you one.'

'Not at all!' he said hastily and fled.

Seven

The next day, Tuesday, was New Year's Eve. And a thoroughly miserable New Year's Eve it promised to be, thought Meredith, notwithstanding Alan's invitation to join him for a drink. A blight lay over it. The New Year would bring the inquest on Harriet and the funeral and the beginning of a regular slog up to London every weekday for herself. The weather was grey, dreary and lowering to the spirits. However, as it was Tuesday and thus Mrs Brissett's day for cleaning at Rose Cottage, she duly appeared, in bobble hat and zipped boots.

'It's really very good of you to come in over the holiday period,' Meredith said gratefully. She was glad to see the cleaner, less for any work Mrs Brissett might do, than because she was glad of the company.

She was realising what a very lonely spot indeed Pook's Common was. The Haynes had not reappeared. The people who owned the garage and the wishing-well cottage did not appear to be about either. Perhaps they had also gone away for New Year. With Harriet lying dead, Meredith realised almost with horror that she was the sole present inhabitant of Pook's Common. Unless one counted Tom Fearon down at the stables.

'It's no trouble,' said Mrs Brissett firmly. 'No point in leaving it and then I've got twice as much to do when I do come. That's what I said to poor Miss Needham. Don't you trouble to come on Boxing Day, she says. Never you fear, I said, I'll be there. And I was – and saw her for the last time, just before she left . . .' Mrs Brissett sniffed and dumped a large shopping bag down on a kitchen chair with unnecessary violence.

'I do try and keep the place tidy, Mrs Brissett,' Meredith said humbly.

'Yes, dear. I know you do. But tidying up and cleaning properly aren't the same thing. Not by a long chalk, they aren't.' Mrs Brissett hung up her coat, took off her boots and produced a pair of pink slippers trimmed with nylon fur from her bag.

123

Wheezing with the effort and being bent double, she pulled them on. 'Our Dawn give me these for Christmas,' she sat up and held out one solid foot in a crepe stocking and pink slipper for inspection. 'Nice colour aren't they? I like pink.' She lowered the foot. 'Our Dawn was that upset to hear about poor Miss Needham. There now. Well, work won't wait. This won't knit the baby a new bonnet, as my old mum used to say.' She stood up. She hadn't taken off her bobble hat which seemed a permanent fixture but next tied on her apron. 'Finished your breakfast, have you?'

'Yes, I was just going to clear away.' And clear myself away, thought Meredith, which is what she means! Out from under her feet!

'You leave it to me, Miss Mitchell.'

'Mrs Brissett,' Meredith said cautiously. 'About Miss Needham. When you said you'd be here this morning, I did mention it to Chief Inspector Markby. Because he'd quite like to have a word with you. He's coming over later. Would you mind?'

'I don't gossip!' said Mrs Brissett fiercely. 'And not about poor Miss Needham, dead and gone as she is!'

'It's not gossip, Mrs Brissett. Chief Inspector Markby is trying to find out just how Miss Needham died. You'd want to help, wouldn't you?'

'I don't mind talking to Mr Markby,' said Mrs Brissett graciously. 'Because he's a gentleman. Not all the police is. But he is. I wouldn't necessarily talk to some of them others. When our Dawn had her trouble and that fellow she was married to broke the house up – that was before he run out on her altogether – Fred went to the police and told them. "Domestic incident!" they said and just sat on their hands and did nothing. I lost confidence then, as it were, in the police. But Mr Markby is different and he can ask away. But I know how Miss Needham died. It was that wicked boy frightened her horse!'

'There's the question of the drugs, the tranquillisers, Mrs Brissett.'

'She never took none! She never took them pills!' Mrs Brissett burst out. 'I tole you so before. I tole everyone. And I'll tell Mr Markby, if that's what he wants!'

Markby drove up shortly before eleven. Meredith met him in the hall and said quietly, 'I'm just about to make coffee and Mrs Brissett is all primed to talk to you. But you won't upset her, will you? She was so fond of Harriet. She won't want – ' Meredith paused. 'She won't want to tell you anything that she would consider cast a bad light on Harriet. And she's got her own notions of what sort of thing that might be.'

'Won't want to talk about men, you mean?'

'Probably not.'

Markby found Mrs Brissett sitting regally in the middle of the kitchen, bobble hat set firmly aloft like a crown and her hands folded in her lap. She had taken off her apron but not the pink slippers.

'I'm very obliged to you, Mrs Brissett,' Markby said, seating himself at the table.

'We're more than pleased to help,' said Mrs Brissett, adding in explanation of the royal plural, 'Fred and me. Fred used to do odd jobs for Miss Needham, mend things, put up shelves, bit of decorating. Fred always thought very highly of Miss Needham. He'll confirm anything I say. All our family was fond of Miss Needham. She was very good to our Dawn when she had her bit of trouble.' Mrs Brissett paused for breath. 'What is it you want to know? If it's about them pills, it's like I told Miss Mitchell. Poor Miss Needham never took 'em.'

'I'm afraid she did,' Markby said gently. 'But we agree that it seems out of character and we would like to know where they came from and how she came to take them. You see, she must have taken them that morning. I understand you went to the cottage to clean after breakfast?'

'Yes, I did.' The bobble on the top of the hat vibrated frantically. It's going to fall off, thought Markby, diverted. He clung to his purpose. 'When you cleaned up, do you recall seeing or throwing away a medicine bottle or packet, or a paper bag with a chemist's name on it?'

'No. Nothing like that and I'd have noticed because there never was anything like that around the cottage! She'd said not to come, being Boxing Day,' went on Mrs Brissett. 'But I said I would, just for an hour, straighten things up, wash up breakfast dishes, that sort of thing.'

'Ah yes, breakfast dishes . . .' Markby murmured.

Mrs Brissett cast him a wary look and redoubled her regal manner.

'Many dishes?'

'A few.'

'For how many people?' Mrs Brissett's mouth set tightly. 'Mrs Brissett,' said Markby. 'I'm not prying into Miss Needham's private life because I'm just curious. Someone took those pills to the cottage and if they were in, say, a box, took the box with any unused pills away with him or her. Someone gave them to Miss Needham. What I want to know is, how? Had she asked for some and took some deliberately – or what?'

Mrs Brissett's workworn hands clasped and unclasped nervously. 'I'll tell you, sir. It's been worrying me. I've got that I can't sleep because of it. Fred will tell you. You ask him. Fred, I said to him, she never had none of those pills of her own. I know. I'd have seen them. I never saw not one. Someone must've given them to her, I said. And Mr Markby – ' Mrs Brissett leaned forward earnestly. ''Ooever it was done it, done it on the sly, because she wouldn't have taken 'em knowing what they was, not Miss Needham!'

Bingo! exulted Markby silently. 'Mrs Brissett, will you tell me now about the breakfast dishes?'

'It was for two,' said Mrs Brissett. 'I'll tell you fair and honest, I don't know who he was. But it wasn't the first time I'd washed up for two or made the bed – ' Mrs Brissett put a hand to her mouth and coughed discreetly. 'When it had been used, if you take my meaning.'

'Quite.'

'She had a number of gentlemen friends, Miss Needham. She was very popular.'

I bet she was! thought Markby's *alter ego* rather ungallantly.

'But that morning, although there were two of everything, cups, dishes and that, the bed . . . I don't think he'd slept there. But of course, I couldn't be sure. There weren't,' said Mrs Brissett in practical tones, 'no hairs in the washbasin from shaving and there was only one pile of pillows on the bed.'

'So he'd called in for breakfast, you fancy, and left?'

'That's it,' said Mrs Brissett. 'No harm in that.' She paused. 'Or perhaps there was, you might be thinking?'

'We don't know. Did Miss Needham have a habit of say, tossing off a glass of something to keep out the cold before she left to go hunting?'

'Yes,' said Mrs Brissett simply. 'Afore she left to go anywhere. She was a real lady and could hold her drink. Never fell over nor anything.'

Markby stared desperately out of the window. When he could speak he said, 'Well, thank you, Mrs Brissett. You've been very helpful. I'd be grateful if you didn't repeat the substance of this conversation – except to Mr Brissett, naturally.'

'We can hold our own counsel, sir!' said Mrs Brissett, regal again. 'Me and Fred.'

'Quite so. Oh – just out of interest, what had Miss Needham and her visitor had for their breakfast, bacon and eggs?'

'No – she was a lovely cook, Miss Needham. She'd taken one of them cording blue courses and made all kinds of fancy things. They'd had that fish thing. Kedgeree, it's called.'

'Kedgeree,' said Markby, thumbing through the cookbook Meredith had found in the kitchen. 'Let's see. Oh, hurrah, hurrah. Boiled rice, cooked dried haddock, chopped boiled eggs, salt, pepper and cayenne, all mixed up together in a lovely muddle and served up piping hot! I'll check with Paul, but if someone slipped half a dozen tiny tranquillisers into that lot when her back was turned, she'd never have noticed. Eaten them down with the rest!'

'And you think that's what happened?' Meredith asked soberly.

He closed the book and grimaced. 'I don't know. I've no evidence. But he could have done. One thing we have learned incidentally, Mrs Brissett's statement confirms what Jack Pringle, who was Harriet's doctor, has been telling us. Harriet was next to impossible to treat for anything because she wouldn't take any medicaments. He didn't prescribe any tranquillisers for her and he's prepared to say that forcefully at the inquest. What we have to find out is, who was the phantom breakfast visitor?'

'If we find him,' Meredith pointed out. 'He could say she asked for the pills and took them voluntarily with a glass of water.'

'So he might. But where is he? Why hasn't he come forward?'

'Scandal. Perhaps he's married.'

'You are absolutely sure that whoever was there the previous evening – the man you saw kissing her silhouetted on the blind – you are sure he left?'

'I heard a car leave. He might have come back later when I was asleep. There was no car there in the morning, but I was late getting up. Again, he might have left early and I missed him. That's possible.'

'Or he might have been on foot . . .' Markby murmured.

Meredith wriggled uncomfortably. 'Tom Fearon?'

'Why Tom?' he looked up sharply.

'He's just down the road. They had a bit of a quarrel on the

Monday at the stables, I only heard a bit of it.' She recounted the scrap of conversation she had overheard. 'She did say he could come and see her when he'd calmed down.'

'Well, I'll talk to him. But she'd have seen him anyway when she went to collect the horse for the Boxing Day meet.' He frowned. 'No one hacks to a meet nowadays. They all have horse-boxes and take the animals there on wheels. What did Harriet mean to do?'

'Tom's got a horse-box, a small one, two-horse affair.'

'Mmn . . .' Markby put away the cookbook. 'I'll tackle Tom today or tomorrow.'

'I'm not saying it was Tom!' Meredith said hastily. 'Only that they knew each other well and they did have a mild spat.'

'Which wouldn't lead him to put pills in her kedgeree. That doesn't fit Tom's style. Tom charges at everything like the proverbial bull at a gate. What we have here is a premeditated act. Someone took the pills with him, waited his chance. But why? And what did he hope to achieve?'

'He knew she was going hunting and hoped she'd take a fall.'

'Yes – he'd know that she'd drink a stirrup cup or two and the mix of pills and drink would start to make her unsteady.'

'But she was unsteady before the stirrup cup came round,' Meredith pointed out. 'We both saw her. So did Dr Pringle. He told her not to drink any more. He thought she'd been over-celebrating.'

'Don't forget we know from Mrs Brissett that Harriet had a glass or two before she set out from Pook's Common! That would explain why she became whoozy so soon. I wonder,' Markby frowned. 'I wonder if he realised that? If he realised she'd start drinking before she got to the Market Square? Let's say, for the sake of argument, that some man – or it might equally have been a woman – unknown called on her by arrangement to have breakfast, slipped pills in her food and then went on his way. He might have reckoned she'd drink a stirrup cup or two, become unsteady after a while and fall, very likely at the first fence she came to.' Markby stopped. 'At the first fence she came to,' he repeated. 'Damn it, I said that to Pearce! But she didn't – she fell in the Market Square. I wonder if he'd anticipated that, the breakfast-guest. I wonder if that didn't mess up his plans a little. She fell off too soon – thanks in part to Simon Pardy and his crazy antics.'

'Why did he do it?' Meredith demanded. 'If he did, this hypothetical man. Why try to harm her at all?'

'Ah, now we're in really deep water. How did Harriet strike you, Meredith? Likely to make enemies?'

'She was nice. I liked her. She was welcoming to me. She was kind to the Brissetts. She was forthright, though. She didn't like the idea anyone might get the better of her. I would have thought that if she did take a dislike to you, she'd be a formidable enemy. She'd be like a terrier – she wouldn't let go.'

She thought of Frances Needham-Burrell and her threat to take her demand for permission to bury her cousin at Westerfield to Lambeth Palace if need be. Family trait. They got what they wanted and they did things the way they thought they should be done and everyone else could go hang. Though she had taken a liking to Harriet, Meredith had to admit that was very much the impression Harriet and Fran both gave.

'The first person we have to find,' Markby said, stretching out his legs. 'Is the man who was at Ivy Cottage on Christmas Day evening. You heard a car but you didn't see it. You don't know for a fact he left. He may well have done so. Mrs Brissett was nicely discreet about the bed but thought it hadn't been slept in by two. One lot of pillows, she said.'

'Harriet might have moved the pillows.'

'I fancy Mrs Brissett really meant that there were no stains on the sheets, but didn't want to mention it.'

'Oh,' said Meredith, reddening, 'Oh, yes, I see.'

'Sorry!' Markby exclaimed, aghast and turning crimson in his turn. 'I forgot I wasn't just rambling on aloud, trying out my thoughts on Pearce.'

'Don't apologise!' Meredith said crossly. 'I'm not that naive!'

'Okay. Well, Mrs B. thinks he didn't sleep there. But perhaps he did. Who and where is he?'

'You know,' Meredith said softly, 'Funny thing about Harriet. When she spoke to the horse, Blazer, it was as if she spoke to a friend. A real human friend, who just happened to have four legs. She appeared jolly and outgoing. But I wonder if secretly she only really trusted animals? Was only really at ease with them? She was a sad person in a way. I'd like to think justice was done by her. And I'm a bit inclined to feel as she would have done, if she'd thought someone she knew had been done to death ahead of her time. She'd have kept after whoever was responsible and I'm going to keep after this, Alan.'

'Police job, leave to the professionals.'

'Yes, but if you can't come up with the answer it will get filed away and forgotten. Like Mrs Brissett's Dawn and the domestic incident. You involved me in the first place and if you can't, then I am going to get to the bottom of it all!' She stared at him defiantly.

She has, he thought despondently, wonderful hazel eyes. I don't suppose we'll ever get any further on than we are. Doomed to stay on our respective side of whatever fence divides us. Aloud he asked, 'I don't know what Mrs Brissett's Dawn has to do with it. But you are still free to come and have a drink tonight, aren't you? See in the New Year? I shall be working until late. I could meet you in Bamford at say, half-eight. We might find a pub which would give us a bar-meal, but they lock the doors on New Year's Eve at most pubs after nine-ish, to keep out trouble-makers. If you're not inside by then, you've had it.'

'I'll meet you at half past eight at the pub, if you tell me which one.'

'Bunch of Grapes,' said Markby off the top of his head. 'It's not far from the station.'

It was only as he was driving back to Bamford that he remembered that The Bunch of Grapes was where Simon Pardy claimed to have been drinking on Christmas Eve.

Bamford on New Year's Eve was busy. All the pubs were packed and one or two were admitting revellers by pre-purchased ticket only. All of this ought to have been a balm to a policeman's soul but Markby was alarmed to find, when he reached The Bunch of Grapes, that its wooden door was firmly shut and a notice pinned on it announced that no new drinkers would be admitted. From the other side of the door came the sound of chatter, laughter and good cheer. He supposed Meredith was in there. And he was out here. He supposed that was par for the course as far as they were concerned. He raised a fist and hammered on the door.

After a while it opened a few inches on a chain and the landlord's face appeared, peering suspiciously into the night. 'We're closed to newcomers. You'll have to go somewhere else.'

'Do you remember me?' asked Markby, manoeuvring himself into the light falling from a street lamp and fumbling in his pocket for his identity card.

'Oh – Mr Markby, isn't it? Didn't recognise you, sir. I didn't send for the police. We haven't any trouble. Not so far, anyway.

That's why I put the notice on the door.'

'I'm not here officially. I have, actually, just come for a drink and I'd arranged to meet a friend inside. She might be there.'

There was a rattle of a chain and the door opened. 'Be quick!' ordered the landlord. 'Or someone else will want to slip in behind you!'

Markby squeezed through and found himself in the packed public bar. If Meredith was here, he couldn't see her. He peered over heads and round bodies. It was unbelievably hot and airless and a minor miracle anyone had enough room to lift a glass to his lips.

'Your friend wouldn't be a lady?' the landlord asked. 'Tallish, brown hair?'

'That's the one? She hasn't been and gone?' Alarm returned.

'No, she's in the snug at the back. She said she was waiting for someone.'

Reaching the snug was a battle but he got there. Meredith was wedged in a corner at a table occupied by a group of other people. A glass of cider stood in front of her and a half-eaten packet of crisps. When she saw him she looked relieved and picked up her folded anorak from the settle seat beside her.

'I saved you a place.'

'Sorry I'm a bit late. I'll go and get myself a drink – what about you? Are you hungry?'

'They're not doing food except sandwiches. I don't mind. I've had these crisps.'

'Hang on,' he muttered. He fought his way to the bar and back carrying a pint, another cider and a packet of ham sand-wiches wrapped in cellophane, all balanced on a tin tray. 'A bit primitive but better than nothing. I don't know why I suggested this pub. But they will all be the same.'

'Are you busy at the station?'

'I've got my immediate tray cleared up but the station as a whole is busy. New Year's Eve always is. It's early yet but give us time and we'll get the drunks, the fights and the car crashes. Generally someone else deals with them.'

'Oh dear!'

'That's life. You didn't have any problems driving in to-night?'

'No. I'm parked just down a little way outside a shoeshop. The shop windows are lit and it throws light on my car so I thought it was a good place and no one would try and break into it and drive off.'

'Sound thinking. Well, here's to a Happy and Prosperous New Year!' He raised his glass.

'Same to you. Cheers.' She sipped her cider and put it down again. 'I have to admit I don't feel much like celebrating. I know I should. But to be honest, New Year always is a depressing time to me. And this time, in the circumstances, more than usual. Sorry, I'm being a real wet blanket.'

'You can't do anything about it, what happened.' Markby tore open the sandwich packet. 'Want one of these?'

'Just one. Have they got mustard in them?'

He peeled back the uppermost piece of bread on the top sandwich. 'No, some sort of pickle.'

'Okay, just the one.'

'Excuse me munching away but I didn't have any lunch.'

'Oh, well, you can have all the sandwiches, then!'

'No . . .' he waved away her hand, offering a sandwich, and spoke indistinctly. 'It's all right.'

Famous last words. From the public bar came a sudden roar of sound and a crash of glass. Everyone in the snug looked up alarmed and interested in equal part. The crowd between the two areas surged back and forth. A girl screamed and there was a heavy thud of a body falling to earth. The landlord's purple sweating face appeared – 'Mr Markby!' – and vanished.

'Sorry – I'm needed! They're starting early!' Markby swallowed half-masticated bread in a lump, jumped up and deserted Meredith. He barged his way through the crowd to the public bar.

There a confused sight met his eye. The drinkers had pressed back against the walls to form a circle. With a mixture of dismay and glee they were watching, trying to keep out of the way of, and here and there encouraging, a turbulent mêlée taking place on the floor. Bodies swore, panted, twisted, turned, kicked and punched. The landlord grabbed at clothing and tugged ineffectually before it was wrenched from his grasp. It was difficult to see exactly what was happening. Was he, Markby wondered, going to have to call for assistance?

He now saw that there were two men on the floor fighting. Two girls in black leather, metal rings and spiked hair appeared to be attacking both men. Colin Deanes with his spectacles awry was trying to grab one of the participants and a third youth lunged in and out of the scrum, shouting, 'Stop it, you stupid sod! Simon!'

At first – until he recognised Deanes – he thought it was just the usual New Year punch-up and prepared to join the landlord in his attempts to pull the participants apart. Then he caught a glimpse of the face of one of the brawlers.

'Tom!' Markby roared, leaping into the fray in his turn. 'What the hell are you doing?'

'Let go of me!' yelled Tom Fearon, 'I'll kill him!'

'He attacked that boy!' howled Deanes.

'Get out of my way!' shrieked Simon Pardy, rising up from the floor and swinging a fist wildly at Tom. Because Markby had grabbed Tom, the stable-owner was unable to protect himself. Simon's fist connected, striking Tom beneath the left eye.

'Let me get at him! Let go of me, Alan, you idiot!' Tom tore himself loose and flung himself on Simon, gripping him by the throat. The whole motley tangle of bodies subsided to the floor again in a struggling heap. One of the black-clad girls grabbed a tin tray and struck Tom over the head with it. It bounced off with a resounding echo, like the opening of a J. Arthur Rank film. Deanes paused fractionally to secure his spectacles and hurled himself into the middle of the mass, trying to extricate Simon but arguably doing more harm than good.

'Cut it out, Tom!' Markby managed to grab Fearon's arms again, break his grip on Simon and haul him out of the fray. 'Deanes! Get hold of Pardy!'

Colin flung both arms round Simon who was coughing and choking, imprisoning him and dragged him back. The two black-clad girls stopped dancing up and down. The one who had wielded the tray, her eyes ringed with black circles which Markby at first took for signs of violence but then realised were make-up, said aggressively. 'He done it!' she pointed at Tom, struggling and swearing in Markby's grip. 'He slugged Simon.'

'A witness!' shouted Colin Deanes. 'You heard what the girl said, Markby! This boy wasn't doing anything.'

'He was boasting!' yelled Tom. 'The little snake was boasting about what he'd done to Harriet!'

'I told you to shut up!' said the third youth angrily to Simon. 'Now look what you've done!'

'You!' bawled the landlord, pointing at Simon. 'Out of here!' He turned to Tom, 'And you, Tom Fearon! Much obliged, Mr Markby!' he added politely and dived towards the front door, opening it. Markby holding Tom, Deanes clinging to Simon and Meredith who had emerged from the snug, bringing up the rear, stumbled out of the door and landed together on the pavement outside The Bunch of Grapes. The door slammed behind them.

'Deanes!' panted Markby, struggling to restrain Tom who had burst out in renewed fury and was trying to get at Simon Pardy. 'I'm making you responsible for that lad! Take him back to wherever he lives!'

'It wasn't his fault – ' Deanes began.

'I don't care whose fault it was! Do you want me to run him in? No? Then take him home! Now!'

Deanes departed, dragging a loudly protesting Simon down the street with him.

'All right, Tom!' Markby turned to Fearon, who leaned against the closed door of The Bunch of Grapes, panting. 'I'm driving you home.'

'I've got my own car!'

'So you may have. You can't drive it.'

'I'm not over the limit!' Tom yelled furiously. 'I'm not bloody drunk! That little weasel was actually boasting to his appalling chums about what he'd done! He just stood there in the bar and said she deserved it! He said Harriet deserved it! Are you going to let him get away with it?'

'I don't know nor does it matter right now whether you're over the limit. I'm satisfied your mental state means you can't be put at the wheel of a car! Now, Tom, either I drive you back to the stables and you promise to stay there or I'll make this official and arrest you!'

'Arrest me?' Tom appeared about to have an apopleptic fit. 'Why don't you arrest him? Why haven't you got him behind bars? He killed Harriet! He's got away with it and he knows it! If those two weird-looking girls hadn't joined in and that other fellow with the glasses hadn't come hurtling out of somewhere and got in the way, I'd have settled Pardy's hash, I can tell you!'

'Then thank your lucky stars Deanes was there to stop you. Don't be stupid, Tom! And come along – my car's down here.'

He pushed Tom with some difficulty along the pavement, opened the front passenger door of his car and shoved him in. Then he went round to the other side and took the driver's seat.

Meredith's face appeared at Tom's window as she stooped

down on the pavement outside to peer in. She tapped on the glass. 'Excuse me.'

'Oh, Christ,' said Markby. 'I'd forgotten her. Wind the window down, Tom.' Tom obliged. 'I'm very sorry about this,' Markby shouted across towards Meredith. 'I'll take Tom back to Pook's Common and come back.'

'No point in it! We're locked out of the pub. All hooligans together. If you're going to Pook's Common, I'll follow behind in my car. If you've time later, call by Rose Cottage.'

She vanished. Markby switched on the ignition. 'Tom,' he said in carefully controlled tones, 'you disturbed my Christmas Day by ringing me up about lost horses. You've ruined my New Year's Eve. You do realise this, don't you?'

'You can – ' growled Fearon and broke off, folded his arms and glowered through the windscreen. 'You know what you can do, Alan,' he finished more mildly.

Markby drove slowly back to the stables. Going along the B road from Bamford to Westerfield in the darkness, frost-touched fields glimmering to either side, he could see in his driving mirror the headlights of Meredith's car cleaving the night behind him. Tom, beside him, had fallen silent and introspective in a 'mood' of more than ordinary virulence. There you have it, thought Markby with resignation. Another proposed tête-à-tête which might have led to situations only dreamed of – ruined. There was a jinx on the whole business of his friendship with Meredith. There was a jinx on him.

'I don't know why I joined the police force,' he said aloud.

Tom growled.

They turned off at Fenniwick's garage, plunged into darkness, and down the lane to Pook's Common. He saw Meredith draw up before her cottage. He drove on down the lane until they reached the stables where he turfed out the morose Tom and told him in no uncertain tones that he was to stay there.

Tom's reply was difficult to make out, which was probably just as well.

When Markby got to Rose Cottage, he found that Meredith had established herself in the kitchen before a large brown earthenware pot of tea.

'I'm really very sorry,' he said abjectly.

'Not your fault. Would you like a cup of tea?'

'Yes, please. It's just, I could have called up help and sent both Pardy and Tom to the nick, but they only have a couple of cells at Bamford station and they'll need them tonight – and it wasn't a regular fight, more – ' he paused.

'More in the nature of a domestic incident?'

'That's it,' he said gratefully. 'Glad you understand.'

'Don't mention it. Has Tom calmed down?'

'Not so much calmed down as sulking. But he can't get into any more trouble tonight. His car is in Bamford and I've taken the keys off him for good measure. I'll see his car is taken to the police pound tomorrow and he'll have to come and see me before he can get it back.'

'He might saddle a horse and gallop back to Bamford across the fields by moonlight. I can imagine Tom doing that.'

'Can you imagine him slipping tranquillisers into Harriet's kedgeree?' Markby asked her quietly.

There was a pause. 'No,' Meredith said a little regretfully, 'I could imagine him grabbing a shotgun and firing off a few rounds in temper.'

'Tom occasionally acts as though his brain had cut out, but not that badly. Tom is an impulsive man, not a planner. And he wouldn't do anything which would get him a custodial sentence. The horses, you see. Whatever else, Tom is primarily concerned with the welfare of his horses. Someone has to muck 'em out and take stones out of their hooves with a penknife or whatever it is he does all day long. I've warned him to stay at home for the rest of the night. I think he will.'

'Hope you're right. Impulsive people can act awfully oddly.'

'I get the impression,' Markby said slowly, 'you don't much approve of Tom.'

'Don't know him well enough to judge,' she said aloofly. 'Well, here's to a happy New Year!' She raised her teacup. 'It's after midnight. Fifteen minutes past, in fact. It is New Year.'

Markby looked at his watch. 'So it is. Happy New Year!'

Eight

New Year's day. The morning was clear and fresh, and undisturbed quiet reigned everywhere as Bamford slept in late after its celebrations. Alan Markby wandered out into his backyard – the local house agent described others in the road as 'patios' – and contemplated his limited desmesne. Coffee cup in hand he cast a speculative eye over walls and paving, planning where, come springtime, hanging baskets and tubs of shrubs would take their appointed place. Oh, for a proper garden. Oh, for the time to be able to concentrate on some proper gardening. He had once toyed with the idea of taking on an allotment, envisaging rows of beans, potatoes and lettuce. But it had to remain a pipe dream. When did he have time to potter all day long in the sunshine, hoeing up weeds and carefully planting out seedlings? The most he could hope for at the moment was to be able to take early retirement and find himself some place out in the countryside with a decent bit of ground.

That made him think of Pook's Common. It was a lonely spot. He was not all that keen on Meredith living out there really, despite the attractions of Rose Cottage itself. He had been quite shocked to learn that at the present point in time she was the only resident of the place, except for Tom away down at the stables and too far away to hear any cries for help – although Tom could get there fairly rapidly if summoned by phone. On the other hand, given Tom's reputation as the local rural Don Juan, perhaps the idea of Tom galloping up to Rose Cottage on a foaming steed looking like young Lochinvar was not exactly the sort of protection he, Markby, fancied for her. And thinking of Tom, he had to drive out and see him this morning. Happy New Year, hah!

The telephone's shrill cry broke into his musings. Secretly hoping it would be Meredith, he walked briskly back indoors and grabbed the receiver. 'Alan Markby!'

'Ah, Alan, just the chap. Happy New Year, and all that.'

Colonel Stanley. What on earth was he doing ringing up at – Markby consulted his watch – ten in the morning to wish him seasonal greetings. Was the old boy sloshed?

'Alan . . .' the Master's voice was muffled and conspiratorial. 'I was wondering, perhaps you could stop by for a drink this morning, welcome in the New Year.'

'Very kind of you, sir, but actually I've got to drive out to the stables and have a word with Tom.'

'If you could . . .' the Master was almost inaudible. 'I've got another of those confounded letters here.'

'What!'

'Can't talk on the phone – don't want my wife to find out about it. Oh, hullo there, my dear! I was just asking young Alan if he'd like to pop in for a glass of sherry . . .' The Master's tone sounded as if he had been caught ringing up a call-girl agency, pitched too high, too jovial and ill-controlling an insane cackle of laughter. Guilty as they come. He had probably grown up on a diet of Bulldog Drummond and believed all villains wore slouch hats.

Muffled female voice in the background, sounding eminently practical and down-to-earth.

'Wife says, would you like to come to lunch?' asked the Master in more normal tones.

'That's kind of her but I really have to go and see Tom and I don't know how long I'll be out there. But I'll stop by for the sherry. Can it be earlier rather than later? Because once I get to the stables – '

'Come round any time, any time. What, Charlotte? Well, how should I know? Yes, all right. Wife says not to rush if you're not ready yet. She thinks perhaps you saw in the New Year rather well.'

I saw it in, if she really wants to know, drinking tea in a kitchen, after breaking up a scrap in a pub and providing a taxi service for Tom Fearon. Aloud, he said, 'I'll be there about ten to eleven if that's all right. And please keep the envelope!'

Colonel Stanley lived on the outskirts of town. At one time his house had been in the country but, during the last fifteen years, Bamford had crept out sideways and caught up with it. Markby fought off the enthusiastic greeting of a pair of spaniels and wished Mrs Stanley a prosperous and healthy year to come.

'And all the very best to you, Alan!' she said, gripping a gin and tonic in her left hand and mangling his fingers with her right.

'Excuse me – I've got to chop up some wood. Come along, boys!'

The boys – the spaniels – lolloped off beside her as she wove her way out.

'Will she be all right chopping wood?' asked Markby uneasily. 'Would you like me –?'

'Oh, she can manage. Dab hand with an axe, Charlotte.' The Master looked and sounded relieved to see his spouse depart. 'Sit down – I'll fetch the blasted letter.'

It was much like the one Tom had received in wording and appearance. Scrappy snippets of newsprint, fairly fluent and correctly spelled which in itself was interesting. Whoever he was, he was literate. Pardy was literate.

'I'll take it away if I may.'

'Please do. I don't want it round the place!'

'You say this came this morning?' Markby frowned. It was a public holiday, no postal service, he thought. Am I not a member of the public? Don't I get a holiday? No, he was a policeman and he didn't.

'Ah, now that's interesting and I can more or less tell you exactly when it came!' The Master nodded and now that the letter was to be removed from his house and responsibility he had resumed something more like a normal, practical manner. 'The thing is, Charlotte and I saw in the New Year with some friends and we didn't get home here until getting on for two this morning. We came in by the front door and there was definitely no letter lying about on the mat then. Went to bed but about oh, four in the morning both damn dogs started to bark. I got out of bed and had a look out of the window but couldn't see anything. So I went out on the landing and leaned over the banister. The dogs both sleep down in the front hall, you see. I called down and they both stopped kicking up a fuss, so I decided there was no intruder. They had just heard a noise outside, probably some people going home after a New Year party. Once upon a time this house was as quiet as the grave at night, but now we're practically built round – got those new houses just behind us. We get noise all night long, car doors, engine noises, headlights playing on the windows . . . And of course, if one dog starts up, the others join in. Anyhow, I'd had a late night and I wasn't prepared to traipse downstairs and investigate so I just went back to sleep.

'This morning I came down about half past eight to let the dogs out and make a cup of tea – and there it was, on the mat.

I couldn't have missed it if it had been there earlier. A good thing I came down and not Charlotte. I wouldn't want her to read that. Disgusting stuff.'

Markby privately thought that the Master's wife was probably pretty robust and not that easily shocked, but he nodded sympathetically. 'So it seems likely it was delivered by hand at about four in the morning.'

'Exactly.'

Markby carefully put the letter and its envelope in a larger envelope. 'I'll drop this in at the station and then I must get out to the stables. I've got to bring Tom in to Bamford so he can collect his car.'

'Oh, not been in an accident, has he?'

'No, he just left it in Bamford last night very wisely, not wishing to drink and drive.'

Colonel Stanley saw him to the door. 'Pity you can't stay for lunch. Frances Needham-Burrell is coming over.'

'Is she?' Markby stifled his enthusiasm, 'Oh yes, I've met her.'

'Nice girl. Good looker, too.'

'Yes, I'll just nip round the back and say goodbye to your wife.'

He followed the sound of chopping wood and hailed his hostess. She stopped work, both arms held above her head brandishing an axe. 'Oh, are you off? Pity you can't stay for lunch. Fran Needham-Burrell is coming.'

'Ah, so I've learned. But I must go, really.'

'Shame. Nice girl. Awfully pretty.'

'Yes.'

Escape.

At the station he marked the letter for forensic examination, not that it was likely to produce much information, then he picked up the phone and dialled Colin Deanes.

'Yes . . .' Deanes sounded sleepy. Markby thought he had probably got him out of bed. Good.

'Markby here. Did you manage to take that lad home all right last night?'

'Yes, I did.' Deanes' voice became more alert. There was a pause and Markby imagined him putting on his glasses. Without them Deanes probably felt at a psychological disadvantage. 'That little fracas was not the boy's fault. We have a witness – three witnesses. He was just having a New Year drink with his friends.'

'And shouting his mouth off in an inappropriate fashion, I understand.'

'Now look here, Chief Inspector,' Deanes said reasonably. 'It was New Year's Eve and perhaps the boy had drunk a couple of pints and was talking foolishly. But more than foolishness it wasn't. He wasn't being malicious. Just a little silly. And that other fellow attacked him. Quite viciously.'

'I'd say he was provoked.'

'His attacker is a friend of yours, I understand!' Deanes snapped.

'It's the first day of the year and I'll do you the courtesy of ignoring the implication in that remark.'

'No offence intended!' Deanes said hurriedly. 'But neither of us wants to take this any further, I fancy. The boy won't do it again.'

'I trust not. His behaviour could be construed as likely to provoke a breach of the peace. And leaving aside the legalities – it was extremely tasteless.'

'He was very sorry afterwards.'

I bet! thought Markby grimly. 'Did you actually see him into his house?'

'Yes, I did. I sat him down in his kitchen, made him some coffee and talked to him like a Dutch uncle. As I say, he regretted it. I left him there about, oh, a quarter to two in the morning.'

'Had his friends come home?'

'No, they hadn't. I had rather hoped they would, but Simon said they intended all going on from the pub to a party somewhere.'

'What about him? Wasn't he going to this party?'

'No, I gather he wasn't invited. The boy is rather a sad case, you know. He needs encouragement, a friendly interest taken in him.'

'Quite possibly he does, but in the meantime he's got to restrain his instinct for stirring up trouble!'

'I think you're being unfair, you know.'

'Yes, I know you do. I'll see you around, no doubt. Best wishes for the year and so on.'

'Oh, yes. Happy New Year.'

Markby put down the receiver. What was the betting that as soon as Deanes had left him, Simon got his revenge on the world he saw as against him and provided salve for his humiliation at The Bunch of Grapes, by glueing together another foul letter

141

and going out and pushing it through the Master's door? It would take Pardy about half an hour, perhaps less at that time of the morning, to walk from Jubilee Road to the Master's house. Deanes left him at about two, the letter was delivered at about four. Plenty of time. He would have to have another word with Pardy. But first of all, he had to drive out and see Tom.

He stopped off on his way down to the stables at Rose Cottage. He wondered first of all it would be disturbing her and she, like Deanes, might be sleeping in. But then he saw that the curtains were drawn back and looking down the pathway running down the side of the cottage, he saw something flapping. He got out of his car and made his way round the cottage and into the back garden.

She was pinning up washing on the line. She wore navy-blue cord pants, a red cotton shirt and a navy-blue cardigan. The wind caught at her dark brown glossy hair and tossed it playfully around in a way he would dearly loved to have done but was unlikely ever to be given the opportunity to do.

'Hullo,' he said. 'Aren't you poaching on Mrs Brissett's preserve?'

'I can wash out my own smalls. Anyway, I've got nothing else to do. Hang on a jiff – I've nearly finished. Do you want to go in the kitchen? It's warmer.'

'I'll wander round the garden if it's all the same to you.' He strolled past her and with his hands in his pockets, inspected the back garden of Rose Cottage in a leisurely fashion. Like many cottage gardens it had been intended originally to feed a labourer and his family. It stretched back a remarkable length and, although most of it was now laid to lawn, it was not difficult to imagine where the vegetable beds had been. Soft fruit bushes still grew there, no more than pruned-back stumps at the moment, imprisoned in a chicken-wire cage to protect them from the depredations of blackbirds and thrushes. There was the remains of a strawberry bed but no one had prepared it for the coming season.

Meredith joined him. 'You'd like to get your hands on this garden, wouldn't you?'

'Not half.'

'You're welcome to come out and dig it up while I'm in residence. I don't mind picking my own strawberries and blackcurrants provided someone else has organised them.'

142

'I doubt you'll get many strawberries out of this bed, not good quality ones. You might get the jam sort.'

'What on earth makes you think I know how to make jam?'

'I tried growing strawberry plants in one of those special earthenware pots,' he remarked wistfully. 'But the snails decided it was a highly desirable residence and moved in.'

'Oh, Alan . . .' she said suddenly and fell silent. He looked up, surprised, and she added quickly, 'Are you coming in for a cup of coffee?'

'Much as I'd like to, I really don't have time. I'm on my way to see Tom and I'll have to take him into Bamford to pick up his car. And I've already stopped off and had a glass of sherry with the Master.' He hesitated. 'He's had a letter.'

'One of the obnoxious variety, I suppose. How did he get it? There's no post surely.'

'Pushed through his letterbox in the early hours of the morning. He lives just on the edge of town.'

'So the writer could be living in town or in the country?'

He shrugged. 'I'll call by this evening.'

'Fair enough.'

He drove off as she stood by the front gate, her arms tightly folded against the chill breeze, and watched him. He wished he could sit and drink coffee with her. As it was he faced a probably acrimonious exchange with Tom. He pulled off the lane and parked on the grass verge beneath the notice reading 'Pook's Stables'.

Markby got out, wondering if Tom had heard the engine or the slam of the door. The yard appeared deserted as he opened the gate and let himself in. Underfoot was trampled mud, dotted with puddles, scattered with straw and imprinted with hoofmarks. A galvanised bucket, kicked into a weird metal sculpture by a contrary hoof, lay abandoned by a loose-box door. But the midden steamed in the cold air, indicating Tom had been up and at work, and from within the loose-boxes, the top half of all the doors open, came various stamping noises and snorts.

'Anyone home?' Markby called.

Two intelligent equine heads appeared over loose-box doors, ears pricked enquiringly, to see who the visitor was. From a third interior came the sound of a man swearing softly. The door opened and Tom appeared in the aperture, scowling. He was wearing aged blue jeans and gumboots, with an open-necked check shirt under an ancient sweater with holes in both elbows and a check cap was pulled down over his black curls. His left cheekbone was swollen and reddened.

'Good morning, Tom,' said Markby. 'Got time for a word?'

'Going to arrest me for disturbing the peace last night?'

'Think yourself lucky I didn't. Give me one good reason why you shouldn't be up before the magistrates tomorrow morning with the rest of the local lager louts.'

An angry red flush crept over Fearon's swarthy features. Then he shrugged. 'Fair enough. I asked for that. But it got my goat to hear that weedy little bastard gloating over what he'd done to Harriet.' Tom came out into the yard, closing the lower half of the loose-box door behind him. The horse inside followed him to the doorway and now put its head over the bottom half door.

'Blazer . . .' said Markby, recognising the horse.

Tom turned and put up a hand to stroke the chestnut's white-streaked nose. 'Yes, poor old bugger. He knows something's wrong. They always do. He keeps throwing up his head and listening for – ' Tom turned back to Markby. 'Come up to the house.'

To describe Tom's kitchen as untidy would have been the understatement of all time. A single man himself, Markby appreciated the difficulties, but Tom seemed to have abandoned all attempt to organise his domestic arrangements. Unwashed crocks were piled on the draining board. A rubbish bin over-flowed. There was a broken bridle hanging over the back of a chair and on the table were scattered a roll of twine, a tin of dubbing, feed bills and other correspondence, a tin of odd tacks and nails, a pair of clippers and one odd glove.

Tom went to the fridge and brought out two cans of beer. He cleared a space by carelessly sweeping aside some of the bric-à-brac and put a can before his visitor. Then he took the seat opposite and jerked open the ring pull of his own can. He had kicked off his mud-encrusted gumboots at the door and now, as he leaned back and propped one foot on the other knee, a large hole in the end of his sock came into view.

'Not got anyone to do for you, Tom?' Markby enquired, raising his can of beer in salute. 'Happy New Year.'

'No, I can manage. Prefer my own mess to some old woman fussing round with a vacuum cleaner, putting everything away where I can't find it. Cheers and sod the New Year.'

A moment's silence while they both drank.

'I'm hoping you can help me, Tom. I'm trying to put together a picture of Harriet's last movements, over the Christmas period.' Markby set down his can and wiped his mouth with the back of his hand.

A gleam of humour showed briefly in Fearon's dark eyes as he raised his can to his lips. 'Oh yes? That should prove interesting.'

'*De mortuis nil nisi bonum!*' said Markby. 'I haven't come to dish the dirt.'

'Like hell you haven't!'

'Okay, then. I have. I'm a policeman. I frequently behave in ways of which my mother would not have approved.'

'My old lady,' said Tom reminiscently, 'was generally too plastered to approve or disapprove anything I did.'

'I remember your family. I particularly recall your maternal grandmother. She lived out there on the common in a caravan, wore a man's cap and boots and smoked a pipe. As a kid I was scared stiff to walk over the common in case I met her. She was like the old witch in the gingerbread house. I thought she'd cook and eat me.'

'Oh, the old 'un!' said Tom appreciatively. 'She was a true Romany, born on the road. She'd never have harmed a child. I used to go and hide out with her when things got rough at home. She was a marvellous story-teller. She used to sell spells locally, a shilling a time. When she died, nigh on a hundred of her relatives came from all over the British Isles to attend her funeral. There were so many wreaths and flowers it looked like the Chelsea Flower Show. They gave her a real gipsy send-off and when it was over they went up on the common, piled all her belongings into her caravan and set fire to it, Romany tradition. And do you know what happened? Some busybody saw the smoke, phoned the fire station and Bamford fire service came charging along, bells clanging, and put the whole lot out.' Tom stretched his arms above his head and grinned, his white teeth gleaming in his walnut-hued face. 'Now I, Alan my old china, represent the respectable branch of the family!'

'God help us!'

'So what makes you think,' Tom asked, 'that I know Harriet's shady secrets?'

'Come off it, Tom,' Markby said mildly. 'You and she were "very good friends", as the old Sunday newspapers used to put it, from the day she arrived in Pook's Common.'

'Possibly. I wasn't the only one. She had a number of very good friends.'

'Let's start with Christmas Day,' Markby said. 'Did you see her then?'

'No.'

'You told me when you telephoned about the horses that you were made late for Christmas lunch with a woman.'

'Yes. The woman in question wasn't Harriet, if that's what you mean.'

'You know, don't you, Tom,' Markby said, suddenly hating all of this. 'That in the normal course of events your word would be good enough for me. But this is a police enquiry. I have to ask for the name of the woman.'

'Ask away!' Tom retaliated sourly. There was a pause and he relented. 'If you must know, it was my ex-wife, Julie. You can check with her. I usually spend Christmas at her place, not because I give a toss whether or not I ever see her again, but because of my kids. I want to be with my children at Christmas.'

'I see.' Markby shifted in his chair. 'I understand. How old are they, Tom?'

'Girl's seven and the boy is nearly nine.'

'I'm divorced too,' Markby said to him. 'Rachel and I had no children which is just as well. It made things a lot easier. We could make a clean break.'

Fearon drained the last of his beer and sat silent.

'All right!' Markby began again briskly. 'You didn't call by to see Harriet in the evening?'

'No, and I wasn't there all night either. I'll answer that one before you get to it and save you the trouble.'

'Then let's move on to Boxing Day. The horses – how did you take your horse and how did Harriet take hers to the meet?'

'I drove both horses there in my horse-box.'

'Harriet go along with you?'

'No. She came over to the stables early, about six-thirty in the morning, to help get the horses ready.'

'Did you breakfast together?' Markby asked, feeling deceitful.

'No. She left about seven-thirty, seven forty-five, to go back to her place, bath and get ready and so on. Breakfast too, I suppose. I finished up in the yard, came in here – ' Tom waved a hand at his higgledy-piggledy kitchen, 'fried up a pan of bacon rashers, cleaned myself up, changed, loaded the horses and drove to Bamford. Harriet made her own way there. That's where I met her again.'

'How was she early in the morning here, mucking out? Well? Cheerful?'

'About as cheerful as anyone can be, mucking out nags at six-thirty on a winter morning in the freezing cold and dark, trying to plait manes and tails while the brutes plant their great muddy hooves on your feet and trying to keep upwind of them in case they behave in anti-social fashion.'

'Anti-social?' Markby asked without thinking.

'So would you on a diet of grass.'

'Oh, right.'

'She wasn't ill!' Fearon said abruptly. 'She wasn't the way she was at the meet.'

'Sure of that?'

'Swear it on a stack of Bibles.'

It was at breakfast then, for sure, thought Markby. It was at breakfast someone slipped her the tranquillisers.

'Did she have a drink here with you, early on? Alcohol, I mean.'

'No – we brewed up some tea in here. I dare say she had a snifter before she left home to go to Bamford. And since your prurient mind seems to be running on sex, I might as well add that we were far too busy with the horses for anything in that line. I didn't even pinch her backside. We were both working.'

'You said she had other close friends – ' Markby began.

Fearon interrupted. 'Yes, but I'm not naming anyone for you. Ask someone else. You've had my information. I'm not a stool pigeon.'

He meant it. Tom had served due notice he would now clam up and to question him further would be pretty well useless. But Markby did have one last question, even so.

'Okay, Tom – but just one other thing, on another subject. Have you heard of anyone else getting any letter like the one pushed through your door on Christmas Eve?'

Tom took off his check cap and studied the lining of it. 'I fancy one or two have. Ask around the hunt subscribers.'

'It may interest you to know the Master has. He got another this morning. You haven't had any more?'

'No.' Fearon ran a hand over his curly black mop. 'All I've got is a bruise on the back of my head. Someone brained me last night in that pub.'

'One of the girls hit you with a tin tray.'

'That's what it was . . . peculiar couple of girls, weren't they?

All that black leather and studs in their noses and muck all over their faces.'

'Modern youth, Thomas. You and I are getting old.'

'Speak for yourself. I hit that creep Pardy and then those two females came at me. Gave me a heck of a shock. I thought I was being attacked by the Undead.'

'It doesn't seem to have done you any harm. Come on, I'll take you back with me to Bamford and you can pick up your Merc.'

'All right, wait while I find some shoes.' Tom tipped his check cap to the back of his head and tugged it forward, resettling it. He disappeared into another room and came back with a pair of shoes in his hand. Propping his foot on the chair to tie up his laces, he said, 'There's something you can tell me. Frances – Harriet's cousin – is she still staying at The Crossed Keys?'

'As far as I know, yes. But she's lunching today with the Master.'

'Good – I'll give her a buzz on the phone.'

'Tom . . .' said Markby reproachfully.

He had made a mistake and saw it at once. Tom looked up quickly from his shoe. His swarthy features had harshened and an unfriendly glint entered his dark eyes. For a moment his seventy-five per cent Gorgio blood seemed to have drained away and left only the twenty-five per cent Romany he had inherited from his grandmother.

He said evenly, 'I understand she is Harriet's executor. As such she'll probably be selling Blazer. I'd like to buy him. He's a good horse and I feel I owe it to Harriet to look after him.'

'I apologise, Tom,' Markby said with sincerity. 'My mistake. I spoke out of turn.'

Fearon relaxed, put his foot to the floor and straightened up. 'I think,' he explained more mildly, 'Harriet would have been pleased to know old Blazer could stay on in his familiar stable with people he knows around him.'

'Yes, I'm sure she would, Tom.'

They walked out of the door and Tom turned to lock it behind him. 'Never bothered to lock it at one time,' he observed. 'Not a soul around in Pook's Common. Now even I am getting jittery. You know . . .' They were now crossing the stable yard and Tom indicated surrounding buildings as he spoke. '. . . I wanted Harriet to come in with me, in the business, build the place up – extend it. But she wouldn't take me up on it.'

Markby glanced at him wryly. 'Perhaps it was your lifestyle, Tom, which put her off.'

'Perhaps. But as things turned out, she could have done worse than take me on, couldn't she?'

Markby stopped, his hand on the handle of the car door. 'Meaning just what?' he asked sharply.

'Come on,' Tom said, 'You're not snooping around for nothing. Asking a load of questions about where I was, she was – who was – what was . . . You think someone slipped Harriet those pills, don't you?'

'I don't know, Tom. But we are looking into it.'

'If someone did,' Tom told him, 'I hope, for his sake and yours, you find him before I do.'

'Don't make threats, Tom . . .' Markby warned. 'Not even just in front of me. I have to take note of them.'

Tom grinned unpleasantly. 'When my old granny was buried, it wasn't in Westerfield churchyard, that was just the church service. It was out there on the common. No one knows where the grave is except those who laid her in it. Gorse and brambles grown over now, most likely. Born on the common, died on the common, laid to rest on the common. Plenty of room up there for another one. You'd never find him, Alan.'

Markby drove them both to Bamford, returned Tom his car keys and watched him drive off in his Mercedes with a flourish. The station was busy but none of it was directly his business, so he slipped out quietly before anyone realised he was available and went home.

It was two o'clock. At the Master's they would be finishing lunch. A decent lunch with a decent wine and a bottle of decent port. Markby rummaged in his larder and opened a tin of baked beans and pushed two slices of bread in the toaster. He ate this frugal meal, made a pot of tea and went into his living room and switched on the television. Sport. He was not a TV sports fan. The relentless chatter of the commentators got him down and the boring pontifications of innumerable experts and inarticulate 'stars' unburdening themselves of their opinions to pally interviewers. He changed channels. More sport. Horse racing. He'd had enough of horses for one day, thank you. He switched the set off.

As he did so, his front-door bell rang. He made his cautious way towards it, mug of tea in hand, and opened it.

149

'Hi!' said Fran Needham-Burrell. 'Tracked you to your lair. Are you busy?'

'No,' he replied foolishly.

'Can I come in, then?'

'Yes – yes, of course.' Markby pulled himself together and stood back to let her into the hall. He put down his mug and asked hurriedly, 'Can I take your coat? Sorry to look so surprised. I thought it might have been Laura – my sister.'

She was divesting herself of a cream-coloured wool coat. He took it from her to hang it up and noticed the continental label in it. It weighed a ton. Probably cost a month of his salary. 'In here,' he opened the living-room door. 'I was just having a cup of tea – '

'Not for me, thanks. I'm awash with food and drink. I just had lunch with Bungy and Charlotte.'

Bungy? The Master? Lord.

'So I understand. I called by to wish them Happy New Year this morning.'

'They told me. You turned down an invitation to join us at lunch – was that because I was going to be there?'

'No!' he said too vehemently. 'It was because I'd already arranged to see someone else this morning and I couldn't guarantee to be able to turn up on time at lunch. It was work-connected.'

'I see.' She settled herself on his sofa, crossing her legs and tapping one tan-booted foot. She wore some kind of peasantry skirt which went well with the boots and her corn-blonde hair was twisted into a long rope and secured with an orange silk scarf tied in a bow. 'I thought you might be lunching *à deux* elsewhere.'

'I had beans on toast here in my kitchen, as it happens.'

She gave her throaty chuckle which was singularly effective. 'We had roast pork and apple sauce, lovely crispy roast potatoes and Queen of Puddings which I hadn't had since I was a kid.'

'Have you,' Markby asked her, 'come here to gloat?'

She shook her head. 'I thought we ought to have a word. Bungy's had one of those anonymous letters you were asking me if Harriet received, hasn't he? I mean, he's had another one.'

'Did he tell you that?' Markby asked cautiously.

'No, of course he didn't. Charlotte did. Don't look so surprised. I know she isn't supposed to know but he's hopeless at keeping anything secret. He acts so furtively that she always knows at once something is going on and she's got her own methods of finding out what. She knew about the previous one, too.'

Markby, remembering the Master's cloak-and-dagger manner on the phone, sighed. Most wives were natural detectives. 'Yes, but he doesn't want it discussed openly. He thinks, rightly I'm sure, that if it gets about someone else will get the idea to write a few letters. We'll be snowed under with the things.'

'Is this,' Fran asked coolly, 'connected with Harriet's death?'

There was a silence. 'I don't know,' Markby said at last.

'You do think, then, there is something fishy about the way she died? About the pills.'

'I think there is just a possibility but I have to stress that I have no evidence, certainly nothing I could put before a coroner or my immediate superiors. All I have are verbal statements made by people who knew Harriet, yourself included, which suggest she never took pills of that kind or any kind. Nor can we find the packet or bottle, or trace where she got them from. She wasn't prescribed any by her regular doctor. You can't find any in the cottage and my sergeant went through the household rubbish and there was no discarded wrapping or chemist's bag in that. We even went through her car and didn't find a thing. It's a mystery and I don't like mysteries. As for the letters, they may be totally unconnected. Until I find out something about Harriet's movements and meetings over Christmas, I shan't be any the wiser.'

'You haven't traced the boyfriend, then? The one who was there on Christmas Day?'

'No. We have eliminated one possibility, however.'

'Don't tell me. The handsome gipsy? But whoever slipped her the pills – supposing someone did and I, for one, am more inclined to believe that than that she took them voluntarily – he must have been there on Boxing Day morning to do it.'

'Yes, she had a guest at breakfast. We can't find him, either.'

'Not the same chap?'

'Not necessarily. The Christmas Day visitor drove off late at night. He might have come back, of course.'

'How long,' Fran asked in her direct way, 'will you spend going into all this, before you file it away and forget it?'

'The inquest was put off because of the holiday period. It's scheduled for Friday. As things are, it's going to be pretty routine. Medical evidence. Eye-witness account of the accident. A question mark over the pills but well, there's an open grate in Ivy Cottage. She could have burned the box. As for the incident in the Market Square, given her dodgy medical condition it was only a matter of time before she fell off anyway – and her drinking habits were well known. I'm afraid there's not enough to bring in a verdict of unlawful killing of any kind. Much less – ' he broke off.

Fran finished for him. 'Murder by person or persons unknown? We're talking about murder now, aren't we?'

'It's possible.'

A flash of annoyance showed in her sea-green eyes. 'You people are always so damn cautious! So as I understand it, if you don't come up with something concrete by way of evidence by Friday, that's it. Harry's buried and forgotten.'

'I can't make bricks without straw, Frances.'

'No, I dare say you can't.' She tapped one tan boot sharply on the carpet. 'It is possible to get away with murder, isn't it? It does happen, all the time, doesn't it?'

Markby smiled. 'No one can say, can they? If foul play isn't suspected – '

'Even when it is suspected, as now? And I know of it happening before! Well, that's got nothing to do with this – ' Fran hunched her shoulders. 'I'm not driving. I walked from The Crossed Keys to lunch and from there to here. You can offer me a drink.'

Markby blinked. 'Certainly. My pleasure.'

'Whisky, if you've got it.'

When she had sipped at her drink, she asked with a malicious gleam in her green eyes, 'Where's Meredith?'

'At Rose Cottage, I assume.'

'All alone? Don't you worry about Tom Fearon? I would, in your boots.'

'I don't think she's overly keen on poor Tom. I don't know what he's done to upset her. But I don't, actually, like her being on her own out there. It's very lonely.'

'How do you come to be friends? I mean, she's always been working abroad, as I understand it.'

'We met on a case – when she was last in England.'

'And is she going to carry on living out there in Pook's Common and you here?' Fran waved a hand at their surroundings. 'Nothing more permanent?'

He felt himself flush. 'Things are likely to stay the way they are. We don't have any plans to change them.'

'Fine. I like to know where the boundaries are in any situation. Nothing to stop you taking me to dinner, then?'

'I can't afford you!' he said, returning her some of her own coin. 'On my salary? You must be joking.'

'Oh, come on. If it's that bad, I'll take you out to dinner.'

'I have already got a dinner date for tonight.'

'Meredith, I suppose. Well, we can make it another night. I shall be at The Crossed Keys until the beginning of next week.' She tossed back the remains of her drink and stood up.

As he helped her on with her coat, she said seriously, 'I'm relying on you, you know.'

'I'm doing my best. But at the moment, there isn't even a motive. That's the worst.'

'I'm Harry's principal heiress, apart from some bequests she made to animal charities. I stood to gain but I didn't slip pills to her – and I was skiing in Switzerland at the time.' Green eyes mocked him.

'Something tells me,' Markby said to her, 'that you like living dangerously.'

She burst into a peal of laughter. 'You mean I'm a bit of a bitch. Well, thanks for the drink and the words of wisdom. Happy New Year!' She leaned forwards. A cloud of expensive perfume enveloped him and firm, warm lips planted a kiss on his cheek. 'Don't forget me, now. Cheery-bye.'

He closed the door on her with relief. Life was getting altogether too complicated.

Nine

When Markby had left her to drive down to the stables, Meredith went back into the kitchen and made coffee for herself. She took it into the living room, lit the gas fire and picked up the local paper which she had bought the day before in Bamford, but had not yet got round to reading.

She felt unsettled and it was due to more than the unforeseen events which had taken place since she arrived in Pook's Common. She was sure now, more than she had ever been, that coming back here was a mistake. She had been afraid of this. She should have known on the day she arrived and found the welcome card from Alan on the doormat. Alan was, of course, hoping that one day . . . and it was impossible.

She didn't want to hurt him. She didn't want, truthfully, for their friendship to end. But, deep down, she was frightened by the prospect of its progressing into anything more 'meaningful' as an agony aunt would have described it. She just couldn't cope with a further development. But nothing stood still and her friendship with Alan couldn't stand still for much longer either. She was going to have to do something about it. She was thirty-five years old, she'd always been on her own and looked after herself. It was too late to change and tie herself to someone else. But she knew that was untrue. Of course it could be done. People married or entered into permanent relationships later in life and thrived on them. But it would turn her world upsidedown.

What worried her most was how much longer she could put off the fateful moment when he, quite fairly, would try to pin her down, tell her she had to make up her mind. Some people would say she had already made up her mind – but she hadn't. Nor could she. But in all fairness neither could she keep the poor man dangling at the end of a rope. With so few close friends and family she was loath to break off any relationship which offered friendship and companionship. She was, to be honest, lonely. He was lonely too, but what he wanted was something all too

155

orthodox – a home, a garden, the traditional setting for a pipe-and-slippers life. He might not realise this himself yet, but Meredith could see it all too clearly. She liked him – very much. She respected him. 'But I'm not in love with him!' she said aloud.

Or was all that just a lot of nonsense? Some of the best and most lasting unions were founded on common sense and mutual respect and interests. Love came along later. Some of the most passionate encounters, on the other hand, fizzled out leaving nothing but regrets. And some, like that other one which had dominated her life and thinking for so many years, remained unfulfilled, unfulfillable and in the end, nothing perhaps but a sheer waste of time, emotion and commitment. That one was over and done with, gone and surprisingly seldom thought about now.

That left Alan. She had to get a grip on all of this before it careered out of control. Tonight, he was coming tonight and would probably want to go out and eat somewhere, she'd tell him tonight. She'd make it clear just where she stood. Disabuse him of any lingering hopes. Having made this resolution, far from feeling better, she now felt like a monster. And also as if she was about to do something very rash.

Meredith sighed and opened up the *Bamford Gazette*. Harriet. Right there in a large photograph in the middle of the page under the heading 'Local rider dies in tragic accident'. It went on to describe the events in the Market Square and added a potted history of the Bamford Hunt. The hunt's history had in fact been singularly uneventful. The only previous time it had gained itself headlines in the paper and invoked the word 'tragedy' had been when some hounds ran on to the railway line in 1904.

Meredith checked the date on the paper. The *Bamford Gazette* was a weekly sheet. Normally it appeared on a Wednesday but this year, the two public holidays falling on a Wednesday, the Gazette had appeared early on a Tuesday. The accident had happened the previous Thursday so naturally it was reported in this edition, still quite hot news from the *Gazette*'s point of view.

She turned back to the picture of Harriet and studied it. It appeared to have been blown up and taken from a larger group, photographed at some horsy event, probably a local gymkhana. In it Harriet was wearing a riding hat and jacket. Her hair was tied back at the nape of her neck and cascaded down between her shoulder-blades in a mane. She was laughing and looked as if she held out her hands to receive something – a cup? That bit of the picture had been chopped off. She looked so happy. In her mind's eye, Meredith saw the toppling figure fall from the rearing horse and plunge to the ground. She saw the blood, seeping out from beneath the red hair, the pale, frozen face, the eyes open in blank surprise. Obscene. It was obscene. Death was obscene. There had been so much life in Harriet and it had just been snuffed out in an instant, purposelessly. Meredith, still studying the picture, moved on to scrutinise the figures in the background.

Yes, the *Gazette* had dredged this picture up from their files. A local event and someone must have been presenting some trophy and the other competitors were gathered behind to watch and applaud. All wore riding gear. One – Meredith brought the paper nearly up to her nose to squint at it – was familiar. It was a man, a burly man in a hard hat which cut off the top third of his face and to make things more difficult, the figure of Harriet in the foreground obscured part of the right-hand side of his features. But what remained visible seemed known to her, though Meredith could not, for the life of her, identify him. It wasn't Tom Fearon, at any rate. Tom's swarthy, handsome features would mark him out in any crowd instantly.

Meredith threw the paper aside. If she sat here the whole thing taken together with her other worries would just get her down. What she needed to do was get out in the fresh air. She fetched her anorak and pulled on her boots and let herself out of the cottage. At the gate she paused for an instant – which way? The common – dank and forbidding though it had seemed on the brief visit she'd paid to the edge of it – remained to be explored. The common, then.

To get to the common she had to walk past the stables. Alan Markby's car was still parked outside but the yard looked empty. Meredith hesitated and found herself listening for men's voices, upraised in argument. But all was quiet. They had probably gone to Tom's ramshackle bungalow behind the stable yard. And men being more inclined to give and take in their relationships with one another than women sometimes were, they had probably forgotten the dispute of the previous evening and Tom's behaviour at The Bunch of Grapes – to say nothing of a New Year's Eve ruined for both Markby and Meredith – and were sitting in Tom's living room, sinking cans of beer. Men! Why, last night Alan had nearly driven off and left her standing outside the pub! He'd been completely taken up with getting Tom home safely and she had been relegated to 'also ran'.

They take you for granted, that's what! thought Meredith, irrationally annoyed now though the previous evening she had been quite equable about it. Harriet had been right when saying that it was advisable not to let Tom get the better of you, only she should have said, don't let men get the better of you. You ended up like Geoffrey Haynes and poor Lucy. Keep your independence, Meredith!

Caught up in this mental diatribe she had reached the edge of the common without realising and now stopped abruptly, hands in pockets, to stare out across it.

What a scene of desolation. Perhaps in summer it was prettier and more inviting. Now it looked like a setting for some Victorian melodrama, such was the indefinably sinister air of it. Yet perhaps the sensations it inspired were much older, reaching down into a heritage of folk subconsciousness. Tales of witches' sabbaths and hallowe'en nights and cadavers creaking on gibbets in the moonlight.

'Stop this!' Meredith admonished herself aloud. If she let herself go on thinking this way, she'd turn tail and run home. She walked on purposefully. The wind with no impediment blew strongly across the flat heathland. The grass beneath her feet was brownish-green and the shrubs and trees dotted about leafless and ugly. She found she was following a narrow bridle track – a true bridle track at that for in the soft mud the imprint of horseshoes could clearly be seen. Tom Fearon rode out this way and often, from the number of tracks. Harriet, too, must have ridden here, sometimes with Tom and sometimes alone. But Harriet wouldn't have scared herself with superstitious fancies.

Meredith walked on. Gradually the roofs of Pook's Common's cottages vanished from view. She might have been on the moon, it was so lonely, bare, untouched. Here and there scraps of fur or feathers marked where some night-hunting predator had caught its prey. After a while the ground beneath her feet became soggy and she was glad of the boots she wore. Then she heard water running and came across a narrow brackish stream bisecting the common from east to west. To her right hand a line of dark trees marked the beginning of a plantation of conifers – regimented intruders which did not belong here – and on the muddy banks of the stream itself were several small, sharp, cloven hoofprints. Not pookas. Not fairy horses, but deer. They must lurk over there in the plantation and come out early in the day to forage about on the common, nibbling at the few shrubs and trees and the coarse grasses.

Far enough for one day, thought Meredith. She felt better now. She had conquered her fear of the common and blown her cares away for the time being. She turned.

A man stood behind her. Meredith gave an involuntary shriek. He started forward, hand outstretched and exclaimed, 'I'm so sorry! Please forgive me! I didn't mean to startle you. I was just going to call out to attract your attention – but you turned suddenly – '

It was Colin Deanes, in his fur-trimmed parka, his spectacles reflecting the pale sunlight so that she could not see his eyes, smiling anxiously at her and with head pushed forward as if peering short-sightedly to see if she accepted his reassurances.

'Oh, Mr Deanes . . .' she said. 'I didn't realise anyone was out here.'

He smiled. 'Yes, it's a lonely spot. I see you know who I am – and I know that you are Chief Inspector Markby's friend – but I'm afraid I don't know your name.'

'Meredith Mitchell.' They shook hands formally. 'I'm living over there – ' she pointed. 'At Pook's Common.'

'Oh, indeed? Have you been there long? I must admit I don't know it – except by name.'

'It's very small. Only half a dozen cottages, a garage and a couple of council houses on the main road. Oh, and the stables. I haven't been there very long, no. About two weeks.'

'I live over there – ' he pointed beyond her further out into the common. 'It's a tumbledown old place but I rented it extremely cheaply to write my book.'

'No disturbance out here, I imagine, good place!' she observed.

He chuckled. 'True. But actually my house is not as remote as might seem from this aspect. There's no direct access to it from this direction. But on the other side there's an unmade road which runs for about half a mile to come out and join the tarmac road at The Black Dog pub – where I saw you with Markby.'

'Oh, yes – I see. It seemed to me that we took a very round-about route to get there when Alan drove me there from Pook's Common.'

'Yes, he would need to. There aren't any roads right across the common and to get to the other side you have to go round it. It's a very ancient piece of open land. And remarkable, I'm told, for its fauna and flora.'

'You could have fooled me!' she said ruefully, looking around at the desolation.

Deanes laughed again. 'You should meet Dr Krasny. He's something to do with the university and last summer I bumped into him several times out here. He seemed to be able to name every blade of grass. I gather he came out to gather specimens and information for his work. I used to see him creeping about bent double. At first I couldn't imagine what he was up to. After a while I got to know him quite well and he'd call in at my place for a cup of tea and tell me what he'd managed to see on his expeditions. Usually I don't walk out in this direction – I go the other way and finish up at The Black Dog. In the summer, it does look more attractive out here, quite pleasant on a sunny day.'

'How's the book going?'

'Oh, I finished that quite some time ago and that's all behind me now. Look out for it in the bookshops! I always take the opportunity to plug my works if possible!' He smiled nervously again. 'I'm living here under false pretences to some extent although I've started to put together a few notes which I hope will eventually turn into the next book. I've the lease on the house until spring so I've stayed on. I quite like it down here. And I've become involved with one or two local problems.' He gave her a look in which a kind of defiance was mixed with a nervousness. 'I know,' he said, 'that what I try to do isn't always popular. The public often don't understand and very often, I'm sorry to say, the police don't.'

'Ah . . .' murmured Meredith awkwardly.

'There are causes which are popular and acceptable,' Deanes went on. 'And those which aren't. Often the ones further afield call up more sympathy than the ones near at home for the simple reason the nearer ones can be seen first hand and the imperfections in them are all too visible. You were at The Bunch of Grapes last night, weren't you?'

'Yes, I was. You're referring to the young fellow Pardy, I suppose.'

'Yes – not an attractive youth I'm the first to admit. They never are. They have problems and one of them is that they present themselves to the world as so unlikable. If they have a cause they don't know how to present it. They don't inspire generosity or forgiveness. They handle their own defence badly. They're aggressive when they ought to be conciliatory. They offend needlessly. Pardy's not an exception, he's fairly typical. He takes the attitude that if the world doesn't like him, he can get along with it. But of course, he can't. He is very young – only twenty.'

'I suppose it is young. But he behaved very badly, didn't he – I'm talking about the affair in the Market Square on Boxing Day. I was there – I saw it happen.'

'Did you?' Deanes pushed his spectacles further up his nose in what seemed a habit. 'I didn't. That puts me at a disadvantage – but I have been spending some time with young Simon. He's a sad, muddled, lonely person underneath the brash exterior.'

We're all sad, muddled and lonely, thought Meredith. Some of us cope better than others, that's all. 'He shouldn't have been saying the things he was in the pub last night. It was asking for trouble.'

'He does – he does ask for trouble!' Deanes said eagerly. 'That's just the point! He goes out looking for trouble and he finds it. Then he becomes more introverted and bitter. What we need to do is to get him off that path. He's basically an intelligent young man and at the moment he's throwing his life away.'

Meredith studied him thoughtfully. His face was flushed. His eyes shone behind the lenses and there was an intensity in his face and voice which couldn't be ignored. He cares, she thought. He really cares.

Aloud she said slowly, 'You must have your share of failures. Don't you ever get discouraged?'

Deanes grimaced. 'I'd be lying if I said, no. Of course I do. But the successes more than make up for it. The thing to do is to break the cycle. The very worst thing which could happen to Pardy is that he could serve any kind of custodial sentence. It would put him in the company of people who would encourage the worst in him. He'd be lost for good.'

'Some people might disagree.'

'They don't work with these youngsters!' Deanes said passionately. 'They don't know!' He seemed to become aware of the vehemence in his own voice and looked embarrassed. 'Forgive me for bending your ear with my views. I can't help it, I'm afraid.'

'That's all right. I'm interested to hear them. I'm glad I met you,' Meredith said sincerely.

161

Deanes smiled, more relaxed and looking suddenly quite an attractive man. It's the specs, Meredith thought, together with the sombre expression and all the nervous tics which make him look plain. He really isn't bad-looking and he isn't that old. Younger than I thought at first. Thirty-nine? Forty? Not more.

'I must get back,' she said. 'We'll meet again, no doubt.'

'Yes – I certainly hope so!' He hesitated. 'If you walk out on the common again and get a bit further, call in at my place for a cup of coffee. I'm generally there during the day.'

'I will, thanks – Happy New Year.'

'Oh yes, I keep forgetting – ' he grimaced again. 'Happy New Year!'

When she walked past the stables on her way home, she saw Markby's car had gone. He'd taken Tom back with him to Bamford. Meredith hesitated, pushed open the gate of the stable yard and walked in. Blazer put his head over the loose-box door and snickered at her.

'Hullo, old chap,' she said, patting his nose. He pushed his head against her chest and snorted. 'I haven't brought you your titbit, I'm afraid. Sorry. You miss her, don't you?' Blazer shook his head up and down for all the world as if he was nodding agreement. 'I wish you could talk,' she told him. 'You could probably tell a lot we'd like to know.' She gave his neck a last pat and went on her way home.

When Alan arrived that evening she still hadn't decided what to say to him and as it was, he put in a pre-emptive bid.

'It's difficult to find a place open today – so many are closed after staying open late last night. But there's a little Italian restaurant on the Cherton road and they're open. I booked a table – I hope that's okay?'

'Oh – yes,' she said weakly. Perhaps it would be better at that. Easier to talk on neutral ground.

The restaurant was benefitting from being one of the few open for business. It was full and obviously booking a table had been necessary.

'How is Tom?' asked Meredith a trifle archly as she plunged a fork into a steaming dish of *tagliatelle al forno*.

'He won't cause any more trouble.'

'You sound so sure.'

Markby pulled a face. 'Let's say then, I am reasonably confident he won't.'

Meredith sipped at her glass of wine and peeped at her companion over the rim. It was a face she already felt she knew so well, all the little lines and wrinkles, the untidy lock of fair hair. This wasn't going to be easy. It was going to be murder. An unfortunate word. She sought for some kind of opening to the subject, dodged it at the last minute, and said instead, 'I met Colin Deanes out on the common today.'

'You did?' He looked both surprised and displeased.

'Yes, don't glower. He's actually a very nice man. He's got a bee in his bonnet about his cause, that's all. A lot of what he says makes sense, you know.'

'I never said it didn't. It's the way he says it which bugs me. We're not going to talk about him, are we?'

'No – no we're not.' Time to grasp the nettle. Meredith put down her fork. She rested her elbows on the table and placed her fingers together carefully steeple fashion, staring at them intently as she did so. 'Alan, there's something I've got to say. It's difficult and I'm sure I won't say it well. Like Deanes, I'll phrase it all wrongly and you'll take offence. The thing is – I – we – I don't think our relationship can develop into anything other than it is now.' She waited to see what he'd say, hoping he might nod understandingly. He didn't.

'Go on,' he said expressionlessly.

'I value our friendship, truly. I like your company. I like you – oh, this is awful. Alan, maybe I'm wrong but I feel that you hope that – well – we might get a lot closer one day.'

'Suppose I do? Is it that dreadful? Look, Meredith – ' he leaned forward. 'I told you, right at the beginning – when you were last in England – that I was prepared to wait – '

'Yes, I know and you have. But no one waits for ever. You won't – you'll get fed up with it.'

'Allow me to decide when I'm fed up!' he said, annoyance sounding in his voice and showing on his face.

'You see, I think you really need a wife!' Meredith plunged to the heart of the matter. What was the use of pussy-footing about, after all? 'And that can't be me. I couldn't take on that kind of thing.'

'I've been married!' he snapped. 'It was an unmitigated disaster!'

'Probably because you married the wrong woman and if you took up with me permanently – in any way – you'd be repeating the mistake. I'm the wrong woman.'

'Listen – ' he hissed, glancing at the next table. 'This is not the place – '

'Where is, then?'

'All right. There are two points to answer in what you said. One, it wasn't Rachel's fault my marriage headed straight for the rocks. I dare say I drove her round the bend. Being married to a policeman is difficult and if the strains proved too much for her, she wasn't the first. Policemen's marriages often founder.'

And she wanted a different kind of life, he thought, remembering. Parties, her friends, a diary of social engagements. And he had always been dragging his heels, pleading pressure of work, wanting to spend his spare time gardening, embarrassing her by turning up in old clothes when she was entertaining her friends. He thrust the memories away.

'Secondly, I know what kind of woman I want. I want you.'

'You see? There you are! You've said it! Oh, Alan, it's not that it isn't flattering – '

'It's not meant to be flattering!' he snarled. The woman at the next table cast him a startled look. She leaned forward and whispered to her companion. He sneaked a sideways glance at them.

'You know what I mean. I wish I hadn't started this.'

'So why did you?'

'Because I'm trying to be fair to you!' The man at the next table met her eye. His was unfriendly. He was closing ranks with the male under attack at the next table to his. 'Mind your own business!' said Meredith to him crossly.

'I beg your pardon!' exclaimed the man's companion, bridling. Sisterly sympathy vanished before instinct to defend her menfolk.

'Meredith!' said Markby in agony. 'It's all right – ' He smiled placatingly at the couple.

An uneasy silence fell during which they ate determinedly, doing scant justice to a very good meal. She looked surreptitiously at Markby. He looked miserable. It was all her fault.

'I didn't mean to make a scene . . .' she began in a whisper. 'I was only trying to tell you what I thought.'

'No, you weren't.'

'What?' She gaped at him.

Markby put down knife and fork and met her eye squarely, his expression grim. 'You were telling me what Harriet thought. I'm seeing you but I'm hearing Harriet Needham. The other day you were in a tangle because you couldn't cook like her. Now you feel you've got to imitate her lifestyle.'

'That's unfair and untrue!' she gasped, appalled.

'Is it?'

The waiter was making his way toward them. Was he, wondered Meredith, about to ask them to leave? He bent over Markby. 'There is a telephone call for you, sir.'

Markby groaned and threw down his napkin. 'I left this number just in case there was a genuine emergency. Excuse me, Meredith I'll have to go and answer it.'

Perhaps, however, they were both of them grateful for the interruption. Left alone at the table, Meredith found herself under the frank scrutiny of the couple at the next one. The woman looked offended. The man looked belligerent. I've messed up our evening, she thought, and I've messed up theirs. They'll go out of here now and have a blazing row about nothing.

Markby was coming back. He looked businesslike but he also looked as if the business concerned something other than their interrupted conversation. He stooped to murmur in her ear. 'I'll have to go straight away to The Crossed Keys. Fran Needham-Burrell has been attacked.'

'What?' Meredith looked up at him shocked, all else immediately forgotten. 'Is she hurt?' She jumped to her feet and grasped her shoulderbag. 'I'll come with you!'

Some confusion reigned at The Crossed Keys. A uniformed policeman stood in the doorway of the hotel entrance. Would-be customers making for the bar entrance further along edged cautiously around him. Sergeant Pearce, snappily dressed, slouched disconsolately by the reception desk, obviously dragged away from some New Year festivity, and the manager stood in the middle of the lobby, wringing his hands. Meredith had never seen anyone do that before – only read it – but he was. The hands twisted in and out of one another, the palms rubbing with a soft, rasping sound which set her teeth on edge. He appeared unnaturally pale – but that was probably distress. The distress was two-fold. On the one hand he wanted to deal with the upset – on the other hand he wanted to keep knowledge of it from the patrons of the public bar and the other hotel guests.

Pearce, when he saw Markby, straightened up and said briskly, 'Good evening, sir. Sorry to interrupt your evening but I thought you'd want to know.' He caught sight of Meredith and added, 'Good evening, ma'am!' which seemed very formal and made her feel like the Colonel's lady. 'Sorry about this.'

'That's all right, Sergeant Pearce,' she said, trying not to sound grand. 'One of those things.' Daft remark. But for a policeman it was, it was just one of those things. For consular officials too. It didn't make it any the less distressing.

'Where is she?' demanded Markby.

The manager darted forward. 'The lady is upstairs with Dr Pringle! I wanted to send for the ambulance but she wouldn't hear of it. She insisted on Dr Pringle only. She's a very strong-minded lady. But really, I know I ought to have sent for the ambulance because of the insurance. We have to cover ourselves and – '

Markby broke rudely into the explanation of his dilemma. 'I'll have a word with you later.'

He ran up the service stairs two at a time, Pearce and Meredith hard on his heels. The door of number twenty stood open. Framed by the doorway they saw as in one of those Victorian paintings which tell a story, Fran sitting on a chair and Jack Pringle bending over her. He was carefully taping a gauze pad to her forehead and she was saying with some asperity, 'Mind my hair, Jack!'

Meredith felt a surge of relief. She wasn't badly hurt.

Fran looked up and saw them. She gave them a wan travesty of her smile and said, 'Ah, visitors! Sorry to break into your evening! Hope I didn't ruin anything promising.'

'You didn't!' Markby said with what Meredith felt was unnecessary frankness. He crossed to bend over her and Meredith looked curiously round the room.

The wattage in the central light bulb was low so the whole scene was lit by an orange murk. The room represented a far cry from anything Fran must be used to. In fact she'd come to The Crossed Keys from the luxury of Klosters and it must be hard to think of a more extreme swing of the pendulum. Room twenty was adequate but no more. It badly needed decorating. The wallpaper was faded and the furniture looked like the sort of thing sold after the war against austerity furniture dockets. On a dressing table lay a document case, open and with papers spilling out higgledy-piggledy. There was quite a hideous picture on the wall showing a row of children asleep all in one bed, each face more grotesque than the one next to it, and by Meredith's foot lay an ugly glass vase. Automatically she stooped to pick it up.

Markby's voice prevented her, ordering sharply, 'Leave it!'

She flushed and straightened up. 'Sorry.' Stupid – obviously it was the weapon.

'Do you feel you can tell me about it, Frances?' he was asking.

Pringle interrupted to say crossly, 'She's had a nasty biff on the head and can do without being badgered. Can't it wait until morning?'

'Don't fuss, Jack. I'm all right!' said Fran. Her unwitting echo of the words of her cousin jolted Meredith unpleasantly. Pringle, too, looked taken aback and then upset.

Markby had drawn up a chair. 'Off you go, then, Fran.'

'Well, as I didn't have anyone to dine with – ' Fran said in a way which struck Meredith as having some meaning which was not immediately apparent to her – 'I thought I'd eat here, downstairs. I wasn't very hungry anyway because Charlotte cooked such a huge lunch. I went down – '

'Lock the door?'

'Yes – yes, I did. Not that I've got any jewellery or anything with me. I went down and started to eat but the food wasn't very good and I wasn't very hungry as I said, so I changed my mind in the middle of the meal, told them to take it away and came back up here.'

'Up which flight of stairs?'

'The main ones. They're the nearest to the dining-room entrance. I was thinking about this and that – not paying much attention to anything. The lighting is pretty poor outside in the corridor. I didn't notice anything until I actually put my hand on the door handle. Then the door swung open. I thought, that's odd – and just walked in a step, putting my hand out for the light switch – and he leapt at me from nowhere. Well, obviously from somewhere – he must have flattened himself against the wall when he heard me coming. He hit me with something hard. I fell flat on the carpet and he was away – gone. I didn't see his face. I can't tell you a thing about him. And I'm not hurt, despite this great big lump of wadding Jack's stuck on my head. I'm just surprised and extremely angry!'

'I see.' Markby stood up. 'Probably a petty thief. Have you had a chance to check and see if anything is missing?'

'I haven't got anything. I had my handbag with all my money and credit cards with me downstairs. All I had up here were my overnight things and my document case with all the papers relating to Harry's estate. Over there – ' Fran turned too quickly and grimaced.

'Steady!' warned Pringle, putting a hand on her shoulder.

'On the dressing table.' Fran pointed. 'You can see he was going through that. But there was nothing in there which could possibly interest a thief. No valuables. Just Harry's papers and all my correspondence which in the case of a death, you will know, is considerable.'

Markby turned towards Pearce. 'Take charge of that vase. Mind how you pick it up, it may have fingerprints – but they all know to wear gloves these days. Still, might be lucky. But he was probably just some yobbo in the public bar who saw Miss Needham-Burrell go into dinner and thought it might be a chance.'

'How would he know this was my room?' Fran asked pertinently.

'True. He may have tried other doors and only got this one open.' Markby walked over to the door. It brought him to stand by Meredith but he took no notice of her. She realised wryly that, as at The Bunch of Grapes when he was dealing with Tom, she had become invisible. That put her in her place, she thought. Flattering herself he was carrying a burning torch for her. Well, he wasn't. His work, that was his first love. And a load of plants his second. No wonder his wife had divorced him.

Markby was studying the door and surround. 'Old,' he said to Pearce. 'Warped. The door doesn't fit the frame, must be a half-inch gap at some points. Even if it were locked, the spring-bolt would scarcely connect with the mortise on the frame meant to receive it. One good push would break it open. It wouldn't even be a noisy break-in. Just a snap of wood. In this old building, wood's creaking and crackling all the time. Look here, you can see where the wood's splintered on the frame round the mortise.'

'I had a word with the manager before you came, sir,' Pearce said. 'It seems there was no one on duty in reception. They don't bother in the evening. It's a holiday anyway and they couldn't have got a receptionist in to work. Anyone could walk in off the street and nip up those back stairs by the reception desk. He probably ran out the same way. No one in the public bar would notice him. No one in the dining room would. The only risk he ran of being seen was if someone was actually coming out of the dining room into the lobby. Not many people staying here tonight and I shouldn't think anyone saw him.'

'You'll have to ask them all, anyway. That constable is stopping any diners leaving, I hope?'

'Yes, sir. And he's asking them all if they saw anything unusual. But it's unlikely they did.'

Meredith crossed the floor towards Fran. 'Would you like to come back to Rose Cottage, Fran? There's a spare room and I don't like to think of you staying on here, not after this.'

Fran smiled. 'I'm okay, truly. Only my dignity upset, nothing worse! Thanks for the offer but I'll stay on in town – it's easier to get hold of people.'

Meredith went back to Markby. He looked slightly surprised as she came up. She repressed an urge to say snappily, 'Yes, it's me!' Instead she said, 'I'd like her to come back with me, but she won't. You talk to her.'

'If she wants to stay, she will,' he said simply. 'We'll have to move her to another room anyway, one with a lock which isn't broken. We'll seal this one up until tomorrow when we can get a good look at it by daylight.' He hesitated. 'I have to talk to the manager and get a look at the stairs. Do you mind very much if Pearce walks you down to the taxi-rank?'

'I can get a cab home, certainly – and I don't need Pearce. You want him here really, obviously.'

'I'll call you – ' he said a little awkwardly.

'I'll drive in tomorrow, anyway, to see how Fran is.'

'Fine – goodnight, then . . .'

She took her farewell of Fran and Pringle, promised to come in the next day, and set off down to the taxi-rank. As she passed the manager in the lobby he was saying to the uniformed constable, 'But we've never had an incident like it! Never! We're not a big hotel. We don't have the sort of people staying here who attract thieves!'

Sitting in the back of the taxi on the starlit drive back to Pook's Common, Meredith turned the incident over in her mind. What if the intruder had not just been an opportunist petty thief? What if he had waited his opportunity and made for Fran's document case looking for – for what? A copy of the will? Why? Post-mortem report? The inquest was due to be held on Friday. All he had to do was attend, sit at the back and listen. What then?

She wriggled on the seat and glanced out of the window at the night-veiled fields and hedges. There was something else, too, which niggled at her mind. What was it? It had almost come to the surface when she walked into the hotel room, but concerned to see how badly hurt Fran was, it had been pushed back down again. It was – Meredith tried to visualise the scene. Fran sitting, Pringle stooping – '

'Dr Pringle!' she said aloud, suddenly.

'What's that?' asked the taxi-driver.

'Sorry, thinking aloud.'

'Turn off down here somewhere, isn't it?'

'What? Oh yes, by the garage. Just a bit further – here!'

They bumped down the lane to Rose Cottage. She got out and paid him.

'Bit lonely, isn't it?' asked the driver, looking about them at the darkened windows of the other cottages and sounding concerned.

'Yes, it is a bit.'

'You go on indoors, Miss. I'll wait until I see you put the lights on.'

'Thank you.'

She went in, switched on the hall light and waved to the driver from the open doorway. He turned his car as Markby had done, by driving on a little way and using the verge beyond the Haynes' cottage. That would be something which would further annoy Geoffrey when the Haynes moved in permanently. The taxi drove past with a toot of its horn. Meredith hurried into the living room and snatched up the *Bamford Gazette*.

Where was that picture of Harriet? Yes – no mistake now. Half his face hidden but the burly build was recognisable and the visible features clear enough. Jack Pringle. And hadn't he said something in the Market Square about once being a hunt follower? Dr Pringle. Dr Pringle?

Ten

When Markby returned to The Crossed Keys on Thursday morning, he found the manager in furious argument with the scarlet-taloned receptionist.

'All I'm asking, Lisa, is for a little cooperation!' the manager was saying in an aggrieved voice.

'I'm not staying on at this desk late at night, Mr Perkins, it's not safe! I can't stop thieves and muggers getting upstairs. I'd only get hit over the head myself like the woman in number twenty.'

'How about another, say, oh – ' the manager wrestled with his instinct for economy and immediate necessity – 'a pound an hour extra for work after seven in the evening. Say you came in from seven to ten, that's three pounds a night on top of your regular wage, Lisa! Fifteen pounds a week more – just think.' He thought himself and added hurriedly – 'just for a limited period, until the end of January.'

'My boyfriend,' said Lisa crushingly, 'wouldn't hear of my doing it. And that's that.'

'Good morning, Chief Inspector!' Mr Perkins had spotted Markby. He hurried forward. 'The lady is much better this morning. Dr Pringle has been to see her already. She's now in number twenty-eight at the end of the corridor. You haven't, I suppose,' he looked mournfully at Markby, 'heard anything – found out who he was?'

'Afraid not yet.'

'It's not fair, you know,' said the manager fretfully. 'We've never had anything like it before but no one remembers that! All they remember is this one episode. *Bamford Gazette* will stick it on the front page. Business representatives who've stayed over here for years on regular visits will take their trade to The Royal Oak, just like that, for no other reason.'

Markby left him lamenting and pleading with Lisa and made his way along the gloomy, creaking corridor to room twenty-eight. He tapped at the door.

'Come in!' invited a mellifluous voice.

'Good morning!' he said opening the door and adding immediately to himself, 'Oh, Lord!'

Fran Needham-Burrell was sitting up in bed in what looked to him like a turquoise silk karate suit. The large sticky plaster on her forehead had been replaced by a slightly smaller one – witness to Dr Pringle's ministrations earlier – and she was perfectly made up and coiffed. Her corn-gold hair spun a radiant halo round her head and some kind of perfume, he was sure very expensive, permeated the room. The room itself was similar to number twenty but possibly slightly more ramshackle. She looked completely out of place in it, like a goddess descended among unsuspecting peasants in some ancient Greek legend.

'Oh, good!' she said, holding out both hands towards him. 'Company! I'm so bored. Jack Pringle says I've got to stay in bed all day. Such a lot of nonsense. I wouldn't have agreed, but Charlotte has got to hear of this and she rang up and suggested I go and stay with her and Bungy. It's kind and I love them both dearly, but I love my independence more so I've settled for taking Jack's advice and staying in this very uncomfortable bed.' She paused. 'You should try it,' she added with the very faintest flicker of eyelashes.

'Glad to see you're feeling better,' Markby said politely, feeling like a prize lemon, 'I've come to see whether you've remembered anything about your assailant or found out if anything is missing.' To his own ears his voice sounded like that of a more old-fashioned type of High Court judge.

'Sit down!' she patted the coverlet. 'I'll tell all.'

Markby somewhat ostentatiously drew up a chair. He wouldn't have minded so much, but she was laughing at him for his pompous manner; he could see the merriment gurgling away in the depths of her green eyes.

'I can't actually tell you anything more about him, Alan. I'm very sorry. I've tried to remember. But it was so quick. He just was there, hit me and was gone.'

'Was he tall – taller than you are? Heavily built?'

'About the same height as me – I'm five-ten. Not particularly heavy in build, I think, but it's difficult to say because of his overcoat.'

'He was wearing an overcoat?'

She stared at him in unfeigned astonishment. 'Point to you!

172

Yes, I think he was! I did know something I hadn't told you, didn't I? I didn't realise I knew it.'

'People often don't. Why do you think it was an overcoat and not say, a raincoat?'

'Because, as I fell, my hand just brushed against it and it felt tweedy.'

'Not many young men wear tweed overcoats, do they? They wear leather jackets, even in quite cold weather. It suggests he was older, don't you think?'

She was nodding but reluctantly. 'It did get quite a fashion to buy old overcoats at jumble sales once. Lots of kids I know of were wearing them, down to their ankles and sleeves all too long. A goddaughter of mine was going round in a coat which had belonged to her grandfather the last time I saw her, a sort of Sherlock Holmes affair with a cape on the shoulders.'

'So he might have been a younger man, eccentrically garbed to follow some youthful fashion, you mean?'

'He might – I don't know.' Fran folded her hands on her lap and wriggled back against the plumped-up pillows behind her. The silk karate suit gaped invitingly, just enough. 'I did check my document case and nothing was missing. That's not surprising – it was all to do with Harry's estate and private correspondence. I've been writing to lots of people to tell them what's happened.'

'Have you?' Markby frowned. 'And these letters were in the case? They'd been disturbed?'

'It was all disturbed.'

Markby was silent. Our intruder might have wanted to know if she had any suspicions about her cousin's death, he was thinking. He might have wanted to know what she'd written to others – or if Harriet had written to her about something – something the police didn't know about yet.

'Penny for your thoughts,' she said huskily.

'Just idle speculation. Nothing missing, then?'

'Not a sausage.'

'To come back to this tweed coat – as you fell, did you happen to smell it?'

'Smell it?' she asked, surprised.

'Yes – I was thinking that if it came from a jumble sale, it might have smelled a bit frowsty.'

She frowned, forgetting the patch on her forehead, said 'Ouch!' and put up one hand to the dressing. 'Now you mention it – it did have a funny smell. I can't quite place it. A bit damp, perhaps . . . you know, as things smell when they've been in an old house.'

Jubilee Road . . . Markby found himself thinking. Pardy wore an old army greatcoat.

'Okay, Fran – I won't pester you any more about it. But if you think of anything – let me know.'

'Sure.' She pulled a wry grimace. 'I messed up your romantic evening, didn't I?'

'No – quite honestly, you didn't.'

'Oh.' The green eyes contemplated him. 'Lovers' spat?'

'Not even that. Just a general bad-tempered sort of argument.' He was surprised to hear himself tell her that much.

'Sorry to hear it but that's the way love goes, I'm told. It wasn't about me, was it?' Eyebrow flickered.

'No – as a matter of fact, it was about Harriet, in a way.'

'Harry? Don't tell me you were one of Harry's merry circle of admirers?' Now Fran really was surprised and curious.

'No, I wasn't!' Markby said crossly. 'What I meant was, Meredith seems to have got Harriet on the brain.'

'Harriet had that effect on people.'

'What circle of admirers?' he demanded suddenly.

She wriggled on the pillows again and the karate suit gaped a bit more. And, he thought, impervious to it now – she knows it and is doing it on purpose. He must be a pretty obvious target. She knew how to distract him with a twitch of her shoulders! And him a copper with how many years experience?

'Stop doing that,' he said sternly.

'Spoilsport.' She didn't even try to deny it.

He had to laugh then. 'Come on, Frances,' he said, growing serious again. 'If you do know of any of her boyfriends. . . .'

'Lots, but not round here. Not current anyway. Well, I could name You-Know-Who down at the stables but you know about him!'

But he was a copper with years of experience, after all. 'Not *current* ones, okay. So name me a past admirer who's local and I might know of?'

For the first time she showed some sign of unhappiness. 'I feel a sneak.'

'If he's got nothing to do with it, it won't matter.'

'Yes, it will. You'll go and badger him and upset him. He's a nice man and he's easily upset.'

'Who, Frances?' he almost yelled at her.

'Well – Jack, Jack Pringle – he wanted to marry her once but she turned him down.'

'What?' Markby sat and glared at her. 'I wish you'd told me before.'

'Why? Anyway, he could have told you if he'd wanted to.' The green eyes pleaded with him. 'Don't go and accuse poor old Jack of things, will you?'

'What things?'

'How should I know? Anything.' She thrust out a pearly-pink lipsticked lower lip. 'Wish I hadn't told you now.'

'Your mother should have told you about men,' he said heartlessly.

'Oh, she did – lots of good advice. Wish I could remember some of it.' She put up both hands to push back the spun halo of hair. 'I'm serious about you finding out who doped Harry. But it wasn't poor old Jack, I'm sure of it.'

'If anyone doped her.'

'Yes – ' Suddenly she was obstinate and as hard as nails. 'Yes, someone bloody well did!'

'If someone did, I hope to find him. But the chances are slim. The inquest is tomorrow. I've nothing I can put before a coroner. I need evidence if I'm to ask for an adjournment.'

'I'll tell him, your coroner!'

'Yes, I'm sure you will. Don't send his blood pressure up too high while you're doing it, will you?'

She lowered her arms. 'Don't you fancy me at all, Alan?'

'Now what on earth do you expect me to say to that?'

'Yes or no, would do nicely.'

'Any man would probably fancy you. I, however, am a servant of the public, an arm of the law – and I've got a prior commitment.'

'She doesn't appreciate you.'

'Well, we'll let her sort that one out, shall we?' he said gently.

'Okay – I stand corrected. I will not criticise Meredith. I think she's nuts.' She put out a hand. 'Pax.'

'All right,' he took the hand she held out. 'We'll call it quits and leave it at that.'

There was a knock at the door.

'My mid-morning coffee,' said Fran. 'It tastes like stewed seaweed. The Crossed Keys is looking after me! I think they're trying to finish off what our pal last night started. But they've offered to make a reduction on my bill! Come in!'

The door opened. Markby turned towards it, still absently holding on to Fran's hand.

'Oh,' said Meredith in the doorway. 'Good morning. Am I disturbing you?'

'You aren't, are you, imagining secret passions?' Fran asked Meredith when Markby had taken himself off in something of a hurry. 'The man is sea-green incorruptible and I've tried! I've got nowhere. He's utterly true to you.'

'I don't want to know!' Meredith said starchily.

'Why not? I would. Anyway, you do know. I've told you.'

'I came,' Meredith said determinedly, 'to see how you were this morning, Fran. Not to discuss my private life.'

Fran sighed and spread out turquoise-silk-clad arms to either side. 'I *am* treading on toes this morning. Metaphorically, that is. Stuck in this bed I can actually do damn all – on my own, anyway.'

'You're impossible!' Meredith said, exasperated and trying not to smile.

'But you've cheered up!' Fran said triumphantly. 'Thank God for that. I thought I had you on my conscience there for a bit. Thanks for coming along. I'm really okay. I'm bedridden because of Jack Pringle's instructions. But I'll be up tomorrow. Well, I've every intention of getting up this evening, actually.'

'Oh, Jack Pringle . . .' Meredith paused. 'He used to be a hunt subscriber, didn't he? Why did he give it up?'

'Oh,' Fran looked vague. 'He kept falling off, I think, and couldn't see his patients because he was in plaster. Either that or he couldn't afford to keep a horse and other outgoings. He hasn't got any money, Jack. Nice chap.' She twisted on to her side and began to delve in the shoulderbag on the bedside table. 'Listen, Meredith, you did offer to help if you could with clearing out Ivy Cottage. Is the offer still on?'

'Yes, of course.'

'Because I'd like you to have the spare set of keys.' Fran dragged a bunch out of the bag and handed them to her. 'I'm laid up here today, tomorrow is the inquest and on Monday I have to go back to London. I'll be back for the funeral which I hope to fix for the end of next week if the coroner tomorrow will give clearance for it to take place. They're letting me bury Harry at Westerfield after all, in the Markby plot. Will you be able to come?'

'I'd certainly like to. But I start work in London on Monday and I'll have to ask for a day off, straight away. They might be difficult.'

'Do try. And if you'd keep an eye on Ivy Cottage of an evening – I realise you won't be there during the day. And there is one little job you could do if you've a spare moment, no rush. I've taken the couple of Harriet's books I'd like to keep and the rest can go to the League of Friends of the Cottage Hospital. So if you could go over and pack all the books you can find into a box or something and just drop them in at the medical centre – Jack Pringle will deal with it.'

'Certainly.'

Fran leaned forward and stretched out her arms. 'This bed is utterly diabolical. Blow Jack Pringle. I'm getting up. Do stay and have a Crossed Keys lunch with me, Meredith. They're so afraid I'm going to sue them that they're giving me a reduction on everything and I'm jolly well going to take advantage of it. Serve them right – letting me get bashed on the head!'

When she left Fran after lunch, Meredith walked slowly back into the town's main shopping area. For all her determination to quit her sickbed, Fran had begun to look distinctly wan by the end of their meal and had several times put her hand to her forehead. Meredith had managed to persuade her to go back upstairs and take a rest during the afternoon. It was a measure of how poorly Fran was feeling that she agreed without too much fuss. Although, thought Meredith, as soon as the headache passed off, she'd jump up and start dashing round again.

It was no use denying that the moment when she had opened Fran's door and beheld Alan Markby holding Fran's hand had been a nasty one. The jolt had been severe, much more than she would have imagined. Of course, she had only to expect it. She herself had told him bluntly the evening before that he had nothing to hope from their relationship. All the same, he hadn't delayed setting about finding a replacement! None of this was doing her self-esteem any good. But she couldn't grumble if the man took her at her word. She paused. She didn't mind really, did she? Did she? Yes, she did. The truth hit her like a palpable blow. Yes, she did mind. She minded like hell. She was suffering from a severe bout of good, old-fashioned jealousy!

She had drawn level with a bookshop and stopped, as was her habit with bookshops, to study the display in the window. It appeared a serious book store with a range of topics in stock from novels to non-fiction. Attracted by the reassuring warmth of the interior, she gave way to the impulse to push open the door and go in.

'Can I help you?' asked the very nice young man at the cash desk, moving out from behind it to greet her.

A thought occurred to her. 'I was wondering if you stocked the most recent book by Colin Deanes. I believe it's called *Revolutionary Youth*.' Alan had told her that. It would be interesting to know more about Deanes' theories.

'Oh, Mr Deanes!' said the young man enthusiastically. 'He wrote that book while living very near Bamford, did you know? He does come in here from time to time. But you can't buy the book yet, I'm afraid. It's not due for release until February. I've been on to the publishers because Mr Deanes was keen to set up some kind of publicity morning here in the shop: Mr Deanes talking about his work and perhaps signing a few books. But we won't get copies of the book until later this month. I'll reserve you one, if you like.'

'Yes, all right.' She gave him her name and address.

'We'll send you a postcard, Miss Mitchell, just as soon as we get our copies in.'

'Thank you.' Meredith turned round to leave and bumped straight into Lucy Haynes. 'Oh, good afternoon, Mrs Haynes! Do you remember me?'

'Oh, yes! Miss Mitchell, isn't it? How nice. . . .' Lucy peered up at her nervously. 'How are you? I was thinking about you and really I'm quite pleased to see you and know you are all right. It must be very unpleasant living out at Pook's Common now, especially directly opposite poor Miss Needham's cottage. I know I couldn't. To be frank, I don't like Pook's Common and I never did. It was all Geoffrey – well, he's always fancied being somewhere uncluttered, not crowded with other people. But I never wanted to buy that cottage. I'd like to move to Bourne-mouth. The climate is nice and I do love the seaside. The shops are lovely there and our daughter lives nearby. Pook's Common always seems to me such an eerie sort of place! Perhaps it's just my imagination.'

'No, I don't think so,' Meredith confessed. 'I find it a little creepy, too.'

'Do you?' Lucy was pathetically pleased to have confirmation of her own impressions. 'Geoffrey says I talk nonsense. But since poor Miss Needham met with her accident, so dreadful, somehow the idea of going and living out there seems worse than ever.'

'It is lonely, to be sure.'

Lucy moved closer confidingly and whispered, 'It's the common itself. It's so sinister and our cottage is right at the end of the row of buildings and so there's nothing between us and the common but those stables. Sometimes at night – '

'Yes – ' Meredith prompted.

'My imagination again, as Geoffrey says, I'm sure. But when we've weekended there I've hardly been able to sleep a wink. I just lie awake and listen and sometimes I could swear I've heard footsteps.'

'At night? You haven't heard the horses, down at the stables, stamping in their stalls? They did get out one night recently, too.'

'No, I don't think so. Footsteps, walking footsteps. Geoffrey says what nonsense, because there's nowhere for anyone to walk to down there. Unless that fellow from the stables has walked up to visit Miss Needham. He was a friend of hers. Yes – ' Lucy considered. 'I suppose it could have been him. Or just the wind bowling some leaves along the lane. I do imagine things. Geoffrey's always telling me off about it.'

Meredith took leave of her thoughtfully and walked on along the pavement. Parked by the kerb a little way further on from the bookshop was a large, shiny black Granada. She drew level with it and stopped. The first time she had seen a car parked outside Harriet's she had had the impression it might have been a Granada. But in the darkness it had been difficult to be sure. All the same, here was one, standing out in this country-town high street by its city-smartness. It was certainly the first she recalled seeing in Bamford. How many were there around? Could it be more than coincidence? Meredith moved towards the window of a butcher's shop and turned ostensibly to study the array of pork chops and best mince, but actually to keep a surreptitious watch on the car. A fixed notice on a metal pole announced that waiting time for vehicles here was limited to twenty minutes in any hour. The driver had to come back soon.

However, she had almost given up and the butcher within was directing some unfriendly glances her way through the plate glass, when a man appeared, striding briskly along. He stopped by the Granada and put a key in the door. There was a limit to coincidences and it had just been reached.

Meredith stepped out and faced him across the car roof. 'Good afternoon, Mr Green.'

Rupert Green stopped in mid-action. His dark eyes studied her suspiciously, trying to place her and failing. 'I'm sorry,' he said coldly, 'you have the advantage of me.'

'My name is Meredith Mitchell. I've rented a cottage at Pook's Common.'

Something flickered in the depths of those dark eyes. His wariness increased. But Meredith felt a thrill of approaching triumph. She'd hit the mark here. She knew it and was emboldened to gamble.

'I believe you were a friend of Harriet Needham's!' she declared with jaunty assurance.

It flummoxed him. 'What makes you say that?' He was too clever to deny it before he found out more about her.

'I've seen your car – parked outside Ivy Cottage.'

Green slowly withdrew the key he had put in the doorlock. 'I'd rather not talk on a public pavement, shouting across the top of a car. There's a café behind us. Perhaps we can go there?'

Meredith preceded him into the Cosy Corner Coffee Shop. Green glanced round the interior and pointed silently to a discreet table behind a pillar. When the waitress came up he ordered brusquely, 'Two coffees!' without asking Meredith what she preferred. The waitress departed and he put his forearms on the table, clasping his hands loosely. They were broad hands with spatulate fingers, coarse hands. Though a good-looking man, his handsomeness was a florid one, impressive but making Meredith think of a canvas to which the artist had applied the paint with a knife. 'What do you want?' he asked coldly.

Meredith felt herself flush. 'I don't want anything except to have a word about Harriet. I'm sure you must be upset about her death and I don't want to distress you unnecessarily, of course.'

Green thought out his answer to that one, his eyes unfriendly and his manner tense. He'd like to bolt, she thought. He couldn't so he'd talk his way out. 'That's very considerate of you,' he said coolly at last. 'Naturally I am upset at her death and particularly at the manner of it. It was a great shock and a disgraceful piece of hooliganism on the part of the youth involved. However, I have been assuming that the relevant authorities have everything well in hand regarding any future proceedings. Are you about to tell me they have not?'

'Yes, they have. But it's all turning out to be a little more complicated than it appeared.' Green's eyes narrowed. He tightened the clasp of his hands on the table-cloth, lowered his head and watched her from beneath thickly marked brows. Boardroom manners, she thought. She pressed on. 'As you may know, the post mortem on Harriet found traces of tranquilliser in her blood.'

'So?' he raised the thick eyebrows. He was either a very good actor or he really didn't know what she was driving at.

'No one I've spoken to who knew Harriet can understand that. She didn't take those pills. She didn't take any pills. She was not, as far as anyone knew, depressed. We can't find any empty boxes or the rest of the pills anywhere.'

'Who,' enquired Green, watching her closely, 'are we?'

'Myself, her family – the police.' Meredith tossed in the last word after a perceptible pause.

'And this has something to do with me?'

'You might be able to help explain it. Did she talk to you of being depressed or taking pills? Did you see any pills of that kind in the cottage?'

'The answer to all those questions is no.'

The waitress brought their coffee. Green dropped two pound coins on the tablecloth and waved the surprised and delighted girl away. He's giving his feelings away, thought Meredith, highly satisfied. He was the sort who normally checked his change if he bought a box of matches. He's rattled.

'I can tell you, Miss – ah – Mitchell, that I don't much like the way you're asking me these questions. You had better have some convincing reason.' The voice and manner were designed to make lesser mortals quail and probably had been very effective on past occasions. But not now.

Oh, don't try that one on me! thought Meredith almost joyfully. She was not the office junior. She'd dealt with much worse than him! He wouldn't bully her.

'I thought,' she said demurely, 'you'd like to know exactly how Harriet died, since you were such good friends.'

'Perhaps I thought it was already obvious how she died, and perhaps you exaggerate that friendship.'

'You were with her on Christmas Day, weren't you? You were there in the evening, at any rate. I think that indicates closeness.' Meredith sipped at her coffee in order to show him her hand wasn't shaking.

'Other than a neighbour of Harriet's, who are you?' he asked abruptly.

Meredith told him and Green's gaze grew more cautious. He raised his clasped hands to rest his chin on them, his elbows on the table. A skin had formed over his untouched coffee. He wasn't prepared to take the same test she had. 'Listen to me,' he said quietly. 'I will tell you exactly what that friendship was. Then, perhaps, you'll leave me alone. If you don't, I shall take legal steps to stop you harassing me. I've no intention of discussing details of my private life and business affairs with a stranger, but I'll tell you this much. My wife and I have a civilised agreement to go our separate ways. She is a partner in several of my business ventures and her father also has a considerable holding in my various business concerns. It is in the interest of neither Felicity nor myself to divorce.'

Meredith put down the coffee cup abruptly. She had completely misunderstood Aunt Lou. Not green politics, but Green, the surname. That green man. That Green man.

'But if there were to be a scandal . . . and this accident of Harriet's has unfortunately a lurid aspect to it as I'm sure you appreciate. If the national press got hold of it – and I'm now talking of the more sensational tabloid newspapers – if they found out my friendship with Harriet, you can imagine the kind of news story they'd make of it. "Top city man's mistress in dramatic death fall from plunging horse!" and who knows what else? Felicity wouldn't stand for that, nor would her father. She'd sue for divorce and the old man would pull out all his investments in my companies. Felicity would want and make sure she got half of everything. I might even be forced into bankruptcy, ruined, I can't let that happen, naturally. There is nothing I can tell you or the police which would throw any light on Harriet's death. And as I am aware that the popular press pays for such titbits as I've told you, I should advise you not to be tempted to contact them. I doubt your superiors at the Foreign Office would approve of your actions, anyway. Gloat over what you've learned for your own delectation if you will.'

Meredith's face flamed and her mouth opened.

Green forestalled her, leaning across the little table and holding her gaze with his. 'If you try and use your knowledge to embarrass me in any way, Miss Mitchell, you'll regret it. And I'm sure you're far too intelligent to think of blackmail.'

'Harriet was my friend!' Meredith said tightly.

'And to me a mistress,' Green said calmly. 'Nothing more. Just that. A mistress.'

You rat, thought Meredith. You miserable wretch. May you rot in your miserable little grave.

'Is that how she saw your arrangement?' she flung at him.

'Of course. Please don't act the affronted romantic, Miss Mitchell. Harriet was nothing if not exceedingly clear-headed. She knew that if she had attempted to change the rules, our affair would have come to an immediate end.'

'How convenient for you!' she snapped. 'I wish I could believe it was so nicely cut and dried!'

Green's lips twisted in a brief, mirthless grimace. 'All lovers quarrel occasionally, Miss Mitchell. It adds a certain spice to a relationship. It does not necessarily alter the nature of it. But if you need further advice I suggest you write to a lonely hearts column. I can't say it's been a pleasure . . .' He made a movement to rise from the table.

'I believe,' Meredith said mildly, 'an elderly relative of mine is a friend of your father-in-law's. Your father-in-law is Mr Ballantyne, isn't he? Living near Newbury?'

It's not much, Harriet, she thought. It was a small revenge but it was the best she could do.

Green froze poised halfway between sitting and standing. His florid face drained of colour and became ashen. 'You should have informed me of this at the outset! This conversation has been conducted on an entirely false premise! I assumed you knew almost as little about me as I about you! How much do you really know about my affairs?'

'Mr Green,' Meredith said rising to her feet with dignity. 'I really have no interest in your affairs, of any nature. My interest is solely to discover where Harriet obtained the tranquillisers. But there is one question you could answer, if you would.'

'Yes?' he said hoarsely.

'Did you breakfast with Harriet on Boxing Day morning?'

'No!' Green snapped angrily. 'I left around midnight on Christmas night!'

'And you didn't come back?'

'No! Why should I? It was the morning of the meet. I had to get ready. I would be seeing her at the meet in any case.'

'Fine. Well, thank you, Mr Green. And thank you for the coffee.' She smiled glacially on him and walked out leaving him silent, furious and, she was pretty sure, scared out of his wits.

183

But as she drove back to Pook's Common, a pall of discourage-
ment settled over Meredith. It had nothing to do with discovering
how Harriet died, but much to do with Harriet herself. What
price your independence, really, Harriet? Meredith wondered
bleakly. She had been so keen not to let anyone get the better
of her. She, who had kept Tom Fearon so firmly in his place.
Yet along that wretch Green had come and she fell for whatever
his charms had to offer. And now all he wanted to do was pretend
he never knew her. It had been him she'd cooked her cordon
bleu meal for on Christmas Day. Now he said she was a mistress,
nothing more. In time he would have traded her in for a newer
model, just as one day he'd trade in that Granada car. How
could Harriet have fallen for such a type? Or had she known?
Had she known and not cared? She wished she knew. Oh Harriet,
she wished she knew.

But supposing . . . Meredith changed gears with a crunch and
slowed at the turning off to Pook's Common by Fenniwick's
garage. There was a man in the forecourt and it appeared to be
open for business again. Supposing Harriet had minded? Supposing she had expected Green to divorce Felicity and marry her?
Or even suppose she had just become fed up with playing such
a cloak-and-dagger role in his life. 'Don't act as though you're
ashamed of me! Take me out and introduce me to your friends!'
she might have demanded. Green couldn't and wouldn't have
done that. He would have refused. She might have been angry,
realising how little she meant to him really. She might have made
threats. That would have given him a powerful motive to shut
her up – for good.

Markby had made his way to the medical centre after leaving
The Crossed Keys. Such a stupid thing – to be caught holding
Fran's hand like that. Meredith surely wouldn't think . . . would
she?

'I'd like a private word with Dr Pringle,' he told the receptionist. 'What time does he see his last patient this morning?'

She looked at him suspiciously. 'Dr Pringle's surgery is fully
booked this morning. He can't see anyone else. You'll have to
make an appointment for the five o'clock surgery.'

'I don't want to consult him. I'm Detective Chief Inspector
Markby,' he produced his card. 'It's a word about a case.'

'Oh,' she thawed. 'Well, he has just one more person to see
this morning before lunch. If you like, I'll just call him – '

She put out a hand for the phone but he stopped her. 'No, I'll wait outside his surgery door.'

He walked down the corridor which smelled of disinfectant and sat down outside the door marked 'Dr J. Pringle'. The medical centre had only been open two years. All its paintwork was nice and fresh, its carpets unstained. But its plastic chairs were already showing signs of wear. Markby shifted unhappily in his and it creaked. Above his head the fluorescent lighting strip made a soft, singing noise and flickered occasionally.

From behind the closed door of Pringle's room he could hear voices, Pringle's and a woman patient's. After a while there was a movement and the door opened. A woman of depressed and depressing appearance came out and scurried away down the corridor. Pringle, his bluff form filling the doorway, saw Markby and exclaimed in surprise, 'Hullo, Alan! Gone sick?'

'No – I've just dropped in for a word, if you've a moment.'

'Come in. I'm on my lunch hour. Then it's home visits, a quick cuppa and back here for five o'clock surgery. Who'd be a GP?' He indicated a chair and sank back in the one he had just quitted. 'Is it about the inquest tomorrow?'

'Yes – you're going to give medical evidence, I understand.'

'That's right.'

'Jack – ' Markby hesitated. 'I don't mean to pry but I know that you and Harriet were pretty friendly at one time, a couple of years ago.'

'I suppose you could call it that.' Pringle's geniality had gone. 'It won't stop me giving an objective medical opinion.'

'I wasn't going to suggest it would. There's no way I can ask this except bluntly, Jack. Did you visit her at Pook's Common on Christmas Day – in the evening?'

'No.' Pringle stared hard at him. 'As it happens, I was called out on an emergency on Christmas Day. You can check.'

'And Boxing Day morning, before I saw you in the square. You hadn't been out and breakfasted with her?'

'No!' There was a pause and then Pringle asked in a quiet voice, 'But someone had, hadn't he? You don't know who and you'd like to. She had a man friend there on Christmas Day – and in the morning on Boxing Day.'

'I'm sorry, Jack,' Markby said contritely. 'I don't like having to bring it up if it's painful.'

'It's not your fault. You have to do your job. No, I wasn't there, on either occasion. Whoever he was, he wasn't me. I don't mind telling you that I wish it had been.'

'Sure, Jack, I understand.'

'And you're right, it is painful. It's two years ago now since Harriet and I were friendly, as you put it. But it never stops hurting, Alan.'

'You didn't decide to do something about it, did you, Jack?' Markby found himself praying that Jack wouldn't reply in the affirmative.

'No. I didn't go down there and feed her tranquillisers. I have access to the things – ' Pringle waved a hand at the shelves around him. 'But I didn't. And I don't much like the thought that anyone else did.' He paused. 'She was like the personification of life itself. I would have done nothing to snuff that out.'

Women, women, women . . . thought Markby as he made his way back to the station. Well, they all seemed to be in a mess in that respect. Now there was the coroner's inquest. He supposed he could ask for an adjournment on the grounds that criminal proceedings were to be taken – meaning against Pardy for criminal recklessness. But those damn pills . . . any good defence counsel would tear the case against Pardy apart if it came to court. Harriet Needham had certainly caused a lot of trouble.

There was a certain awkwardness between herself and Alan Markby now, thought Meredith, and she couldn't help but admit it was entirely of her making. Finding him tenderly holding Fran's hand hadn't helped, but the basic situation was one she had created. Which made it difficult to pick up the telephone at Rose Cottage and ring him, but she had to.

'Meredith?'

She heard the eagerness in his voice and cut in quickly before he could say anything more. 'I wanted to tell you, I've found out the identity of Harriet's guest on Christmas Day. It was Rupert Green. I've spoken to him and he admits it.'

'Does he, indeed?' she heard him give a low whistle.

'He says he left late – at the time I heard the car drive away – and he didn't come back. He knows nothing, or so he claims, about pills. He says Harriet didn't mention any or claim to be depressed and he wants to be kept out of it. If his wife finds out she'll divorce him and his father-in-law will discontinue his financial backing. All in all, he's very nervous is Mr Green.'

'I'd better have a word with him.'

'Be careful. He'll threaten you with his lawyers.'

'Is that what he did with you?'

'More or less.'

'You watch yourself!' he said censoriously. 'He could prove a tricky customer.'

'He blusters. He puts up the big bold image. In my experience that kind is hiding something and is looking for a way out.'

'So long as all he's hiding are his extra-marital affairs. Thanks for finding out – but couldn't you have brought your information to me and let me sound him out?'

Meredith stiffened. 'I didn't have it to bring until this afternoon. I just saw his car and then him in the High Street and I'm afraid I got a gut feeling about it. I gambled, if you like, and I was right. Anyway, you couldn't have seen what I saw. Your aunt doesn't live next door to Rupert's father-in-law.'

'You've lost me,' Markby said.

There was an embarrassing pause as the double meaning sank in for both of them.

He began again hurriedly, 'I mean I don't – '

'It's all right, Alan. I know what you mean.' Meredith put the phone down.

Markby, at the other end of the line, replaced his own receiver as the familiar burr of a cut line sounded in his ear. Clearly Meredith did think he was romantically entwined with Frances Needham-Burrell. Oh, what the hell! he thought angrily, grabbing a pile of papers from his In-tray. He couldn't help what she thought. He wasn't going to run round to Rose Cottage to explain himself. She didn't want a closer relationship, fine. She wasn't getting one.

'You go on home!' he said sourly to Pearce who ventured to put his head round the door. 'I'm working late!'

'Old man's in a bad temper!' warned Pearce downstairs, on his way out.

The 'old man' – whose temper would not have been improved by the description – had set himself to work and work he did, solidly with a couple of brief breaks for coffee until late. Which was how he came to be in the building when the 999 call came in.

Simon Pardy was also having problems with being rejected. He was used to it, mind you, but it still made life just that little more difficult than it already was. The facts of the situation simply were that he was barred from nearly every public house in Bamford. Simon was not sociable by nature but even he was surprised at the inconvenience caused to him by the new restrictions on his already limited social life.

The first to bar him had been The Bunch of Grapes, following the affray on New Year's Eve there. This Simon found completely unfair because after all, he was the one who had been attacked by that prat from the stables, and so it wasn't his fault, was it? All he'd done was defend himself. Colin Deanes agreed with him. He was all right, was Colin. But barred from The Bunch of Grapes Simon remained. Micky, Tracy and Cheryl, on the other hand, had let him know in no uncertain terms that they were not barred from The Bunch of Grapes, and had every intention of continuing to drink there. Their disloyalty did not surprise Simon – he had been mildly surprised when the girls came to his aid when Fearon attacked him, though he realised that was a matter of principle with them as he was a member of their party at the time. But their attitude now did make him bitter. They ought to continue to stand by a mate, shouldn't they? Someone who shared a house with them? Had their situations been reversed, Simon would not have dreamed of standing by them, but this thought did not trouble him.

However the unjust discrimination against him had begun earlier; it had begun the day after Boxing Day. It seemed that since that business in the Market Square when that silly bitch fell off her horse and cracked her head open, the mark of Cain was on him. No one wanted him around. Others felt they could not drink in comfort knowing he was there, ill-omened, accursed. In addition, Harriet Needham had had a surprising number of friends and admirers and he had been getting some threatening looks and words. It wasn't just that fellow from the stables he had to worry about. Yes, the word had gone out. A rotten, decadent society had closed its ranks against him, the reformer. He was out.

As a result, Simon found himself reduced to drinking alone in Bamford's least popular tavern. It was run by an elderly curmudgeon who could expect to see half a dozen in his public bar on a good night and treated these few hardy souls with fierce disdain. He didn't mind Simon drinking there. He didn't care who drank there. He didn't care if no one drank there. His was not a tied house, he was answerable to no brewery and he could and did do as he liked.

That Thursday evening, a week to the day since the accident, found Simon sitting on his own in the gloomy corner of the above pub which he had made his own. Not that there was anyone to challenge his right to it. The misanthropic publican leaned on the bar and read the paper. Two old men in caps drank in the far corner and by the door sat a bleached blonde who had been banned, like Simon, from a good few bars in her time but whose luck had turned tonight. She had succeeded in picking up a lonely, bored businessman on a sales trip, and was downing Cinzano and lemonade as fast as she could while her new friend was paying.

The pall of gloom and bitterness thickened about Simon, helped by the unpleasant, bitter-tasting, weak-tea-coloured brew – claimed by the landlord to be lager – which he was drinking. The misanthrope seldom washed out the pumps. Tomorrow was Friday and there would be the inquest to get through. He'd be asked to give evidence, explain his actions. The coroner would keep on at him, asking what was in his mind. Trying to make him say things to trap himself. Trying to trick him into saying he meant to injure her. He'd tell them nothing. Colin had warned him, just stick to the basic facts. Remember they saw the accident so you can't deny your actions, but you can deny you meant any harm. Speak up clearly, be frank and look straight at them. Don't say anything controversial. Include an apology. That last would stick in the throat but Colin insisted. Say how sorry you are. You hadn't realised she would fall off.

A wave of self-pity swept over Simon. You'd think, seeing that he had all that to get through tomorrow, Micky at least would have come out tonight and had a drink with him. Even the girls' company would have been something. They'd let him down. Not that he expected anything better of them. They wanted to be rid of him. He set down his half-finished lager with a grimace and got to his feet. He'd had enough. He'd go back to Jubilee Road where he'd have the place to himself. The others would have gone out by now. A picture of them enjoying themselves at The Bunch of Grapes flashed through his head and sourness tightened his stomach, encouraged by the drink. At that moment, he hated everyone. And he had work to do at home. He lurched across the floor and rudely pushed by the couple sitting by the door as he went out.

'Look at that!' said the blonde indignantly, brushing contact with Simon from her sleeve. 'No manners and he looked like something the cat brought in!'

'I've got two at home like that . . .' said the businessman gloomily. 'Cost me a fortune in fees for private education, piano lessons, trips abroad – now neither of them can hold a job down or speak a civil word. Loaf round the house all day . . . never do a hand's turn to help their mother. I don't know why.'

'Don't tell me, dear!' said the blonde, patting his hand. A real sympathy glowed in her mascara-caked eyes replacing the purely professional concern with which she had earlier been listening to his woes. 'I know! I've got a daughter – nineteen, she is. Gone off up to London and never writes or picks up a phone! Went off with a feller, of course. He was no good, I warned her, but she wouldn't listen. Now I don't know where she is or what she's doing. And yet when she was a little girl, she lacked for nothing! I bought that kid everything she wanted. I had to go without myself to pay for her dancing lessons and the tights and tutus and shoes and whathaveyou. Look . . .'

She fumbled in her plastic handbag and dragged out a folder. Photographs tumbled out of it on to the greasy, beer-stained table. 'That's my Cindy when she was six. I kept her looking like a little princess.'

The businessman had produced a photo folder of his own. 'That's my two boys taken five years ago, on a family holiday in Majorca. When I think of what I spent on those family holidays . . . if I'd known then what I know now, I'd have kept the money and bought a sports car!'

Their heads touched, bent over the jumble of photographs representing their past lives, their dashed hopes, their spurned love, united, for a quarter of an hour at least, by their sense of loss and grievance.

Simon had gone back to Jubilee Road. The house was in darkness. He opened the front door and its stale air struck his nostrils. The place was a dump. He put out a hand to switch on the hall light and nothing happened. Bulb had gone again. The way the wiring was in this place, light bulbs lasted two minutes. He made his way up the groaning staircase in the darkness, steadying himself by grasping the rickety banister which moved beneath his grip, and pushed open the door of his room, the one at the top facing the stairs. As he did, he heard a faint creak from the next room, Micky's. He called, 'Mick?' Despite himself, a faint note of hope sounded in his voice.

There was no reply. No one there. The brief flicker of antici-pation at the possibility of some companionship was cruelly extinguished, added to the pile of other burnt-out hopes. Simon threw open his door and switched on his light. The room was as he had left it, that is to say a shambles, the bed unmade, sheets unwashed. Soiled linen was piled in a corner and across the table was scattered his work. Simon stood looking down at it and smiled. Yes, he'd get a good few done tonight. Some coffee would help him along. He'd go downstairs first and make a cup.

He stepped out on to the gloomy landing and hesitated at the top of the stairs, trying in the faint glow coming through the open door of his room behind him to make out the steps descending away from him into black nothingness. And then quite abruptly the light from his room was extinguished, leaving him in utter darkness.

'Bloody hell!' he muttered, 'That bulb's gone too . . .'

And that was the last clear, conscious thought he had.

Eleven

When the call came in, its contents were passed to Markby straight away. He left orders for Pearce to be contacted and told to meet him at the scene – and left for Jubilee Road prey to an emotion he had not felt for a number of years.

No policeman ever gets used to sudden violent death. If his career leads him to deal with it fairly often over a period of years he grows a protective carapace which shields him against the trauma. He may sometimes appear to outsiders to be hard-bitten but few are really so on the inside. Most hate it, every time.

Markby particularly hated violent death when it struck down the very old and the young. He hadn't liked Pardy, but it was a young life, snuffed out. A young life misused perhaps, but one day the boy might have found his way, given time. But time had run out for Simon Pardy. Markby felt a dull anger burning inside him.

There was a patrol car before the house in Jubilee Road and a light in a bay window downstairs. The front door stood ajar with a uniformed man guarding it but no light shone in the hallway behind him. In nearby houses curtains twitched at bedroom windows. The neighbours were watching, curious, apprehensive, appalled, jubilant. Plenty of people enjoyed a good disaster provided it didn't affect them personally and they could walk away from it, or close up the newspaper, when they'd had enough.

'Good evening, sir,' said the uniformed man. 'You'll need a torch in there. There's no light bulb in the hall. We've switched on the light in the living room and opened the door but it doesn't throw much light on the body.'

Markby paused. 'No light bulb at all?'

'No, sir. Looks like someone took it out. Perhaps it was broken and they meant to replace it. They're all in the kitchen, sir, with Wpc Jones. She's very good with shock.'

'They?'

'The other youngsters. Three of them. They all live in this house. You know how it is . . . they club together to pay the rent. Mind you, looking at this place, I'm surprised the landlord found anyone who wanted to live in it!'

'Who found him?' Markby asked, cutting off the constable's observations on the state of the property. He could see that for himself. 'Who reported it?'

'One of the youngsters, one of the girls. They all came home and found him together, they reckon.'

Markby nodded, took the torch the constable offered him, and went into the frowsty-smelling hall. There was another smell in it, too. Faint, but he recognised it. Blood. And death!

Simon was sprawled on the hall floor at the foot and to one side of the staircase. He had landed face down. Blood had poured from a smashed nose and leaked horridly from his ear. His head was crookedly set on his shoulders. His eyes and mouth were open. He looked surprised. Halfway up the staircase, the banister was broken. 'Fell from the top,' muttered Markby, judging it with his eye. 'Grabbed the banister or fell against it but it gave way and he crashed through to the bottom. Rotten wood.'

He put out a hand and cautiously touched the unbroken banister nearest to him. It rocked. The whole edifice was as rickety as a matchstick construction. The stairs themselves were carpeted after a fashion, but the carpeting was so old and threadbare it was little more than a hessian backing full of dust and holes, and more dangerous than it was useful. The state of decoration of the place, or lack of it, was disgusting and the occupants hardly gave the impression of being houseproud. Living in such a place they might be excused. Although they were way better off here than some of their contemporaries, sleeping in doorways. Markby flashed the torch around the hall area. Light from the living-room door, of which the constable had spoken, did little but throw a gloomy shadow. The kitchen door at the end of the hall was shut but a stronger light gleamed in a strip beneath it and the murmur of voices could be heard behind it.

A car drew up outside and was followed quickly by another. He heard the constable's voice, then Pearce's, then others. Pearce appeared as a dark silhouette in the front doorway, the light from the street lamp outside glowing around him. He peered into the gloom and enquired breathlessly, 'Mr Markby?'

'Good evening, Pearce,' said Markby politely. 'If that's the photographer, he'll need to set up his own lighting.'

Pearce edged past the body, staring down at it. 'Turn up for the books,' he said. He glanced up the staircase. 'What a heap of old scrap! Think it was an accident, sir?'

'I don't think anything as yet. It was a singularly unfortunately timed one if it was – he was prize witness at tomorrow's inquest.'

'Today's,' said Pearce.

'What?' Markby glanced at his wristwatch. Five past midnight. 'So it is. Well, at least I've got grounds to ask the coroner for an adjournment now. Go upstairs and take a look around, mind how you go. Keep an eye open for any sign of a struggle or that he was pushed. I'll have a word with his friends in the kitchen.'

When he opened the kitchen door a bright yellow light suddenly bathed him and made him blink. Wpc Jones appeared in front of him, barring the way. Then she saw who it was and said, 'Oh, good evening, sir.'

'All quiet?' he asked.

'Bit upset, sir.' Wpc Jones lowered her voice even more. 'The lad most of all, actually. One of the girls seems a bit slow on the uptake and the other is a tough little number.'

'The female of the species,' said Markby. 'Okay, Jones. Spare me that feminist glare and nip out there and see what you can do. Call on the immediate neighbours to either side and across the road. They might be a bit slow answering the door but they're all out of bed, bright-eyed and bushy-tailed . . . The net curtains are twitching in unison. Gossip, Jones. I want gossip as well as witnesses who saw him come home and anyone else – you know the drill.'

'Gossip,' murmured Wpc Jones, setting out on her task. 'If I get the neighbours talking about that lot, I'll be here all night.'

'That lot' faced Markby across the kitchen table. He recognised them as the youngsters involved in the fracas in The Bunch of Grapes on New Year's Eve. That was the youth who had tried to pull Simon out of the general scrum but hadn't sounded very sympathetic towards him. He was a young man of about twenty-one or two, slim, pallid, nervous. On his knees he was nursing a baleful-eyed, streetwise tabby cat. The boy's hands smoothed the cat's short stiff fur rapidly and repeatedly.

'Okay, son,' said Markby mildly. 'Take it easy.'

He pulled out a chair and joined them at the table. The kitchen was evidently the main living area of the house. It was fairly clean, reasonably warm, not uncomfortable. The heat, he ascertained, came from a portable electric fire. It looked new. They had probably bought it themselves.

The two girls sat side by side and watched him warily. One had her mouth open. The other glowered at him with eyes encircled with black rings. That was the one who hit Tom with the tray. A real little scrapper. They were both wearing their best going-out-on-the-town garb: black leather jackets, black tee-shirts with gaudy legends emblazoned on them, lots of chains and studs and peculiar ironmongery fastened to their earlobes. He opened his mouth but before he could speak, the scrapper leaned forward. Her chains chinked and her rusty-black cocks-comb of hair seemed to quiver in indignation. She looked like a small but belligerent rooster.

'We none of us had anything to do with it! We found him, that's all. We're all sorry and that – but it's nothing to do with us!'

'I see,' said Markby politely. 'Perhaps I could have your names?'

She was called Tracy, the other girl Cheryl and the boy Micky.

'Your cat?' enquired Markby of Micky.

'No – well, in a way. There are two of them. I don't know where the other one is. They sort of hang around. Live here in a way.' He had a faint Belfast accent.

'Like we do!' said Tracy drily. 'They've not got anywhere better to go!' Markby had unwarily stretched out a hand towards the cat and she warned, 'He bites!'

'Oh, in that case I won't stroke him.'

'He doesn't bite us!' said Mick, defending his pet.

'He bit Simon,' said Cheryl, speaking at last.

'Did he now?' Markby murmured. 'Simon not like cats?'

'Didn't like anything, him. Didn't like people, didn't like animals. Funny sort of bloke.'

'But he campaigned for a stop to fox-hunting, didn't he? Perhaps he liked foxes.'

'Don't know nothing about that,' said Cheryl vaguely. 'He was always spouting about something. I never used to pay much attention. He got you down, always on about things being wrong.'

'It wasn't his idea, that fox-hunting business!' said Tracy scornfully. 'He never had no ideas of his own, Simon. It was all what other people had said. He'd hear someone say something and he'd take it up. He was always repeating what that Deanes said.'

Markby raised his eyebrows. 'Colin Deanes, the writer?'

'Yeah – well, I suppose it's writing. He don't write stories or stuff for TV. It's all dry stuff. Dunno who reads it. No one I shouldn't think. Simon thought Deanes was Batman.'

'Look,' the young Irishman broke into the conversation. 'We honestly don't know a thing. We were all out all evening.'

'Pardy didn't go with you?'

'No, well, he was banned, you see – from The Bunch of Grapes. After that punch-up on New Year's Eve. You must remember it. You were there. But we still went there. They didn't ban us.'

'Where did Simon drink, then?'

They looked at one another vaguely. 'Dunno,' they chorused.

'So who found him?'

'We all did,' said Tracy, the spokeswoman. 'We all come back together.'

'At what time?'

'Oh – ' she glanced at the other two for confirmation. 'It wasn't late, about twenty past eleven.' The others nodded.

'You came here directly from The Bunch of Grapes?'

'Yes – well, more or less. They call time at ten-thirty, but we all stopped on the way home and had a hamburger from the van that parks by the library in the evening.'

'Okay, go on. You came back here and . . . ?'

'Opened the door and fell over him,' said Tracy succinctly.

'Did you touch him?'

They paused and looked shiftily at one another. 'I knelt down and put my hand on his shoulder,' Micky said at last reluctantly. 'I didn't move him. I sort of touched his face . . .' He began to look agitated and pearls of sweat broke out around his mouth. 'My fingers felt all sticky, I knew it was blood . . . I was scared. I sort of jumped back. Then I tried again – to find a pulse. I got hold of his wrist. I nearly threw up.'

'That was courageous of you,' said Markby, meaning it. 'To try again. But you are quite sure you didn't move him, are you?'

'Move him? No! It was all I could bring myself to do to touch him at all!' Micky paused. 'I wanted to be sure because – ' he broke off and looked down at the animal on his knees. His fingers gripped at the loose fold of skin on the back of the cat's neck.

'Because? It's all right, just say what's in your mind,' Markby encouraged.

'I thought – if he was alive but dying – I thought perhaps one of us ought to go for a priest.' The words came out barely audibly. He did not look up. The two girls stared at him.

'What for?' asked Tracy.

'I just thought it,' Micky said unhappily.

'All right,' Markby interrupted gently. 'But then you decided it was too late for that?'

'Yes. I told the girls not to touch him. I guessed he was dead, after all. Trace went out and phoned the police.'

'Where from? Here?'

'No, we haven't got a phone. But there's a public one just round the corner.'

The time of the police call would be logged, the hamburger-seller might remember them, they were probably regular customers, the landlord of The Bunch of Grapes likewise. It would not be difficult to make out a timetable for their movements. That made a nice change. Usually it was more complicated. From outside in the hall came the rattle of metal. The photographer was setting up his lighting. A new voice murmured, the police surgeon had arrived.

'You didn't like him much?'

'That doesn't mean we pushed him down the stairs nor nothing!' snapped Tracy.

'I didn't say you did. I just gained the impression you didn't like him.'

'He was nutty,' said Cheryl suddenly. 'Round the bend, he was. And that posh talk got up my nose. He was a fake, that's what he was.'

Markby stared at her in some surprise, as did her two friends. Not only was it a long speech by her standards but it was surprisingly perceptive.

'Why a fake, Cheryl?' Markby asked her.

'I told you, that posh voice. And he'd been to one of them posh schools. But living here with us and dressing like he did – like he was one of us, but he wasn't. It was just all pretending with him. That's why that Deanes fussed over him. Because he was one of them, not one of us.'

Oh dear, thought Markby ruefully, poor Colin Deanes. So the people he'd most like to help see him as an interfering middle-class do-gooder whose first loyalty is to his own class. Poor Deanes.

'There's no light bulb in the hall,' he said. 'Has it been missing long?'

They stared at one another again. 'It was all right yesterday,'

Micky said. 'I put a new one in last week sometime. The light bulbs are always going in this place. It's the wiring.'

'But they usually last longer than a week?'

'Oh, yes, longer than that. And there was one there, definitely.'

At last . . . thought Markby and the dull anger inside him was replaced by a sense of satisfaction. At long last . . . he's made a mistake. He should have replaced that bulb before he left. He hoped we'd fancy Simon tripped on that ripped stair carpet, just a forseeable accident. Accident, be blowed. Someone had pushed Pardy. And now that someone was starting to make careless mistakes. Just give him time . . . and he'd have him, thought Markby grimly.

'Now think,' he said to them. 'When you came home, who went up to the front door first to open it?'

'I did,' said Cheryl after a pause.

'You're sure?'

'No, it wasn't you,' said Tracy briskly. 'It was Mick.'

'No, it was me. Mick stopped to call Boots.'

'Boots?' asked Markby.

'Him!' said Cheryl, pointing at the cat. 'Micky stopped to call him and I opened the door, honest, Trace, I did!'

'Now, don't quarrel over it!' said Markby hastily. 'What do you think, Mick?'

'I think one of the girls must have opened it,' said Micky cautiously. 'I picked up Boots, I had him in my arms, and I was looking round for the other cat, but I couldn't see him.'

'He couldn't have been shut up in the empty house, the other cat?' Markby asked quickly. It was possible that, after all, Simon had fallen over the animal . . . although that didn't explain the missing light bulb.

'No, he isn't – wasn't. He wanders off for days. We think he travels miles because, when he comes home, he's all dusty and looks as though he's been in fights.'

King of the local tomcats, thought Markby with a moment's amusement. Defending his perimeters! 'So you were carrying Boots when you walked into the hall?'

'Yes – just at first. Then Tracy or Cheryl, one of them, sort of screeched and stumbled. One of them shouted out it was Simon, on the floor. So I dropped Boots and came in to look.'

'All right, so then, Cheryl . . . was the front door locked? Did you need to use your key?'

'Yes.'

'You're sure?'

'Yes, course I am.'

Markby looked slowly round the kitchen. There was a back door, that didn't look very secure, and a window – He got up, walked over to the window and bent down to peer at it. 'Any of you touch this window since coming home?'

'No,' they answered in unison.

'It isn't properly shut, is that normal?'

'Yes . . . we leave it that way,' said Mick. 'In case anyone forgets the key. I mean, no one is going to break in here, are they?'

Aren't they? thought Markby. 'What's behind here? Out the back here, I mean. A garden?'

'Yes, well, not much of one. None of us does any gardening. It's just mud.'

Mud, better and better. Footprints, with luck. 'Does it run down to another garden, or what?'

'No,' Micky said. 'It runs down to a back alley. All the gardens in this street do, on this side.'

That's the way he came and went, then! thought Markby. Even better still. It often went like this. You messed around getting nowhere with nothing but your instinct to guide you, and then your luck changed. 'I don't want anyone to touch this window or the back door or go out in the back garden, all right?'

'All right,' they said obediently.

Markby found himself suddenly liking them all. They were actually quite nice kids. Pity about the chains and the metal studs, but they'd grow out of that. He found the way they clung together rather touching. Cut off from their own families, they'd formed a family grouping of their own, setting up in this disastrous dwelling, adopting the two stray cats, going off together on their evenings out. And into this milieu had come Simon, the outsider, the interloper, the unaccepted.

'How did Simon come to be living here?' he asked.

'Mick met him in a pub,' Tracy said.

'We needed a fourth,' Mick explained nervously. 'He was looking for a place to live. He always paid up his share of the rent all right. We don't know anything about him. He never said anything – about himself, you know.'

'Do you know where he lived before this?'

Micky shook his head.

'Not round here!' Tracy said suddenly in her aggressive way. 'We'd have seen him before. He just turned up, like Micky said, one evening in The Bunch of Grapes.'

'Fair enough,' Markby smiled at them. 'You'll have to sign statements later, but it can wait a few minutes. Make yourselves a cup of tea, why don't you – but don't touch that window frame!'

He went outside and found the surgeon repacking his bag. 'Hullo, Alan,' said the surgeon morosely. 'In the absence of a post mortem, I'd say cracked skull and broken neck, either of which would have killed him. Mind if I go home now? I'll get you a proper report in the morning when I've had a chance to take a good look at him.'

'Fine, thanks for your help.'

The surgeon departed. Markby gave orders for the kitchen window and door to be fingerprinted. The ambulance had arrived at some point whilst he had been talking in the kitchen and waited outside, lights flashing. Pearce came down the rickety staircase, very cautiously.

'Hunt's up!' said Markby to him quite cheerfully. 'Suspicious circumstances, all right! What did you find?'

'One or two things which will interest you, sir.' Pearce led the way upstairs. All the bedroom lights were on now and the landing reasonably lit. 'First of all,' Pearce pointed down at the newel post at the head of the stairs. 'Fibres. Some kind of cloth caught on there. Might just be from their clothes, of course. On the other hand, the damage to the wood looks new.'

Markby stooped and peered. A few rough woollen threads were snagged on a splinter of wood in the post. As Pearce had said, the wood behind the splinter was pale and clean. It was recent. 'Take good care of these. Get them down to forensic. Have them check them against all their clothes, including Pardy's. Pardy had a long overcoat – but these are the wrong colour, to my eye. But check just the same. What else did you find?'

Pearce grinned. 'You'll like this, sir.' He stood back and gestured towards the interior of Pardy's room with a flourish.

Markby walked in with a grimace of distaste. What a mess. 'Hullo,' he said. He walked over to the table, covered with Simon's 'work'. Newspapers, scissors, glue . . . scraps of chopped up print . . . cheap paper and envelopes.

'It was him, all right,' said Pearce. 'Writing those letters.'

'Looks very like it, doesn't it? We'll check that notepaper

against Tom Fearon's letter and the one the Master got. And the type of newsprint – the glue, too.' Markby's eye ran over the untidy room. 'Search this glory-hole and carefully.'

He made his way back down the staircase and stopped on the bottom step to allow Pardy's sheeted body to be carried out on a stretcher. One accident too many. Now he knew he was looking for a murderer. And one who was getting sloppy in his methods, jumpy – it was all snowballing beyond him. Panic was setting in. Markby stared down at the dark stain on the hall floor. But his quarry was getting used to killing. If they didn't find him, he'd kill again.

It was drizzling with rain later that morning when Meredith arrived for the inquest on Harriet Needham. She parked her car in the forecourt of the building and got out into the fine mist of water which worked its insidious dampness into hair and clothing with ruthless efficiency. She had put on a lined raincoat for warmth and because the anorak hardly seemed respectful enough for the proceedings – but the cold damp weather made nothing of the garment and she shivered.

Something seemed to have gone wrong with the heating in the room where the inquest was to be held. The radiators were barely warm. As people arrived they huddled together with pinched faces and grumbled about the cold and rain. Behind all their complaints could be read, in their eyes, their apprehension at the proceedings about to start.

Frances Needham-Burrell, splendid entirely in black with her corn-blonde hair swept up into a pleat, said fiercely, 'If that coroner tries to fob me off with some damnfool verdict of misadventure, he'll soon find out that it won't do!'

Jack Pringle had arrived, lugubrious in his duffel coat, and Tom Fearon, unnaturally smartened up and respectable in a dark-blue short length overcoat and carrying in his hand the sort of trilby hat seen on racecourses. He greeted them morosely and turned his back on them all.

'Tom in a mood,' said Pringle. He blew his nose on a large blue-check handkerchief. 'I can't do with the damp weather. It plays havoc with my sinuses.'

'You're a doctor,' said Fran unsympathetically.

'I still can't help my sinuses.'

Mrs Brissett and Fred arrived looking nervous. Fred's hair had been slicked down and he'd cut himself shaving. Mrs Brissett had exchanged the bobble hat for a jersey turban and her zipped boots for shiny black court shoes on which she teetered uncertainly and which were obviously excruciatingly uncomfortable.

Colonel Stanley appeared accompanied by his wife, he in what was obviously his funeral suit and she utterly immovable in tweeds, brogues and thick stockings and brandishing an umbrella.

'I hope this doesn't drag on too long,' she said. 'We've left both the boys in the back of the car. They get bored and chew things.'

Pringle looked mildly alarmed and the Master explained. 'The dogs . . .'

'Oh,' said Pringle, blowing his nose again.

'Got a cold, Jack?' asked Charlotte. 'Try a tot of whisky in your tea. I don't believe in medicines for colds.'

Meredith was looking round for Markby but so far he had not put in an appearance. But someone else had, much to her surprise. Rupert Green had slipped into the room behind the last arrivals and stood alone at the back in a camel overcoat, his pigskin-gloved hands gripping the back of a chair. He met Meredith's eye and gave her a cool nod of acknowledgement. Meredith returned him a dowager's bow. The two of them would be sending their seconds round to discuss weapons next, she thought wryly, and then wondered where Alan had got to.

At that moment he arrived, hastening through the door looking rather dishevelled and as though he had been up all night. He muttered, 'Good morning, good morning . . .' at them all and disappeared through another door in the side of the hall. Voices could be heard in a further corridor, rising and falling.

A tingle ran up Meredith's spine. Something's gone wrong, she thought. Something's happened . . . something pretty big and important.

In the room where they waited the atmosphere had subtly changed. Fran muttered, 'What's going on? They're late starting!'

'Might as well sit down, Charlotte,' said the Master. 'Going to be here for a bit, I fancy.'

'Oh dear I hope the boys don't chew the armrest again.'

'So do I, ruddy brutes.'

'The leather makes them sick. You should have put down newspaper, Bungy.'

'Oh dash it,' said the Master. 'I've just remembered, I've left my *Times* on the front seat.'

There was a bustle at the front of the room. The coroner had arrived accompanied by a pale man in a shiny dark suit and Markby trying ineffectually to smooth his hair and generally tidy up his appearance. Everyone sat down hurriedly. The inquest was opened with the usual preamble and Meredith tensed, waiting to hear the first witness called.

It was at that moment that she realised Pardy wasn't there. But surely, he was the principal person to give evidence? She looked round but only caught Rupert Green's eye. He gave her a steely look.

The coroner leaned forward. 'Detective Chief Inspector Markby, I believe you have a request to make of this court?'

'Yes, sir . . .' Markby got up. 'I'd like to ask for an adjournment.' A sigh ran round the courtroom followed by utter stillness.

'On what grounds?'

'There has been a sudden death overnight, in suspicious circumstances, of someone who would have been a main participant in the proceedings today. There may be a link with the death of Miss Needham. The police are conducting enquiries and it's possible criminal proceedings will result.'

'Very well,' the coroner said. 'In view of the likelihood of criminal proceedings at a later date, this inquest is adjourned for the time being to allow the police to complete their enquiries. It will be reconvened at a future time and persons concerned will be informed.'

Small-scale chaos broke out as soon as the coroner had retired and Markby found himself mobbed.

'Where's Pardy?' Meredith demanded. 'What's happened to him?'

'What do you mean, he's dead?' Fran was not beating about the bush. 'Who killed him?'

'I can't discuss it, I'm sorry.' He tried to extricate himself from the crowd about him.

'You've got to discuss it with me, I'm Harriet's nearest relative!' Fran insisted.

'I'll call round at The Crossed Keys, but not today probably. I'm very busy today. I'll call tomorrow.' Markby pushed a way forcibly through for himself. Catching Meredith's eye he opened his mouth, closed it again and gave her a meaningful look which probably meant he would telephone later, she thought – or hoped? She watched him disappear through the main door.

Somehow they all squeezed out behind him in a disorganised hubbub. Green walked quickly away into the rain. Slowly the others dispersed, having asked each other fruitlessly several times what had happened and speculated wildly on the cause of the delay.

Meredith walked slowly to her car. In the estate car parked behind her, Charlotte's boys barked wildly as they saw people come out of the building. The interior of the estate car was scattered with confetti of shredded newspaper. The boys had happily dismembered the Master's *Times*. She reached her own car, put the key in the lock and then suddenly realised that Pringle's car was parked alongside hers and the doctor sat in the driving seat motionless, his hands resting on the wheel, staring fixedly down at the dashboard.

Meredith, alarmed, stooped down and tapped on the window. 'Dr Pringle? Are you all right?'

Pringle started and looked up at her. The glazed look faded from his face and he wound the window down. 'Yes – sorry, Miss Mitchell. I was just thinking . . .' He fell silent again.

'You are sure you're all right?' she asked, unconvinced.

'Yes . . . yes. It's just that I was wound up to give evidence – about Harriet . . . and it wasn't necessary. I'm suffering a little from the reaction.' He glanced at her almost timidly. 'I was rather dreading it, to tell you the truth. I was – I was very fond of her, you know.'

'I didn't know,' Meredith confessed. 'But I can understand it. I didn't know her for very long, but I liked her very much.'

'I loved her,' Pringle said simply. 'I wanted to marry her. Just a foolish dream on my part. I mean, I had nothing to offer. I did ask her once – but she turned me down. Only to be expected. She was quite right, of course. Still, it rocked me at the time. I'd been a hunt subscriber but I gave up after that, sold my horse and all the rest of it. I just couldn't bear to be where she was, in company, hunt balls, point to points, that sort of thing. Seeing her with others . . . I'm sorry, Miss Mitchell, I'm rambling.' He smiled in a strained way.

'That's all right, Dr Pringle. I am sorry, really.' Meredith looked at him in helpless despair. There was nothing she could say which would make any difference. Pringle had loved and lost. There was no lonelier situation in the world. She put out her hand and touched the rain-damp shoulder of his duffel coat. 'I am truly very sorry.'

The rain eased as she drove home and she switched off the

windscreen wipers as she turned off the main road on to the B road. Glancing up into the driving mirror immediately afterwards, Meredith saw another car turn into the B road behind her, the easily recognisable Mercedes of Tom Fearon. She pulled over so that he could overtake her but he didn't, he seemed content to follow her at a steady distance. Perhaps, she thought, he's going to stop at Fenniwick's garge for fuel. But at the garage he turned off down the lane to Pook's Common behind her. Meredith drew up outside Rose Cottage and got out. The Mercedes slid past and she was not surprised to see it stop a few yards down and Tom get out and walk back towards her. She waited for him.

'Do you know anything about all that – back there?' he asked her without any preamble, jerking his head in the general direction of Bamford.

'No, should I?' she asked, nettled.

'You're Alan's girlfriend, aren't you?'

'Friend, not girlfriend – ' She saw the ironic expression in Fearon's dark eyes and her annoyance increased. 'He doesn't discuss his work with me and, in any case, I haven't seen him to talk to properly since the day before yesterday.'

No, I haven't, thought Meredith crossly. We're not exactly talking at the moment – but that was none of Tom Fearon's business.

Fearon muttered and pushed his hands into the pockets of his blue overcoat. 'If someone has got Pardy, I'm not surprised, but it wasn't me. I suppose the adjournment means Alan will be going round asking us all where we were every minute of every blasted day and night!' He stared at Meredith truculently. 'I was waiting to hear what they were all going to say about Harriet – all those people back there who reckoned they knew her!' he said suddenly.

'Reckoned?' Meredith raised her eyebrows. 'You think they didn't know her really, then?

'No!' said Fearon in some disgust. 'Look, I saw her every day more or less for five years. I knew Harriet. She came over as full of herself, confident, independent, difficult – but it wasn't confidence, it was defensiveness.'

'It did seem to me,' Meredith said slowly, 'that she might have been shy, underneath it all.'

'Did it now?' That gained her a shrewd look from Fearon. 'You were probably nearer the mark than most, then. Harriet always had to prove something -- not to others, although I did think that at first, but to herself.'

'What makes you say that?' Meredith supposed she could invite Fearon in for a cup of coffee but prudence warned that he might not prove so easy to get rid of afterwards. It had stopped raining. They could talk as well out here.

'The way she acted. When she first came here she turned up at the stables one morning enquiring about livery fees. She wanted to buy a horse and needed nearby stabling. We sorted that one out and she asked me if I knew of a likely animal for sale. She wanted a lightweight hunter. I didn't but I told her of a couple of stock sales coming up. I offered to go with her to them if she wasn't sure about bidding. She said she could manage – told me so pretty sharp, actually. So I thought, right, you get on with it then, and don't grumble to me if you bring back some sway-backed, knock-kneed brute with one blind eye and a mean disposition! But she came back with Blazer, nice sound horse, good temperament – bit out of condition from neglect but nothing which couldn't be remedied with feeding and general care. So I realised she knew a good horse when she saw one.'

Meredith repressed a smile. Presumably one went up or down in Fearon's estimation according to whether one knew a good horse or not.

'But she had to do it herself, you see? And it was the same with everything – take that fancy cooking. Why couldn't she turn out meat and two veg like any other woman? Prefer it myself, personally. I don't like these sauces – you can't see what's underneath. I like my food recognisable. No, Harriet had to be the best cook around. She hated things going wrong. She hated making a mistake. So I reckoned that at some time in her life she'd made a beauty – and she was still trying to live it down.' Tom shrugged. 'She needed someone to look after her, I reckon.'

'Not you, I shouldn't think!' said Meredith, she realised very rudely. However, Tom would probably claim to appreciate plain speaking so he might as well hear some.

'I didn't suggest me!' Fearon growled. 'Although what's wrong with me? Got mud on my boots, I suppose? Smell of horses, do I? Pardon me!'

'That's not what I meant.'

'Yes, you did. Well, it's mutual, sweetheart – you're the sort of woman I find aggravating without any compensatory virtues.

Harriet could drive a man barmy – but she made up for it in other ways!'

'You make me sick!' said Meredith furiously. 'All of you! You mean she was beddable! That's all that matters to you, isn't it?'

'Try it – before you dismiss it!' said Fearon. A mocking gleam showed in his eyes. 'You know where to find me.' He turned and walked back to his Mercedes.

Meredith stormed indoors. Her eye lighting on the telephone, she prayed, 'Don't call me now, Alan, please! I'll say a dozen things I'll regret afterwards!' Mercifully the phone stayed silent. After a while, as questions about Pardy grew in her mind, that seemed less of a blessing.

But Markby had other concerns. When he returned to the police station he found Pearce hovering in the corridor waiting for him.

'Mrs Turner is here, sir. Wanting to see you. She's Pardy's mother. Pardy's father was her first husband. Wpc Jones is with her at the moment.'

'That was quick!' Markby exclaimed. 'How did she hear about it so soon?'

'I found a letter from her amongst Pardy's effects and I rang up the local nick to send someone round to see her,' Pearce said.

Markby nodded. 'Good work. What's she like?'

'Nice woman – not what I'd have expected somehow.'

Markby opened the door of his office. Wpc Jones sat talking with a small, pale, neatly dressed woman in her forties. A half-drunk cup of tea was on the desk. Wpc Jones got up as he came in and Markby nodded his acknowledgement and dismissal. He pulled up a chair and sat down by Mrs Turner who gazed at him with bewildered and frightened eyes, red-rimmed from crying.

'I'm very sorry, Mrs Turner,' he said. 'A terrible shock to you.'

'Reg – my husband – is in Scotland,' she whispered. She cleared her throat and made an effort to speak more loudly. 'Otherwise he would have come too. I didn't have time to contact him – he's on a business trip and it's difficult during the day. So I came down myself by train. I didn't want to drive – I was too upset, my concentration all over the place, and we live near the station. My neighbour kindly telephoned British Rail Information and they said there was a good connection.' She fidgeted with the handbag resting on her lap. Her fingers must have become thinner over the years because her engagement solitaire and wedding ring were both loose. 'I'm a supply teacher. Luckily there's no school requiring me at the moment so I could come at once without having to make arrangements, you see.'

'Yes, I see. Were you – forgive my asking – were you in close contact with your son?'

She shook her head miserably. 'No, he was always a problem. But it wasn't entirely his fault.' She added the last words quickly and defensively, darting a nervous glance at him. 'You see his father died when he was three and I had to manage on my own. He was a very withdrawn child. I think because I had to leave him at day nursery and with minders while I went out to work. Some children become independent that way, but some just close up. Simon was one of those. Later, when he went to proper school, he never really had any friends. It used to be quite awkward when his birthday came round. I'd give a little party but it was a job to know which children to invite. I finished up inviting the neighbourhood children – but even at his own party, he never seemed to play with them.'

She fell silent and reached for her cup of tea, her hand shaking. Markby waited patiently. But the story already had a familiar ring to it.

'I worried about him and I thought that perhaps he needed a male influence in his life. A boy being brought up by a mother alone, perhaps it wasn't the best thing, and a different environment might suit him better. So I sent him to boarding school. It cost a lot of money but because of my circumstances – I should have explained I was an army widow. My husband was killed as a result of an accident on Nato manoeuvres in Germany. The school gave Simon a bursary which helped quite a bit and I was working fulltime once he'd gone there so I was earning more money. The school was not very far away. He could come home at weekends if he wanted to.

'I thought it might bring him out. I was taking a gamble really, I suppose. With him away at school, I had more free time myself and I was able to go out a little, join a few local societies. That's how I met Reg, my second husband. He was a widower and a fellow member of the local historical society. We got along well, had a lot of common interests. We got married.'

'How old was Simon then?'

'Oh, fourteen – quite old enough to understand, I thought. And Reg took a real interest in him, tried to be a father – but Simon just rejected all his efforts.'

Not surprisingly, thought Markby. The boy had never had a father-figure in his life and being suddenly presented with one at fourteen was bound to go down badly.

'He just dropped out of school altogether at sixteen – failed all his exams. Not because he wasn't bright – but he – well, I have to say, I think he failed them all on purpose. Out of spite – to punish us. It sounds awful . . .' her voice trailed away, 'I think he hated us.'

'He was probably going through a phase,' Markby said encouragingly. 'Lots of youngsters rebel against their parents.'

'Yes – ' she brightened. 'Yes, they do, I know. Well, Simon left school and he ran off down to London. Luckily we were able to find him and bring him home. He was still under age. The police in London said we were very fortunate. So many of the youngsters who run off down there just disappear and the parents can't find them. Simon stayed home for about six months after that and then ran off again. That time we couldn't trace him.

'Then, when he was eighteen, he just turned up again one day. I think he had been sleeping rough and he was broke and not feeling very well . . . We took him back, of course. We hoped . . .' She drew a deep breath. 'It didn't work out. He wouldn't get a job, just hung about the house. Reg started grumbling at him. There was a terrible row and Simon just packed up his things and walked out. After that he lived here and there in all kinds of places. Sometimes he'd come and see me – generally when he wanted money.' She gave Markby a very direct look. 'I do realise why he came. I used to tell Reg when he'd been to see me – but I never told Reg I gave Simon money. Reg wouldn't have understood.'

'I see,' Markby said. He had heard similar tales a hundred times before but they remained as heart-breaking as ever.

'I used to worry,' Mrs Turner said, 'about the kind of company Simon kept.'

'If it's any consolation, Mrs Turner, the three young people he was living with here in Bamford are all quite nice youngsters – if rather oddly dressed and so on. I don't think there's any harm in them.'

'It's nice to know that . . .' she said gratefully. 'When – when can we have the body? When can we bury Simon?'

'Not yet, I'm afraid. I hope fairly soon. There will be an inquest.'

'Yes – of course. It's odd, one worries about so many things.

210

I used to worry about drugs. I was afraid Simon would take to using drugs. I never thought – your sergeant said Simon's death was suspicious. That means murder, doesn't it? I mean, one just never thinks about murder, does one?'

Markby shifted awkwardly on his chair. 'In my line of work, Mrs Turner, I'm afraid we often do.'

'Yes, of course. What I can't understand is, why anyone should want to kill Simon. I know he was difficult – but he wasn't a threat to anyone and I don't see how he could have done something to make anyone that angry with him, do you?'

'I don't know yet, Mrs Turner. But I am trying to find out,' he told her.

When she had left, Markby sat silent at his desk for a while, doodling daisy plants in pots on a scrap of notepaper. At the end of his third row of daisy plants, the telephone at his elbow rang. It was the pathologist.

'Hullo, Alan – I've finished with your young victim and I'm sending over a report as soon as I can get someone to type it up, but I thought you might like to know straight away that there's a contusion behind the right ear.'

'Not from the fall?' Markby asked sharply. He dropped the biro, leaving the last daisy without a pot to stand in.

'It's an outside chance, but my own opinion is that it's unlikely. From the angle and nature of the wound I think that we have here your old pal and mine, the Blunt Instrument.'

'Haven't found one yet.' Dash it, have to go back to Jubilee Road and search the garden and that back alley again.

'As I read it,' the voice in his ear continued, 'someone right-handed came up behind him and struck him behind the ear as he stood with his back to his attacker. He would have been temporarily stunned and fallen down the staircase like a sack of potatoes.'

Markby replaced the receiver. Words come back to haunt us. Simon's words came back to haunt the man whose task it was to find his killer. 'She went down like a sack of spuds.'

'Who says,' murmured Markby aloud, 'that Fate is blind?'

Twelve

The dustcart hove into view at the corner of Jubilee Road late that same Friday morning, moving slowly and running well behind schedule. It was always the same after a major public holiday, and Christmas and New Year were by far the worst. Regular collections of household rubbish had been interrupted, people had been supplied with black plastic sacks to take the resulting overflow and the amount to be collected from each house was doubled.

They began on Jubilee Road as they began on every road. Two dustmen in their yellow council overalls moved quickly and efficiently down, one on either side of the street, collecting up the plastic sacks and other receptacles and piling them in neat heaps at intervals. Then the lorry began its stately progress along and as it reached each heap, a yellow-overalled man picked up the sacks and boxes and threw them into the back where a set of metal teeth dragged them into the dustcart's interior.

There was a certain poignancy to this post-festive rubbish. Gaily coloured wrapping paper, besprinkled with reindeer and Father Christmas figures, protruded in crushed wads from plastic sacks which had split or been torn open by cats. Here was an empty 'sparkling wine' bottle which had heralded the birth of another year sticking up amongst the gnawed remains of a turkey, a string of Christmas tree lights which had failed to work, a toy expensive but already broken beyond repair.

Between the sodden tea-bags and potato peelings could be glimpsed fragments of Christmas cards depicting people plodding to church through snowdrifts, although it was years since Bamford had had a White Christmas. There wasn't much church-going from Jubilee Road, either.

Before number forty-three the dustman gathering up the bags stopped and found himself exchanging appraising looks with a uniformed police constable barring the entrance. A tabby tomcat was prowling around the torn plastic bag of the rubbish put out

213

by next door's gate but there was no bag in the gateway of forty-three.

'What they done, then?' enquired the dustman of the policeman with a jerk of his head towards forty-three.

'Never you mind,' said the constable.

'Where's their bag? If they don't put it out I can't take it. I haven't got time to go knocking on the door and asking for it. We're not supposed to. Council policy. Wastes time.'

'You can't have it,' said the constable.

This gave the dustman something to think about. 'Why not? Got the crown jewels hidden in it?'

'It's being examined . . .' said the constable loftily. 'Your mate is waiting for you in the lorry.'

'All right,' said the dustman, reluctantly moving towards next door's sack. 'Git out of it!' He aimed a kick at the tabby tomcat which dodged him and jumped over the wall carrying a mangled piece of chicken carcass dragged from the bag. 'Them cats,' said the dustman in disgust. 'They tear them bags open every week.' He collected the plastic sack and hurled it into the back of the lorry. Then he came back to the constable. 'What you looking for?'

The constable was a bright young man and he wanted to transfer to CID. He could have told the dustman to move along but an inner prompting stopped him. 'Something heavy, hard . . . a weapon,' he said in neutral tones.

'Go on . . .' The dustman was fascinated. 'Someone get murdered?'

'Might have been,' said the constable.

There was a shrill whistle and an unintelligible cry from the lorry as it moved on.

'All right!' bellowed the dustman and followed it.

In the back garden of number forty-three Sergeant Pearce had earlier arrived hot-foot from the station, dispatched by his superior as soon as the pathologist's phone call had terminated. 'Find it!' Markby had ordered him crisply. Pearce had rushed over to Jubilee Road with two extra constables and proceeded to comb the back garden and alley. Now he was helping an unhappy constable to finish sorting through the last contents of forty-three's bag of rubbish. 'Don't half smell, dunnit?' mumbled the constable. 'Yah – what's that?'

'Rice pudding . . .' said Pearce after inspecting the hand the constable held out. 'Tinned sort. I like that myself.'

The constable muttered and wiped his hand on a rag. They shook out the last of the contents. Beer and Coca-Cola cans rolled away in all directions. Cigarette ends fell on to the muddy paving stones of what had once been a patio and stuck there. Baked-bean tins oozed red gore.

'Nothing!' said Pearce in disgust. 'Nothing he could have been hit on the head with!'

'We've been over the garden, not that there's much of it,' said the constable obstinately. 'There's nothing here. We went all through those overgrown flowerbeds. And that back alley is clean and all.'

A footstep was heard and they both looked up. 'Oh, hullo, sir . . .' said Pearce, glancing at his wristwatch. It was almost one. 'No luck, I'm afraid. Not a thing. We've searched in the garden, the back alley there and this was the dustbin bag. We rescued that from collection. Bin day today.'

'You mean,' Markby said slowly. 'All the other bags on this side of the street have been collected – taken away?'

An uneasy silence fell. 'Um, yessir,' said Pearce, turning scarlet.

'The weapon could,' Markby said with increasing ire, 'have been thrown into any of them! All the gardens have gates into the back alley! He needn't have thrown it away in this one! In fact, it's far more likely he chucked it in another, if he chucked it anywhere!'

'Sorry, sir,' said the miserable Pearce. 'I should have thought of that.'

Markby growled and walked back through the house and out of the front door to join the constable on guard.

'Dustcart?' he snapped.

'Just been past, sir!'

Markby swore and looked disconsolately along the pavement. It was bare of plastic sacks, but a torn Christmas card, a chicken bone and a piece of tinsel ribbon marked where a rubbish bag had stood next door. Similar odd bits of debris appeared at intervals down the pavement.

'Cats tore the bag open before the lorry came,' said the constable in explanation. He hoped he wasn't going to get the blame for this.

'Gone,' said Markby. 'If it was in any of them. Gone to join the rest of the rubbish on the municipal tip. Damn, damn, damn . . . ! He strode away towards his parked car. Pearce wasn't normally incompetent, but this morning he'd made a bad mistake – partly because of the time factor. They hadn't known that Pardy was struck over the head until Markby's return from the adjourned inquest. If Pearce could have got to Jubilee Road an hour earlier . . . It was no good, Markby was the one who'd have to take responsibility.

A yellow-overalled figure had appeared at the corner of the street and was walking quickly down it towards them.

'Here, mate!' the dustman hailed the constable, 'You know you said you was looking for something like a weapon . . .'

'Yes?' the constable cast a nervous eye towards the chief inspector. If the old man heard, he'd tear him off a strip for chatting about the search to an outsider.

'Well, down at the corner house another of the bags was torn open,' said the dustman, 'and when I picked it up, this fell out . . . I'd told my mates what you'd said and Baz, that's the driver, said we ought to hand it over to you, just in case.' He held out a small woodwork hammer.

'Mind how you handle that!' exclaimed the constable. 'Mr Markby, sir, wait a minute!'

Friday evening it began to drizzle with rain again and Meredith turned up the gas fire and switched on the television. From time to time she sneaked a look at the telephone but it refused to ring and as a matter of principle, she wasn't going to be the one to pick it up. She was not normally a great television-watcher on the grounds that she found it stopped her thinking. But just now to stop thinking seemed highly desirable. She turned on the set in the corner of Rose Cottage's living room and, sitting with her feet tucked up under her on the sofa, became hypnotised by the succession of flickering coloured images and the curiously adenoidal dubbed voices of the Channel Four screening, an incomprehensibly surreal Spanish film. If the plot seemed disjointed and punctuated by dream sequences, it hardly mattered. Most of it drifted by Meredith's ear unabsorbed.

Here she was, sitting in someone else's home on someone else's sofa watching someone else's television set. All this because in her mid-thirties she didn't own a thing of her own except an ageing car and a couple of suitcases of clothing. True, she had got a box of household utensils and bed linen somewhere between Eastern Europe and the Channel ports which, when it finally arrived, she wouldn't open because here she had plenty of household items ready supplied, and when she did eventually open it she'd wonder why on earth she ever bothered to ship all that stuff home. But she did know why she bothered. She shipped it home to prove that she did have a home. She carried it about like a snail or tortoise on her back. Shipping a crate home, even full of junk, was making a statement that her life had substance. Going through the absurd ritual of insuring it even more so. But if it all fell off the lorry somewhere along the Autobahn it wouldn't have mattered a jot.

But it was what she'd wanted, wasn't it? When she first left England (fled England might be a better way of describing it), she'd said she didn't want ties. She didn't want memories. She wanted to be able to pick up a suitcase and walk away from anything which ruffled the surface of her own little pond.

Well, she'd learnt two things. One is that you never walk away from your memories. The other is that the walking away slowly becomes a marathon solo affair. No roots, no ties stops being fun and independent. No roots, no ties starts to get a bore. But, like anyone who has travelled a long way along one road, you grew afraid of turning back and looking for another road, another direction.

But all this introspection was thoroughly unhealthy. The screen was transmitting the advertising break. Meredith uncurled and went to peer out of the window of Rose Cottage into the murk. A yellow light across the lane and down to the right indicated that someone had returned to live in the cottage with the wishing well. The Fenniwicks, presumably. At least she wasn't now entirely alone in Pook's Common. The gleam of yellow was comforting. Of course there was Tom, down at the stables. She wondered whether tomorrow, Saturday, the Haynes would return for their usual weekend. Poor Lucy.

Meredith glanced at her watch. Getting late. But it was a dirty night and she was loath to go up to bed. She watched the film to its mystifying end, and the programme which followed, made some cocoa and sat up until the early hours watching, and thoroughly enjoying, an elderly horror film. By the time she went to bed at two the light in Fenniwick's cottage was extinguished. The rain was still coming down, harder now. Not a night to be out and about. A night for rolling yourself up in the duvet and trying not to wish that when you stretched out your foot, it made contact with another body.

The next morning the sun shone but Meredith got out of bed

feeling tired and irritable. Partly, she told herself, that was because Alan hadn't phoned, partly it was going to bed so late and watching too much television, partly not knowing what would happen now that the inquest had been adjourned. Besides which she had only this weekend left of her leave. On Monday would begin the daily haul as a commuter up to London and back. There was nothing to do in Pook's Common today. Meredith put on her anorak, went out, got into her car and switched on the ignition with some idea of driving to Bamford or even as far as Oxford.

The ignition coughed, spluttered and fell silent. Panic seized her. The car had to be running all right! On Monday she'd need it to get in to Bamford station! She tried again. Nothing at all. It was dead. Meredith got out and opened the bonnet, peering doubtfully into the engine. She was no mechanic but there was just a chance that some obvious disconnected wire or other visible mishap might spring to the eye. It didn't, but a probable explanation was moisture. The poor car had stood out all night in the teeming rain and resulting dampness had wreaked some havoc. Meredith shut down the bonnet, wiped her hands and sighed. There was, however, help at hand in the form of Fenniwick's garage up on the B road. She set off to walk there.

Joe Fenniwick was under a car. At least she supposed the feet sticking out belonged to him.

'Mr Fenniwick?'

'Oh, right you are..' said a muffled voice. He wriggled out and sat up, a small, thin-faced man with a gingery crest of spiky hair. 'Oh, ah . . .' he said, greeting her with a wave of a spanner. 'What's up, then? Want some petrol?'

'No, my car's broken down. The ignition. Either that or the battery is flat. It's down the road at Pook's Common, outside Rose Cottage.'

Mr Fenniwick scrambled to his feet. 'You're the lady then, what's taken Dr Russell's place? Pleased to meet you.' He extended an oily hand, thought better of it and withdrew it. 'My wife would have been over to welcome you, like, but we've been away for the holiday. At the wife's sister's. She hurt her leg, the wife's sister that is, so my wife she went to help out and me and the boy, we went too and celebrated our Christmas over there. The wife will be back tomorrow and the boy . . . but I had to come on home earlier because of the business.' Mr Fenniwick looked vaguely about him. 'Ignition, ah. I'll tell you what, 'tis more like the battery. Got no cover down there – car's out in the open, that right?'

'Yes, I'm afraid so.'

'Might be your wiring. Tell you what, I'll come down later with my breakdown truck and bring your car up here to have a look. I can't be fixing it down there, you see, because of being on my own here.'

'Yes, I quite understand, Mr Fenniwick, but I need the car on Monday first thing as I have to go into Bamford and catch the early London train.'

'I got a taxi service,' said Mr Fenniwick. 'So you're not desperate, as you might say. But like as not, I'll be able to fix it before then.' She thanked him and he said, 'You didn't have the chance to meet the lady opposite to you, did you? Her as had the accident?'

'Miss Needham? Yes, I did. It was a dreadful thing.'

'Ah . . . Pook's Common, you know,' said Mr Fenniwick. 'It's an unlucky place. All the old folk round here will tell you so. Some of them are surprised my wife and I want to live here. Still, touch wood,' Mr Fenniwick gravely tapped his own forehead, 'we've not come to grief yet!'

Meredith walked back to Rose Cottage. A little later Mr Fenniwick appeared driving a smart little breakdown truck and towed her car away, promising to see to it right away. Meredith was left marooned in Pook's Common with nothing to do. She looked across the lane towards Ivy Cottage. It was not surprising Harriet had spent her time down at the stables. There was precious little else to do here. Harriet – Fran – the keys – the books for the cottage hospital. But there was something she could do.

Meredith went indoors and collected the keys Fran had given her and crossed over to Ivy Cottage. She let herself in and closed the front door. The drawing-room door was open and she went in and surveyed the desolate scene with sinking heart. There was a strangely neglected air about Ivy Cottage now as if it knew its owner had quitted it for good. The furniture was dusty, no Mrs Brissett coming to polish it up any more. Fran had collected up all the photographs and put them in a cardboard box on the floor. Meredith stooped over it and picked up the topmost frame. Three little girls. Fran had changed quite a bit. She hadn't been a particularly pretty kid, rather scrawny, but my, she'd blossomed! Harriet with her red hair. And the other child . . . Caroline Henderson, the unlucky little heiress. Of the three little girls, two were now dead. Meredith shivered and put the photograph back.

Most of the books were in a glass-fronted bookcase. Meredith went in search of a box and found one upstairs in the bedroom. Fran had been busy up here. All the bed linen in the cottage had been packed in bags and tickets tied to the necks saying 'WVS'. She carried the box downstairs and began to stack the books carefully into it. As she did, she checked the titles to see if there were any she hadn't read. There was a copy of *Briony Rides at the Horse of the Year Show*. Meredith put it to one side, meaning to ask Fran if she might keep it. She picked out the next book to it and stood with it in her hand.

The cottage was quiet. Pook's Common was deserted. When she opened the book, the pages rustled and the noise seemed exaggerated in the stillness. Meredith sat down on the nearest chair and began to read, skipping pages here and there. The binding was stiff. No one else had read this book. She had to force the pages open against the rigidity of the spine and they smelled new in the way paper does the first time a spanking new book is opened. Meredith turned back to the beginning and read the publishing information, names of publisher and printer, date, copyright notice, ISBN . . .

Crack! It came from the kitchen. Meredith's heart skipped a beat and she froze, book in hand. 'Mrs Brissett?' she called. There was a faint gasp and a muffled exclamation from the direction of the kitchen. A moment's silence and then a creak and a scuff of a footstep. Whoever was in the kitchen, it was not Mrs Brissett but an intruder who had forced open the back door, not knowing Meredith was here. But he knew now. Meredith waited, watching the drawing-room door. Another step outside in the hallway. The door opened slowly.

'Good morning, Mr Deanes,' Meredith said, no longer really surprised, not now. 'I expect you've come for this.' And she held out the copy of *Revolutionary Youth* which she had been reading.

He was wearing his fur-trimmed parka today. He pushed up his spectacles on to the insignificant bridge of his nose and peered at her perplexed. 'Miss Mitchell? What are you doing here? I thought you'd gone to Bamford . . . your car isn't there!' He sounded slightly irritated, as if she had made the wrong move in some game.

'No, Mr Fenniwick is bringing it back some time today. Soon I hope.'

The sooner the better! she thought suddenly. She was alone here with him, with no one else to hear if she shouted – and Tom down at the stables . . . Harriet's telephone was outside in the hallway but Deanes still stood by the door.

Deanes was looking at the book in her hand. 'Yes . . . that's mine. I was worried that someone might throw it out . . . I came for it, as you say. I had to force the back door catch but I fully intended to fix it again before I left.' He held out his hand.

Meredith held tightly on to it. 'I'd like to read it, I've started . . . look. Would you mind if I hung on to it for a bit?'

'Yes, I would. I'm afraid you can't, I must have it back!' He began to sound agitated. His pale cheeks flushed.

'It's an advance copy, isn't it?' Meredith said. 'I tried to buy it in Bamford but they told me it wasn't due out yet. Harriet must have got this one from you.'

Deanes sat down on the chair by the hall door. His spectacle lenses gleamed and, as on a previous occasion out on the common, she couldn't make out his eyes.

'I can explain, Miss Mitchell.'

'I'm sure you can, Mr Deanes.'

He hesitated. Suddenly he leaned forward. 'I'm sure you'll understand, Miss Mitchell, you're a sensible woman. You were sympathetic when I spoke to you of my work. You understand how important my work is. Those young people depend on me! Whatever else happens, my work must go on! If you'll listen, you'll see that this whole thing has been a terrible – ' he broke off.

'Mistake?'

'No – just a piece of truly rotten bad luck. Everything that followed stemmed from that. It was all forced on me by that woman. Everything was going so well and then . . . she found out. She hounded me.' Deanes raised a hand and gestured at Ivy Cottage about them. 'She was a terrible woman!'

Joe Fenniwick knew she wanted the car urgently. He'd bring it back today but when? Soon, Mr Fenniwick, please! In the meantime, she had to keep him talking.

'Please tell me, Mr Deanes,' she urged.

He leaned forward and his gaze fell on the box of photographs in their frames. Something happened then, she was not sure what. He twitched. His manner changed. He no longer looked agitated and anxious to explain himself. He looked quite clear in his mind – although how that mind was working who knew –

and he looked angry. Very angry. He jumped up, seized the topmost photograph of the three little girls and brandished it under Meredith's nose.

'This!' he shouted. 'This is the cause of all the trouble! Three women who have ruined my life! Her!' He jabbed a finger at the picture of the young Harriet. 'The harpy! She persecuted me! This one . . .' The finger stabbed at Fran in turn. 'Just like her. I got rid of one and the other turns up! I should have expected that!'

'And the other child . . .' Meredith whispered.

Deanes' forefinger moved to rest on the likeness of Caroline Henderson. 'Oh, Caro,' he said sadly. 'Caroline, my wife.'

Alan Markby sat with Fran Needham-Burrell in the gloomy lounge of The Crossed Keys. A tray with coffee cups and pot stood on the low table between them. No one else was in the room. It was clean and tidy enough, but the furniture was dull in colour, the carpet worn, the potted plants dusty. That in particular annoyed Markby. In putting a duster round the furniture, it wouldn't have been that much of an extra effort to wipe off the leaves of the rubber plant next to him.

'Why are you scowling at that plant?' Fran asked. 'Would you like some more of this coffee?' Her hand hovered above the pot.

'No, thank you.'

'Don't blame you.'

'It's not bad – it's just I don't have a lot of time.'

'I understand.' Her green eyes surveyed him. 'I'm grateful to you for taking time to come over here to see me.'

'You said you would be leaving on Monday. I didn't have the chance to talk either to you or Meredith – ' He hesitated slightly but hurried on ' – at the inquest. It seems too much of a coincidence that Pardy should be killed as he was on the eve of the inquest. Why should anyone kill Pardy? It seems it could only be that the murderer was afraid of what Pardy might blurt out in court. Youths like Pardy are unreliable – they get carried away when cross-examined by the coroner . . . The trouble is we don't know what he might have said. It's frustrating. But we're getting there. We've got what we're sure is the murder weapon – the forensic evidence matches and the owner of house in whose dustbin it was found denies all knowledge of it. We have the young man Michael Leary to swear to having replaced the light bulb in the hall just the other day. We have further forensic evidence from the house . . . I'm currently tracing back Pardy's movements that day. Or rather, Pearce is. He's also tracing all Pardy's contacts. I'm modestly optimistic we'll get our man and when we do . . . we can work back to Harriet's accident.'

'You're sure there's a connection?'

'There has to be!' Markby said vehemently. He smiled, a little embarrassed. 'Well, just possibly there isn't, but I'm fairly sure.'

'How will you find out about Pardy's contacts? Apart from what the three youngsters in the house can tell you?'

'I'm hoping a chap called Deanes will help me. I've tried to get hold of him. I've rung his place this morning but he's not there. Deanes is a kind of sociologist and writer who took an interest in – '

But Fran was leaning forward, sea-green eyes gleaming. 'Colin Deanes? You mean Colin Deanes, don't you? You don't have to tell me who he is! I know Colin all right! What's he doing down here?'

Markby looked at her, surprised. She had clenched her fists on her knees and her face was flushed. Corn-blonde hair tumbled unheeded over her forehead.

'He rents a house out on the common – Pook's Common itself, not in the hamlet of Pook's Common. He's been living there nearly a year.'

'Well I'll be damned,' said Fran flatly, sitting back in her chair and throwing up her hands in a gesture of disbelief. 'I bet he didn't know Harriet was living so near when he took on his house!'

'Why?' Markby demanded sharply. A tingle ran up his spine. 'What's Deanes to do with Harriet? I didn't even know they'd met.'

'Met? You bet they'd met! He would have wanted to keep out of Harry's way! Mine, too!'

'You?' Markby frowned, suddenly struck by something. 'He wasn't at the opening of the inquest yesterday! Why not? Pardy was his protégé. He's been acting as Pardy's solicitor.'

'He was keeping out of my way, you bet!' said Fran firmly. 'He's found out I'm here!'

Or did he know . . . ? wondered Markby. Was it too preposterous? Did he know Pardy no longer required his services and support?

'All right, Frances!' he said briskly. 'Start at the beginning and tell me everything you know about Deanes and Harriet.'

'You don't think . . . ?' She paused. 'You don't think he did it again?'

'Did what, Frances?' Markby urged.

'I'll tell you the whole thing, but it goes back a long way, several years!' she warned. 'Well, in fact it goes back before Deanes actually came on the scene. It started when Harry and I were at school and we had a chum called Caroline Henderson, we all called her Caro. The three of us were pretty well insepar- able, the Three Musketeers some people called us. Caro was a pretty kid but a bit sickly – she was a diabetic. She was also rich. Due to family history she finished up as heiress to her grandfather's estate. I don't just mean she was well off, I mean she was seriously wealthy! But she didn't have any family, only a guardian and some trustees with regard to her money. It was in trust until she was twenty-one.'

Fran paused. 'I can't tell all this with a dry throat and I can't drink any more of this coffee. I fancy a G and T.'

'I'll go through to the bar,' said Markby, rising to his feet. 'It will be quicker than trying to get service here. It's almost eleven, they'll be open.'

He came back shortly with a pint of beer and the gin and tonic. 'Carry on, Fran.'

'Right!' Fran sipped appreciatively at the gin and tonic. 'We left school and we did what young girls like us do. I went abroad to a Swiss finishing school but at the end of the first term they asked me to leave – I'll tell you that story one day, but not now and not here – and after that I travelled round a bit. Caroline took an art course. Harry took up good works and went to work for a charity which dealt with delinquents. That's where she met Colin. He was newly qualified as a solicitor and giving his time free to the charity. Harriet was really impressed with him. I don't mean – ' Fran grew emphatic ' – that he was any kind of boy- friend! She just knew him and worked with him and she admired him. She brought him to some parties and introduced him around her friends. She introduced him to Caro. It was the biggest mistake of Harry's life and she never forgave herself for it. If I'd been in England at the time I might have been able to warn Harry. She was naive in some ways. She didn't realise that what Deanes was looking for when she took him to parties and intro- duced him around was a wealthy wife. He had no money and he needed money. Not for himself – he was in his way quite altru- istic. He wanted it for his work, the kids he helped. He had all

224

kinds of projects of his own, quite distinct from the work of the
charity, but without solid and continuous financial backing he
hadn't a hope of getting any of them off the ground. He saw all
those well-off young girls at the parties Harry took him to and
he saw that there was the money he wanted! I'm sure he felt –
and who is to say he was wrong? – that the money they spent
on frivolities would be better spent elsewhere. They were wasting
it: he could use it for good. He could single-handedly redress the
social balance, as it were. The snag was that most of those girls
had families who kept their eyes open for fortune-hunters. If he
had shown interest in practically any one of them he would have
been warned off. But Caroline Henderson was an orphan without
family of any kind. She was twenty-one and had come into her
own money. She was what you might call a sitting target. There
was a whirlwind romance and she and Deanes were married.'

Frances drank the rest of her gin and tonic slowly. Her green
eyes were veiled, inscrutable. She was remembering and the
memories were painful. 'They were miserable,' she said brusquely. 'Or at least, Caroline was! Colin Deanes was in seventh
heaven because he had the money to do as he wanted at last! It
wasn't his, of course. But he could persuade Caro to sign the
cheques, it wasn't difficult. Caroline began to realise that he saw
her as a lady bountiful, not a wife. He didn't love her, he didn't
much care about her at all. I think he hardly saw her – even
when he looked at her, if you know what I mean. She was
the lady who funded his projects, that's all. Caro became very
depressed. She had one or two bouts of illness connected with
the diabetes as well. Things were bad for her. I came home
about then and found out all this. Harriet was distraught. She'd
introduced Deanes to her circle, she'd praised him up to Caro
and others, she'd vouched for him – and this was the result.

'Then one day Caroline came to see Harriet. Harry had given
up the charity work herself. She really wasn't cut out for it and
she and Deanes had quarrelled over his treatment of Caroline
so it was best if they kept out of one another's way. This particular day Caroline turned up on Harriet's doorstep unexpectedly
and seemed – so Harry told me later – excited. She said she had
finally made up her mind. She was going to divorce Deanes. She
should have done so earlier, she said, but had been frightened
to suggest it to him. He had a temper and he could lose it with
her. She was a little scared of him. But now she'd made up her
mind and she'd spoken to him about it at breakfast. He'd taken

it quite well, better than she'd expected. She'd offered to make a financial settlement which would allow him to carry on his work for a while, until he could find other funding. He'd accepted. She was so happy, Harriet said. It was the last Harriet ever saw of her. The last anyone did. That evening Caroline overdosed. She was alone in the house. Deanes was out with the family of one of his good causes, dispensing advice. He could prove it, could produce the family in question. But if you had seen them, Alan! You wouldn't have taken their word about anything! The mother was simple, the father a crook and the kid was a pathological liar. They would have said anything Deanes asked them to say! Harriet always believed Deanes was at his own house at the time he claimed to be with his problem family. That he contrived Caroline's overdose. That he killed her. The difficulty was, Caro hadn't spoken to anyone else of her decision to divorce Deanes. She hadn't yet seen her solicitor. Deanes, when he was questioned, denied divorce had ever been mentioned. Harriet accused him to his face of lying. She told him Caro had been to see her and told her about the divorce plans the day she died. But Deanes only said Harry must have got it wrong, that Caro was a depressive and often made wild statements off the top of her head. Caroline had had treatment for depression in the past – there was really no reason for anyone to disbelieve Deanes' story. Only Harry. And me. I never believed him because I believed Harry – and I never liked Deanes. Harry never got over Caroline's death and always felt responsible. She sold up her family house which she'd inherited and moved down here to the cottage at Pook's Common, right away from everything which could remind her of Caro and everyone she knew . . . only she didn't, it now seems. She didn't leave behind everyone she knew. Deanes turned up. Talk of bad pennies. The one person guaranteed to bring all the bad memories flooding back. She always believed he got away with it. She always believed, I think, that she owed it to Caro's memory to see justice done if she could. I wonder . . . I wonder if she did meet him, down here? He couldn't have been living that far away, out on that common. Good God, it's a stone's throw!' Fran clenched her fists again in frustration.

'She never wrote any letter to you, suggesting she had met up with Deanes again?'

'No – I would have remembered. But then,' Fran hesitated. 'You see, I told her to try to forget it, put it all out of her mind.

She might have thought, if she mentioned it to me, I would just have come down here and delivered another lecture. Although . . .' Fran paused and her forehead creased in a frown. 'She did once put a cryptic postscript at the end of a letter. Several months ago. Something about having a piece of surprise news for me but she'd tell me when she saw me. 'It's a small world!' that's what she wrote, I remember now. A small world. She might – oh, it's so exasperating!'

But Deanes didn't know whether she'd written to Frances or not, thought Markby, trying to control his own excitement. And the thought of Fran's private correspondence lying unattended in her hotel room here while she dined downstairs might have been a tempting invitation to take a look and see if there was any reference to him!

'You mentioned to me once someone you knew getting away with murder . . .' Markby said eagerly. 'Did you mean Deanes?'

'Yes,' she nodded. 'And if I'd known he was around here I'd have told you a lot sooner. He had something to do with Harry's death! The more I think about it now, the more I'm sure of it!'

'I certainly think I shall have to have a word with Mr Deanes very soon!' Markby scowled. 'Excuse me a minute, Fran.'

He went quickly out into the lobby and tried Deanes' number on the public telephone. No answer. Deanes was still out – or had he skipped?

He went back into the lounge to rejoin Fran. 'He's not at home. Or at least he's not answering the phone. I'm going to drive out there. There's a track leading to his house across the common. It starts at a pub called The Black Dog.'

'What about Meredith?' Fran asked, getting to her feet. 'She ought to be told about Deanes.'

'Yes . . .' Markby looked worried. 'She did meet him once out on the common. I'll call by Rose Cottage first and tell her briefly what you've told me. Then I'll drive to Deanes' house. It means going right round the perimeter of the heathland – there's no access by road from the Pook's Common side.'

'I'll come with you,' Fran said determinedly. 'You can leave me with Meredith while you go out to Deanes' place.'

They hurried out of The Crossed Keys into the winter sunlight.

Thirteen

'Your wife,' Meredith said slowly. 'I see.' In reality she did not see fully, but the mist was beginning to clear. Little bits of knowledge began to fall jigsaw-like into their rightful place.

'She,' Deanes said fervently, 'that woman, Harriet Needham, she told wicked, cruel lies about me and about Caroline. She was a wicked, spiteful woman!'

'What did she say?' Meredith asked as calmly as she could. She glanced again at the window and strained her hearing for the noise of a car engine but Pook's Common was as silent as the grave. Unwelcome simile. It was certainly cold enough for a cemetery in Ivy Cottage. The heating had been switched off since Harriet's death. It was clammy and icy and she felt her nose and fingers turning red with cold. She rubbed her hands together surreptitiously, almost afraid to move at all in case he interpreted her action as one of aggression.

'She said I killed Caroline,' Deanes said sullenly. 'She said I lied about where I was that evening when Caroline died from an overdose. I didn't kill my wife!' His voice began to rise on an aggrieved note. 'I didn't kill Caro!'

'All right,' Meredith soothed him. 'Tell me what happened.'

'She took a massive overdose of barbiturates,' Deanes blinked rapidly. 'She suffered from depression. She had always done so. She was a diabetic and had always been sickly. And that Needham woman made things worse, working away on Caroline, telling her lies about me, suggesting things . . .'

'Things, Mr Deanes?'

'Yes! Saying I only married Caroline in order to have the money for my work. I was meant to have that money, Miss Mitchell! Fate led me to Caro. What else would she have used that money for?' He spread out his hands. 'Nothing! It would have been wasted. No, I was meant to have that money. Caroline understood. I explained it to her. She understood – but that woman kept interfering!'

Deanes got to his feet and began to pace up and down the drawing room restlessly. Every time he passed by the box containing the photographs he glared down at the topmost one. Meredith wished she could reach out and remove it from his sight. She did try once to lean forward and put out a hand but he said sharply, 'Leave it there!'

'Would you like me to make us a cup of tea, Mr Deanes?'

'No! Stay where you are, where I can see you! I want to tell you what happened here. How I suffered! You have no idea . . .' He came towards her, head lowered and face contorted. 'You have no idea how she made me suffer!' He sat down again much to her relief, the pacing made her feel dizzy, and clasped his hands nervously together.

'You see, I had no idea she was living here. She left the district where Caroline and I had lived together after she couldn't get her way and persuade people I killed Caroline. People wouldn't believe her lies, you see!' He nodded triumphantly. 'They knew what good work I'd done and they believed me! She was nothing, just a rich spoiled woman but I could point to my work! My work spoke up for me!'

'Yes, Mr Deanes, I'm sure it did.'

He looked mollified. 'I knew you'd understand. I came down here because I was offered the old farmhouse out on the common. It was quiet and I could write there. I really didn't know about her. If I'd known she lived here, so close, I would never have come. I didn't know for a while – and she didn't know about me. But then I had that piece of truly bad luck I told you about. It happened out of the blue while I was sitting in my own kitchen drinking coffee and talking with someone.'

'Dr Krasny!' Meredith was unable to prevent herself blurting.

Deanes pushed his spectacles up the bridge of his nose and stared at her. 'That's very perceptive of you, Miss Mitchell!' Suspicion entered his voice. 'How do you know?'

'I guessed. You told me once about Dr Krasny looking for wild flowers on the common and dropping by to have coffee with you. And – and Harriet told me about the other people who used the cottages in Pook's Common. Krasny used to call on her, too.'

'Yes, a very pleasant man. He had no idea what he'd done. I don't blame him,' Deanes told her earnestly. 'We were sitting in my kitchen and he was talking about Pook's Common and he mentioned her. I thought there must be some mistake. I walked over the common to the cottages on several evenings and hid near this place – ' he indicated Ivy Cottage about them – 'trying to catch a glimpse of her. She had men visiting late. All kinds of men. She was a whore!'

Meredith remembered that Lucy Haynes had spoken of hearing someone pass her cottage late at night. She must have heard Deanes, on his way back to his lonely house after scouting around Ivy Cottage.

'I saw her! There she was! It wasn't a mistake, it was the same Harriet Needham who had persecuted me before! It was like a nightmare come true! But worse, Dr Krasny told her about me and my house out on the common so she knew about me and one day, she came.'

Deanes fell silent for a moment, his last words hanging in the chill air. Their simplicity and the way he uttered them brought to life the real horror Harriet's arrival on his lonely doorstep had represented to him. A figure from his past who had materialised out of the moor to haunt him.

'I was working,' he said quietly. 'I heard hoofbeats and then someone knocked on my door. I went to answer and there she was.' As he spoke Deanes' calm visibly disintegrated and he began to grow agitated, rubbing his hands, jumping up and sitting down again, face twitching. 'She was abusive! She said she'd make a scandal when I tried to launch the new book! I tried to reason with her – she wouldn't listen. She kept coming to the house after that. Not right up to the house, just out there, on the common . . . I'd be working and I'd hear the hoofbeats. I'd go to the window and look out and there she would be, sitting about thirty yards away on that red-gold horse of hers, with her red hair hanging down her back and both of them shining at me in the sun. She was like a Fury set on my track. She persecuted me, destroyed me, day by day, little by little, eating away at my peace of mind, leaving me unable to eat, to sleep, to write! And all of it without a spoken word. She just sat there and waited, watching, day after day, sometimes for as long as twenty minutes at a time. And then she'd ride on. But she'd come back, she always came back. It was a wonder I was able to finish the book . . . I'd be listening for her all the time, imagining the hoofbeats when there were none. Sometimes hearing them and rushing to the window only to see that fellow Fearon ride past. He was in it with her, you know. When she didn't come past the house, he did. I knew I had to do something about it. Between them they were slowly driving me out of my mind! But I'm not a violent man, Miss Mitchell. I'd tried reason but that hadn't worked, so I tried distraction. I thought, if she had something else to worry about, she'd forget about me.'

Deanes' face twisted in genuine misery, 'I thought of a plan involving Simon Pardy. You must believe me, I really would not have harmed him for the world! I wanted to help him! But I thought, he could help me, too! He was looking for a cause as so many of these sad young people are. I suggested to him that a campaign against local fox-hunting might be something he could devote his time and talents to. I knew that woman hunted. She was hunting me! And like the fox I had to be wily if I was to get away! I suggested he try to get up a petition to ban the hunting on council-owned land – that would have barred the hunt from the common for a start! I suggested he wrote a few letters anonymously just to distract her, you understand. But it didn't work.'

Deanes sighed. 'She was implacable, she was fixed on my trail like a bloodhound. Nothing could shake her off! What could I do? When I got the advance copies of my book I made a last attempt at reason. I sent her one through the post, that one you're holding there. I begged her to read it. I wanted her to understand what I was trying to do. I hoped she'd see what damage she was doing. All I got in return was a vile letter from her. I tried phoning her and begging her to read it but she shouted at me on the telephone and hung up. I was desperate, Miss Mitchell! On the morning of Boxing Day I rang her up and asked her, begged her, as it was the Christmas season, at least to see me and talk about it. She was in a good mood. She said to come over and have some breakfast. I really thought, I really thought she was prepared to listen.

'I walked across here. She was cooking the breakfast when I arrived, a substantial one because she was going to be out all day. I began to reason with her and she appeared to listen to what I had to say. She suggested we go into breakfast.

'But it was all a cruel trick. She hadn't changed. When I finished explaining, she said she'd asked me over because she was curious – curious, that was her word! – to hear what I'd say. She said I was a fool to think she would be taken in by such a farrago of lies. She said I was off my head! She said my work had turned my brain! Filthy bitch! But I was ready for her. I never really trusted her so I had come prepared. I'd brought the pills with me. They had been Caroline's. I knew in my heart that

Harriet would never leave me alone and wherever I went, she'd turn up just as she turned up here. I thought if she didn't listen to me and agree she was wrong to persecute me, then I might have a chance to feed her the pills during breakfast. It wasn't difficult because she was getting ready to go out hunting and even though she was shouting her foul accusations and abuse at me, still half her mind was on that. She kept going in and out and upstairs and down, fetching things. She put the kedgeree on the table on the two plates and then went out to the back porch to fetch in her boots which she'd washed off after going down to Fearon's stables earlier. I had plenty of time and it was so easy. The pills were tiny things. I forked them into her plate of food and even I couldn't spot them. She came back, bolted the food down and her coffee, insulted me a bit more and then told me to get out, she hadn't any more time for me. Don't you think it rather fitting that I should have fed her Caro's pills?' Deanes looked ridiculously pleased with himself.

'It's dreadful . . .' Meredith whispered, appalled.

'I knew she'd have a drink of alcohol before going out, she always did, and she'd become groggy. They took effect faster than I'd anticipated, however. And I hadn't realised Simon Pardy would behave as he did. I thought she'd fall off somewhere out in the country and everyone would think it was a hunting accident. I hoped she'd break her neck!' Deanes added viciously. 'A fractured skull was just as good. It shut her up. Shut her up at last!'

Deanes turned his glinting spectacle lenses towards Meredith. 'But I wouldn't have done it if she hadn't driven me to it, Miss Mitchell! It was entirely her own fault, her doing, not mine! I thought it would be over when she died, but it wasn't. People started asking questions. Everyone was meddling. Pardy was going to be questioned at the inquest and he might have told them about me and my idea that he should campaign against the hunting and write the letters. Young people like him are so unreliable! They get excited and may say anything! And the other woman had turned up meanwhile, Frances, her cousin. Just as bad. I didn't know how much Frances knew. I went into Bamford and waited until she was at dinner and forced my way into her room to see if there were any letters about me . . . But she came back too soon!' Again Deanes looked aggrieved as if Fran this time had made the wrong move in a game, breaking the rules. 'She came in while I was there but luckily I was able to knock her down and get away. But I was scared! I kept thinking about

Pardy and the inquest next day. What would he say? I had to stop Pardy giving evidence. I'm really sorry about that!' Deanes sounded mournful. 'That boy was innocent. His blood is on my hands! But she was the cause! She started it all!'

The sad look had faded and the vicious one returned. 'But I had to go to the inquest, even so. Markby knew I was Pardy's solicitor. People would ask where I was. I got to the door of the courtroom. I was a little late and when I looked in I saw you all waiting there. I realised the delay meant they had found Pardy's body. Then I saw Frances! She was directly in my line of sight talking to the doctor. She was all dressed up in black like a great Black Widow spider. I couldn't face her. I knew she'd recognise me, start shouting abuse, accusations about Caroline. Markby isn't a fool. He'd put two and two together. He's never liked me. I couldn't risk facing F-Frances – ' Deanes began to stutter in his agitation. 'I t-turned and ran before she saw me. I knew it would look odd, my not being there to represent Pardy. I thought I could phone and say I was sick or something . . .'

'Had you forgotten this?' Meredith asked, lifting up the book in her hands.

'Oh, yes, I had. I was so anxious to get away as soon as I saw she'd swallowed the food with the pills that I clean forgot to ask her to return my book. It was a direct link between us. I knew that if someone intelligent such as Frances or yourself saw it, or Markby, they'd know at once she could only have got it directly from me, yet without it Markby didn't know I'd ever met her. So I had to get it back. I came across the common last night. A dreadful night, pouring with rain and I got wet through!' Deanes scowled. 'But you stayed up so late! Your light was on! I thought if I started searching in here there was a chance you'd look out and see my torch. I stood about in the rain getting drenched waiting for your light to go out and in the end I went home!'

'I'm so sorry,' Meredith apologised. 'I didn't know you were outside in the rain!' Absurd though the apology was, it seemed quite logical in these bizarre circumstances.

'So I came this morning. I saw your car had gone and I was pleased because I thought you'd gone to Bamford. I thought I wouldn't be disturbed, but you were here, waiting for me! It was a trap!'

'No!' Meredith cried out. 'It was just a bit of bad luck like yours! My car broke down or I should have gone away for the day! I came over here to pack up the books for the Cottage

Hospital, Frances asked me to do it.'

'Meddling,' Deanes said morosely. 'Meddling women, all of you! I'm sorry that you've become involved, Miss Mitchell, because you are a nice woman. But you see, you came under her influence, the Needham woman's. It was always the same. She was a wicked woman and she poisoned everyone's ears!'

'She never spoke to me of you, Mr Deanes, I swear!'

'It makes no difference,' he said. 'You found the book. You understood. I have to kill you, Miss Mitchell.' He sounded apologetic but quite decided. 'It's a pity, Pardy was a pity. All this had been forced on me. You do understand?'

She had to make a break for it. She had no choice left. Meredith had been gripping *Revolutionary Youth* and now she hurled it full in his face with all the strength she could summon. His spectacles were struck from his nose to the floor and as he threw up his hands to protect himself, Meredith leapt up and dashed past him.

She reached the front door, had even managed to wrench it open, before he reached her. His hands gripped her throat. She had no idea he would be so strong. She tried to thrust him away, pushing at his chest, clawing at his face and then kicking out with her feet. But all the time he was exerting relentless pressure on her windpipe. Blood roared in her ears. She could no longer see, no longer distinguish direction. She was choking, her tongue swelling in her mouth and pressing against her teeth. Stars sparkled and exploded before her and then blackness came, swirling up to engulf her.

'Ruddy Deanes!' muttered Markby as they drove at some speed along the B road towards the turning off to Pook's Common. 'You know, when you spoke about the overcoat the man was wearing, the man who attacked you, you said it smelled damp and old. I thought at first of Pardy but after Pardy's death I had another think about it. I actually thought of Deanes and then dismissed him because he always seemed to be wearing that fur-trimmed parka. But that old place he lived in out on the common, that must be damp. Anything stored in a cupboard there would smell pretty fusty. But I couldn't see why Deanes should want to harm his protégé, Pardy, and I crossed him off my mental list! It just goes to show!'

He slammed his foot on the brakes and Fran made a grab for

the dashboard to steady herself. 'Watch out, Alan! I'm all for driving with a bit of style but we do want to get there in one piece!'

'Meredith's car!' came the taut reply. They had reached Fenniwick's garage. Markby drove into the forecourt with a flourish and jumped out.

The car stood at the back of the work area. The bonnet was propped open and a wiry man with gingery hair and blue overalls was peering into the engine.

''Ullo,' he said amiably as Markby strode up. He wiped his hands on a rag.

'Where's the lady who owns this car?' Markby asked him brusquely.

'She'll be down Pook's Common waiting for me to bring it back,' said Mr Fenniwick. 'Most like. Wanted it back as soon as possible, she did. Well, you need a bit of transport living out here. It's her battery got damp though what she really needs is a new one, but I got jump leads on this 'un . . .'

'Thank you!' Markby said hurriedly and strode back to rejoin Fran in his car. 'She should be at home. I hope to goodness she hasn't taken it into her head to go out for a walk on the common!'

'Unlikely, too wet underfoot after all that rain last night,' pointed out Fran practically as they turned off into the lane which led to the cottages.

They drove slowly down. 'Here we are!' Markby said. They got out before Rose Cottage and stood back to allow Fran to precede him to the door. At that moment, as he afterwards described it to Pearce, all hell broke loose.

The door of Ivy Cottage opposite flew open. Meredith appeared briefly in the doorway and then was abruptly jerked back. When she reappeared it was as part of a struggling pair of bodies which stumbled writhing into view. Her congested face, eyes bulging, stared towards his unseeingly.

'Meredith!' yelled Markby leaping towards the cottage. Fran dashed after him and they both became temporarily entangled in the narrow gateway to Ivy Cottage. Belatedly Deanes became aware of the arrival of others. He suddenly released Meredith who slumped back against the doorjamb making grotesque gurgles and clawing at her bruised throat. Deanes stared wildly at the two newcomers and then bolted across the front of the cottage.

Fran dived towards Meredith and Markby raced after Deanes.

With an athleticism his general appearance belied, Deanes vaulted the low stone wall into the next garden and ran across the front lawn past the wishing well and jumped over another low wall into the lane. He was making for Markby's car in which the chief inspector realised he had left the keys. He pelted after Deanes with desperate determination. The fugitive had managed to get into the driving seat and was fumbling with the starter when Markby reached it. He wrenched open the door, grabbed Deanes by the shoulder and hauled him out into the roadway. 'No you don't!' he gasped.

Deanes let out an animal squeal and twisted in the chief inspector's grip. He slipped out of the parka like a trapped grey squirrel shedding its furry tail, and raced away down the lane towards the common, leaving Markby holding the abandoned coat. Markby swore, hurled it to one side and set off in pursuit again.

Quite where Deanes thought he was going was unclear. An animal instinct led him to bolt towards his own territory and it was possible that out there on the common with its wealth of ditches and shrubs he might have given Markby the slip. But Deanes was not to reach the common.

Ahead of them, round a bend in the lane appeared a rider on a grey horse. Tom Fearon. 'Tom!' yelled Markby.

But Tom had already seen and understood. Markby read it on his swarthy features. Read too, something else. Again Markby bellowed, 'Tom!' adding an agonised, 'Tom, no! Don't!'

The grey swung across the fleeing Deanes' path. Deanes at full pelt could not apply the muscular brakes in time. The horse reared up and Deanes found himself beneath the flailing hooves. An unearthly scream split the damp cold air of Pook's Common.

'It was a nasty moment,' said Markby with deep feeling. 'Well, the nastiest was seeing Deanes throttling you in the doorway of Ivy Cottage, Meredith. But I really thought Tom was going to ride Deanes down.' He got up and obligingly adjusted the gas fire.

'You should have let him do it!' said Fran belligerently. 'I wouldn't have shouted out for him to stop.'

'Thank you, Miss Needham-Burrell, I have enough fatalities connected with this case to sort out! Anyway, fortunately at the very last moment Tom pulled the grey's head round and avoided him. But Deanes thought his last moment had come. Frightened him out of his remaining wits. He was ready to beg me to arrest him for his own protection after he'd read what was in Tom's eyes. We'll put Tom's efforts down as a laudable contribution on the part of an honest citizen towards preventing the escape of a fugitive from arrest. The court will probably thank him and award him fifty quid.'

'Hah!' said Fran darkly and Meredith gurgled.

Markby regarded them both with bewilderment and some exasperation. The three of them sat around the fire in the living room of Rose Cottage on Sunday afternoon and had just finished tea and toasted muffins. Or rather, the two guests had finished the muffins. Meredith had enough trouble swallowing the tea and faced living on yoghurt and scrambled eggs for some time.

'I don't know what you two have against poor Tom!' Markby went on. 'What on earth has he done to offend you? He's a rough diamond, I'll grant you, but after his own fashion quite a chivalrous chap. Deanes was more of a threat to womanhood than Tom!'

'You wouldn't understand!' Fran told him coldly. Meredith uttered a corroborative croak.

'Well, he was a loyal friend to Harriet!' said Markby obstinately. 'He knew about her affair with Green, of course. He's told me so now. He wouldn't name names before. That's what I mean about Tom. He's got his own notion of honour. Anyway, he tried to warn Harriet to stay clear of Green but she wasn't taking any advice from him or anyone else. They had a few quarrels over it. You heard a snippet of one of them, Meredith. Tom had had an affair with Harriet himself when she first came to Pook's Common. It was all over and finished but they stayed friends. They had quite a lot of shared interests, horses and so forth. It wasn't sour grapes on Tom's part which made him try to persuade her to ditch Green. He really thought she'd get hurt. He was trying to protect her. He even had a barney with Green himself over it, but the Master stepped in and asked him not to sow dissension among the followers of the hunt.'

Meredith said huskily, 'So they all knew more than they were telling!'

'People generally do,' said Markby gloomily. 'Any policeman will tell you that!' He regarded her with some concern. 'I think you're mad even to think of going up to London tomorrow.'

'Here, here!' said Fran forcibly. 'You're injured, for crying out loud! You can't work! Jack Pringle's all against it!'

'They expect me . . .' croak.

'What does the Foreign Office want, your blood? Let me ring 'em up and tell 'em what's happened.'

'I must just go up and explain and then I'll go sick, promise.'

'Did Jack write you a sick note?' Markby asked her. 'I'll give you a police report that will make their hair curl. After all, you were the object of an attempted murder!'

Meredith stretched out her hand and picked up a sheet of closely written paper. 'Pringle's medical report . . .' she wheezed.

'Jack says,' Fran observed, 'you're lucky no permanent damage was done! Deanes released you in the nick of time!' She sighed. 'Poor old Jack. He's very down in the dumps.'

'Well, at least we have Deanes,' Markby consoled her. 'Smart of Deanes, you know, to realise he was so well known about here in that fur-trimmed parka and to change it for an old overcoat he had before setting out to break into your hotel room. We've found the overcoat out at his house, by the way, and matched threads from it with some found at Jubilee Road. But proof isn't hard to get. Deanes is confessing to Pardy's murder with a wealth of lurid detail. It's on his conscience and he can't stop talking about it. He's decided to be a bit cagy about his feeding of pills to Harriet, though. He's now saying he only meant her to have an accident, not be killed. But the murder charge against him over Pardy is quite clear-cut.'

'Do you think,' Fran asked, 'that he also killed Caroline, his wife, all those years ago? As an expert, what's your opinion? Harriet and I always thought he did.'

Markby shrugged. 'Who can tell, now? He'll never admit it. But he certainly believed he had a right to her money for his work. If she had divorced him and changed her will, the small amount she proposed giving him to tide him over until he found new funding would have been nothing compared to what he would have lost. There are similarities between her death and Harriet's. Both women threatened his work. Both their deaths came about as a result of misuse of medicines. In both cases Deanes contrived either to be well away from the scene at the moment of death or to have witnesses to swear that he was. Multiple murderers do tend to use a successful method again. And he was a violent man, Deanes, for all his mild appearance. His wife had spoken to Harriet and to you, Fran, of being scared of him. Nor did he let finer emotions stand in the way of his killing. He wanted to be a friend to Pardy but he slugged him and pushed him down the staircase and he tried to throttle Meredith, although he liked her.'

'He was very strong,' said Meredith hoarsely.

'Yes, and I'm not so sure you are, my girl. Take it easy!'

'I'm fine . . . tell me, who let Tom's horses out on Christmas Eve?'

'Deanes did. He'd persuaded himself that Fearon and Harriet were in a plot together to persecute him. Tom says not, he didn't know anything about it. Anyhow, Deanes tramped over the common at dead of night with the letter Pardy had made up in his pocket, shoved it through Tom's door and chased the horses out into the lane. Imagine if that had come out at the inquest! To protect Deanes, Pardy had to go, I'm afraid.'

'I've got to go,' Fran stood up. 'I'll be back next week and fix up the funeral. You'll both come, won't you? And I hope I can sell Ivy Cottage but there are now three for sale in Pook's Common!'

'Three?' Markby asked.

'Yes, the one next door to Harriet was already on the market. But now the Haynes have put theirs up for sale, didn't you know? Lucy will be pleased but Geoffrey it was who made the decision, as always! Nothing to do with poor Lucy's wishes. It seems Geoffrey had not realised the rural crime rate was so high! They're now looking for a bungalow on the South Coast.'

'Some benefit's come out of it all, then,' Meredith muttered.

'Don't come to the door!' Fran ordered. 'Too cold! Alan will see me out, won't you?'

He followed her out into Rose Cottage's tiny hallway and helped her into her coat. 'See you next week, sometime, then. I'll be at the funeral if I can. Police duties can always interfere, alas. But I'll do my best.'

'Sure,' she delved into her pocket. 'Here, it's my card. It's got my London phone number on it. If you're ever up in Town, come up and see me, as Mae West put it. We can have lunch – or something!' She winked at him audaciously.

'Er – yes,' he said hastily. He thrust the little oblong of card into the pocket of his green weatherproof hanging in the hall and glanced guiltily towards the open living-room door.

Fran grinned at him and departed. Markby returned to the living room to find Meredith with her back to him standing by the windowsill.

'She's – gone . . .' he said lamely.

'I must be unobservant . . .' came in Meredith's present croak. 'I hadn't realised . . .'

'Look, it's nothing!' he burst out. 'She's only fooling around! She doesn't mean it! By this time next week she'll have forgotten all about me!'

'What?' Meredith turned round and stared at him with puzzled hazel eyes. 'What are you talking about?'

With horror he realised they were at cross-purposes. 'Sorry,' he mumbled. 'I misunderstood you . . . what were you talking about?'

'The plant . . .' she pointed at the windowsill. 'The Christmas cactus you gave me, it's flowered. I hadn't noticed with all the comings and goings and excitement!'

'So it has.' He crossed the room to look at it and then looked at her. 'Oughtn't that to be symbolic of something?'

She shook her head. 'Don't, Alan!'

'New Year is a time for resolutions, isn't it?'

'I never make them. Can't keep them. My resolution is, don't make any. Leave things as they are, Alan, please, can't we?'

'Yes, I suppose we can,' he said after a pause. 'I'll be in touch. Take care. Especially if you do decide to go up to London.'

'I must. Got to show myself.'

'You can post them Jack's report and mine, you know.'

'They'd only get filed away. I'll go and croak at people.'

'Ridiculous!' he muttered. 'If you show you can get there unaided, they'll assume you're okay, no matter how much you croak! You are an obstinate woman!'

'Yes, can't help it.'

'It means a lot to you, your job, doesn't it?' he asked after a pause.

'Yes. Doesn't yours to you?'

'Yes, all right. I'll phone tomorrow evening.' He dragged on the weatherproof, put his hand in the pocket for his car keys and his fingers touched the sharp corners of Fran's card.

Meredith accompanied him to the door despite his objections and watched him drive off.

He'd gone. He'd be back, but he'd gone for now. Perhaps one day he'd drive off and not come back again. Get fed up and go for good. Some people seem to have no trouble at all with relationships. She just couldn't seem to make them work. Harriet had problems too, she reflected. Perhaps that was what drew her to her. Meredith wondered how on earth people saw her. The men in Harriet's life saw her quite differently, each of them. Green saw her as a mistress to be ditched if she got troublesome. Jack Pringle wanted to marry her and would probably have done anything for her. Tom was her loyal friend, come what may. Deanes saw her as a vengeful harpy bent on his destruction, as she probably was. Four different women in one. Meredith really didn't know Harriet very well. Tom was right about that. None of them did.

She glanced along the row of cottages. Normal life had returned in some measure to Pook's Common. Mrs Sowerby had come back from her Christmas with relatives to live next door. She had called round to express concern and sympathy.

'Your poor throat! It makes one quite nervous of living out here, doesn't it? Who would have thought . . . My daughter wants me to go into a sheltered flat in Bamford, but I really don't fancy it. But I depend on my daughter. She brings me my shopping once a week out here. If she puts her foot down now, after all this, I'll have to go. I hope you feel better soon. Would you like me to make you a rice pudding?'

Mrs Fenniwick had also been across. 'Call me Sonia. What a turn-up! You could have knocked me down with a feather when Joe told me! Just shows you. You never can tell. Poor old Harriet. Mind you, I always thought she played with fire. You can't trust men, none of them. Let me know if you need anything. I've got a food blender if you haven't got one. It liquidises everything up into a sort of mush. Looks horrible but you can swallow it.'

Meredith shivered in the breeze and turned to retreat into the warmth of Rose Cottage. As she did so, a clip-clop of hooves became audible. She waited.

Tom Fearon, looking handsome and untrustworthy in equal measure and mounted today on Blazer, came riding up and drew rein outside. 'Hullo there!'

'Hullo.'

He grinned. Blazer was immaculate, gleaming like a burnished copper kettle, and even Tom was looking reasonably tidy today. He'd shaved, his black topboots were polished up and his breeches clean. Only the old cap was the same and the battered Harris tweed jacket stretched across his shoulders over the pullover underneath hadn't changed either. Nor had its owner, she suspected. She thought about Deanes, peering fearfully from his isolated house at Blazer carrying the vengeful Harriet, hating and fearing the sight of the horse as much as that of the rider.

Tom patted Blazer's neck. 'The old boy is looking all right, don't you think? I wanted to buy him off Frances but she insisted on giving him to me on the understanding I never sold him.' He cast her an appraising glance. 'I rode up to see how you were today.'

'Thanks, not too bad,' she husked at him.

Blazer, growing impatient, tossed his head up and down, champing at the bit. He blew noisily through his nostrils and pawed at the ground. Tom leaned forward and crossed his forearms on the pommel of the saddle, reins lying loosely in his well-made but scarred hands. His white teeth flashed in his swarthy face and his dark eyes gleamed beneath the brim of his disreputable cap. 'Anything I can do for you?'

Meredith met his questioning stare firmly and managed to articulate a clear, 'No, thanks!'

'Nasty experience,' said Tom with sympathy. 'I'm sorry now I didn't ride straight over the creep. Still I suppose it was better I left him for Alan to deal with.'

Meredith nodded vigorously.

'I hope,' said Tom, probably intending to sound polite but sounding slightly aggressive, 'that our previous disagreements won't cloud our future relationship? Small place, Pook's Common. If we're to be neighbours – '

'If!' croaked Meredith vigorously.

Tom raised a black eyebrow and Blazer stamped crossly. 'Moving on already, then?'

'Perhaps,' she said hoarsely. 'Thinking about it.'

For a dreadful moment she thought he was going to ask about Alan. He had a funny sort of look in his eye as if he could read her mind. 'Fair enough,' he said at last. He grimaced and picked up the reins.

Blazer twitched his ears as Tom clicked his tongue, rolling his large lustrous eyes in an expression which plainly said, 'About time, too! All this human gossiping!'

'Keep out of trouble!' said Tom with an indescribably lecherous grin. He saluted her with his whip and clattered away briskly down the lane.